PRAISE FOR TRACY CLARK

Echo

"[A] hard-hitting police procedural that examines justice, and who metes it out."

—*Library Journal* (starred review)

"Revenge is served ice-cold during a frigid Chicago winter in Clark's entertaining latest procedural."

—*Publishers Weekly*

"*Echo* is the third in Clark's series focused on [Detective Harriet] Foster, but it stands firmly on its own."

—*The Washington Post*

"An impressively original and thoroughly fun read . . ."

—*Midwest Book Review*

Fall

"Clark's second Detective Harriet Foster title (after *Hide*) provides a compelling plot as well as significant character growth . . . The lead detectives are new to each other and building trust, and readers will become invested in the fragile bond they currently have, as well as the mystery surrounding Foster and her former partner."

—*Library Journal* (starred review)

"Another worm's-eye view of the city . . . marinated in savory civic misdeeds."

—*Kirkus Reviews*

Hide

2024 Anthony Award Winner

2024 Lefty Award Winner

2024 Edgar Award Finalist

2024 ITW Thriller Award Finalist

"A Chicago cop still mourning her late partner transfers to a new precinct just in time to catch a truly creepy case. Solid . . . work from a writer who knows the dark side of the Windy City."

—*Kirkus Reviews*

"[Detective Harriet] Foster's dogged approach to catching killers will resonate with Michael Connelly fans. May the wait for the second Harriet Foster police procedural be brief."

—*Publishers Weekly*

"*Hide* is an astonishing crime novel that broke my heart and then sewed it back together again, stronger than before. It hits all the right notes—a captivating protagonist up against a nightmarish serial killer, their hunt played out across a Chicago so immersive, so flawlessly rendered, that you can hear your own footsteps slapping the streets—while managing to create something completely unique. One of the best books I've read in years."

—Jess Lourey, Amazon Charts bestselling author

"Tracy Clark's not-so-hidden talent is for conjuring characters who are engaging and achingly real. Detective Harri Foster is a stellar recruit to her new team and to our crime fiction shelves. *Hide* is a page-turner with heart."

—Lori Rader-Day, Agatha Award–winning author of *Death at Greenway*

Runner

"You know those books that are wonderful, but that envy, the worm in the bud, makes you shy away from praising because you wish you'd created that prose or those insights? *Runner* by Tracy Clark. She understands the streets, kids, the way a PI and a cop really work. Kudos."

—Sara Paretsky, *New York Times* bestselling author of the V.I. Warshawski series and cofounder of Sisters in Crime

"Clark writes with purpose, her sense of social justice never venturing into dogma but remaining fully rooted in Raines's actions and personality. She saves, but is no savior, because she operates in a world where survival is the benchmark, and pain remains in the aftermath."

—*New York Times*

"Clark has a unique voice in the PI genre, one that is articulate, daring, and ultimately hopeful."

—S.A. Cosby, Anthony and ITW award winner, *Washington Post*

Broken Places

"Engrossing and superbly written—I can't say enough good things about *Broken Places*!"

—Lisa Black, *New York Times* bestselling author of *That Darkness* and *Unpunished*

"Unforgettable . . . Distinctive, vividly written characters lift this promising debut. Readers will be eager for the sequel."

—*Publishers Weekly* (starred review)

"Clark's compelling, suspenseful, and action-packed debut introduces a dogged, tough African American woman investigator who is complex and courageous and surrounded by a family of fascinating misfits. Fans of Sue Grafton's Kinsey Millhone or Sara Paretsky's V.I. Warshawski will welcome Cass Raines to their ranks."

—*Library Journal* (starred review)

"This street-smart first mystery boasts great characterization and a terrific new protagonist. Get this writer on your radar now."

—*Booklist*

EDGE

ALSO BY TRACY CLARK

Detective Harriet Foster Series

Hide

Fall

Echo

Chicago Mystery Series

Broken Places

Borrowed Time

What You Don't See

Runner

EDGE

A DETECTIVE HARRIET FOSTER THRILLER

TRACY CLARK

THOMAS & MERCER

Published by Thomas & Mercer, Seattle
www.apub.com

EU product safety contact:
Amazon Media EU S. à r.l.
38, avenue John F. Kennedy, L-1855 Luxembourg
amazonpublishing-gpsr@amazon.com

ISBN-13: 9781662517358 (paperback)
ISBN-13: 9781662517341 (digital)

Cover design by Damon Freeman
Cover image: © Andrew Vandeford, © Bendi Lukman, © Nature Peaceful, © Sean Pavone, © Spiroview Inc / Shutterstock

Printed in the United States of America

For Mom, who read all the stories and planted the seed

PROLOGUE

The chair had belonged to her father. And the desk. And the house. And the gun. It was throne-like, regal, carved of expensive wood, with a velvet cushion on the seat. At the ends of the armrests there were intricate lion's heads, the mouths open in a roar. The chair sat front and center behind a massive desk in an office full of mementos from a dark life—a 24K-gold-plated handgun; a bloody Chicago brick, aged, pocked, salmon pink and deep red; both gun and brick sharing pride of place in a silver-and-glass display case.

The old greystone, which was more fortress than home, sat entrenched and evil in the heart of the South Side on the teetering edge of ruin and revitalization, a warning, a Brobdingnagian, on a block of houses that matched it only in shape and design. It had been the base of Big Daddy Gamon's empire. Not of industry, not of business, but of crime and power and violence. Cora Gamon ruled here now. Cora sat in the chair. She pushed the pills and the powder, moved the women, used the gangs, piled up the money.

Big Daddy was gone. Her brothers, heirs to the chair, gone too. Violence begot violence, and the Gamon men meant to rule the empire and occupy the seat of power had succumbed to the bullet years ago. That left Cora, who'd watched and learned, and now ruled.

She folded her hands in her lap and stared languidly at the petrified man in the unremarkable chair facing hers. She watched as he shook and sweated, as his wide, agitated eyes ricocheted around her office, taking in the gun and the brick and the other things. Fear, she had learned at Big Daddy's knee, could be as effective as a gun to the head. The time taken to let that fear grow and burrow deep into a man's bones was time well spent and weakened his resistance.

Cora waited. She was in no rush.

She always dressed in black. Big Daddy had, and so had her brothers. Black sent a message that Gamons did not dwell in the light. She kept her makeup simple, her jewelry tasteful, expensive, befitting her status. Her face was dark, her skin unlined, nurtured, glowing for a woman in her mid-fifties. From outward appearances, no one would be able to tell who or what she was, or what she might be feeling or thinking.

The man. Cora watched him without a single hint of expression. He was insignificant, a bug. Cora dealt with a lot of bugs.

Against the wall stood her enforcer, Crow. Big, silent, deadly, an enigma to all, even to her. The opposite of a human billboard, Crow had a stillness and stoicism that almost made him blend into whatever room he stood in. Even his eyes revealed nothing because no one ever saw them, as he wore dark sunglasses indoors and out. His clean-shaven head shone under the light. No mustache, no beard, no bow to trend or fad. Just a big dark man in a dark tailored suit who watched and waited and did not hesitate when the time came. Loyal enough, Cora knew, if the price was right. A killer, if he felt like it on the day. Beside him stood a Gamon, a niece. Patrice. Twenty, untrained, ambitious, a motherless discard.

Cora's eyes slowly shifted to the dead man in front of her. "I *think* you thought because I was a woman, you could get away with selling in my territory, taking money out of my pockets." She glanced down at the desk and at the piece of paper with the man's name written on it. "Is that it, *Andre*?"

Maybe in his mid-thirties, if she had to guess, Andre squeezed his eyes shut and shook his head from side to side with whiplash intensity. "You got this all wrong. It don't have to be all this. Look, I'm a small operator. You got the market cornered. I'm no threat to you." He looked over at Crow. "I'm nobody, *nothing*. You let me go, and I'm out of here, understand? Plus, you got the wrong guy anyway. I did not *do* this."

Cora's brows lifted. "Oh?"

Andre licked his lips, swiped sweat from his forehead. "All wrong. Wrong guy. What I look like coming up on you disrespecting you? I swear. You let me out of here, you ain't never gonna see my face no more."

Cora's eyes never left Andre's. "Crow."

The big man walked out of the office, plunging it into silence. When Crow returned moments later, he was holding a Black man by the back of his hoodie. The man slumped in Crow's grip, having been beaten to a bloody pulp. Both his eyes were swollen shut, his nose had been rearranged, his face covered in snot and blood, every finger was broken beyond repair. Andre took one look at his associate, and his face went three shades lighter as the realization of his fate hit him.

Cora leaned forward; her manicured fingers entwined on the top of her mahogany desk. "This is about honor, Andre. You, your friend there, disrespected me. You stole from me. I can't have that. Can I, Andre? What message would it send?"

"Look, I'm out, all right? I don't know what he said, but I'm *out*. I'm gone."

Cora leaned back and considered his words for a moment. "Okay. I'll take that. You're gone." She raised her hands, palms up. "You can go with Crow. He'll show you and your friend out."

Andre sat stunned, his breath catching. "For real? You're letting me go? I can just *walk out*?"

Cora nodded. "With Crow. Yes. On the promise that I will *never* see you or your friend again."

Andre popped up from the chair but appeared wary of the open door. He looked over at the silent enforcer, his face a blank slate, and at his friend, who was more dead than alive. Andre took two steps toward them, then froze before reeling back around.

"You're not letting me go, are you?"

"You're going with Crow. He'll see that you get where you need to be."

Andre's eyes darted around the room, looking for escape, but there was no getting past the big man or the goons he knew were positioned outside. His shoulders drooped, his will appeared to leave him. He died either here or wherever Crow chose, but he knew for certain in that moment that hubris and greed had condemned him. He took one last look at Cora Gamon, not even having the will to curse her, then turned to meet his fate.

When the door was closed behind them, Patrice smiled and sat in the chair Andre had occupied. "So, you always take them out? No second chances?"

Cora's cold eyes met the girl's cold eyes. Gamon eyes. "No mercy. Disrespect is not tolerated. You show weakness, you've lost. This is business. *My* business."

Patrice's eyes widened. "*Our* business. *Family* business."

Cora let Patrice's words linger for a moment. Those in the chair didn't share. They didn't consult. They didn't rule by committee. This house, this empire, this business were not a democracy. Surely the girl knew that by now? Hadn't Cora fed and clothed and tried to teach the child to know at least *that much*?

"*My* business," Cora repeated. "*My* chair. *My* way. Know that." Patrice pressed her lips firmly together. "Nod that you understand."

Their eyes held.

Patrice nodded. "Blood is blood, Aunt Cora."

Cora squared her shoulders, exhaled slowly, taking the child in without an ounce of maternal instinct getting in the way of her assessment. Blood was blood, but business was business, and the chair was the chair. "Yes," she said, conceding the fact, but not in the context Patrice had meant it. "Back to work. Your numbers are down. Get them up." Patrice opened her mouth to speak, but Cora held up a hand. "Not a discussion. Just do it."

Dismissed, Patrice stood up and left the office, closing the door behind her. Cora stared at the door for a moment, then picked up the phone to make her money. Like a Gamon.

CHAPTER 1

Harri walked the lakefront path on her day off, counting her dead, rain tapping the hood of her jacket, the dull plink resembling the sound of dropped nails meeting a coffin lid.

It was spring, a season of renewal, but the gray sky and the rain and her unease belied the optimism of rebirth. She had shoved her star and her gun in its tuck holster into the pocket of her jacket before she left the house, because she was a cop, off duty or on. Now the weight of both dragged that side of her coat down, slightly affecting her gait. Nearly every jacket she owned had one torn pocket where gun and badge had stressed fabric over the years. Occupational hazard. Harri dropped her hands in after the hardware to warm them, fists clenched. Early spring in Chicago was just winter light.

She'd hit the wall two months ago. Right after Eddie Noble was killed. Her reservoir of avoidance, that gut pit where she dumped and buried all those things she chose to ignore, had reached capacity. The word *fine*, her standard response to those asking how she was doing, now caught in her throat like a tough piece of meat cooked to death. She was angry but knew she couldn't *be* angry. Anger and cop didn't work.

Her pace quickened as though speed could get ahead of the feeling, as if the heavy slap of her Nikes against the puddles could flatten the emotion as easily as it could an ant. Harri wasn't an idiot. She knew you couldn't outrun life, that you couldn't bargain away death. Still, there had been that sly *perhaps* that had made her believe if she mourned enough, suffered enough, grieved enough, the gods would be kind and all would be restored. She'd buried that fantasy in the pit too.

What was she going to do now that she couldn't stuff it all down anymore? The walk was meant to order things, to stop her fists from clenching, but it wasn't working. It wasn't working, because Noble was dead, and though she had the answers she'd needed, she'd been denied the satisfaction of seeing justice properly carried out. *Justice.* She struggled with its meaning. What accounted for justice was often weak, impotent, and empty, changing nothing in the end. The bullet to the dirty cop's head had released him from all accountability, but her partner was still dead. Detective Glynnis Thompson's family, her husband, her boys, they still had to go on without her. And Harri had to find a way to live with the uneasy fix without letting rage, clenched fists, and a filled gut pit lead her down a road she couldn't come back from.

Ducking her head, she focused on the tops of her shoes, pointing them south toward Oakwood Boulevard. She'd stop there, then turn and head back. One foot in front of the other, a metaphor for life itself. Forward because forward was the only way, but not without doubt or struggle. Forward one day, one thought, one footstep at a time. Peace by the second, knowing an end wasn't always the balm it promised to be.

Harri peered out under the bill of her hood at the light traffic up the Drive, light even for a Sunday. The flatness of the lake to her left should have been calming, but the slowly undulating hue of gray toad and spilled green paint had no effect. She thought of the alewives that had once littered the beaches and wondered where they'd gone. Dead too. Change and constancy were twin demons.

As she got closer to the skate park at Thirty-First Street, something on the lip of one of the deep concrete bowls caught her eye. Perhaps a jumble of blankets belonging to the unhoused? Garbage from an overturned city cart, dumped by late-night miscreants? It was only when she got closer that she could clearly tell it wasn't either of those things; it was two people lying on the cold ground getting rained on. There was no movement from either of them, which set an alert ringing in her head. No movement could mean sleeping, though she could see no good reason for anyone to choose such an exposed spot to take a nap. No movement could also mean dead. She didn't want it to mean dead, not today, not on her day off, not when her gut had taken all the punches and delusions it could withstand.

Tentatively, she walked toward the metal fence that ringed the park. Stopping for a moment to look for a twitch or a jerk from the prone bodies. There was nothing. Harri sighed, knowing her day off was probably over almost as soon as it began. The shift from off duty to on would have gone unnoticed by most, but Harri's back straightened. She pulled out "cop face." Suddenly, different, harder, assessing eyes scanned the area for things out of place, things not normal, things criminal. Clenched fists and uncertainty gave way to steel and training and service.

Her hands on the fence, she turned slightly to check the small parking lot a few yards north. There was a banged-up Hyundai sitting in it, nothing else. Did the car belong to the two she was looking at?

Everything about this was odd. Nobody would choose this spot to party in, not with a cruel wind flying off the lake in early April. No homeless person would choose it, either—too exposed, too easy to be spotted and rousted by cops and forced to move along. And neither scenario made sense in the rain.

"Hey," she called out, her eyes on the two unmoving forms. "Hey," she repeated, this time a little louder.

No response. The imaginary alert in her head, the sense she got from a cold chill down her back, confirmed that her hope that this was nothing was not to be.

The two—one male, one female, both white, and from Harri's vantage point, young—lay on their backs, their arms out to the side, like human crosses nailed to the lip.

"Hello? You two in the park."

When she got no response a second time, she found the gate and tried pushing through, but it was locked. Harri glanced at her watch. City parks opened at 6:00 a.m. and closed at 11:00 p.m. Or were supposed to. Somebody was late with the key. Not that a locked gate would be much of an obstacle for a truly determined fence hopper, she thought. What the gate and the fence did was cover the city's ass in the event of injury and lawsuit if somebody cracked their head or broke a bone when the park was closed, supposedly. Harri looked around for skateboards. None. So, either the gate stayed locked, with no one from the park district bothering to open and close it on a regular basis and the two jumped the fence, or the two jumped the fence *after* the park closed at 11:00 and the gate was locked. She gave the fence a good going over. It appeared doable for the young and hearty. Harri was forty-three and beginning to feel it. Fence hopping was not high on her list of preferred activities.

"*Police.* I'm coming over."

She wasn't sure what this was yet, but she didn't want either of them to wake up in surprise, assume she was a threat, and strike out. Harri eyed the fence again, looking for the easiest access point. Gate locked. There was no way but up and over. She sighed, resigned to the effort.

"Police," she called again; this time it was more of a bark.

Harri's rain jacket hit mid-thigh, so she hiked it up to climb over the three-foot fence. Getting as good a grip as she could on the wet, slippery metal, she swung her left leg over, hung for a second, then pulled her right leg over too. Both feet landed in a cold puddle, soaking her socks and the bottoms of her jeans. She clenched her fists, then unclenched them, before reaching into her pocket for her star.

Taking a look around, Harri noticed there was no one on the path she'd just abandoned, no one else in the park but these two, and only the sound of the lake and traffic along the Drive to distract from what was in front of her. As she approached slowly, ready to identify herself, there was still no movement. The uneasy feeling she'd had before she'd climbed the fence grew into something more, a sense of dread and inevitability.

She held her badge out in front of her. "Police," she repeated. "Do *not* shoot me."

There was no response.

She stood over them, her assessing eyes making a full sweep. Barely twenty, she guessed, still babies. Both were dressed in jeans, sweaters, running shoes, light jackets, like kids, everything now soaked from the rain. White, yes. Male and female. The young man with dark hair and long lashes, the young woman blond and thin. Both out of place here. This was Thirty-First Street. Bronzeville. East of The Gap. Wrong hood.

The two were side by side as if they'd simply lain back and fallen asleep together. Odder still. Not in the rain. Not with the wind off the lake. Harri knelt between them, scanning the ground they lay on and the area around it. A purple backpack sat next to the girl; two half-empty beer bottles next to the boy. By the bottles, a small light-blue plastic bag, just the right size for a hit of cocaine or a pair of party pills. The bag was empty. The fact that she could see no residue inside the bag indicated to her that they'd likely taken pills, not powder. There was something faint stenciled on the packet, but Harri couldn't make out the small lettering without her reading glasses, nor did she want to touch the bag and contaminate it.

"Damn it," she muttered, slipping her badge back into her pocket.

The pair were strikingly pale, their lips blue. The young man's eyes were half closed; a trickle of vomit had dried at the corner of his open mouth. Blood that had oozed out of each narrow nostril had darkened to the color of clay brick. Harri knew dead. She worked with it every day, all day. Dead was cold and vacant and unalterable. It couldn't be undone by vow or bargain or prayer. Still, she pressed her fingers to the boy's neck to check for a pulse she knew she wouldn't find, then did the same to his thin wrist before laying a hand on his chest for a moment. One last human touch. There was nothing else she could do for him. Without taking a second to think, Harri turned to the young woman. Seeing her this close, Harri put her age closer to eighteen, nineteen. Her baby face and full cheeks were now chalky white and waxen. Like with the boy, she checked for a pulse at the young woman's neck, expecting nothing. She drew in a surprised breath when there was a faint report. Very faint, thready.

The girl was alive.

"Yes, keep breathing," Harri muttered as she reached into her pocket for her cell phone, a sense of relief flowing through her, though she knew the situation could turn at any moment. She shook the girl gently, hoping to rouse her at least a little, but she got no response.

The girl's nose had bled, like her friend's, but it had had time to dry and clot. There were no wounds that Harri could see. There'd been none on the young man either. She was certain the drug bag was the answer. OD.

She punched the numbers for 911, put the phone on speaker, and set it on the cold concrete beside her as she scanned the path, looking for help. A rainy Sunday morning. Perfect for walking alone, not so perfect for finding Good Samaritans, especially a doctor or nurse. Miracle thinking.

As the phone rang, she turned the girl over on her side and leaned down closer to her ear on the off chance she could hear her. "Hang in there. I've got you."

Harri rolled the girl back, then rubbed her knuckles across her sternum. Again, no response.

The dispatcher's flat voice broke the silence. "911. What's your emergency?"

"This is Detective Harriet Foster. District one." She checked on the girl again while relaying her star number for authentication. "I have a suspected OD at Burnham Skate Park at Thirty-First." She glanced over at the dead boy. Full lips. Dark hair. Gone. "One female unresponsive. Approximately nineteen. One male, about the same age. Deceased. I'm off duty and on scene. It looks like they've been out here some time. The female's pulse is very weak, almost nonexistent. She doesn't look likely."

She listened as the dispatcher directed the call to emergency services. "Response en route," the dispatcher reported. "Three minutes out. Stand by."

Three minutes? She looked down at the young woman, wondering if she had that long.

Harri ended the call. "Help's coming," she told the girl. "Three minutes."

She held the girl's hand. It was cold to the touch, but there was still life in it. Scanning around again, she looked for an AED box, though she wasn't even sure a defibrillator was the right move to make in this situation. She wasn't a doctor, and the girl's heart was beating, though not well. A plunger of Narcan would maybe help, Harri thought, but no first aid box meant no can of Narcan either. Waiting helplessly was all she could do. Harri hated the feeling.

Traffic whizzed past them on the Drive. Cars driven by live people on their way to wherever. Maybe nothing bad would happen to any one of them all day, she mused, though if anything did, she was sure it wouldn't be half as bad as a dead kid lying in the rain. For her own peace, Harri avoided looking at the dead boy, but it didn't stop her from feeling his absence or thinking about the boy *she'd* lost. Three minutes. She kept repeating it in her head. One hundred and eighty seconds. Not a long time, though it felt like an eternity.

"Hey, what's going on over there?"

Harri turned to see an older white man on a bike stopped on the path, his phone out, the camera pointed at her. Her first thought was *Who bikes in the rain?* Her second, *Why was he recording this?*

"Put your camera away," she snapped, biting off the reproach and the fury that accompanied it. Whippet thin, dressed in full racing gear, including a sleek helmet, the man stood there, his bike between his legs, his camera trained on the skate park and her.

"I've got you on video," he snapped back. "I'm calling the police."

She pulled her badge out again, held it up for him to see it. "I *am* the police. Turn your camera *off*! Would you want somebody recording *your* kid lying here dying?"

The man lowered his phone and stood with his mouth open. "They're dead? What happened? You shoot them?"

She fought hard to say nothing. Of course, it's the first thing people thought when they saw a cop. That they're maniacs who randomly shoot kids down in skate parks on lazy Sunday mornings. Harri gritted her teeth, then turned her back to him. She had more important things to do.

"Stay back, out of the way," she ordered. "Nobody needs you blocking things up."

"I'm not blocking anything, and I've got a right to record. I'm a citizen."

Harri bolted up. "Move! Away! *Now!*"

The man jumped at the ferocity of her delivery and meekly pedaled his bike farther down the path but didn't leave. Harri knew it was the best she would get.

"Ghoul," she muttered as she went back to the girl.

A rattle came from the girl's throat. Harri recognized it, and her blood froze.

"No, no, no-no-no-no. Don't you *dare* die on me," she warned. "You hear me? I *forbid* you to die on me."

Sirens wailed in the distance. Help was coming. Her heart literally leaped in her chest. She focused on the girl struggling to live.

"How could you do this to your mother?" she whispered to her. "You have no idea what—"

She couldn't finish. The lump in her throat was too large. It felt as though the dead boy's spirit sat on her shoulder, like a ghost haunting her soul. One death, she thought, but it would change many lives. The mother who bore the young man and carried his heart in hers would never be right again.

The sound of sirens grew louder. Harri spotted the first flashing lights of the emergency vehicles. Seconds later an ambulance, fire truck, and two squad cars barreled into the lot, speeding toward her. Her sense of relief was almost overwhelming.

Harri looked down at the girl. "They're here. You made it."

Dialed-in paramedics, firefighters, and cops bolted out of their vehicles and raced toward her, the paramedics laden down with bags full of lifesaving equipment and medication.

"Happy to see you," she said as the first paramedic reached her. "She's still breathing. The boy's not."

She picked up her phone, stood, and then pedaled back to give the experts the room to assess and work. It was only then that Harri realized how tense her body had been, how tightly her jaw had been clenched.

"Whadda we got? OD?" the female paramedic asked as she knelt down beside the two.

Harri met the woman's serious brown eyes and found competence in them. She'd no doubt faced this particular situation many, many times before. Her eyes wandered down to the nameplate on the woman's chest . . . Carlson . . . then to her black hair pulled back into a short ponytail, which had a prominent streak of magenta running through it.

"Suspected," Harri said.

Her partner, Latino, with biceps the size of juice cans, moved to take a look at the boy, but it didn't take long for him to discover what Harri had already told them. Not wasting time, he swiveled around to assist his partner with the one they had a chance of saving. He grabbed things out of his bag—blood pressure cuff, a syringe, tubing, and the blessed plunger of Narcan, which Harri would have given almost anything for earlier.

"What the hell were they doing out *here*?" he asked as if Harri would know. "The dumb things dumb kids do to themselves."

His name was Arias. And Harri, standing in the cold wet, her hands deep in her pockets, faced with senseless death yet again, was finding it difficult to disagree with his assessment.

Pedaling back farther out of the way, she eyed the young woman's backpack, and keeping well clear of the activity, she picked it up and carried it with her as she took a few more steps away. Both victims would need to be identified, their families notified. The boy's ID was likely in his pocket, but she didn't want to disturb the body any more than she already had. His ID would have to wait. The last thing she needed was an ME tech breathing down her neck. She could justify the pack. They needed a name for the girl, a starting point.

Glancing over toward the path, she saw that her biker videographer was still there. It never ceased to mystify her why some people were so invested in other people's tragedy. She'd called him a ghoul, but there had to be more than that to it. Harri turned her back to the biker and began picking through the pack, looking for a wallet. While she felt around the bottom of the bag, she kept her eyes on the paramedics and the work they were doing for the girl. She was still unconscious but not as deathly pale. Maybe the Narcan was having some effect?

Her hands hit something leathery, and she drew it out. The wallet was a small red deal with some kind of anime sticker plastered to the back of it. Still a child, she thought.

Harri was right. Holding the girl's driver's license in her hand, she read her age—nineteen. Ella Louise Byrne. The license photo revealed a full-of-life ash blond with bright-green eyes and a cute smile. Somebody's baby. There was a school ID too. Byrne was a sophomore at the University of Chicago. Though the school was only about four miles south, it was worlds away from the skate park.

"Whadda we got?"

She looked up at the uniformed cops. She read their nameplates. Officers Pappas and Seaver, respectively. Both white, both burly, both looking as though they'd been ground down by endless bullshit, stress, and futility. She dug into her pocket and retrieved her star. She couldn't recall ever having had to present it so often on a day off in her entire career. They would have gotten her name already from dispatch, but they still needed to confirm it, and she had no problem with that. This time, she clipped her star to the pocket of her jacket, where everyone could see it. The two nodded an all clear, dialing some of the cop back to stand waiting for direction. Harri was first on scene, and she outranked them.

"ID on the girl," Harri said. "A start, anyway."

Her eyes cut to the lot as an unmarked car rolled up. She watched as the doors opened on a tan Crown Vic to see if they were detectives she knew, but they weren't.

She went back to the girl's wallet. There were a couple of credit cards and money, $400. The amount surprised her. What college kid carried so much or even *had* so much? Harri also found a wool hat with a white pom-pom on top. In a side pocket were photos of a family—parents and three kids. Harri easily picked out Ella smiling among them.

Her search was interrupted when two detectives walked up and took a good long sweep of her, the scene, the dead boy, and the young woman still struggling to live.

"Breathing's better," Carlson announced. "Narcan's working. Good signs."

"She going to make it?" Harri asked.

Carlson winced. "Still not out of the woods. A lot could happen."

The detectives walked up.

"Detective Streeter," the taller one said. He was solid and thick, with a square jaw, bold stance, and comic book–hero looks. Batman without the mask. Dick Tracy without the raincoat and techie watch. Streeter cocked a thumb toward his partner. "Evans."

Harri put the half-searched wallet back into the pack and handed the pack to Streeter. This wasn't her crime scene. They were now in charge. "Foster. The young woman is Ella Byrne, U of C student, nineteen. I couldn't access the boy's ID. He didn't make it." She eyed them both. Evans was Black, broad, shorter than the hero by only a few inches, but formidable looking, as though he could lift a Buick without straining a muscle. Harri could tell by the look in his eyes that not much got past him either. It wasn't difficult to tell a dialed-in cop from one who just ran out the clock on their shift. Evans was dialed in.

"We don't usually roll out on OD calls," Evans said, flicking a look at his partner.

"We were close, though," Streeter said. "Thought we might as well stop by and see what was up."

Evans shook his head. "An OD." He looked everything over, a scowl on his face. "Private party gone wrong, it looks like." He turned to Harri. "Anything look like somebody else had a part in this?"

She shook her head. "Not that I could see." She told them about the blue bag, pointed to where she'd found it by the boy's body, empty. "Pills or something else. Can't say."

Streeter looked down at the pack in his hand. "Was this all you touched?"

It was a valid question, one she'd ask if she were in his position. But something in the way he asked, accusatory, didn't sit well.

"The pack and the victims were all I touched," she said, "only enough to render aid."

Streeter searched the pack himself, again something Harri would have done. Cops couldn't rely on a person's word, not even another cop's or their own mother's. They had to see it, hear it, know it for themselves. Solid evidence was king. "Not much," he determined far too quickly in Harri's opinion. She would have spent a lot more time on the bag.

Evans flicked a thumb toward the path. "Who the fuck is that guy on the bike?"

"Gawker," she said. "I didn't have time to deal with him too."

Evans huffed. "Hell, *I* got time." He turned around, glared at the biker. "Fuck off or go to jail, man."

"He's not committing a crime," Harri said. "He's just a looming presence."

Streeter smirked. "We know. But Evans doesn't like anybody looming. It makes him antsy."

The biker stayed put, camera still going. That was until Evans took a threatening step toward him. Suddenly the camera dropped, and the biker took off in a hurry, going south down the path.

Evans turned back around grinning, dusting his hands. "See? Problem solved."

Harri wished everything were that easy, especially for Ella Byrne. "Mind if I take another look at that pack?"

Streeter gave it to her easily, then moved past, along with Evans, toward the young man. "Well, since we're here, we may as well do what we do. The sooner we get him off the ground, the better I'll like it."

Pack in hand, Harri followed them, wanting to know who the boy was. She watched as they gloved up and then gently turned the body over to slide a wallet out of his back pocket. The rest would wait until the ME's office came out. Harri avoided looking at the boy's face, concentrating instead on the leather billfold in Streeter's hand.

"Robert Mitchell," Streeter said, reading the details. "Michigan license. Twenty." He checked the rest, then looked over at Harri. "You say the girl goes to U of C?"

She nodded.

Streeter held up an ID card from the wallet. "Him too. Damn shame. What's that go for? Fifty K a year?"

Evans moved around him. "Try closer to ninety."

Streeter whistled. "That's a chunk?"

Evans snorted. "And a half."

Harri tried blocking out their conversation. What did it matter how much the school cost? A kid was dead, lying on the cold ground. She concentrated on Byrne's wallet, checking it more thoroughly this time. Maybe something there would explain what had happened. She needed to understand the why.

She looked over the scene. "Anybody finding cell phones?"

"One in the girl's pocket," Carlson answered.

Harri looked down at Evans and Streeter. "Him?"

She watched as Streeter felt the boy's pants and jacket pockets. "Yep." He pulled the phone out. "Locked."

"Biometrics?" Harri asked.

Streeter lifted the boy's hand, held his index finger and pressed it to the phone's screen, then shook his head. "No such luck. Password protected."

Following his partner's lead, Evans moved over to retrieve the phone from the girl's pocket. "Same here."

Harri sighed. Why could nothing ever be easy? She went back to the wallet. It had a lot of sleeves and slots and hidden pockets. In addition to the license, the money, and the school ID, there was a cafeteria meal card, an ATM card, a card for a fitness center, and a couple of business cards, one belonging to an attorney on LaSalle. It was the second business card that pulled her up short. It held the CPD seal, like the one she carried in her bag. But it was the name on it that flipped her stomach and made her feel nauseous. She stepped away from Evans and Streeter, then turned her back to them altogether. Aware that the two POs were still standing by, she avoided them as well.

The card belonged to Detective Matt Kelley, a member of her own team. The department didn't issue courtesy cards, but a cop's business card often served the same purpose. It identified the holder as a friend or family member of a cop, and it was enough most times to get the bearer out of minor infractions—a ticket, a traffic stop, a nuisance offense—with only a slap on the wrist or a sly wink and an order to move along and sin no more.

Behind her, the young woman began to cough. Harri reeled around to see Byrne's eyes begin to flutter and her body jerk and move and thrash around. Arias placed an oxygen mask on the girl's face as her drowsy eyes searched for a hint as to where she was or how she'd gotten here. She began to whimper softly.

"Let's get her out of here," Arias said as he pulled the gurney in closer, ready to lift Byrne onto it.

Harri knew they'd take Ella to the closest hospital. That meant Mercy, or whatever they called it now. As she watched them get ready to move, Harri dialed Matt's number. She was off today, but he wasn't. Ella started to moan, and her head lolled to the side. She wasn't fully conscious. Matt answered on the second ring.

"Oh, no," he said jovially. "You're off today. That means *off*, Harri, not just *not here*."

Harri hesitated, not sure where to start. "I ran into a bit of a situation."

"What's up?"

She stared at the card of *her* Matt Kelley, holding it tightly in her hand. "Do you know an Ella Byrne?"

Kelley went quiet on the other end. The quiet stretched far beyond what felt comfortable. "What's going on?" His voice had changed, no longer jovial. Now it was all cop, all business.

"Matt?"

"She's my niece. My sister's oldest. Nineteen last June. Tell me."

There was no play in his voice. No more lightheartedness. Even over the phone, she could feel him tense and brace himself for bad news. Harri explained what had happened as clearly and thoroughly as she could, like she was giving a report to a superior, knowing that was the best way to do it, knowing that even so, every word she uttered would hit Kelley like a round between the eyes.

"I'll hand off here and meet you at the hospital," she told him. "I'll stay with her until you get there."

"Yeah. Got it. On my way." He paused, his voice softened. "Thanks, Harri."

He ended the call. She put the phone away, then stood for a moment to settle herself. She watched as they rolled Ella toward the ambulance. Harri looked for Streeter and Evans while fishing in her pocket for her own city cards. She raced over and handed them each one.

"If you need me, I'll be with her. Turns out I work with her uncle. She's one of ours."

She didn't need to say anything more. She ran to catch up with the gurney, flagging down the paramedics.

"Hey," she called out to them. "I'm riding along."

Both Carlson and Arias looked confused as they lifted Ella inside.

"Above and beyond?" Arias asked.

Carlson's brow furrowed. "Yeah, we don't usually carpool it."

Harri ignored them and climbed in the back. Tight squeeze, but that's what it would have to be. "Her uncle's on the job."

They nodded. It was all Harri needed to say. "Let's go then," Arias said, strapping Ella Byrne in while his partner jumped out and closed the back doors. When he was ready, he slapped the side of the ambulance, and Carlson drove off, sirens blaring.

Ella's eyes opened. She looked up at Harri. "Uncle Matt?"

She'd heard her. Ella was coming back. Harri leaned down closer to her ear. "He'll meet you at the hospital. Everyone will, I'm sure. Until they get there, *I'm* with *you*. I'm Harriet."

The girl looked up at her, but her eyes were still jumpy and unfocused. She reached out her hand, and Harri held it tight, finding it blessedly warm instead of deathly cold.

"I've got you," Harri said. "You're going to be fine."

As she held Ella's hand, Harri's mind flooded with other things. Why were Ella and Mitchell in the skate park to begin with? What had they taken? Where had they gotten it? Why was there so much money in Ella's wallet?

"No use trying to make sense of it."

She looked over at a smiling Arias.

"I can see you're trying to figure out what happened," he said. "There's no use trying to make sense of it. All the talking, all the information, the school programs, but they never think it's going to happen to them."

Harri nodded, knowing he was right, gripping Ella's hand tighter. "Until it does."

CHAPTER 2

Harri stood outside the ER bay, pacing. Doctors and nurses were inside with the drape pulled closed, working on Ella. The place was packed as always. Close to midday on a Sunday, there was a crunch between new arrivals and those who'd spent the night being administered to and were now just being discharged. Every patient slot was full, and when she'd walked out to the waiting room to stretch her legs and get some fresh air, every plastic chair had calamity sitting in it.

Harri hated hospitals. She hated their smells and strangeness. She hated that they were where hope and people died. For her, anxiousness was ground into the tiles and paint. It lived in the steady beeps of every lifesaving machine. Back outside Ella's bay, standing sentry at the curtain, she waited for Ella's people to get there. There was no limit on how long she'd stay. The minutes ticked by as she stood and hovered and watched.

"Harri."

She turned to see Matt barreling toward her with a panicked middle-aged couple right with him. Ella's parents. She recognized them from the photos in Ella's wallet. The woman looked a lot like Ella, ash blond, thin. Her husband was darker, thicker, beginning to gray.

"Where is she?" the woman asked, her voice breaking. She was crying. Her blue eyes swam with tears, and it appeared she'd long ago cried away her eyeliner and mascara, leaving her stricken face haunted by fear. "Where's my *daughter*?"

Kelley put his arms around the woman before Harri could answer. "This is my sister, Maggie. Her husband, Joe. How's Ella?"

Harri thought she knew Matt pretty well. He was a smart, dedicated cop, a bit of a jokester around the office, easygoing. But this was a different Matt, stern of face, deliberate, ready to step up for the family.

"They're in with her now," Harri said. "She was in and out in the ambulance. Not very clear in the head. They administered Narcan on scene. I don't know how much she'll remember."

That was all Maggie Byrne needed to hear. "Narcan. Oh, my God." She brushed past Harri, flung back the privacy drape, and burst inside unannounced.

"What the hell happened?" Joe asked, his hands on his hips, a disquieted crease between his eyes. Harri could see that he and his wife had dressed hurriedly. Their clothes were slightly wrinkled, jeans, sweatshirts. Things they'd likely grabbed because they were the first things they could find before rushing out of the house after Matt's call. Joe eyed the curtain apprehensively, no doubt wanting to join his wife and daughter yet wary about doing it, afraid of what he'd find.

Harri repeated what she'd told Matt and what Matt had undoubtedly already shared with them. She left nothing out.

"She wasn't able to answer any questions in the ambulance," Harri said.

Joe bristled. "You *questioned* her? Like she's a criminal?"

Matt put a steadying hand on Joe's shoulder. Harri focused on Joe, giving him a pass because he was helplessly out of his element. "I asked her if she knew her name. If she knew what day it was. If she could tell me what happened. She couldn't."

Joe ran his hands through his hair, squeezed his eyes shut. "Sorry. *Sorry.* Of course. I didn't mean that. Dear God. I can't believe this is happening. Ella's a good kid. We've never had to deal with anything like this. What about the boy you found her with? Who the hell is he? Did he do this to her?"

Harri shook her head. "All we have at this point is an ID."

"What was she *thinking*? She's a good student. She's working. She's got friends. She's well adjusted. Where's all this coming from all of a sudden?"

Harri thought of the wallet full of money. "Where's she working?"

"She's a research lab assistant somewhere on campus. Chemistry's her major." Joe Byrne scanned the activity around him, seemingly confused. "I don't know the place. Maggie would, I guess. I know Ella was lucky to get the spot. It sure beat flipping burgers or waiting tables. We wanted her to work. Be independent. Learn how it feels to earn a dollar." He stopped suddenly. "Sorry, I'm rambling." He eyed the drape. "And stalling. I don't want to have to deal with this. Maggie's a lot better at this stuff. I never thought we'd ever be here."

"Go in, Joe," Matt said gently. "See what they're saying."

Joe eyed the curtain like he was torn between going or staying. "Yeah, yeah. I should go in. Be with Maggie." He turned to Harri. "Thank you, Harriet. Matt says we got lucky you being there." He reached out and grabbed her hand to shake it. "I don't even want to think about what would have happened if . . ."

Joe looked like he was on the verge of losing it. "Go. Be with your family," Harri said.

He pulled the curtain back and stepped inside, then drew it closed behind him. When he was gone, Matt blew out a loud breath, tilted his face up toward the ceiling, looking as though he wanted to be anywhere else but here at any other time than this one. Of course he did, Harri thought. This was a parent's nightmare.

"I can't believe this," he whispered. "*Ella.* Joe was right about her being a good kid. There has never, *ever* been anything like this going on with her."

"Experimentation?" Harri asked. "Peer pressure, maybe."

Matt's face fell. "We've worked so many cases like this. Never in a million years did I ever think *Ella* would wind up in such a mess. What the hell was she *thinking*?"

Harri assumed the question was rhetorical, so didn't try to answer it. Instead, she stood quietly as Matt worked through what he needed to.

"And we have *nothing* on the other kid?" he asked.

Harri shook her head. "Just a name. I'm assuming the car in the lot was his, unless Ella drives a beat-up Hyundai?"

Matt shook his head. "Maggie and Joe bought her a nice little Honda when she graduated. They didn't want her relying on the bus or L to get around."

Harri had a feeling, one she couldn't dismiss. "There was four hundred dollars in her wallet."

"She was *working*," Matt responded, a hint of defensiveness in his tone. "You heard what Joe said. They didn't want her dependent on them for everything. They wanted her to learn how to make her own way. Are you saying—"

"Nothing. I'm saying nothing. Just trying to figure it out like everybody else."

"Okay," Matt said. "I get that. Always straight A's. She doesn't even drink *beer* . . . as far as I know. She's just a kid, for Christ's sake. Out there all night." His eyes met hers, cautious. "You would have said if . . ."

Harri knew the questions he would ask. "I would have. I saw no evidence of assault, but only the doctors can say for sure."

"Good. Okay." Matt nodded, let a moment go. "And just the two of them, far as you could tell?"

"Just the two beer bottles and the bag," she said, "no evidence of a larger gathering. We can check to see if any reports came in about kids in the skate park, but with the rain last night, I don't think that's going to be likely, do you?"

"No, that wouldn't make any sense, but frankly neither does this." Matt groaned. "Jesus. I can't even keep my own family safe from this mess. *Ella.* Are *my* kids next? What good are we if we can't even keep our own kids safe?"

He realized too late what he'd said and looked to Harri in shock and apology. "God. Sorry, Harri. I can't believe I just said that. I didn't mean to—"

She waved him off, suddenly exhausted now that things were out of her hands and the adrenaline rush had dissipated. "Nobody died and made us invincible. Our badges don't shield us, or our families, from the bad things in life. I've come to accept at least *that* much. We do our best and hope it's enough."

He gave her a strained smile. "We can't heal the world?"

"Not even ourselves," she said, letting the truth of it sink in. "Another recent discovery."

"Well, then, somebody should tell Symansky, because that crusty old-timer thinks his star makes him king of the world." He eyed the curtain, wary, as though it might actually bite him. "I'll hang here. Don't want to crowd anything."

Harri smiled. "You'll now be the sentry at the gate, then?"

"Kinda tailor made for it," Matt said. He paused. "I owe you one, big-time. If anyone else had stumbled on them, Ella might not be here."

"You don't owe me anything. I'm glad I was there."

"Still, if you're ever short a twenty before payday or need a kidney, or *anything*, I'm your guy."

She grinned. "Good to know."

"Okay. You need to get out of here. It's your day off, and we've wrecked enough of it. I already let the boss know what was going on, asked her to spread the word, so I wouldn't have to."

"You didn't have to do that. We're not entitled to your family business."

"You're all family too. We hold each other up, don't we?"

It was another thing she'd come to accept. "She's in good hands, so are you. Whatever you need ask for it."

"It'll be okay," he said. "Ella's a fighter. But I want *you* to get out of here. No more cop today, Harri," he said. "Promise?"

She rolled her eyes at the impossible ask. "Sure." She gave him a playful punch to the shoulder as she moved to walk away. "Keep us posted?"

"I will. Definitely."

She gave him a thumbs-up, then headed for the door, out of the smell of sickness, out of the orchestrated chaos, into the rain.

Stepping through the ER's automatic doors, Harri took a deep breath and watched a steady sprinkle beat down on the street from under the overhang as Matt's words echoed in her head. *No more cop today,* as though she could distinguish what she did from who she was, as though she could take off the cop as she would a sweater and hang it up in a closet until *cop* was needed the next time.

There had to be more.

"Baby steps," she muttered. "Progress. You can do it, Harriet. *Goddamn it.*"

She got her phone from her pocket to call for a ride home, flipped her collar up, closed her eyes, and waited to step out into the rain.

It was a fretful sleep. Harri simply could not settle. Fighting the blanket, punching the one pillow she owned, she rolled over in bed in the dark room to glance at the alarm clock on the nightstand, the clock a remnant from her old life, the one that had been full and normal and meaningful to her. Three a.m. At least the tenth time she'd checked the clock. Five hours until she was due for her shift. Rolling over on her back to stare at the ceiling, not wanting to close her eyes, knowing what she'd see, the dead boy's eyes. She knew that Mitchell was not her son, so why did it feel as though *she'd* lost him? Why was she so certain that she was sharing this sleepless night with the mother who had?

Sleep was not coming, and there was nothing Harri could do about it. She flopped over on her side with an unuttered expletive of frustration and futility on her lips, resigned to the fact that she would not get any rest this night. As her eyes scanned the darkened room, they stopped on what looked like a figure standing in the corner, watching her. She startled. In one seamless move, she bolted out of bed, grabbed her service weapon from under the mattress, and then flicked on the bedside lamp, only to find the corner empty, the window closed, no one in the room but her. The hammer strike of panic, the adrenaline-spiked beat of her heart, was as intense as the frenetic flapping of a hummingbird's wings. The room appeared to undulate.

Still, she stood ready for a moment longer, sure her eyes were just not seeing what had clearly been there in the dark moments ago. Somebody. Watching her. Harri listened to the old house, for creaks across the floorboards, the sound of footsteps, anything. As her fear subsided, as her heartbeat slowed, she had the eerie feeling that though she was clearly alone, she was not in fact alone.

That's when the cop clicked in. She started the search, though the gun in her hand felt weightless. Bedroom clear. Bathroom clear. She slipped down the stairs, quietly, stealthily, flicking the light switch on at the bottom to reveal her empty living room and kitchen. No one. She checked the back door. Locked, secured. She checked the alarm. Activated, untriggered, though she would have heard the alarm sound had it been tripped. She paused in the middle of her underutilized kitchen and stood guard over the place, her gun at her side. It was then that her eyes swept over the small table, beneath which just one chair was slid. She'd made no accommodation for visitors because she never expected to have any. One chair. One small table. One chair in the living room facing the picture window. A case board, much like the one she used at work, hung from her wall instead of paintings or lithographs. Near the front door a standing vase filled with colorful glass marbles, one marble dropped in to mark each day since her son Reg's murder. Her eyes took in all of it. But it was the table that got her attention. On it sat a marble. Just one. And she hadn't put it there.

An alarm sounded. It got louder. It rattled the windows. Red light bounced off the walls. She bolted up, bathed in sweat. Awake. The alarm, the lights, belonged to a passing ambulance. Heaving, trying to catch her breath, she leaned down to see if her gun was still under the mattress, its grip pointed outward. It was. She turned to look. The corner was empty. She had been dreaming. Harri dropped back, her eyes pinched closed, trembling. Was this what she wanted? she thought, running her hands through her damp hair. *This?* She knew the answer.

CHAPTER 3

Harri walked into the office Monday morning, her bag slung over her shoulder, a cup of hot coffee warm in her hand, as ready for the day as a woman with fifteen years of cop work under her belt could be at five minutes after 8:00 a.m. She was still a little disquieted by the night before but had settled on the certainty that the dark figure in her bedroom had been a figment, the result of an emotional day and an impossible night. The marble from her dream still loomed large in her mind. Was she supposed to interpret its meaning? If so, there was no chance of that. All she was left with was an eerie feeling. But Harri could compartmentalize. It's how she lived. It's how she kept moving when she didn't want to.

The first person she saw was Detective Matt Kelley, hunched over his computer, dressed in the same clothes she'd seen him in at the hospital the day before.

"What are you *doing* here?" As she stood over him, her mouth open, she realized the words had come out of her mouth far sharper than she'd intended.

He looked up, unshaven, his eyes bloodshot, like he was just off a two-day stakeout.

"Don't tell me you've been here all *night*," she said while searching his tired face, with its stubble and bleary eyes. "Matt, come on. This is not good."

"I know. I know. I just thought I could try and run down a few things and then touch base with the guys running Ella's case. The more eyes, right?" A large coffee stain ran down the front of his button-down shirt, the sleeves rolled up just past his elbows. His hair was askew, as though he'd run his hands through it a million times or more since Sunday morning. Ella's case? What case? It was an OD. A tragedy, nine times out of ten, something they would never be able to hold anyone accountable for.

"How is she?" Harri asked.

"Alive. Not making much sense yet."

"Then there's nothing else you can do, is there? You should go home, get some rest. Streeter and Evans have it." She said it gently because she knew he wasn't thinking like a cop right then. "If there's something they need, if it looks like it could turn into something, they'll let us know."

"You sound like this is a victimless crime. One kid dead? Ella nearly there? Who sold it to them? Where are they right now? They could be out there this minute selling the same stuff to somebody else. We have to get on it. I'm fine, really. I'm clear." She stared at him, knowing full well what "I'm fine" meant, knowing that it pushed people away and masked hard things. Matt was worried about his family. Nothing she could say could touch that.

"I actually put a call into Streeter already," he said. "I know it's early. Ella's still not up for questions, so we're going to have to tackle this from the other end for the time being." He checked his watch. "Her doctor plans on doing another scan, or something, in a couple hours.

"Maggie and Joe are there, and Annie went over this morning to sit with them while the kids are in school. We're all good. Everything's covered. We just need to know *how* this happened. Who's responsible." He turned back to his computer. "I've been running Mitchell. Maggie says Ella never mentioned him before, so they weren't dating, as far as she knows. She swears Ella tells them everything, though obviously she left a few things out. Mitchell's clean. *Was* clean. Just a regular college kid. No priors. The Hyundai was his. Nothing on it. Mom's a CPA. His father's an orthodontist. They're clean too. Just normal, all of it." He flicked a look at Harri. "It would help if we knew what they took. The test at the hospital showed it was some kind of opioid. Maybe something new on the streets, or a bad batch of something already out there? If we knew who they scored it from even . . ."

He was talking too fast, hyped up on fatigue and bad coffee. Harri decided to let it go. This was something he would have to work out on his own.

"Ella should be able to add something to that," she said. "When she's ready."

"Definitely," Matt said.

"Meanwhile, what can we do to help you?"

He shook his head. "You've done enough. You *saved* her. I have to do something besides sitting around waiting, though. Waiting's sucking the air out of me."

Harri glanced around the room at the change of shift, overnight cops going off, day ones coming on. Li and the others would be clocking in soon to find Matt hovering over his keyboard like a man possessed, and not a single one of them would *not* understand why.

The room smelled of old cop sweat and musty heat from the dirty ceiling vents. The city wasn't going to invest in any Google-like amenities like carpet, espresso stations, or complimentary Fiji water in the old beater fridge. They were city workers and got what city workers got year-round, every day, all day—a spot, a stack of open cases large enough to pound the life out of them, and a bimonthly paycheck. And when they eventually put in their papers, she pondered cynically, all they'd get was a hastily planned retirement party at a local cop bar and a pension that city aldermen would spend their careers whittling away at, so they'd end up with next to nothing to die on. All that hadn't bothered her much before, but it was beginning to bother her now.

The feel of the large room changed. Without turning around, Harri knew Detective Al Symansky and Detective Vera Li had walked in. She had picked up Al's heavy approach as his hard-soled shoes clunked and slid along the gray linoleum, and then there was the smell of fresh doughnuts, which told her Vera had stopped at her usual place for her usual dozen. Crullers for Al, jelly for Detective Tony Bigelow, chocolate for her, and whatever else she added to the box for Kelley, who strangely didn't have a preference. *Their* arrival also meant that Bigelow was still five or six minutes out and that he would be coming in and grumbling until his first cup of free CPD coffee from a scorched pot hit his full lips.

It was interesting how much she had learned about them all in the relatively short time she'd been with them. She'd transferred in just over a year ago, but it felt like she'd known them much longer than that. She knew that both Symansky and Bigelow were divorced with grown kids, but that only Bigs was actively dating (with dubious results). She knew that Vera pulled triple duty with cop work competing with a husband, a three-year-old, and a mother living at home. Symansky was their resident curmudgeon, Bigelow the one unfazed by anything around him. And Kelley, a detail-obsessed cop who could have been anything else from an astronaut to a neurosurgeon but instead chose city pay, overwork, and flat feet. They were a weird group, but they worked.

"Why am I seein' Matt sittin' there?" Al asked, his gruff voice carrying even over the low din of the retreating cops. He took off his tweed newsboy cap and tossed it over on his desk, then worked his way out of his rumpled grandpa jacket. "I mean, I'm seein' what I'm seein', ain't I?"

Vera shifted the pink bakery box in her arms. She and Harri exchanged a look. They both knew no amount of coercion or cajoling would move Matt from his chair.

"All righty, then," Vera said. "What are we doing? What do you need? Who's doing what?"

"I'm taking it," Matt said. "You all have enough to do without this on your plates too. I've got it. I'm just going to ask a few questions. Get a better handle on things."

Al glowered down at him. "Since when does anybody around here go solo?"

Matt stood up, rolled down his sleeves. "Look, I appreciate all this, really, but I'm on it. If I need you, I'll ask, promise." He reached for his jacket slung over the back of his chair and slipped into it. "I'm taking a couple hours PT. I want to see Streeter and Evans face-to-face."

"Why?" Al asked. "It's an OD case. Not to be blunt or anything, but they probably just filed it if nothing looked off. And if there was, Harri woulda said."

"I didn't see anything, but I also didn't map the whole area," Harri said. "Ella was the priority."

Matt was undeterred. "No one files this one. *I'll* work it if I have to." They all knew what was going on. Vera opened the bakery box and let the aroma of warm sugar and yeast rush out. She thrust the box at Matt. "At least fortify yourself with empty calories."

Matt grabbed a long john and then his notes from his desk. "I'll be back."

"Call if you need backup," Vera said.

"Don't do nothin' dumb out there," Al added.

Matt stopped. "Like what?"

Al wasn't shy. He never backed down. Close to retirement, stocky, with wonky knees but a mind like a steel trap, he boldly went up against those half his age and twice his size. His confident swagger and no-nonsense approach were the first things Harri noticed about him when she joined the team. He was Southwest Side tough and didn't mince words or suffer fools, much like their boss, Sergeant Sharon Griffin. "Like flush your job down the crapper."

"This is my family," Matt snapped back.

Al considered for a moment. "Part family," he said, "and part you wantin' to put somebody in your cuffs for jeopardizin' it. Smart move here is you at that hospital, not on some vigilante mission. That only leads somewhere you don't want to be."

Matt flushed red, anger simmering below the surface. "I said I'll be back."

The three of them watched him go.

"Poor Matt," Vera said. "This is awful."

Al shook his head. "Yeah, both parts. The kid and now him loaded for bear. Old days, no problem. It was like the Wild West out there, in here, too, matter of fact. Now? He so much as spits on the sidewalk with his star on his hip and he's got a rip comin'. He can't be out there Rambo-in' it up."

"I don't think you're giving him enough credit," Harri said. "He knows where the line is. He won't cross it."

Al rolled his eyes. "Yeah, let's hope. But in my experience? Lines don't mean nothin' when your head's not on straight."

"I bet there's a Shakespeare quote just right for this moment," Vera mused.

Al whipped his head around to glare at her. "Don't you friggin' dare. One Poindexter on this team is enough for me."

Vera raised her shoulders and grinned. "Just trying to help."

She turned to wave the doughnut box under Harri's nose to entice her, but she was gone, already sitting at her desk and hard at work.

Vera dropped the box on the corner of her desk and plopped down into her saggy chair, eyeing Harri over a short pile of interdepartmental paper. As she did it, she reached up to smooth her hair, which today was pulled back in a tight bun. "You know you should really wear a bell or something? You're as sneaky as an alley cat. One minute you're there, next minute you're not."

Harri plucked a chocolate doughnut from the box and took a slow bite. "You weren't paying attention, that's all." She yawned.

"Rough night?" Vera asked.

Harri flashed back to the marble. This time she was ready to share. "Not a lot of sleep, that's all. Had a weird dream." She briefly recounted the figure and the marble on her table. "It sure felt real."

Al walked up, took a doughnut from the box, seemingly in no hurry to get his shift started. Licking sugar off his pudgy fingers, he said, "Sounds like one of them God winks."

Harri looked up, cautious about what was coming. "A what?"

He bit into his breakfast, deep-blue eyes twinkling. "God wink. When weird stuff happens or strange occurrences you can't explain. People swear up and sideways it's either ghosts of their dead relatives visitin' or God tossin' a divine hand in. That kid bein' in distress and you just happenin' by knowin' what to do? God wink."

Vera leaned back in her chair, a skeptical look on her face. "Hmm. I'm leaning more toward fortunate coincidence in the case of Ella, and a bad dream on the other thing. The one marble, though, sounds kinda spooky."

The air shifted. They all noticed at once and turned to see Tony lumber in, all six foot, three inches of his linebacker self. Per usual he looked half asleep, his dark face zombie-like, but Harri knew that meant nothing. He was all there, ready to go, only not yet fully caffeinated. She suspected his outward appearance of languidness was an energy-saving thing. A former marine, Tony had probably learned to power up only when he needed to. With him, it was all about the timing.

He walked over to them without a word, plucked a jelly doughnut out of the box, and then kept walking toward the back to the small kitchen, where the coffeepot sat. A deep grunt passed as a morning greeting.

"Gang's all here," Vera announced, smiling. Then her eyes traveled and landed on something over Harri's and Al's shoulders, and her expression darkened. "Uh-oh. The bone pickers are back."

They turned to see what had gotten Vera's attention and saw Detectives Arlene Dillard and Frank Tomczak from Area 2.

"Not today of all days." Harri sighed.

Concern blanketed Al's grumpy face. "They got the nerve to waltz in here *again*? I thought we were cleared on this? They're still thinkin' you popped Noble? I mean, sure, you had good reason, and plenty of opportunity, as a matter of fact, but we all know you didn't do it."

Harri watched as the detectives strode up to the boss's door, knocked, and went inside. Then she turned to Al. "Thanks. Good to know you *don't* believe I'm a cold-blooded killer."

The detectives in Griffin's office were, they all knew, working Eddie Noble's case, and from Dillard's and Tomczak's perspectives, Harri seemed like the likeliest suspect, and why not? Noble was stalking *her*, not anyone else. He had killed *her* former partner, not anyone else's. It was Noble and not anyone else who had vowed to kill her and everyone she loved.

She glanced at her team, at Tony who'd joined them in the interim, instantly brought back to full life by the coffee and the sugary doughnut, and now firing on all cylinders. She didn't think they needed to hear it again, that she hadn't killed the man, but she opened her mouth to say it one more time, only Vera broke in first.

"Save it," she said. "Not necessary."

Al nodded agreement. "Yep. You ain't made that way."

Tony scoffed. "You serious? We're *all* made that way. Human beings do all kinds of messed-up shit to each other. Just look at the cases on our desks right now. Since when do our badges make us Jesus? Look, that scumbag put a gun to Harri's head. He *killed* Thompson, the vengeful fuck, then he goes threatening Harri's *mother*? Hell, any one of us *should* have taken his ass out."

Vera stared shocked at the two of them. *"Oh my God."*

Al drew up his shoulders, took another swig from his chipped CPD mug. "Can't fight the truth, Vera."

They could all hear murmuring from Griffin's office, even with the cheap door shut. None of it could be good for Harri.

"Couple of idiots, them two," Al groused. "Just tryin' to clear the case without workin' too hard for it."

"Just doing their jobs," Harri offered, readying herself. She flexed her fingers to keep from clenching them and focused on keeping herself steady, even keeled, and calm. She felt like a pot boiling on a stove, its top rattling from the steam.

She sat there, a little left of a good place, knowing that she had wanted Noble dead, that she'd wished him there often, and that she'd come closer than she'd ever thought possible to becoming someone else. Her team was not wrong to doubt. She doubted her own motivations more times than she could count. It's what happened when you got pushed to the edge and anger became a dangerous fire you couldn't put out with reason or temperance, principle or will. This was why she feared for Matt. It wouldn't take much for one wrong move or decision to derail everything.

Harri had wanted Noble dead, but someone else had taken him out. Done deal. She felt released from the burden of retribution, but strangely, she also felt robbed, cheated. Why did it feel like someone had denied her a thing that was rightfully hers? That the circle wasn't quite closed? She had wanted Noble to pay for killing Glynnis. A quiet grave wasn't payment enough. Death was an end, but not a reckoning. Death was peace, not punishment. Anger killed; she knew it. It gnawed at the heart and turned a soul as black as pitch. She wondered how long it would take to find a place for all this. Though she was a good cop, she was not a perfect one. No cop could ever be perfect. Harri heard Griffin's door open behind her. She waited for her name to be called.

"Not for a minute did I think it was you," Vera said.

Harri's eyes met hers, a slight smile. *"Liar."*

"Well, maybe for a half second. Tops. Just because, well, I'm a cop and completely jaded. But never seriously. Not like Tony here, who, apparently, hangs with Satan and probably doesn't trust his own brother."

Tony harrumphed. "If you knew my brother, you wouldn't trust him either."

Harri knew they were kidding. Trying to lighten the mood to distract from the just-opened door and the cops in the boss's office. She also knew they believed her and that she didn't have to say another word about it. She stood up and straightened her jacket and the collar of her blouse before taking another cleansing breath.

"Foster, my office," Griffin called, her commanding voice cutting through the room like a freighter's horn on a foggy night.

"You shouldn't go in there without your union rep," Al whispered to her. "They're sharks. You walkin' in there alone is like dumpin' blood in the water."

"I don't need a rep," Harri said.

Al threw his arms up. "Wrong move. I can't tell you how many cops I seen mosey into a room like that all cocky and come out twisted in knots, their pensions hangin' by a thread."

Vera stood in solidarity. "Harri knows what she's doing."

"Not if she walks in there without a FOP rep," Al snapped. "Don't let 'em tie you up."

Harri nodded. "I'll be okay."

Tony took a sip from his mug, flat eyes peeking over the rim. "Vaya con dios. Whatever you do, don't FUBAR yourself. You have the right to remain silent. Name, rank, and serial number only. Make them go fish."

Harri's eyes held his. *"Really?"*

Tony grinned. "Yell if you need us to cover your six, oorah."

Harri headed for Griffin's office, knowing halfway there that her Monday, already a steep hill she didn't have the energy to climb, was about to get a lot steeper.

CHAPTER 4

Harri found Griffin sitting at her cluttered desk, her face stern, a leprechaun bobblehead dressed in CPD dress blues holding down a stack of departmental folders. Dillard and Tomczak, a fit pairing, as far as Harri was concerned, stood silently in front of the boss's desk, the smell of frost clinging to their wet wool coats. Detective Arlene Dillard, Black, thickset, and Dennis Tomczak, white, thickset, matched in height, five five, five six, and looked like two human fireplugs, squat, wide, inert. They were even dressed alike in dark overcoats, cop shoes, dark pants, and crisp white shirts, only Tomczak wore a tie. Harri wondered fleetingly what impression she and Vera made to others. Harri had never worked with Dillard and Tomczak, so she only had one previous unpleasant encounter to go by, but that hadn't left her with a very good feeling for either of them. She knew for a fact they hadn't cast a wide net once they found out she had a motive for wanting Noble dead. They'd stuck with easy, hoping easy would work for them. Dillard and Tomczak were lazy cops.

Griffin stared at Harri, her frosty blue eyes fixed on Harri's even-leveled brown ones. *Stern* was an understatement, Harri concluded. Griffin wasn't happy, which surely meant Harri would soon share in the emotion. The only thing she could do was wait.

"There've been developments in the Noble case," Griffin said, leaning back in her chair, her hands folded across her middle. "Thought you should hear them firsthand."

Harri stood with her back straight, her face unreadable. If they were waiting for her to ask what the developments were, they would all be there until the polar ice caps melted. Harri had a stubborn streak that ran long and deep. Dillard and Tomczak were dinnertime cops, cops who didn't stretch too far or probe too deeply, cops who waited for leads to fall at their feet wrapped in a pretty bow and tied to an easy confession. Always home in time for dinner, clocking the hours until the pension kicked in. Slow-burning candles, Harri thought, when an actual fire in the gut was required.

Dillard looked amused, the coy expression on her face almost playful, like she'd caught a rabbit in a snare and wanted to parade it around by the fluffy tail. "Not even going to ask, are you?"

Harri's answer was a subtle shake of the head and a look of sheer disinterest. This was their show. Her flat eyes held Dillard's, then shifted slowly to Tomczak before sliding away to land on a green fedora that smelled of stale Guinness, which hung from a peg behind Griffin's head. A silent dismissal.

Tomczak frowned. "Yeah, whatever, Foster. We're doing our jobs just like you do yours, okay? We're not supposed to ask questions when the guy after you gets it right between the eyes?"

Griffin shifted in her chair. "Easy, Tomczak. We're all badges here. Watch the tone and the delivery."

Tomczak gave the leprechaun a dirty look, as if he and not Griffin had admonished him. "We work facts, not badges." He turned to Harri. "You lied about Noble. You were following him, like he was following you. Your own game of cat and mouse, was it? We even found an incoming call from your phone to his. That's more than you said happened. When we talked to you last, you didn't mention the shadowing *or* the call."

"Seems all that sneaking around was news to Griffin here too," Dillard added. "So, what about it?"

Harri looked over at her boss. That explained the scowl and the blue thunderclouds. She looked away, back to Dillard.

"I was keeping an eye on him," Harri said. "Seemed the smartest thing to do, since he was doing the same to me. Know thy enemy, right? Much better than a sneak attack and a cold grave."

Tomczak sneered. "You sure that's all?"

"Yes."

"Looks like you did a good job of keeping an eye on him." He pulled a pair of 8 × 10 black-and-white photos from his folder, then displayed them side by side on Griffin's desk. "Take a look."

Harri stepped forward and glanced at the images. One photo was of her car parked in front of the warehouse where Noble was killed, the other of her car parked in front of Noble's sister's house. She stepped back, unfazed.

"They confirm what I just told you," Harri said.

Tomczak cut his eyes at her. "We have more."

"IDOT cameras got you coming off the Bishop Ford the night Noble was killed," Dillard said. "Heading east toward the warehouse. And a neighbor's Ring camera got you at his sister's place, where he was staying."

"Doesn't that just corroborate the photos you have here?"

"So?" Tomczak said, a little peeved. "What do you have to say?"

Everyone waited for an explanation Harri knew she wasn't going to offer.

Tomczak pointed at the photographs. "*These* say you had motive, means, *and* opportunity. They also say you don't know how to disengage. You make things personal."

"You were there the night he was killed," Dillard said. "Stalking him."

"Right day, wrong time. Check the time stamps," Harri said.

Dillard grimaced. “You could have doubled back.”

Harri stood defiant. “Show me those photos, then.” Harri knew they couldn’t produce any additional photographs. This was all just a show. There was more they weren’t saying, of course. Batting her around like a ball was the warm-up, a power play, wholly unnecessary. But not all cops were right cops, and not all cops were friends. Look at Noble, a dirty cop twisted by greed and hate and evilness. His oath hadn’t meant a thing to him. He’d done the unthinkable and appeared more than willing to do the unthinkable again.

“You had us chasing our tails,” Tomczak said. “Had us looking at you when we should have been looking someplace else.” He sneered. “You wasted our time.”

Harri glared at him. “*You* wasted it, I didn’t. Nothing you found tied me to Noble, but you kept at it.”

The room fell silent. When no one spoke or moved, when it was quiet enough to hear a handcuff key drop, Harri turned to them and said, “Someplace else? Now I see. This is just you two throwing weight around . . . you already know this isn’t me. You just wanted to play it big.” She shook her head, disheartened. “Does this make you feel important?”

“Get over yourself, Foster,” Dillard said. “We lost time because of *you*.”

Harri turned. “Laziness lost you the time, Dillard. Why pick apples when you can catch the ones that fall from the trees and bonk you over the head, huh? The time lost? You didn’t lose it, you squandered it.”

Tomczak studied her. “I’m still getting the feeling you’re holding out.”

Harri met his eyes and held the connection. “You can stuff your feeling. I followed him and knew where he hung out. I followed him to his sister’s place. I called him to confirm the number he called me from was active, and that it belonged to him. That’s it. No contact beyond that." She pointed to the photos on the desk. "I never got out of my car at either place. I never got within fifty yards of Eddie Noble, except when he broke into my car right out there in the lot and put a gun to the back of my head. That's all you need to know. That's all I have to say. Get off my *back*."

Something had shifted since Noble's death. Harri had felt it the moment she learned he was dead. It was freedom, release, then something darker. He'd killed Glynnis, G, and he'd only done it to hurt Harri. In her opinion, he'd forfeited the right to breathe.

He was dead, that should be the end of it, but the missing pieces of her life were still beyond her reach. A dirty cop's karma hadn't changed much for her, not yet. It had done nothing to banish the overwhelming impulse to scream, loud and long, until her voice gave out. Harri could feel it coming, the tipping point. She could see the steady approach when she closed her eyes, a looming shadow of some monumental endgame. There was nowhere she could run where there wouldn't be hurt waiting for her. But she couldn't cry about it here, or now. This was not a building she could be weak in.

Griffin, who had been watching Harri closely, turned and fixed Dillard and Tomczak with a long, cold stare. "I don't like games. Never did. Even as a kid. Monopoly was the worst. That fuck-all game took *forever*, and being the youngest of six, I never got the Scottie *or* the thimble." She leaned forward, all ice and flint now. "I have a short attention span. I like things to move along, for people to get to the point. Time wasted is time you never get back." Griffin checked her watch, then eyeballed Tomczak and Dillard like they'd stolen her car from the cop lot and wrecked it on I-94. She twisted the bobblehead around to face them as though it were a tiny inquisitor with a stopwatch running. "You two are pissing me off and harassing my detective. She's not your killer. You'd better have something else in that folder, Tomczak, and it better be damned good. You got five minutes."

Dillard and Tomczak looked as though they didn't know which way to jump. Neither responded, but Harri did.

"I can think of at least six people off the top of my head who would've wanted to kill Noble," she said. "You need a list?"

Dillard huffed. "We have our own list, thank you, and a name at the top of it."

Griffin shook her head, then leaned back again. "Personally, I would have led with that and ditched the slideshow. For future reference."

Harri watched Dillard and Tomczak squander future capital with the boss. She then locked eyes on the folder in Tomczak's hands before flicking a look at the bully leprechaun standing in for Griffin. "Who?" Harri asked.

Griffin tapped the leprechaun's service cap, sending its tiny head shivering, folded her hands in her lap, and waited. Dillard and Tomczak got the message loud and clear.

Tomczak pulled a couple of more photos out of his folder and dropped them on the desk like he was slapping down a winning poker hand on a green baize table. "*This* guy."

Harri rushed forward for a look. "Leonard Krieg. Noble's partner?"

"How do you know *that*?" Dillard asked.

Harri ignored her, explaining to Griffin instead. "Noble threw Krieg under the bus, and Krieg served eight years. When he got out, he went under, completely disappeared. I tried tracking him down but couldn't find him anywhere."

"He didn't want to be found," Tomczak said. *"Obviously."*

"Until he came out of nowhere to shoot Noble," Dillard said.

The first photo was of Krieg, dark, angular, in a black hoodie, walking down a shadowy sidewalk with his hands deep in his pockets. He'd grown a mustache and beard in prison, but his face was the same, if maybe a little gaunter. Krieg had lost everything when Noble pulled him into his dirt—wife, kids, job, home. Krieg had as many reasons to want Noble dead as Harri had. The second photo was of Krieg making his way through what looked like a park, head down, seemingly moving at a fast clip.

"First one was taken from a street camera," Tomczak said, "half a block from where Noble got shot. Two minutes after his body hit the dirt. Second, him booking it through Woodline Park two blocks over." He pulled another photo out. "This? It's Krieg getting into a Scion. Stolen. He drives off west. That's the last we pick him up. He likely ditched it soon after that. No reports of any other vehicles stolen in the area that night, but there are half a dozen bus lines running right through there. Or he could have legged it. He looks prison fit."

Harri shook her head. "None of that's rock solid. You're making the same assumption you made with me. Proximity means nothing."

Tomczak pulled a report from the folder. "His prints on the dime he tossed on Noble's body work for you?"

"Why would he be so sloppy?" Harri asked.

"There's more," Dillard offered. "There was a fire at Noble's sister's place two nights ago. Total loss."

Harri reeled, shocked. *"What?"*

Griffin leaned forward, the temperature in the room suddenly felt like it had plummeted into negative numbers. "Krieg."

Tomczak nodded. "It was deliberately set, so yeah, that's our thinking. The sister isn't exactly on anybody's enemies list."

"Was anyone hurt?" Harri asked, knowing that Noble's sister had sons, one away at college, the other a teenager still living at home.

"One fatality," Dillard said flatly. "Household cat named Poncho."

Harri gave Dillard a dirty look, wondering what was wrong with the woman. Dillard had the good sense to look embarrassed and avoided Harri's contemptuous gaze.

"How do you know for sure it was Krieg?" Harri asked.

"Neighbor's Ring camera caught him booking it away. Looks like Krieg hung around long enough to make sure the house went up before he got out of there," Dillard said, now all business. "Same hoodie, but the facial hair was gone. As the neighbors flooded out into the street to watch the fire and call for help, he slipped away."

"He's vengeful enough to want Noble and everyone important to him gone," Harri muttered. "Eight years is a long time to hate someone's guts."

"We thought maybe he was planning on going after Noble's whole gang, at first."

Harri shook her head, adamant. "Going after Noble's gangster friends would be suicide. And what do you mean 'at first'?"

"We found the Scion parked in a long-term lot at Midway," Dillard said. "Assuming it wasn't a ruse to throw us off, we ran facial rec. He boarded a plane with phony ID to LA, then from there to Honiara. Solomon Islands."

Griffin's frown deepened. From the look on her face, Harri could tell she didn't think much of the two detectives in front of her. "How the hell did we let Krieg get all the way to the Solomon Islands without anyone flagging him?"

For a moment there was only silence in the close room, only Harri's thoughts weren't quiet. Krieg was gone. There was no way to catch him. They'd been too slow, or at least Dillard and Tomczak had. Krieg was free as a bird lounging around in paradise. "Where's the sister now?" she asked. "And her son?"

"She's at Northwestern," Tomczak said. "Smoke inhalation, but she'll pull through. The younger kid wasn't home at the time. He's staying with friends till she gets out."

"A family for a family," Harri muttered. She looked over at Dillard and Tomczak. "Facial recognition, flight manifests, both after the fact, and useless. A fake ID and passport. He had help getting out of the country. Now we have a killer on the loose. A dangling thread." She studied the duo disdainfully. "With no way of tying it off."

Griffin's fingers were busy on her cell phone. Suddenly she let out a growl. "No extradition agreement with the Solomon Islands. Now how did I know *that*? Krieg did his homework." She tossed her phone down on the desk. "Hell, he had eight years to google the hell out of this." She glowered at Dillard and Tomczak. "You know when slow and steady doesn't win the race? When you have a murderer out there ticking names off a hit list. Get out."

"We can still get him," Dillard said. "We know where he is."

"I know where the moon is too," Griffin shot back, "but that doesn't mean I can sling a rope around it and pull it into my backyard. Get out."

Dillard's eyes fired. "Look, Griffin, with all due respect—"

"You finish that sentence," Griffin said, "and I feed you both to the banshees."

Tomczak, fuming, gathered up his photographs. "Unbelievable," he mumbled under his breath as Dillard began angrily buttoning her coat, obviously having had enough of the second-guessing. "Thanks for the critique, like we just started this job yesterday. Foster wouldn't have done any better."

"I'd have been quicker," Harri said. "Once I ID'd him through his prints, after the fire, through the car at the airport, I would have assumed he was planning to board a plane, and it would have been all hands on deck. Might've had a shot at stopping him."

"Supercop, are you?" Tomczak said.

"There's no such thing," Harri said. "All you have to do is give a damn." She turned to them. "And if you had all this, Ring cameras, prints and all, why were you sweating *me*? Showing up here, trying to shoehorn me into this?"

"You looked good for it at first," Dillard said. "You hated the guy. And you were stalking him. Then you popped up everywhere he went.

Noble was dirty. Who's to say you weren't dirty too? We're not going to apologize for the heat we gave you."

Harri took a menacing step forward but then took it back. "You two need to grow up." Tomczak scowled at the leprechaun. "Well, you're up to speed," he offered with an air of finality. "Obligation *met.*" He turned to Harri. "No more piling on required." He smiled smarmily. "We wouldn't want you staking us out, would we?"

"Hey, Tomczak," Griffin barked, her freckled cheeks aflame. "Can the dumb shit or I'll shove one of my shillelaghs up your nostrils."

Tomczak blanched, then winced before looking about the room warily, no doubt wondering which of Griffin's festooned walking sticks (and there were many) she would use. Dillard appeared offended on her partner's behalf.

"Your reputation precedes you, Griffin," he said. "Right down to the knobby sticks and all the Lucky Charms crap."

Dillard tugged Tomczak by the sleeve of his coat. "That's all," she said. "We're good."

Dillard swept past the desk, past Harri, toward the door, an angry Tomczak following her out, and closed the door behind them.

"Took them weeks to pull street cameras?" Griffin said. "Needling you meanwhile, just for chuckles? Took them even longer to think airport escape? The Solomon Islands, no less. Jesus H. Christ."

Taking a deep breath, Harri turned to leave too. She didn't want to think about Krieg or Noble anymore, at least not today.

"Nuh-uh. Not yet," Griffin said.

Harri reluctantly turned back and watched Griffin tap the leprechaun again. "Two things," Griffin said. "First, Kelley."

Harri gave her the latest update on Ella, then stood waiting for the second thing, only Griffin just stared at her, giving nothing away.

When she'd had enough, when all she wanted was to get out of there and get back to work, Harri said, "I did what I needed to do. And you would have done the same, and you know it."

Griffin smirked. "I would have gotten out of the car. *Second*, it ends here. The bastard's gone. He's not coming back. And third."

"You said two."

"I lied."

Harri knew Griffin could see how tense she held her body, as though she were coiled like a snake on the inside. Efforts to hide it had obviously failed. A long look from Griffin was as good as an X-ray.

Out of frustration, Harri closed her eyes and whispered, "Stop it."

Griffin sighed, averted her gaze, but Harri could still feel the laser. "Third . . . consider a vacation. *Not* to the Solomon Islands. You and Krieg do *not* meet, here or in the next life. Got it?"

Harri opened her mouth to speak, but Griffin put her hand up to stop her. "Not a discussion. You're not the first cop to stand in front of my desk hollowed out and running on fumes. You think you know what you're doing, but you don't. You think you're handling it all just great, but you're not. The short temper. The fists. Not good. You're letting this job bury you."

"Boss, I don't think any of this is your business. What I do—"

Griffin unclipped her star from her belt and slammed it on the desk. "Boss my ass. This is me talking to you. No rank. No bullshit. The first day I met you, I told you that if I found you hanging from a belt in the john, that I would cut you down and kill you again myself. I meant it then; I mean it now. I am not going to let you mourn yourself to death, Harriet Foster. You want to be among the walking dead, you won't do it here, not while I'm watching. I don't want ghosts on my squad, and I sure as hell don't want ticking time bombs. Talk to somebody. Get your head on straight. Deal with it, or it'll deal with you, then *I'll* deal with you."

Harri stood reeling on the edge of something she didn't want, couldn't voice, didn't want to show, not here. "I'm—" She had begun to say *I'm fine*, her standard response, the one that had been able to close down all conversation and give her room to breathe. But she couldn't bring herself to tell the lie anymore, even to herself. Griffin was right, and Harri knew it, and that made her even angrier with herself. Now what, she thought? Now. *What?*

"Question," Griffin said. "You and Li go through a door. Li goes down. What do you do? Do you leave her there and save yourself?"

"That's a stupid question," Harri said. "You know what I'd do."

Griffin nodded. "And anybody out there would do the same. We never leave *anyone* behind." Her eyes bore into Harri's. "Because I'm sitting here and you aren't, I'm not leaving this to chance." She reached out and picked up a business card, which she handed over. "You've got an appointment with counseling tomorrow. Since you never seem to leave this place, it's at seven a.m. Be there or don't bother coming in. Understood?"

"Wait a minute, you can't just order me to—"

Griffin held her hand out to stop the flow. "Technically? You're right, I can't. I can only suggest it." Her icy eyes bore into Harri's. "I'm suggesting it, hard. Talk or walk, Harri. You're too valuable to lose, but I'd take that over the alternative."

Harri shifted her eyes to the bobblehead, but even he seemed to concur with what Griffin had just laid down. Slowly, Griffin picked up her badge and put it back on her belt. "All I've got, unless you want to say something?" She waited a beat, but nothing came back. "No? Then go do what you're good at." Harri turned to leave, having given up any hope of responding. Out in the hall, she took a moment to exhale before running her hands across her face and finding it damp with sweat. She read the card. The roiling in her stomach and the flutter in her chest were unwelcome, but Griffin and her leprechaun had been too on the money for Harri to take offense. She didn't want to be anyone's pity project. She didn't need saving, didn't want to be handled or worried over, but here she was.

Heading back to her desk, she felt it coming. She turned and double-timed it down the hall the other way. Out of sight, away from the team, she slammed her fists against the wall. There was more, but she managed to catch the worst of it before it escaped. After a few moments, Harri breathed in, then out, then shoved the card in her back pocket, composed herself, and looked to make sure no one had seen her lose it. No one had.

"Move," she ordered herself, the word barely audible. *"Move."*

She walked back to her desk, Griffin's words ringing in her ears. *Deal with it, or it'll deal with you.* Harri could feel her colleagues tracking her with their eyes. What was she going to say to them? She swept her jacket off the back of her chair.

"Need a minute," she announced without breaking stride as she made for the door.

She ran down the stairs, through the lobby, and out the side door to the cop lot, cold, raw air coming at her with as much force as a boxer's roundhouse punch. At least the rain had stopped, though the sooty clouds and the weatherman's prediction promised more soon.

Head down, she paced as cops went in and out around her. No greetings, no nods, no smiles from her this time. A minute meant a minute. How far could she go? Not far. How could she leave things as they were? She had no clue. It wasn't like her to leave a thing unfinished. "The Solomon Islands, for God's sake." A world away. And Griffin thinking she was flirting with a full-on breakdown. What else could happen? Vera's voice broke through her thoughts clear as a bell. "Minute's up."

She turned to find her partner standing behind her, burrowed into her jacket. No hat, she noticed, but she knew why. Vera didn't want to mess up her bun and have to redo it. She was efficient to a fault, even with hair.

Harri shook her head emphatically. "Nope. Not doing this." She walked toward her car, only to remember she'd left her bag in her bottom drawer with her keys inside. She turned to face Vera. "I didn't mean literally a minute, you know that, right?"

"Sure. What am I, stupid?" Vera pulled her keys out of her pocket and clicked the key fob. The gray Mazda SUV chirped a row over. Harri's eyes hardened. "In case it started raining while we were out here," Vera explained. "Or you needed to scream the f-word, or anything."

They sat for a moment inside the vehicle, silent. There was a car seat in the back for Vera's three-year-old, Wynton. The interior smelled like cookies and juice boxes.

"Some weather, huh?" Vera said.

"I refuse to talk about the weather."

"Fair enough." Vera checked her nails. According to regulation, they were short, and the polish was a conservative color, in this case, a pale beige. "So, you *didn't* need a rep?"

Harri turned to Vera, ready to kick out at her because she was close, and Krieg and Griffin were not, but she lost her nerve before she got a single word out. She turned back, resigned to the inevitable.

"Noble's partner killed him and got away," Harri said simply. "So, it's over . . . and not over. Noble was *mine*."

"Hmm."

"Griffin has also ordered counseling . . . for *me*, not her, though I could argue a case for her benefiting from it as well. She's talking to leprechauns now."

Vera turned to look at her. "She's what?"

Harri waved the question away, then unloaded it all. Dillard and Tomczak, the fire, the airport, the escape, Griffin's badge on the desk. It was more than she'd intended to share, but everything she no longer had the space to carry. When she'd finished, she stared out the windshield at the cops coming and going and at the building where they were expected to perform miracles for city pay, then at the confounded rain that had started *again*, and at her life that was a mess years in the making. It was as though she were just now waking up from a long sleep and couldn't quite get her bearings.

Harri let out a long sigh, having prepared for Vera's take but getting nothing. *"Well?"*

"So, they actually talked *directly* to the bobblehead?" Vera asked. "Is that going to be a new thing we're going to have to do every time we go in there?"

Harri looked over at her. Vera grinned back. Harri lifted the lever on the door, but the doors were locked.

"Let me out of this car," Harri said.

"You're doing okay," Vera said seriously. "You'll do better when you've dumped the baggage and talked it out." Vera adjusted her rearview, then checked the lot behind her. "There's light at the end of the tunnel. And you're closer to the end than you were a year ago." She considered things for a moment. "I think it's okay to let Krieg and Noble go, don't you? Noble's definitely in hell, and Krieg's created hell for himself right here on earth. He's a killer now, and that leaves a mark. None of that's got anything to do with you."

Harri stared out the window at all the cars in the lot, at all the cops. "I did this to myself. I laid down in a coffin and nailed the lid shut, only I kept breathing." She watched the rain run down Vera's windshield. "I made a mess. I couldn't let go. Still can't."

"There's no living in a box," Vera said. "Letting go doesn't mean forgetting . . . I wonder what Thompson would say right now?"

Harri smiled. "Likely the same as you, only she'd be a lot more colorful with the language."

"I can blue it up if that's what you need."

"No, leave it." She let out a sigh. "I didn't know partnering with you would include a deep dive into my personal issues."

"Well, they do."

"Your turn next time," Harri said.

Vera gave her a thumbs-up. "We can do me now. When I told my mother I was going to become a police officer instead of going to medical school, she started to cry. In her mind, and I know this to be a fact, because she has said it to my face, police work is not a suitable profession for a woman. I may as well be turning tricks on Cicero."

Harri faced her, shocked. "She actually said that?"

Vera smiled. "I added the tricks part. The best I could do for her was to marry a doctor." Vera shrugged. "That calmed her down a little bit."

"We sure make a pair," Harri said.

"Sure looks like it."

CHAPTER 5

Reuben McClintock fumbled with his door keys, trying and failing with calloused hands to get the damn key in the lobby door of his apartment building. He'd been calling his wife, Marie, for nearly an hour without a pickup or a callback. That wasn't like her, especially now.

Halfway through his overtime shift at the garage, he'd begun to get a strange feeling, and then to worry that something was wrong. That's when he started calling. Since the baby six months ago, Marie hadn't been quite herself, jumpy and unsure, stressed. It would pass; everyone they knew had said. The malady even had a name, the baby blues. Reuben had never heard of such a thing before, but this was their first baby. There were a lot of firsts.

Scanning behind him, his eyes sweeping up and down the haggard block, he wondered if maybe Marie had gone out? He dismissed the thought. She had the baby, and it was cold and damp, and there was rain coming by noon. Marie was home. She was always home.

The doctor had prescribed something for the anxiety and the depression. Low doses. It seemed to be working. Marie was perfectly okay when he left the house for work twelve hours ago. *So where was she?* Reuben wondered as he pushed the door open and rushed up the stairs to the second floor.

It would have helped if they had family close, but they didn't. Marie's mother was in California, Reuben's in Dayton. They'd both visited when the baby was born, but only for a few days, just to get them and the baby set up. The couple couldn't afford a babysitter, even for a couple of days a week. They were saving every penny for a house, a home, for the family. Reuben banged on the apartment door. "Marie? *Marie.*"

Nothing.

He unlocked the door to 2C and swept inside, dropping his tool bag at his feet. The front room was empty, nothing out of place, the secondhand furniture and handful of things to make the place look nice, the same as when he'd seen them last. Reuben turned toward the bedroom, his heavy boots clomping along the uncarpeted hallway, loud to his ears, in the eerie stillness of the place.

"Marie."

He could see the kitchen at the back of the apartment. There was no one in it, no food cooking, the lights were out. The apartment felt abandoned, as though Marie had just picked up and left with all their things still inside.

Reuben flicked a look at the scratched Timex on his wrist, the one Marie had given him for his birthday three years ago. Not expensive, but reliable, a working man's watch. It touched him that she'd saved to have it engraved—*My dearest one. M.*

Dread overtook him, fear. Why wasn't Marie in the kitchen warming up bottles? Why wasn't the baby crying? *"Marie?"*

He turned the knob on the bedroom door, the only other place Marie and the baby could be. For a moment he stood there, afraid of what he might find inside. If only they hadn't needed the overtime pay, he thought, cursing himself now. But they were behind on their bills, and things were extra tight with a new mouth to feed and all the things the baby needed. He leaned his sweaty forehead against the door and whispered his wife's name. *"Marie."* It was half prayer, half plea, and the world snatched it away a second after he'd said it.

He found Marie on their bed, lying on top of the floral spread they'd gotten at the bridal shower. Dressed in her nightgown, her arms outstretched, her hair disarranged, she wasn't asleep. Reuben drew in a deep breath at the streaks of blood coming from her nostrils, at Marie's stillness, her big brown eyes, the eyes that had stolen his heart years ago, fixed, half open, unseeing. She was ashen, her caramel skin no longer exuding warmth.

Marie. *His* Marie was dead.

He moved to approach the bed but couldn't bring himself to do it. This was all he could take.

As if a spell had broken, he turned toward the baby's crib, suddenly panicked. But as he ran to the side and looked down, there baby Emmanuel lay, cooing and playing with his fat toes. Reuben smiled at his son, at his chubby cheeks and toothless grin. He didn't even realize he was crying until his tears hit the baby's blanket. He'd never known babies could be so cute, so special, or that you could love one quite so much, but from the moment Emmanuel was born, he was everything Reuben worked for. *His* son, *his* baby. His and Marie's.

He reached down and picked the baby up to find him drenched, his diaper sodden, his onesie soaked through. He'd been alone in the crib for hours, it appeared. Hours.

Reuben blew out a breath, calming himself, not wanting to distress Emmanuel. Babies could sense when things weren't right, when those holding them were unsure, unsteady, or in a state. He didn't want his son to be afraid. He turned his back to the bed, so Emmanuel couldn't see, and calmly walked his son out of the room. Reuben knew that Emmanuel, at six months old, wouldn't remember this day, or recall seeing Marie on the bed, but if there was even a small chance, he wanted to shield his son the best he could. It was his job, his sole responsibility to protect him now.

Marie was dead. The words echoed in his mind because he couldn't say them yet. His wife was dead. His family was dead. Leaning back against the wall in the hallway, he slowly slid down to the floor, kissed his son on the top of his head, and cradled him in his massive arms. "It's okay, buddy. You and me. All safe with Papa."

The apartment felt as cold as a grave. Reuben didn't know what to do next. Who should he call? What should he say? Was it the baby blues that had killed her? The medication the doctors had given her? Did Marie do this to herself?

He stared down at little Emmanuel, his son's wide, bright eyes happy and innocent. Reuben should call his mother, and Marie's, he thought. Other people. But he couldn't move yet. Right now, all he could do was bury his face in his baby's small chest.

CHAPTER 6

"Damn her," Harri muttered as she stormed into the building to talk to a stranger who didn't know the first thing about her. "Damn *this.*" She stopped at the front desk, staring at the young smiling woman sitting there. "Damn *all* of it," she muttered before drawing in a deep breath and getting it done.

Harri's first cynical impression of the place was that it was trying too hard to be comforting. Everyone spoke in soft tones, the walls were a calm color, the carpets were pale and calm, even the air smelled unoffensive, clean with just a hint of flowers, like it was worried about offending somebody's lungs.

"Fantasyland BS," Harri groused as she sat in the session room waiting for someone named Dr. Roxanne Parker. Probably some old white woman with all kinds of letters after her name but not a lick of common sense. She'd probably come at her with breathing exercises and pills to keep her mellow. Band-Aids on a gunshot wound. What did some Roxanne Parker know about what she had to do? The room felt tight, like a cage. She was the piece of raw meat thrown inside to await the ravenous tiger who'd soon be let in.

Harri stood up from the chair, flexed her fingers, and walked over to the window that overlooked the street that she knew for a fact was anything but calm and sedate. Calm in here, she thought, killers and cruelty outside.

Harri turned when the door opened to see a Black woman on an old wooden cane walk in smiling. She was dressed in a camel-colored cashmere sweater, black pants, and flats. The woman looked to be in her mid-sixties, she was light skinned, her hair cropped short. She seemed instantly familiar, though Harri was certain she'd never met the woman before. This couldn't be her shrink, she thought.

"Good morning. I'm Dr. Parker." She eyed the two chairs in the middle of the room. "Where're you sitting?"

For a moment, Harri blanked, then pointed to the chair she'd just gotten out of. "There." She then watched Parker sit in the one opposite it. Too close was Harri's first thought, and her second.

There was no desk, no seat of authority. Just the chairs, a small couch, about a dozen folding chairs leaned against the wall, and a niche with a coffeepot and paper cups. There was no coffee brewing, though. This was a room for spilling your guts, Harri reasoned, so apparently not much more than that was required. Harri sat down and studied the woman, the cane, her eyes.

Parker leaned her cane against her chair, crossed her legs, and placed her hands in her lap. She hadn't come in with a clipboard or folders or anything. Just herself. "You're Detective Harriet Foster."

"I am."

Silence hung in the air.

"Typical cop response," Parker finally said. "I asked a simple question, you gave a simple answer." When Harri said nothing, she continued. "What do you need to talk about?"

"This wasn't my idea," Harri said.

Parker nodded. "Okay. Whose idea was it?"

"A leprechaun bobblehead's and my boss."

Parker cocked her head, confused. "Not enough information."

"Maybe later."

"All right. Well, there's no trick to this. We just talk about whatever it is you need to talk about. Everybody comes in here with their stuff locked up tight. The only person who can unlock yours is you. First thing people usually ask is what gives me the right to pry into their business. Your mess is your mess, right? True. But sometimes everybody needs a little help getting back on track. There's absolutely no shame in asking for that help."

Harri looked over at her. "Shouldn't you be taking notes, or something?"

Parker smiled. "On what? You haven't said anything." She glanced over at the coffee maker. "Want coffee?" Harri shook her head. Parker's eyes held hers. "I don't take notes. I listen. We talk, work it out, you feel better. You go home."

"I know it's not as simple as that," Harri said.

"I gave you the nuts and bolts."

Harri looked down at the cane. "How old is that cane?"

Parker looked where Harri looked. "I don't know, actually. *I've* had it for twenty-five years now. My partner gave it to me when I got out of rehab." She turned back to Harri. "The bullet lodged close to my spine. There was a good chance I wouldn't walk again, but I did. Wrong alley. Wrong day."

There it was, Harri thought. Why Parker felt familiar. "You were a cop."

Parker chuckled. "Oh, *now* you're interested? I was twelve years in when I got shot. My partner and I chased a banger into a gangway. There was a bad outcome. Banger died. I didn't. That was the one good thing. I wasn't paralyzed, that was another. But the wonky legs, the weakness? That took me off the street. I couldn't see myself riding a desk for the next thirty years, so I left the job and went back to school. Then I got divorced. I raised my kids. I did what they tell you to do. I pivoted. Made a new way out of no way." She patted the cane. "I could get a prettier one, I suppose. But I like this one, it shows its age. It's imperfect. It's scarred and not quite straight. It's a daily reminder to me that life is just like that. Nothing is going to be always pretty or good or right. But you can be strong and not perfect."

"What about your partner?"

"Still on the job. Rising through the ranks. Still family. But you know how it is—one bullet, two nightmares."

Harri could feel the sting of tears in her eyes but held them back, refusing to let herself go in front of this woman in this BS building. She stared down at her hands in her lap, getting herself together. Dr. Roxanne Parker. She repeated the name in her head. For what seemed like an eternity, neither of them said a word.

Finally, Parker said gently, "It's your vault. Only you can open it."

Harri looked up. "So, I open it. What changes?"

Parker stared back at her. "If you *don't* open it, what *doesn't* change?"

Harri frowned. "This is how it's going to be? This vague guru-riddle stuff?"

"You're in charge here, not me. I'm just ears."

Harri could sense she was far more than that. "How did you feel when you had to quit the job?"

Parker hesitated. "Lost. Broken. Like I'd never find a single thing ever again that mattered to me, aside from my children. Do you feel lost, Detective Harriet Foster?"

Instead of answering, Harri reached into her pocket to feel the paper clip hidden inside. It had been her coping mechanism. Secreting small things in her pockets, using them to calm herself and get her through the day. She pulled the clip out and held it tight, aware that Parker was watching.

"I lost my son." She spoke barely above a whisper, each word seeming to scorch her throat as it came out. They were words she didn't want to say, ones she couldn't yet accept. "And my partner. I would rather it had been me . . . both cases." She squeezed her eyes shut. "I've lost myself." It was a simple declaration, and after she'd made it, Harri set the clip down on the table between them, and sat back in the chair, ready to face whatever painful thing came next.

"How do you feel right now?" Parker asked.

"Like an idiot."

"Deeper," Parker said.

After a second's hesitation, Harri said, "Like I'm living on time that shouldn't be mine . . . and it's crushing me."

Parker took in every word, every nuance, ever watchful. "Do you prefer Harriet, or something else?"

Harri breathed in deep as her vault opened a fraction of a fraction. "Harri."

Parker picked up the paper clip and looked at it. "Then, Harri, let's get this party started. You've got a lot of ground to make up."

CHAPTER 7

Two hours later, Harri and Vera stood over the bed of Marie McClintock, staring down at the young woman's body, their hands in nitrile gloves, keen eyes assessing the details in the room, the body, the feel of the space, their human hearts guarded by procedure and routine, yet heavy, nonetheless.

Standing behind the ME tech, Harri eyed the neat bedside table and the three medicine bottles lined up on it. The names of the medications meant nothing to her, and she couldn't touch the bottles to see if they were empty or full until they'd been dusted, logged, and cleared. Still, she jotted the names in her notebook, then shifted her attention back to the bed. McClintock was in full rigor, her face ashen and gray, her lips blue. The blood dried beneath her nostrils reminded her of the skate park, of Ella and her friend. Too early to assume a connection, of course, but she couldn't ignore the similarity either. Ella had taken an opioid. Had Marie McClintock? Not with the new baby, Harri thought, but, again, she wouldn't know until she knew.

She was unsettled from her session with Dr. Parker. She'd gone places she hadn't allowed herself to go in years, and it had scared her. Parker had been patient and wise. Harri liked her. But for her, an open vault after all this time felt dangerous. She hadn't mentioned the nightmare of the dark figure in her room or the marble left on her table.

She wasn't ready for their explanation, yet, and didn't want Parker to think she was losing her mind.

"Any clue what the medications are for, Vin?" she asked. Vincent Studdard, the ME tech called out for this one, was a thin rake of a man, a marathon runner who didn't eat anything that a food-processing plant had touched. "The blood from the nose is not usually what we see."

Studdard was taking body temps but looked over his shoulder to answer. "No idea yet. Husband might know. But preliminarily, dilated pupils, blood could hint at some kind of cerebral damage. Could also be drugs. Could be a lot of things."

"Like?" Vera had been standing at the foot of the bed, taking in every inch of the room just like Harri, looking for anything out of the ordinary, signs of violence, blood anywhere else but on the victim.

"Aneurysm comes first to mind," Studdard said. "Stroke, maybe. Internal bleeding, unknown cause. But, like I said, too early. You know the drill."

Vera stepped to the bedside table and with her phone snapped pictures of the labels on the bottles, sliding Harri a look. "Google's faster."

Harri angled her head. "What's it say, then?"

Vera scanned her screen, her thin finger scrolling up. "The meds are prescribed for postpartum depression." She looked at Harri. "New baby. A lot of pressure, stress. Accidental dosage, maybe? Something else."

Studdard continued his examination of the body as the crime scene photographers snapped away for the record. This was a death investigation for the time being, not a homicide, but the step by step was the same. They could never know what they needed until they needed it.

"On the other side," Studdard reported, "no visible signs of injury. No petechiae, no signs of restraint, no handprints around the neck, no bruises." He let out a long sigh. "I'll roll her over in a bit." Harri stood ready, her face expressionless. "When you're ready."

Studdard continued his methodical work as the sound of a fretting baby crying came from the other room, casting a chill over the bedroom.

"Feel sorry for that kid," Studdard mumbled.

Harri didn't respond. She didn't want to think about the baby, even though she couldn't stop thinking about the baby. She stepped away from the bed to check the bedroom closet, only to find the usual items—shirts, shoes, dresses, slacks. Nothing expensive, nothing flashy, just the bare essentials and a couple of nicer things. She ran her hands through every pocket, too—nothing. The baby's things were in a small portable changing table all neatly folded and clean and ready for use. There were diapers stacked inside, and the usual assortment of infant powders and lotions, creams for minor rashes. Familiar things, soothing. Harri picked up a pale-blue baby brush with rubber duckies on it, its whisper-soft bristles smelling of lavender. How many times had Marie McClintock lovingly brushed her baby's hair with it? she wondered.

She turned back to look at the dead woman. The young mother. Accidental or on purpose? The pressure of the new baby too much to bear, or something else? Tragic either way, she knew.

"Bathroom medicine cabinet holds no secrets," Vera announced from behind her. "Nothing hidden anywhere either. I even checked the toilet tank."

Harri put the brush down, faced her. She hadn't realized Vera had left the room to check the bathroom, but she wasn't the least bit surprised that she had. After all, they weren't joined at the hip, neither did they need each other's permission to move independently. Vera covered a scene all 360 degrees and didn't miss a thing. They each held up their ends, and Harri never once worried that Vera would drop hers. She hoped Vera felt the same, though she couldn't imagine bringing herself to ask.

"I'm not sure if that's good or bad news," Harri said, avoiding the bed and the tragedy lying in it.

"Anything in here?" Vera asked as her eyes took another sweep.

Harri closed the drawer to the changing table, then shook her head. "No red flags. Just normal."

"All right," Studdard announced. "Turning now."

Harri and Vera stood behind Studdard as he gently rolled McClintock over on her left side to reveal rumpled bed linen. Studdard scanned the skin, looking for anomalies and injuries. "No needle marks, no punctures. Probably wouldn't be on the back, though, right? Unless someone came up behind her and . . . doesn't make much sense."

Harri's eyes took the same tour Studdard's had made, but as he was about to turn her back over, Harri spotted something that made her hold her breath.

"Stop. Wait," she said. "Hold her there, please."

Harri stepped a little closer and leaned down to see clearly what she thought she had. A small blue plastic bag, big enough for a snort of powder or a handful of pills, half hidden by the top sheet. Blood from the nostrils. A blue drug bag. She snapped a picture of it on her cell phone.

Vera slid in beside her. "Something *not* prescribed by a doctor?"

Harri looked over at her. "I've seen a bag like this before, at the skate park. Same color, size as this one. I did make out a circle on the bag with some faint lettering stenciled inside it, but I couldn't make anything out. I left it and focused on Ella instead."

With one gloved finger, Studdard cautiously pulled the bag out from under McClintock before gingerly placing her back down. Pulling a small magnifier out of his kit, he leaned over to inspect the bag more closely. "Definitely a circle, with something etched inside it. An *M*, or a weird *E*? The lettering's so light. Not an expert job. Crude, like somebody stamped it out with an ink stamp." He looked up at Harri and Vera. "Mean anything to either of you?"

Harri loomed over his shoulder, eyes on the bag. "Show me."

Studdard angled the glass so Harri could see. He was right, either an *M* or a strange *E*. Faint and inexpert, like the bags had been produced in a basement somewhere, which was likely the case. Harri stepped aside so Vera could take a look, her mind busy.

"Nothing I've seen before," Vera said, "but these things pop up all the time. Same poison, cut with whatever. Could be the hot new thing? Party drug. Cheap, easy to get." She took a photo of the bag, then stepped back. "Doesn't really fit this, but we've been surprised before."

Harri heard her, she always listened, but her mind was on the connection, the bag. Slowly, she moved away from the bed. College kids out for a thrill, one gone, one holding on. A blue drug bag. A young mother—her infant son fussy in the next room—suffering, it appeared, from postpartum symptoms. Connected.

Vera broke into Harri's thoughts, doing that thing she always did, as though she were actually reading her partner's mind. "You're right," she said. "They're connected."

Harri's eyes locked on Vera's. It was on, and they both knew it. For a moment, the only sound in the room was the police photographer moving around the bed, finishing up with her photos.

"We need everything you've got, Vin," Harri finally said to Studdard. "Don't miss anything."

CHAPTER 8

Harri and Vera found Reuben McClintock sitting on a radiator in the front room, clutching an infant in his arms for dear life. Two POs stood over him, not for comfort, Harri knew, though from their pained expressions she thought they would have been more than willing to provide it. No, this was procedure. Until they knew what had happened to Marie in the bedroom, Reuben was an unknown, possibly a suspect. You didn't leave unknowns alone in an apartment where a weapon might be hidden. No cop wanted a bullet to the back.

The apartment was tidy, clean, homey, with a comfortable-looking couch and matching love seat in a pale-green color. No drapes, but there were white blinds pulled down halfway. The one floor lamp in the corner next to an end table leaned a bit, she noticed, but most of the light was coming from the recessed fixtures overhead. The place smelled of baby powder and furniture polish. And there were baby toys, little soft balls and stuffies strewn about, joyful things, happy things, unless you were a mother like her who'd lost a child.

But nothing stood out in the room or in the apartment that would indicate trouble. Everything pointed to the McClintocks being a young family, just starting out, their entire lives ahead of them.

Harri was familiar with the spot where Reuben McClintock now found himself. She recognized the mile-long stare, the shock, the brokenness. Like a sin-eater, she stood over him as he rocked his baby and she consumed the man's misery, grief, and despair, quietly stacking it on top of all the other miseries she'd taken in at scenes like this, in apartments like this, on worst days like this one.

Harri didn't drink to push it all away, though too many cops chose that route. She didn't take pills to sleep or wake or function, she just stood and took it. She ate the sins, then buried them and didn't deal with them. Stacking up miseries was a slower death, a quieter one, one that now bothered her when it hadn't before. She'd actually had Noble's gun to her head, and recalled the flicker of a moment when she would have welcomed the bullet if it meant seeing her son again. An eater of sins and miseries, she thought, standing silently in front of the broken man and his baby. That's what she'd been. What was she now that she wanted to change?

Back in the present, she looked over to find Vera watching her. Again. Harri swore the woman could see into her very soul. It was unsettling, it was pressure she didn't want, even if maybe she needed it. She frowned, looked away, and went back to the job at hand.

Harri's eyes swept over the POs' nameplates. Two males, both mid-thirties, maybe, Perez and Blake. She gave them a nod, and they both took a few steps back, seemingly relieved. The duo, first on scene at about 6:00 a.m. this Tuesday morning, gave their brief report of finding Marie McClintock in the bedroom and her husband and son where they were now. No one else was found on the premises.

"Thanks," Harri said. "Stand by, will you?" She turned back to McClintock.

Harri could see the baby was wet, but McClintock, his eyes dazed and fixed, didn't appear to have noticed. The baby squirmed in his arms, fussed, but he didn't appear to realize that either. The big man with the rough hands, dressed in grease-splotched work clothes, rocked gently, maybe to soothe the baby, maybe to soothe himself, his mind somewhere distant, a happier place, perhaps, or else in the bedroom where his wife lay dead.

The baby needed to be changed, but she didn't dare reach for him, not until McClintock was ready to let him go. Harri could feel Vera break off and knew exactly where she was going without having to turn around to see. She waited for her partner's return before she started with the questioning. Vera was quickly back with a fresh diaper, powder, wipes, and a clean onesie. She gave Harri a nod. They could begin.

"Mr. McClintock, I'm Detective Foster. This is my partner, Detective Li." She paused for a moment, not sure if what she'd said registered. "Mr. McClintock?"

He stopped rocking and looked up at them with a bewildered expression on his face, as though he couldn't believe what had just happened to his world in the span of a few short hours. Harri repeated the introductions.

"We'd like to ask you a few questions, if that's okay?" Harri looked down at the baby and smiled. "What a beautiful baby. What's his name?"

McClintock looked down at his son as though he had to think about it. "Emmanuel."

"What a wonderful name," Vera said. "Mr. McClintock? Can I help you with Emmanuel?" She held up the diaper and baby things. "He'd be a lot more comfortable with a change, don't you think?"

McClintock clutched the baby tighter, as though Vera might snatch him right out of his arms. "I . . . I . . ."

"We'll stay right here," Harri assured him. "Emmanuel won't be out of your sight for even a second." She pointed at the couch. "Right here. Where you can see."

McClintock appeared to think about it as Harri and Vera and the two POs standing back waited for him to decide if he was ready to let the baby go. Finally, he handed the baby to Harri, who held him in sure arms for a moment before passing him over to Vera. McClintock's rattled eyes following Emmanuel the entire time.

"We're sorry for your loss," Harri said. "Is there anyone we can call for you? Someone who can be here for you and Emmanuel?"

"I called Pastor Pope," he murmured. "We don't . . . *I* don't have anybody else close. I called Marie's mother when I found her. She's getting on a plane. My mother too." He nodded. "They're both coming back."

Vera looked up from changing. "Back?"

"When Emmanuel was born, they both came and stayed for a few weeks, just until we got used to everything. Feedings. Bottles. Schedules. And then Marie had a tough time getting adjusted. She wasn't sleeping. Me either, much." He lowered his head and picked at the calluses on his palm. "We thought the worst was over. The doctors said she was better . . . anyway, the pastor's coming."

"Good." Harri checked in on Vera on the couch, the smell of baby powder and aloe filling the room. Emmanuel now cooed instead of fussed. She motioned for Perez. "Have somebody outside let us know when a Pastor Pope gets here, please."

Perez nodded and left the room to relay the message. "Good," she repeated.

"What a good boy," Vera said to the gurgling Emmanuel. "Look at that smile, would you?"

McClintock stood and squared his shoulders, ready to answer questions. "I don't know what happened. This doesn't make sense."

Harri could feel the notebook in her jacket pocket but left it there. If she pulled it out and began taking notes, McClintock might spook and shut completely down. She'd have to write her notes later in the car. Meanwhile, she knew Vera wouldn't miss a single syllable. "When was the last time you spoke to Marie?"

He thought about it for a moment. "What's today?"

"Tuesday," Harri answered.

"I worked double Monday, so maybe eight last night? She sounded fine. She told me she was going to bed. But when I called later to check that everything was okay, she didn't answer. That wasn't like her. I kept calling, but she never picked up. I got worried and told my boss I was clocking out."

Vera bounced a drooling baby on her knees. "What times did you call?"

McClintock shrugged. "At eight. Then again around eleven, when I thought the baby might be up to be fed. Again, around two. I worried for maybe another hour before I clocked out. I work at the airport. I got here a little before three . . . and found her like that."

"Officers Perez and Blake arrived a little after six a.m.," Harri said. "What'd you do for three hours?"

McClintock drew in a breath. "I held my baby. I sat with my wife. Then I called."

Vera handed Emmanuel back to his father with a smile. Efficiency personified. "Back to Papa."

"Thank you," McClintock muttered, rubbing his son's head. "I couldn't bring myself to go back in there to . . ."

"We understand," Harri said. "How was Marie when you talked to her at eight?"

"She was okay."

Vera watched him. "We noticed the medication on the bedside table."

McClintock nodded. "She was having some issues, postpartum, but it wasn't as bad as it could get with some women, and her doctor, Dr. Weltz, said she was doing well." He looked from Vera to Harri. "If she weren't, I wouldn't have left her by herself. I'm telling you she was *fine*."

Harri thought of the blue bag. "Was the medication all Marie was taking?"

"Vitamins too."

"Was she breastfeeding?" Vera asked.

McClintock shook his head. "We went with formula. Emmanuel just wouldn't do it. That's partly what stressed Marie out. They told us at the hospital that breastfeeding was better for the baby, but it wasn't working. Marie was afraid we were hurting Emmanuel by going with the formula, though. Nobody could get her off that."

"So, the medication and vitamins." Harri persisted because it was her job to. "Nothing else?"

McClintock stared at her; his brows knit together in consternation. "What are you saying?"

Harri lifted her phone and showed McClintock the photo she'd taken of the drug bag beside Marie. "We found this. Any idea where she might have gotten it?"

McClintock's eyes widened. "What is that? Where'd that come from? That's not Marie's."

"We're hoping you can help us with that," Vera said calmly.

"It was found in the bed next to your wife," Harri said bluntly.

"Marie did *not* do drugs," McClintock shot back. "Never. And not with the baby. What *is* that?"

Harri put her phone away, her eyes fixed on McClintock. His reaction appeared genuine. He was quick to defend his wife. Maybe he was telling the truth. She softened her tone. "We don't know yet. Can you think of anyone who Mrs. McClintock might have gotten this from? A friend?"

"What kind of friend would give her something like *that*? No, I'm telling you Marie didn't do drugs. We don't know people who do drugs. We would never let anything like that in our house."

Yes, maybe the truth, though Harri knew that often lies came first, the truth only later after they dug for it. For sure, the blue bag didn't waltz into the McClintock apartment on its own. And no signs of force pointed to the fact that Marie McClintock had ingested it herself. "Dr. Weltz, you said?"

"Thomas Weltz. He's at Rush. Ask him if you don't believe me. He knows everything Marie's taking . . . took."

"We believe you, Mr. McClintock," Vera said gently. "But we had to ask. Would you mind if we talked to Dr. Weltz if we need to?"

McClintock frowned. "Yeah. You talk to him. He'll tell you the same thing I'm telling you. *Not* Marie." He glared at Harri as though *she* were the enemy, not death. She looked back at him, unbowed.

Vera reached over and toggled Emmanuel's tiny hand, making funny faces at him. "Did Marie go out much? I know that right after I had my son, I often needed to take a break, get some air, be around adults who could carry on a conversation."

He shrugged. "Marie's the same. She goes out to the store, to walk around the park, church, out with her girlfriends for a lunch, or coffee. She wasn't cooped up in the apartment all day if that's what you're thinking. She wasn't totally out of it, just a little stressed and down sometimes. And it was passing, like I said. We had it under control."

Harri stood silently, observing. She had expected McClintock's shortness. Now that the shock was wearing off, she knew he was feeling all kinds of ways. That was normal. Guilt, maybe, for leaving his wife alone with the baby? Anger would come next, a kicking out at things he couldn't change. He caught her staring.

"You two have kids?"

His words sounded like a challenge, but before Harri could think of how to answer, Vera answered for them both.

"We do, so we know how important it is for you and Emmanuel to get the answers you need. In order to do that, we have to risk you thinking we're complete monsters by asking questions you don't want to answer at a time like this."

Reuben McClintock's eyes glinted, but he seemed to ramp down. "I get it." He repositioned the baby in his arms. "Go ahead. Ask your questions. But I have to feed Emmanuel soon."

Harri continued. "Is there anyone Marie might have confided in besides you? A friend? Pastor Pope?"

McClintock lowered his head. "Marie had friends from her job and a few ladies from the church. Also, Sister Pope, the pastor's wife. Marie always liked talking to her."

"Where did your wife work?" Vera asked.

"She was an administrative assistant with the water department. After her maternity leave ran out, she wasn't ready to go back, but they wouldn't give her more time, so she had to quit. There was no one to take care of the baby while I worked. We couldn't afford for anyone to come in. Things have been tight since, but we were making it work."

Perez slipped back into the room and approached Harri to whisper in her ear. The pastor and his wife had arrived. Harri looked back at McClintock, who seemed to have run out of steam in just the few seconds her attention had been diverted. Perez moved away.

"Pastor Pope is here," Harri said. "Just one more question, though?" She waited for McClintock to nod his assent. "Is there anyone you know that Marie would open the door to at night, besides you?"

He thought about it. "Maybe one of the neighbors. We know everybody in the building."

"Anyone in particular?" Vera asked.

"Crystal across the hall," he said. "She and Marie were friends. Crystal's got a few kids. One not too much older than Emmanuel. When Marie had questions, she'd ask her. She wouldn't let in a stranger. The building's not that great, but the door downstairs locks, and I put double locks on the door to our apartment, even though the landlord didn't like it. We were careful."

"Crystal's last name?" Harri asked.

He met her eyes, cautious. "Why?"

"Maybe your wife talked to Crystal last night. Maybe Crystal saw something that might help us figure out what happened. You said she lives across the hall? If someone came in . . . if there was a knock at your door. We don't want to go over there with just a first name, Mr. McClintock. It would be disrespectful."

"Reynolds," he said.

"Thank you."

Harri exhaled, then stepped back to give McClintock more breathing room. "I think that's all we need for now." She looked over at Vera to see if she had anything she wanted to add. When she got Vera's subtle head shake back, she said, "We'll let you take care of your son now. Again, we're so sorry for your loss."

"Here," Vera said, pointing toward the door, "Officer Blake will walk you out."

McClintock balked. "No, I need to stay with Marie. She's in there . . . I need to stay."

"We'll take good care of Marie for you, Mr. McClintock," Harri said, her steady brown eyes holding his unsteady ones.

His eyes welled with fresh tears, and Harri could tell he was fighting like hell to keep from breaking down. She knew what he feared the most, what most people who've lost someone fear.

"She won't be alone," Harri said softly. "She'll be safe with us."

CHAPTER 9

Harri and Vera stayed with Marie McClintock, a pall having fallen over the small bedroom as the quiet ballet of crime scene photographer and ME tech played out. They stayed while Marie was moved from the bed onto a gurney, covered up, and slowly wheeled out into the street. It had taken close to three hours for Studdard to finish.

From what they could see, Marie McClintock hadn't been attacked, there was no evidence of foul play by an intruder; she just appeared to have gotten ready for bed, took something she shouldn't have, and then died. Harri couldn't *not* wonder if it was the same something that Robert Mitchell and Ella Byrne had OD'd on. She had been trained to always look for connecting evidence. But this was not a scene of violent homicide, it was simply an investigation of death by misadventure, to use the legal term. From all outward appearances, a struggling Marie McClintock overwhelmed by a new baby and a chemical imbalance caused her own death, and though sad and tragic, with far-reaching implications for the young family she left behind, there was little they needed to do.

As Harri and Vera stepped out of the building behind the body, it had begun to rain again, a light mist blanketing the entire street in a gray hanging gloom, which made the removal of the body ten times sadder. Though there was no one standing on the street gawking, Harri knew they were behind their curtains and blinds, staring out at the police cars, fire truck, and tech vans, curious about what had happened and what was going on. This time, the sword had missed them, maybe next time it wouldn't.

"Sometimes an OD is just an OD," Vera said, pulling her hood up on her head against the mist. "Doubly senseless in this case, though."

Harri glanced over at Reuben McClintock, who stood on the building's front lawn with a Black couple she assumed was the pastor and his wife. He didn't have Emmanuel with him, and she wondered where he'd gone.

"Guess you're right," she said. "But let's at least talk to the neighbors in the building and to the Popes, before we leave this man to his grief."

Vera sighed. "Self-medicating when the prescribed stuff doesn't work."

"Possibly," Harri said. "It doesn't leave us much to do, does it? Our killer's already in the morgue van." She glanced around the scene as the fire truck and tech vans pulled away, leaving a couple of squad cars and their car at the curb. "Still, *somebody* sold it to her. Either she went out to get it, or somebody brought it here." She stared at the McClintocks' apartment building, then turned 360, her eyes focused on the buildings around them. "No Ring camera on their building. Maybe there's something across the street? A POD camera at the corner. We'd be looking for a needle in a haystack. Plus, we don't work Narcotics."

Vera reached into her pocket and pulled her phone out. "All true, but it's not like we haven't looked for needles before. I'm calling Matt. If we can talk to Ella, she might be able to tell us something."

"Vera, this is not us," Harri said.

"It's us adjacent, though, isn't it?"

Harri didn't argue. There was no point. She knew Vera couldn't do things halfway. Leaving it and turning toward the three stone-faced sentinels standing on the lawn, Harri focused on the couple. The older

Black man wore a clerical collar and a solemn expression. He looked to be in his late sixties, if she had to guess. Portly, not much past six feet, dark, wearing an old driving cap. His wool dress coat wasn't ideal for rain, but its formality befitted the sad situation. A member of his flock was dead. He was here to pray for her soul and to support the family she left behind.

The woman beside him, younger by maybe twenty years, held on to McClintock's arm tightly, as if she were trying to anchor him to the world, to fasten him to the here and now. Her simple coat was much like her husband's, her only bow to the weather, a clear plastic rain bonnet and waterproof ankle boots that left her thin shins exposed. Together they made an odd pair, mismatched pillars of silence flanking Reuben McClintock. Harri wondered about the age gap. It begged the questions of how and why, though neither was her business. Still . . . odd.

"You know if we do talk to Ella, we won't be able to keep Matt out of this," Vera said, punching in his number.

"His niece nearly died. He's already in it."

Harri was sick of the rain and wanted to get out of it. "Let's finish up here." She watched the Popes. "We may be able to consolidate. I'll meet you over there."

They met with Crystal Reynolds, the McClintocks' neighbor across the hall, and with Reverend Clevon Pope and his wife, Faith, in Reynolds's front room. The Popes sat on a sagging navy blue love seat while Harri and Vera stood. There was only one other chair in the room, Reynolds sat there. Emmanuel slept in the next room while his father gathered a few things from their apartment to see them through a couple of days at the home of a deacon from the church. No one could blame Reuben McClintock for not wanting to sleep in his wife's deathbed.

Reynolds's eyes were puffy from crying. She was a sturdy woman in her early thirties, busty, thick, her hair wrapped in a colorful scarf wound tightly around her head. McClintock had told them Reynolds had a lot of kids, but there was no evidence of them in the room they were in. No toys, no small clothes left around. The apartment was economical and underfurnished, just the seat and the chair and a worn coffee table that looked like it had been salvaged from the Salvation Army. But the place was comfortable and warm, and Harri could tell Reynolds took great pride in it. Reynolds offered them juice, which they politely declined. The starkness of the place, born, no doubt, from a lack of money for more things, looked a lot like Harri's place, though her house was empty for other reasons.

Harri glanced at her watch, impatiently, wanting badly for time to fly, but it was just past ten thirty in the morning. Why did it feel as though she'd been at this for days already? She and Vera could have taken the Popes and Reynolds separately, but this way was faster. They still had the upstairs neighbors to talk to.

Harri flicked a look at her partner and got a nod back. They could start. "After eight last night," she asked Reynolds, "did you hear or see anything unusual across the hall?"

"Nah, it was quiet. There's never anything crazy happening over at Marie's."

"When's the last time you spoke with her?" Vera asked.

"Around lunchtime. She came out to get the mail downstairs. We spoke. She was all right then. Like I said, there's never a problem over there. It's upstairs we got to worry about. They keep it lit most days and nights. Music thumping, kids running up and down the floor all hours. Can't talk to them because then they want to fight. The landlord *won't* talk to them. Same reason. Not one of them up there's got an ounce of home training."

"That must disturb *your* children," Vera said.

Reynolds frowned. "No, ma'am. I don't let nothing disturb *my* babies. I got three, and I don't let them anywhere near any of them up there. As for the noise, well, not much I can do about that, so we make do. What they do up there is their business, not mine."

"The McClintocks do the same? Steer clear?" Harri asked.

Reynolds nodded. "Yes, ma'am. They trouble up there, and neither one of us is for it. You all should know. The police up there all the time breaking up fights, carting folks off, but they always come back."

"Where are your children now?" Vera asked.

Reynolds stopped and took a head-to-toe sweep of Vera Li before she answered, distrust in the look. "With their granny. So I can get my housecleaning done without them all under me. She just lives a few blocks over. I take good care of my kids, if that's why you're asking, okay?"

"That wasn't why I was asking," Vera said. "I was thinking about the activity outside and across the hall. It can be upsetting for little ones."

"Hmm. They fine then."

"And *Mr.* Reynolds?" The reverend put too much emphasis on the word *mister* if Crystal's prickly expression was any indication.

"*I'm* Mr. Reynolds," Crystal said, "*and* Mrs. Reynolds. I'm *all* the Reynolds I need, *Reverend*."

"You knew about Marie's postpartum depression, of course?" Harri asked.

Reynolds nodded. "I knew. I went through that myself with my twins. It was hard, but I got through it. And Marie was getting through it too. We talked all the time about it. She was doing what they told her to do and taking time to get herself straight. I'd help with Emmanuel when she needed it, just to give her some time to herself." Her eyes welled with tears. "I don't know what happened."

"Did she say anything about taking something that wasn't prescribed by her doctor?" Harri asked.

Reynolds's defensiveness returned. "Like what? If you're talking drugs, you're talking nonsense. Marie didn't do any of that. *That* business? You need to take upstairs."

"There are drugs upstairs?" Vera asked.

Reynolds harrumphed. "They probably got everything under the sun up there, which is why I stay away from there."

"What about strangers in the building?" Harri asked, probing for an angle, hoping to find something that would tell them how Marie had come to possess the drug that apparently killed her. "Any around the McClintock apartment?"

"No, and I'm here most days. I work part-time at a little piece of job over at the Kwik Mart up on State Street, but that's been off and on lately. I'm looking for better, but . . . I been looking a while."

"Were you here yesterday?" Harri asked. "Did Marie go out?"

Reynolds shook her head. "I was here in the afternoon, then I went to drop my babies off. I didn't hear her go out, or anybody. That front door closes heavy. Makes it easy to know when folks come and go. But Marie doesn't go out after dark unless Reuben or somebody's with her. This ain't the neighborhood for being out like that."

"We didn't see any security cameras outside, or in the hallway," Vera said.

"That's because there ain't none." Reynolds frowned. "They don't do much for this building, but they right on time for the rent, that's for sure. Old Money Bags sends Lewis around every first of the month like clockwork."

"Lewis?" Harri asked.

"The pickup guy. Don't know his last name," Reynolds said. "He's Brown's son-in-law. Willie Brown owns the building. Been owning it, they say, since forever."

"You see Lewis only once a month, never any other times?" Harri asked. "The first of the month was a couple weeks ago, so not since then?"

"He don't come this way until it's money time. He knocks, you pay, he goes on about his business."

"The McClintocks ever have any trouble with Lewis?" Vera asked.

Reynolds shook her head. "Money was tight with Emmanuel, but Reuben's job is good and it's steady. They were making do." She glanced toward her door. "I just don't know what that man's going to do with himself now."

Harri jotted in her notepad, then turned to the Popes, light rain hitting the window, the sound of it like birdseed tossed against the panes.

"This is sad, sad news," Reverend Pope said, his fingers entwined in prayer, his hands in his lap. "So young, such a profound rebuke of God's gift of life. I must say, this truly hurts my heart."

Harri watched as Pope lowered his bald head and closed his eyes to pray. Was he praying for Marie, she wondered, or for himself? To her, it sounded like he was blaming Marie for her affliction, which rubbed her the wrong way, hard. Slipping her pen in her notepad, she closed it and then waited, not wanting to encroach on the man's communion with his Higher Power, if that's what he was doing. She also wanted to watch the man as she spoke to him and not be distracted by her notes. As she waited and watched, she subtly shifted her gaze to Pope's quiet wife, who sat as still as a stone wall beside him, her eyes closed, her hands in her lap. Also praying?

Faith Pope sat with her knees pressed determinedly together, the hem of a shapeless gray skirt hitting just below her knees. The neck of her severe blouse came almost to her chin, achieving maximum coverage, and she wore just a little mascara and only a faint tint on her full lips. Even her black hair, pressed and sheeny, didn't dare flirt for attention. It was pulled back and pinned in a bun by simple plastic combs. Faith Pope, pastor's wife, looked as though she had stepped out of the early twentieth century rather than lived in the twenty-first.

Suddenly, Reverend Pope opened his eyes and unclasped his hands, bringing his palms to his knees, where they rested as he sat as motionless as a sphinx. "As spiritual leader of Holy Land Church, it's my responsibility, my duty, to help Brother McClintock find the light in the darkness at this, his time of great upheaval." He looked from Harri to Vera, righteous eyes probing theirs. "What will be done next for Sister McClintock? When can her church family do for her?"

"Soon," Harri said. "When's the last time either of *you* spoke to Mrs. McClintock?" Harri glanced over at Mrs. Pope. "Mr. McClintock told us his wife often came to *you* for counsel, Mrs. Pope. Maybe she confided in you?"

"If she did," Reverend Pope intervened, "*confide*, that would not be anything my wife could share. We keep our congregants' confidences firmly inside our circle. We're truly an extended family of faith." He clutched his hands to his chest. "We hold each and every sister and brother close and completely, never to forsake them."

Vera's sharp eyes swung toward the plain, quiet woman. "There's *nothing* you can tell us?"

Harri added, "Anything you can think of that might have triggered what happened?"

Reverend Pope jutted his chin out. "We can tell you that Sister McClintock was bathed in the blood of Jesus. She had nothing, *nothing*, to fear." He raised his index finger to the ceiling. "*He* heals the brokenhearted and binds up their wounds . . . *God* is the healer, not man." He smiled. "Psalm 147:3."

Harri's eyes held Mrs. Pope's. "We're not asking for you to divulge confidences. Did she appear well the last time you saw her? Or was she stressed or anxious, overwhelmed. Besides you, was there anyone at church that she would have talked to?"

"Nothing like that at all," Reverend Pope answered. "And any one of us would have jumped at the opportunity to help Sister McClintock."

Harri hesitated for a moment, then her eyes locked on the reverend's. "Do you *always* answer for your wife, Reverend Pope?"

He looked affronted. "I know my wife better than anyone, I would say. And while she is the absolute beating heart of our family and of our church, *I* am the head of both. No Christian woman should have to deal with anything like this, especially the first lady of Holy Land."

Mrs. Pope reached over and placed a gentle hand on her husband's. "Thank you, Clevon, but I want to help, if I can."

Harri was relieved to discover that the woman could actually talk and waited expectantly as Mrs. Pope drew in a long breath, let it go, and then began to speak. "Marie was such a good woman, a truly Christian woman. I just know she's with our Lord, so it would be selfish to grieve. Clevon and I are always available to listen, to do our best to help our people with whatever they need." She gave her husband's hand a squeeze. "Marie came to service frequently, also to a few of my Bible-study classes for the women of Holy Land. It wasn't always easy for her to come with the baby, but she made an effort. I could tell she was struggling somewhat. I encouraged her to speak to her husband, to share the burden with him, and he would lead her through, as a husband should. I gave her one of Clevon's Bibles in hopes that she would find comfort in the Word, and I always kept her and her child in my prayers."

"We all did," Reverend Pope said. "The whole church. We never leave anyone to struggle alone."

"Mrs. McClintock was suffering from a *medical* condition," Harri said. "The symptoms were beyond her control. Postpartum depression isn't a personal failing."

The Popes stared as though they didn't understand the words coming out of her mouth. Harri stared back, firm in her assessment.

Vera let a beat pass, hoping to reset. "How big is your church?" She directed the question at Mrs. Pope.

Reverend Pope shifted in his seat and refrained from speaking for his wife this time.

"We're hundreds strong and growing," Faith Pope offered proudly. "Holy Land is standing proud and always will. The community needs us." She looked at her husband, then smiled. "God wants Clevon to serve. He always knows who's righteous and who isn't."

Reverend Pope smiled back at his wife. "Yes, that's exactly right. I have been called to be a shepherd to my people. There are so many lost souls amongst us. Someone must help them find their way to Christ. We may have lost one to this terrible affliction, but we will not lose the rest. I promise you that."

"Was Mrs. McClintock at church this past Sunday?" Harri asked.

The Popes shook their heads.

"But she was there the week before," Reverend Pope said. "She sat right up front with baby Emmanuel. Emmanuel, truly a blessed name. From *immanu* meaning 'with us' and *el* meaning 'God.' That child is a gift, as all children are." His eyes shifted first to Reynolds, who glared back at him, then to the door of the apartment. "Brother McClintock is rarely able to attend since he is solely responsible for providing for his family. But we know he is a faithful man, a good man. He will survive this and come out stronger on the other side. That's God's promise."

Harri had a problem with God's promises, but the Popes were entitled to their belief. "I think that does it," she said, wanting to wrap things up before another Bible verse came pouring out of the good pastor. Reynolds saw them all out.

Standing outside in front of the building, Harri and Vera watched as the Popes walked down the sidewalk hand in hand and stopped at a late-model Cadillac.

"Bet she's not driving," Vera said.

Harri wiggled her hands into a pair of gloves. "Nothing says she can't."

"Bet you *Pope* says she can't."

Vera was right. Reverend Pope opened the door on the passenger side for his wife and waited until she eased in before closing it behind her, then he walked around to the driver's side.

"Chivalry is not dead," Vera said.

"But it is controlling," Harri said. "You were unusually subdued in there. Why?"

Vera's eyes followed the Cadillac as it pulled away from the curb with the pious Popes inside. "She seemed awfully familiar to me. Like I've run into her before."

"And you were trying to place her," Harri said.

"Um."

"She'd be hard to forget."

"Not the old-timey clothes, the eyes. I never forget eyes."

"Windows to the soul," Harri said.

Vera's phone buzzed in her pocket. "It'll come to me." She punched the screen. "Yeah, uh-huh. Uh-huh. Okay, heading your way now. Give us fifteen." She ended the call, slipped the phone back. "It's Kelley. Looks like the roughnecks upstairs are going to have to wait. Ella's awake and talking. Ready to do this?"

She looked over at Vera. "Who drives?"

"Oh, woe is me," Vera said, the back of her palm to her forehead in feigned calamity. "We have no gentleman to hold our door or drive the big, mean conveyance. Whatever shall we do?"

Harri headed for the car. "We'll go alphabetically, Meryl Streep. I drive."

Vera studied her partner. "You seem different. Your thing was today." Harri pulled the driver's door open, paused. "I'd rather have to clear an alley at two a.m. then go through my baggage."

Vera squinted. "Hmm. You're alone in that one."

"Change the subject?"

Vera eased into the passenger seat as Harri slid in beside her. "Subject changed." Vera peered out the window at the McClintock building. "Poor Emmanuel. One wrong thing, a lifetime of somebody else dealing with it."

Harri started the car and pulled off. "All it takes."

CHAPTER 10

Goodlow Dixon was nervous watching Patrice Gamon storm around his cooking room like an agitated lioness stalking around a small zoo cage. The threat to his life was real and ominous. She'd brought a wide thug in braids who stood in a corner, wearing dark sunglasses under the fluorescent lights. He'd never seen this thug before, but he knew the Gamons had a whole army of them at their disposal.

Patrice wasn't right in the head. He'd always suspected it. At twenty, she took the impulsiveness of youth to heights that scared him. She was mean, quick to temper, petulant. Only five feet five and slightly built, she wasn't physically imposing but exuded an oily air of menace and unpredictability. The ticking bomb wanted what she wanted when she wanted it, and now she wanted Goodlow's head on a plate.

"What the fuck did you *do*, man?" she croaked as she paced his dirty floor. "I asked for a skyrocket, and you give me shit that's dropping people on the streets? I can't make money on dead people, Goody." She stopped and turned to face him. "Tell me. How am I supposed to do *that*?"

"I told you I'd try," Goodlow said. He was twice her age, a grown-assed man, but he was nervous. He could feel the sweat flooding his pits, smell his own fear. "I said I couldn't guarantee the mix was right. It takes time. I *told* you that. You wanted double the strength. You don't know what all goes into this."

She was dressed entirely in black, just like a Gamon, the biggest drug pushers and flesh peddlers on the South Side. There used to be a whole gang of them, now just two—Patrice and her aunt, Cora. And Goodlow had made the mistake of his life by signing on with them. He'd been at a low point all those years ago, almost homeless, even with a degree. He was *still* paying off the loans.

She looked all around the room at the empty long tables. "Where are all your people?"

"I sent them home. Until things are decided."

"They're already *decided.* You didn't get it right," she growled. "If Cora finds out you're out here killing our customers, you know what's going to happen." Patrice extended her arms. "You got all this. Everything you need right here. You know what to do. *Do* it."

Goody nearly lost his breakfast, and he'd eaten it hours ago. "Cora doesn't know? You said you and Cora came up with this together. You *said* she gave it to you to handle. Now you saying she doesn't know anything about it?"

Goodlow felt faint. Cora was far deadlier than Patrice. He could count on his right hand the number of disappeared connected to Cora Gamon's wrath. He wanted to kick himself. Why had he agreed to this? "You have no idea what you just did. Cora's . . . she's . . ."

"I can handle Cora," Patrice blurted out, "you just get me the stuff I need. The *right* stuff. When it hits and we corner the market, Cora won't have anything to say, will she?"

Goodlow turned around in a circle, scanning his small basement lab, the concrete floors, the brick walls, the chemicals, the blue bags in boxes. This was what his life had come to. He was going to die. Cora Gamon was going to kill him.

"Oh my God," he said, his hands scrubbing across his ashen face. "When she finds out. When she *knows*? Okay. Okay. What do I do?" He looked past Patrice to the quiet thug against the wall, trying to look all Secret Service in baggy jeans and a Travis Scott T-shirt, tattoos running up and down his arms and across his neck. He was at least three hundred pounds, so Goodlow was confident he could outrun him if he had to, but he couldn't outrun a bullet. He didn't see a gun on the dude, but he knew he had one.

Money. That's what he'd sold his life for. He couldn't find real work; his bum leg was an impediment to anything physical. He couldn't pay his rent. He had kids, and another on the way. He had one marketable skill—making dope, and he'd sold it to the Gamons. Cora demanded loyalty, and now Goodlow had crossed her without knowing he was doing it. It didn't matter that he'd done it for another Gamon. He was a rat in a trap, and he had deaths on his hands.

"You said you could do it." Patrice circled, getting increasingly agitated. "You took my money. You gave me back *shit*. You killed some rich white boy and some lady with a baby. It's all on the news. *That* gets folks looking and talking. That's got the *police* in it now. I don't need any of that right now, Goody."

Goodlow glared at her. "That's all you're worried about? The *news*? What about the people? They're dead. And what about Cora? She will *kill* me. Hell, she'll kill *you*."

It was as if she hadn't heard him. "You're dealing with me, not Cora. This is my business, not hers. This is going to work. We do this again; this time it will be right." She reeled to face him. "You understand me? We do it again. It works. We get rich. Period."

Goodlow's eyes followed the little menace around the room, and as they tracked her, he worried about the gun he knew she had on her. Where was it? Back of the waistband? On her ankle? And where was Crow? The ten-foot-tall enforcer that made it his life's mission to protect and kill for the Gamons? Goodlow got the low-level thug instead. Maybe that was a good thing? Crow had no soul, no qualms about killing. Goodlow couldn't even swear that he was actually human.

A grown-assed man. He kept repeating it in his head. How was he going to let this child treat him like some fool? He had leverage. He knew how to cook the dope, Patrice didn't. But it was Cora he worried about. He'd exposed her business and involved the police. Goodlow squeezed his eyes shut, feeling sick to his stomach. He had to get out of here.

"We stop," Goodlow said. "End it here. You find yourself some other guy."

Patrice took a step forward, heat in her look, greed and crazy backing it up. "We don't stop *anything*, Goody Dixon. I'm not saying it again. You're going to get this right, and you're going to get it right *right* now. Get your people back here. Fire up all this shit. This time no fuckups."

Goodlow shook his head. "I'm not killing anybody else. I'm out. You know what she's like. You know what she can do."

Patrice grabbed him by the front of his sweaty T-shirt, stunning Goodlow into silence. He could have easily overpowered Patrice, but that momentary victory would ultimately land him in the grave.

"Cora's not who you need to worry about right now. Back to work or . . ."

Goodlow waited for the end of the sentence, it never came. He had a feeling, though, and felt compelled to confirm it. "Or what?"

"I'll let you think about that, Goody." She unloosed his shirt, smoothed out the bunched fabric. "Long and hard."

And still there was the need. The thing that had gotten him into this in the first place. Money.

"How much?" he asked, finding a little spine.

"Considering your fuckup?" Patrice held his eyes in hers. "One life. *Yours*."

Goody backed away from her, though he knew if he backed up a hundred miles, it wouldn't be enough distance between them to make him safe.

"You kill me, you got nobody to mix up anything. The Gamons are out of business."

Patrice smiled. "Who said anything about killing *you*?"

He was here. He was the dead mouse sitting between two killer big cats, Cora and Patrice. He didn't want to end up in a sludgy creek somewhere, his body tied to a tire or a sewer grate. He couldn't risk his kids because of the bad choices he had made. Damn the Gamons, he thought. Damn them all to Hell.

Goody found one final pocket of nerve. "Or I tell Cora you forced me. Put a gun to my head. After that, you won't be my problem, you'll be hers."

Patrice laughed. The sound of it permeated Goodlow's bones and chilled every last one of them. He watched as she pulled a gun from her back waistband, then held it at her side. "Go ahead. Try that."

Goody's momentary boldness melted away. He had few options. Goody swallowed hard and tried to think clearly. It was critical that his brain worked here.

"Well?" Patrice asked, cradling the gun in the crook of her arm. "Which way we going, Goody?"

He let time pass as his mind reordered. No way out. "One more. Then you find somebody else."

"One *good* batch," Patrice countered, "and you keep doing what you're doing. We own you, Goody Dixon. You belong to *us*."

She was wrong, and Goodlow knew it. Nobody owned him. He'd made a mistake, but mistakes could be corrected. He stood watching her, seeing clearly now what he'd failed to see before—a monster in training. An eternity seemed to pass between them in an instant while Goodlow planned.

CHAPTER 11

Matt met them at the door to Ella's private room.

"Good God, man," Vera said. "When's the last time you slept? You look like death warmed over."

He scowled. "Thanks, Vera."

Vera pressed a hand to her heart. "I say it with love."

"How is she?" Harri asked.

Matt exhaled, as though he were throwing off a great weight. "Better. She's good. The doctors say she got lucky, and, boy, do we feel it. This could have so easily gone the other way. I heard from Al you got another OD. You think it's the same stuff?"

Harri pulled out her phone and showed him the photo of the blue bag. "Looks the same to me. We're hoping Ella can tell us something about where she and Mitchell got theirs."

Matt shook his head. "Then you're just in time. None of us has asked her yet, too worried about whether she was going to make it. Now that we know we've dodged a bullet . . . Ella's in for some major parental correction once she gets out of here, but right now she's the woman of the hour. She's still a little fuzzy, but she's conscious, lucid."

"You get anything from Streeter and Evans?" Vera asked.

Matt frowned. "They stonewalled me. Al was right. They're just going to file it. Low body count. They're putting their energies elsewhere. But for me . . ."

Vera studied him. "It's family."

He nodded. "I feel if I don't stay on this, who's going to, right? Ready to go in?"

"Her parents in there?" Vera asked.

"You'd have to blast them out with TNT," Matt said. "Ella's now their top priority." He smiled, but there wasn't a stitch of humor or lightness in it. "Buckle up. Maggie's in full mama-bear mode. One wrong move and *wham*." Matt clapped his big hands together like a tripped animal trap. "She'll have you for breakfast."

Vera jumped at the sound. "*Jesus*, Matt. A little warning next time."

Harri's hand was already on the door, pushing it in. The first thing she homed in on was the hospital bed with the wan young woman lying in it. The last time she'd seen Ella, she was as white as a ghost, today her color had returned, and she was conscious. Harri could feel the muscles in her neck and shoulders ease a little. She'd worried about the girl, and was relieved now that it looked like Ella was going to be okay.

Maggie and Joe stood from their chairs when Harri, Vera, and Matt entered, Ella's mother moving to the bed rail to protect her kid. Ella's eyes tracked Harri's progress to the bed, a quizzical look on her face. Harri knew the girl wouldn't recognize her. She'd been semiconscious at best in that ambulance, but her parents knew who Harri was, and had likely told their daughter a cop had been on hand to get her the help she'd needed.

Harri stopped a safe distance from the bed. "Hi, Ella. I'm Harriet Foster."

Ella's eyes widened. "You saved me."

"A lot of people saved you, especially the ones in this hospital."

Vera moved in beside her. "And I'm Vera Li. We work with your uncle. He's an okay cop." She looked over at Kelley, tilted her head. "Not great, but he'll do."

Matt sighed. "Nice, Vera."

Vera worked her brows up and down like Groucho Marx. "I am who I am."

"Are you up for a few questions?" Harri asked. "We promise not to take too long." The last part was directed at the parents. A signal that they would be gentle and respectful of the situation.

Ella nodded, her parents too. All of them looked as exhausted and as emotionally spent as Matt. "Can you tell us what happened to you Saturday night, Ella?" Harri asked.

Ella flicked a cautious look at her parents, no doubt knowing they were not going to like whatever she said. "There was a party. Off campus. Robby." She looked down at her hands, the left one had an IV port sticking out of it and trailing through a tube to a bag beside the bed. "We decided to hang out somewhere more interesting. We ended up at the skate park. We drank a little." Again, she checked in for her parents' reaction only to find it wasn't great, but she pushed on. "Then he pulled out something and asked if I wanted to try it. At first, I said no. I don't do drugs. Everybody knows I don't. But he just kept at it. He took a couple pills. He said it was like weed, no more dangerous than that. When he seemed okay, I . . . I tried them too."

Harri watched as Maggie's hands grasped the bed rail, and her knuckles turned chalk white. That's what was happening outside, she could just imagine what inner turmoil was going on.

"And then what happened?" Vera prodded.

"He got really blurry he said, and then he couldn't seem to keep his eyes open. He started talking strange, off-the-wall stuff, slurring and everything. Then he laid back and just, like, passed out. That's when I started feeling not so great. It was like my head was a hundred times heavier than it should be, and I couldn't hold it up. My stomach started to feel really weird, and I don't remember anything after that." She stared at Harri, her head angled. "I remember your voice, now that I'm hearing it again. I was so scared. You were nice. Thank you for saving me. I owe you so much."

Harri quickly got back to the details. "Did Robby tell you where he got the pills?"

Ella squinted, as if trying to recall something. "The pills? . . . A friend hooked him up, he said."

"Did he say who?" Vera asked.

"I'm not . . ." Ella paused. "He said Petey, I think. He didn't say a last name."

Harri asked, "Petey go to school with you two?"

Ella lay back against her pillow. "I don't know. He didn't say anything about that. Sorry, I don't know anything else. I shouldn't have taken the pills he gave me. I was stupid. I know better. I figured . . . one time."

"One time that almost *killed* you," Maggie said, anguish seeping through in her voice. "For God's *sake*, Ella."

Ella started to cry. "I know. I'm *sorry*. I'll never do anything like this again. I *swear*."

Joe leaned over and gave his daughter a hug. "We're okay. We've got you, all right? You're still here, we can work on the rest of it."

Behind her, Harri could feel Matt's discomfort, but she wanted to keep going. "Did Robby say how he contacted Petey? Or when he did?"

Ella shook her head. "He just said Petey hooked him up. That's all I know . . . Robby wasn't a bad person. He wasn't some druggie. He just . . . *we* made a mistake. People make mistakes all the time, don't they?"

Harri held up her phone with the photo of the blue bag on it. "Did Robby say what the pills were, *specifically*. Did he explain the markings on the bag?"

Ella only glanced at the photo. "It's a party drug called Edge. Rob said it gave you a quick trip, and then left you totally blissed out. I was curious. And since he said it was as safe as weed . . ."

"Don't tell me you were curious about *that* too?" her mother asked.

"I never did weed. I *told* you."

Maggie kept her voice even and low, and somewhat restrained. "And just so you know, no drug is *safe*, Ella, not even aspirin if you misuse it. To think what could have happened . . . to think what you almost did to yourself just because you were *curious*? I thought you knew better. I was sure we'd done a better job of teaching you." She wiped at her tears. "I don't know what to think now, what to do." She looked over at her brother, the cop, completely at a loss. "What do we do, Matt? Tell us, what?"

"For now," he said, "we let Ella get some rest. There's time for the other stuff later."

Maggie looked over at Harriet, and what passed between them, mother to mother, nearly took Harri's breath away. Hurt, sure, but the fear, the fear of not being able to protect your baby once they were out of your arms, was written all over Maggie's face. She would likely not sleep well tonight, Harri thought. She might never sleep soundly again.

The room grew silent. It was as far as any of them wanted to go for now, and so Harri, Vera, and Matt turned to ease out of the room to let Ella rest.

"Wait," Ella said. "Harriet? Can you stay for a minute?"

Harri was shocked by the ask but turned back and waited while everyone else filed out. When the door closed behind them, Ella said, "Was Robby dead when you found us? I asked everybody, but they won't tell me. It's like they think knowing is going to freak me out . . . or something."

"He was dead," Harriet answered. "He'd been dead for hours."

Tears trickled down Ella's cheeks. "Oh."

Harriet eased closer to the bed. "Had you known him long?"

Ella shook her head. "Not too long. He was nice."

"Something I wanted to ask you about," Harri said. "There was a lot of money in your wallet. Your parents said you had a job?"

Ella lowered her head and picked at the thin hospital blanket. "Yeah. I just got paid too," she said, her eyes sliding over toward the window before sliding back to meet Harri's. "What's today?"

"Tuesday."

"Friday," Ella said. "I got paid Friday."

"Where do you work?"

"Why?"

"Just curious. Your father said you were lucky to find a spot that fit your major. Chemistry, he said?"

"That's right. It's on campus," Ella said. "Part time." She laid her head back on the pillow and shut her eyes. "I'm tired now. I need to sleep. Thanks for telling me about Robby. It seems so unreal."

That was it. Harri would have felt like a heel pressing on, so she left it there. "Take care, Ella. I'll check up on you later."

Ella opened her eyes. "Thank you."

Harri joined Matt and Vera in the hall. Maggie and Joe weren't there. Vera read her mind.

Vera said, "They went down to the cafeteria for coffee and a good cry."

"I think it'll be a while before Ella gets out of the house again," Matt said. "You don't know my sister."

"I'm on Team Maggie," Vera said. "Pills from Petey. Good God."

Matt ran his hands through his hair. "Kids are so trusting."

Harri looked over at him and Vera. "Edge. And they think it's *safe*. We'll pass this along to Narcotics. They may have run into this Petey before. They may even have seen this stuff on the streets already."

"Best they can get Petey for, maybe, is delivery," Vera said. "If we can tie him to Mitchell, more."

Matt shook his head. "Petey's mine. I'll find him."

Harri looked over at him. "Wouldn't it be better to put this in other hands?"

Matt's face went hard, harder than Harri had ever seen it. "He's *mine*. I want the guy who sold this poison. *I* want to shut him down."

"Then what?" Vera asked, concerned. "You know how this goes. Petey's likely a small fish. You get him, all you get is a small fish while the big fish swims away."

"If we don't try, we get *no* fish, and next time, it'll be somebody *else's* kid," he said. "*I'm* going to try."

"When? During all your free time?" Vera asked facetiously. "Your candle's already burned at both ends. Maybe this time, just take the win? Let Narcotics take it?"

Harri stared at Matt and saw only obstinance and determination. Vera was wasting her breath. "ODs are hard to prosecute. It's almost impossible to find the source."

"It's not a victimless crime," Kelley offered defiantly. "Look at Mitchell. A promising kid gone like that? Not to mention the same thing could have happened to Ella. We could be planning a funeral now instead of waiting for her to be discharged."

"We all know there's no such thing as a victimless crime." Harri pushed past him. "We're heading back. I'm glad Ella's all right."

"I wouldn't want to be Petey," Vera told Matt as she turned to follow Harri out. "That little fish picked on the wrong family."

"I *will* find him," he said. "You know I will, and he's going to definitely wish I hadn't."

Harri shook her head but didn't turn back. She saw a long road ahead for the Byrnes . . . and for Matt. Who knew better than she did? Matt and Petey, her and Krieg? Not much difference. But her mind was quickly back in the hospital room, back with the girl in the bed who'd made the mistake of her life. Harri had asked Ella a specific question, one she should have easily been able to answer. *Where do you work?* Instead, Ella had been evasive, then quickly shut down. Was it fatigue, overload, or something else?

CHAPTER 12

Taylor Johns got out of the car dodging raindrops and lugging a ten-pound bag of grocery store ice and a twenty-four-pack of Bud Light, the bottles of amber brew tinkling as he raced up the front stairs to the house of his coworker Bill Clements. Big Bill. He was late. Bill's weekly poker game with the guys from the plant had started an hour ago. Taylor had taken a wrong turn, thanks to the GPS, and missed his turnoff . . . twice. He lived north and wasn't familiar with the South Side.

It had taken Taylor weeks to wheedle himself an invitation to the game. He was just six months into the job at Dietzen's meatpacking, so he was the new kid on the block, running without a crew, until Big Bill gave him the nod. Now Taylor was in with the cool guys, one of the gang. He'd *made* it.

Smiling, he set the case down on the stoop and rang the doorbell, smoothing down his hair in the reflection in Big Bill's security door. He wasn't bad looking for a man of thirty-two, he thought, not that attractiveness was what had gotten him the nod. It's just that he wanted to look decent, not like a weirdo or some friendless clown who lived in his mother's basement, playing video games. Taylor wanted to make a good impression on the guys and had bought a new shirt for the game and had used the cologne he normally reserved for funerals or weddings. He squared his shoulders, prepared to make an *awfully* good impression.

Through the door he could hear the thump of music coming from inside, which threw him for a second. Who played music at a guys' poker game? You put a game on, whatever game you could find on the five hundred cable channels or sports packages you had access to. Music? He grimaced and wondered about Big Bill's commitment to this poker thing. There was no answer to the bell, so Taylor rang it again, then nervously smoothed down his shirt and straightened the cuffs on his jacket a second time. When there was no answer to the second ring, he checked his phone for the text he'd received from his host. Taylor checked the address in the text against the numbers over the door, then he double-checked the date. Right address. Right day. Taylor was exactly where he was supposed to be. He knocked next, but there was no answer to that either.

A sickening feeling came over him. He wondered if he'd been the butt of a joke, if this was some kind of initiation prank. Make a fool of the new guy. God, he hoped not. He'd never taken things like that well as a kid, and he was too old to deal with it now. All he wanted was a group of pals, but he wasn't about to eat shit to get it.

He set the bag of ice next to the case and went down the stairs again and over to the picture window to get a look inside. If the music was on, somebody had to be home. Maybe they just hadn't heard the bell or his knock. He weaved in between the bushes, his shined shoes sinking into the damp, mossy bed of mulch, then he peered in and saw his soon-to-be buddies, his poker pals, slumped over a card table, playing cards and chips scattered everywhere. Three of them. Big guys. The NBA pregame show was on the fifty-incher mounted to the living room wall, the playoffs in full swing. Music, poker, *and* the pregame?

"What the hell?"

He rapped on the window, but nobody at the table moved. Taylor looked around the front room, but there didn't appear to be anyone else inside. He could see right through to the kitchen, too, which seemed to be empty. He didn't know if Clements had a wife. He hadn't asked. He stepped back, not sure what to do. Then he dialed Big Bill's cell. After a click, two, he could hear Bill's phone ring from inside, then the voicemail kicked in, and Big Bill's deep voice ordered him to say what he had to say at the end of the beep.

He ended the call. Three guys were out of it inside. All of them couldn't have passed out drunk at the same time, Taylor thought. Carbon monoxide? He peered through the window again, as though the odorless, colorless gas would show itself. As if the guys would rise in unison and go back to their poker hand. His eyes swept over them. No blood that he could see. Taylor turned from the window and scanned Big Bill's block. Nothing but bungalows and compact squares of brown lawns, just like Big Bill's. If he'd expected an explanation for what he saw inside written on the sidewalk, he was sadly mistaken. He eyed the case of beer, the bag of melting ice. His Sunday afternoon was wrecked, but not as wrecked as Big Bill's.

"Fuck."

He dialed 911.

"What the hell am I lookin' at?" Symansky asked as he stood with the team staring down at a card table with three bodies slumped over it.

It was just past noon on Sunday. Church day. Playoff day. A day of rest, though that never much held for folks with badges. They'd gotten the call just half an hour before, and the mention of a suspected overdose was enough to twist Harri's nerves into knots long before she walked through the door. That twist became a vise grip of foreboding when she caught sight of a handful of small blue bags, empty and discarded on the table amid a scattered deck of playing cards and bowls of chips and browning guac.

Harri couldn't have missed the bloody nostrils either. Robert Mitchell, Ella Byrne, Marie McClintock, and now three more. The better part of a week had gone by and Pease and Narcotics hadn't tracked down a source for Edge. None of their CIs admitted to knowing anything about it, and there was no chatter on the streets. ODs came and went without raising too many eyebrows or concerns. Nobody lost sleep over a lost junkie, except for those who loved them. But when was a simple overdose *not* a simple overdose? When there were six now staring them in the face.

"We're looking at a problem," Vera said.

Bigelow groaned. "A *big* problem."

A patrol officer stood behind them. Officer Bey, the first on scene, the one to call it in, the one who now stood as white as a sheet of composition paper, her eyes darting around the room as if the knickknacks on the mantel might pounce.

Vera looked over at Bey. "Is this it? Anything upstairs we need to know about?"

Bey shook her head. "No other victims on the premises. We checked upstairs and the basement, then secured the scene. The caller, Taylor Johns, is sitting in a squad outside when you're ready to talk to him. He identified the victim in the blue shirt as Bill Clements. This is his place. He and his friends are meat-packers. This is, or *was*, a weekly poker game."

"Johns say anything else?" Harri asked.

"That it was his first time at the game. He didn't know any of the men real well. He called Clements when there was no answer at the door. We came in through the back. That door's not as sturdy as the one in front."

Al's gaze sharpened. "We?"

"My partner, Adams. He's . . . he stepped out for some fresh air."

"Okay," Harri said. "Thanks. Let us know when the techs get here?"

Bey headed for the door. "On it."

"I don't know," Vera said, looking over the victims. "This is supposed to be a party drug we're dealing with? Ella and her friend might fit the demographic, but not these guys or Marie McClintock."

"Since when do drugs have a type?" Tony asked. "They're usually an equal opportunity fucker-upper."

"Yeah, yeah," Al said. "Let's do this before Matt gets wind and comes in here like Batman on a tear. The last thing . . ." His words trailed away when Matt barreled through the door, breathless, like he'd been running sprints in the sand. "And *there* he is."

Matt took one look at the scene and said, "What the hell am I looking at?"

Al raised his hand to stop the rehash. "Been there, done that."

"This the same thing?" Matt stared down at the table, clocked the bags. "Never mind. Asked and answered." He turned to the team. "I heard the call. We're dealing with bad pills." He looked at Harri. "No way we stand back now and wait while Narcotics comes up with nothing."

Harri let it sit for a second. "No," she said. "Now it's ours."

CHAPTER 13

Reverend Clevon Pope stared at his reflection in the mirror in the shabby back room at Holy Land Church, the mirror a scarred slab of cheap glass tacked to the back of a plywood door. The room smelled fusty and rickety, stacks of old hymnals scavenged from another church that'd gone bust pushed against a wall, narrowing the path between a wobbling wooden table Pope used as his desk and a low-end rolling chair bought on sale from Office Depot.

He was an old man, a longtime preacher, but he didn't feel old. He had a congregation, a wife, a calling. The gray hair, the aging body, did nothing to dampen his resolve to serve the Lord until his dying day.

"Despite the unfortunate loss of Sister McClintock," Pope said, "I'm full of the Spirit this day. Death is just a beginning, not an end. I truly believe our troubled sister is with our Lord in Heaven. It is now our obligation to stand by our brother Reuben and lift him up in Jesus's name." He raised hands toward Heaven and said a silent prayer, then turned to his wife. "This, Faith, is the day the Lord has made; let us rejoice and be glad in it. I'm feeling hope; I'm feeling blessed. I feel the Lord's hands pressed down upon my very shoulders." He adjusted his tie, then turned to face his wife, beaming. "Yes, ma'am. I'm feeling the Holy Spirit in my *bones*."

Faith Pope looked down at the pink tie, her husband's favorite, the one that went so well with the gray suit he was wearing. "You say that same thing every Sunday, and every prayer meeting, and in every Bible-study class." She smiled at him. "*Every* day is the day the Lord has made."

He winked at her. "True. True. Psalm 118."

He was testing her, as he always liked to. Faith was saved, and he wanted to keep it that way.

"'Give thanks to the Lord, for he is good; his love endures forever,'" she recited back.

Pope nodded, assured, then checked his gold cuff links, the ones with his initials in cubic zirconia. CJP. Clevon James Pope. Reverend Pope. Leader of the faithful of Holy Land Baptist Church.

Faith handed him his perfectly pressed suit jacket, then gave him a peck on his cheek as music started up downstairs. It was Sister Barrett on the secondhand piano. One day, there'd be a proper organ again. They'd had to sell the old one, to keep the creditors away, but Clevon didn't worry. Their situation would change. The old church would survive. The Lord would see to it.

"You are the shepherd of this flock," Faith said. "And you are doing great things."

"Not for me, though, for all of us, for the entire community, for all the world, as the Lord leads me to do." He held her chin and got lost in her eyes. "And with the perfect wife by my side."

His Faith, he thought, an unexpected gift after his beloved Betty had succumbed to cancer years ago. Though she was quite a bit younger than he was, Clevon believed that when God provided, he never provided the wrong thing. The Lord had sent him a soul to match his own, an angel, when he needed one most.

Faith hadn't grown up in the church like Clevon had. But she was born again, newly consecrated in the Word. Now he had a true helpmeet. He didn't want to talk about Betty, what she'd gone through, and he knew there were things Faith didn't want to relive. Why return to the pain of the past when a new life had begun?

Clevon had been pastoring for more than forty years, first down home in Alabama, then here when his family moved up north for better prospects. He'd gone from outdoor revivals to traveling ministries to bouncing from church to church to Holy Land, starting as an associate pastor to his mentor, Reverend Thomas Mowry III. Now Holy Land was his, Mowry long gone to the Lord. Their congregation was hearty, strong in the faith, numbering nearly two hundred anchored here in the dirt-caked streets on the city's South Side. And their number would grow, Clevon knew it would.

The church was old, it needed repair. The pipes were bad, the wires not so great, but they survived and forged ahead in Jesus's name. Clevon didn't worry about the ominous letters from the bank or the notices of taxes due from the state and city. God would lead them through. They needed money, but money was a worldly need that Clevon made no room for. God would provide. He always seemed to come through at just the right time. The heart of Holy Land still beat. The word of God dwelled inside these crumbling bricks, and he was the right messenger for the right time.

"Sounds like Sister Barrett is in fine form today," Clevon said, checking his watch. "Folks will be coming in anytime. You ready?"

"If you are, I am," Faith answered back. "Clevon, the church *will* pull through. It's too important to our people, to you and me. We will *not* let it fail."

Clevon drew her thin frame into a hug. "I wish you wouldn't worry. Those who live in Christ have no need of worry." He released her but held her by the shoulders, looking straight into her eyes. "Holy Land will not shutter. It will go on and on because God *wants* it to continue His good work. Banish the doubt from your mind. Pray on it, Faith."

He turned back to the mirror so he could see himself and Faith in the reflection. "Reverend Pope and the first lady of Holy Land Baptist."

She smoothed out her yellow skirt, making sure it was straight and proper for the first lady of Holy Land. "I believe in you, Clevon."

It would take all he had, every ounce of faith, he knew, but he did not fear that they would be disappointed. God would clear the path.

"Meanwhile, we got the food bank and the job tutoring to keep going," he said. "Two new congregants came in just last week. Plus, I got that meeting with the alderman coming up. No one wants to see Holy Land go away. There might be something she can do to help us raise what we need. She might even be able to put in a good word for us at the bank." He offered another playful wink. "We must be committed, Faith." He closed his eyes and raised his hands toward Heaven a second time. "Holy Land will be saved. Nothing will flow through it but love and divinity. Hundreds of faithful, thousands will come. So many we'll have to have an overflow space to fit 'em all in. Me up there sharin' the Word, bringin' folks to Christ." He opened one eye, caught Faith looking back at him. "Sounded a little prideful, didn't it?"

Her brow lifted. "I didn't hear anything prideful in that. He'll give you what you need to do what he needs doing. It *will* happen."

Clevon buttoned his suit jacket, took one last look in the mirror. "I hear them comin' in. Let's go save some folks." He held out his hand for his wife's. It was their custom as pastor and first lady to enter the service together and to sit in front, facing the congregation. They would greet every grandmother in her well-appointed Sunday hat, every man, every child, even babes in their mothers' arms. They were family here at Holy Land.

Clevon thought about the church's building fund. There was barely $2,000 in it, and they needed $62,000 to repair the church. But God worked in mysterious ways. Only He could make a way out of no way.

"You have a good sermon for today," Faith said as they walked out.

"The Spirit moved me toward Malachi 3:10." He cleared his throat to test it out for Faith.

"'Bring ye all the tithes into the storehouse, that there may be meat in mine house, and prove me now herewith, saith the LORD of hosts, if I will not open you the windows of heaven, and pour you out a blessing, that there shall not be room enough to receive it.'"

Faith laid her head on his shoulder. "Amen, Pastor Pope. Amen."

CHAPTER 14

Hours later, after the service, after the lights had been dimmed, the piano pushed aside, and the pews emptied, Faith Pope stood at the door of the upper room, her hands clasped in front of her, as she welcomed her young women's Bible-study group.

Clevon left the ministering of the women and girls to her. Who knew better to teach women and children the way, than Christian women, he'd told her. He was such a sweet man, a good man, a decent man. Trustful, in all things. But who knew better than Faith how cruel the world could be? How hard, how cold, how unforgiving.

Faith said a little prayer when she heard the front door open and then footsteps on the stairs. She knew there would be three girls, but never the same three. She watched solemnly as three girls walked in without greeting her, each with a Bible she knew they'd never read. These were hard girls, girls from the street, girls who were at the mercy of whatever man was in their life—an abusive father, mother's boyfriend, uncle, brother. She knew they'd learned early that fighting and clawing and taking were how they survived, and that they'd likely given up, or been forced to give up, innocence for food or shoes or a sense of belonging well before Faith met them. She knew the life. She'd once preyed upon the vulnerable, the weak, the sick, the dispossessed. Sin. But God changed hearts and fortunes all the time. She believed that one Bible verse, one kind word, one good example, could change what seemed unchangeable, and she and Clevon knew how.

"Welcome, welcome, ladies," Faith said as each girl filed into the room. "Thank you for coming. Praise Jesus."

The girls said nothing. They never said much. They were resistant to goodness and kindness, never having encountered either before. Faith had laid out a plate of cookies and cans of pop, a little more sweetness to sweeten the pot. When they were all in, she shut the door behind them and locked it with a key from her pocket.

Three girls, always three, but not the same three every week. It was hard to make a real connection this way, Faith lamented, but she would never stop trying. One girl came more often than the others, the one who called herself Lil Smoke. She was a girl of maybe seventeen, though she looked decades older. Smoke was covered in violent tattoos and wore baggy clothes and severe makeup as striking as a theatrical costume. There were scars on her face that looked like they'd been acquired in a knife fight, one over her left eye, one along her right cheek. Faith had never been able to get a given name out of the girl. It hurt her deeply to have to call her Lil Smoke.

The girls dropped down onto the folding chairs Faith had set out for them, and then waited for Faith to start, as she always did, with prayer. When Faith had finished, there was no amen from the three, just blank, unaffected expressions of boredom.

"I don't know your names," Faith said.

Lil Smoke frowned. "You know mine. Don't matter what theirs is. They just here to *read the Bible*. God know they names, right?"

The girls snickered but offered nothing more. Lil Smoke nudged her friends. "Y'all can do whatever, I guess. We just got to make it look like something." Smoke stood, walked over to the table in front, took a cookie off the plate, and nibbled on it. She then shoved a can of pop into each of her big pockets. Turning toward her friends, she gave them a nod, and they did the same. Lil Smoke was in charge.

"Did you read your Bibles at all?" Faith asked. "It's all right if you only read a little bit at a time."

Lil Smoke sneered. "Too busy." She stared at the single key on the table next to the cans of pop, then grabbed it up and headed to the closet at the back of the room. "And praise the Lord, there's a lot of words in that Bible. Jesus and 'em had a lot to say in them Olden Times."

"Don't mock the Word," Faith said sternly. "If you'd only just give it a chance, it can heal you, like it did me. I once—"

The girl held up a hand, cutting off her words. "Keep it, church lady. You know we not here for all that."

Lil Smoke's unnamed companions joined her at the closet to do what they *were* here for, as Faith watched. It was shame she felt as she stood by and allowed the good she'd done to get overtaken by *this*. Who was she? What would Clevon think? Were there some things even he couldn't forgive? How far was too far to go to do good?

She watched the girls go about their business, knowing none of them questioned their actions. They were ruled by impulse and need and fear. These girls, Faith knew, hadn't been girls in quite a while. They were walking ghosts with feral eyes, feared, discarded, and overlooked. No home training to speak of, they got by on their wits and by opportunity. They were lost.

Faith closed her eyes for a moment to pray for them, and others like them, who didn't know the way, and for her own soul, and to count her own blessings. "God accepts everyone who has faith. He forgives."

"I been baptized," one of the girls offered. "So, I'm good."

"What harm would it do my knowing your names?" Faith asked.

Lil Smoke eyed her friends, gave them a nod. "Go on. It ain't gonna hurt nothing."

The smaller of the two, who looked all of twelve but who Faith hoped was older, answered first. "Do Run."

Her friend, her hair a bright fuchsia, her body too big for the tight jeans and sweater she wore. "Tosh."

Do Run. Tosh. Faith guessed they were no older than eighteen, true children of the dust. They belonged to the Forty-Third Street Double Dees, who ran the neighborhood that folks had to navigate through and controlled the block Holy Land sat on. God was not in charge of the Double Dees, but Faith knew who was.

"The Bible says," Faith began as she stood with her back straight and her hands shaking before these lost children, "in Proverbs 21:5 that 'Good planning and hard work lead to prosperity.'" She stared at the girls. "All things work for good for those who love God. Romans 8:28. If we love God, if we want to do good . . . he understands that."

Faith closed the Bible, gripped it in her hands. "Do you know what the *greater good* means?" The girls didn't answer. "It means that sometimes the things we do we do for other people, to make things better for somebody else, not us, personally. For no other reason than that it's the right thing to do. The good thing."

"For free?" Lil Smoke said, an incredulous look on her face. "Just because?" She lifted the pack onto her shoulder.

"For the good of everyone," Faith said. "For others. Sometimes, the things we do for the good of *others* . . ."

She eyed the girls each in turn. "Lil Smoke? Do Run? Tosh? We would welcome you all here at Holy Land."

When the girls had claimed all three packs. Lil Smoke locked the closet and returned the key to the table. Reaching down, she took the last of the cookies and stuffed them into her pocket.

"That it?" Lil Smoke asked. "No more Bible sayings?"

"I won't give up," Faith said.

Lil Smoke set her Bible on the table, the other two hung on to theirs. Props. That's all they were.

"I respect that about you," Lil Smoke said with a clueless grin. "We see you next week." She looked back at the table. "Have some more of those cookies too. They good."

Tosh glanced down at Faith's Bible. "That book don't pay no rent."

"It saves souls," Faith snapped back. "If you follow the Word, give yourself over to Christ, it will save your life."

Tosh chuckled. "Christ don't pay no rent either."

Faith unlocked the door, and the girls left. She stood and listened as they exited on giggles and titters through the front door, the fun making likely at her expense.

"Galatians," she muttered. "'And let us not grow weary of doing good, for in due season we will reap, if we do not give up.'"

The first lady of Holy Land scanned the now-empty room. The locked closet. The empty plate where the cookies had been. The Bible on the table, left for her.

"For the greater good."

CHAPTER 15

"You haven't said one word in"—Sly consulted his watch—"six minutes."

Harri looked across the table at Detective Colman Sylvester, a little surprised to find him there. She'd been deep in thought and in a place she wouldn't be able to define if asked. She'd been in a state of self-reflection since seeing Dr. Parker, feeling as though she were stumbling aimlessly through some no-man's-land, unsure which way to go or where she was supposed to be.

Why did she always end up at Sly's? As though he were the safe spot, the oasis? She felt guilty about it, feeling as though she were using him and giving very little back. She didn't want to be that person. She didn't want this to be one-sided. Taking a deep breath, she inhaled the scent of sandalwood and spices. Sly's home was a *home*, warm and inviting, colorful, filled with overstuffed pillows and earth-toned furniture and tapestries, African drums and the art of their people, which spoke to her in profound ways. It was a haven, a remembrance of what she'd once had. An anchor, if she were forced to give it a name. And in this place was a good man, who hadn't pulled away from waiting for her to come back to herself. Harri didn't know why but wasn't ready to ask. She also wasn't ready to think about what it all might mean or how she felt about it.

"Sorry," she said, "I was just thinking."

He angled his head. “About?”

Harri took him in. Kind face. Dark skin. Wise ebon eyes that crinkled at the sides when he smiled or laughed, both of which he did often. Sly smelled also of sandalwood. How did she feel about him? How did she *feel* about anything? She was just beginning to rediscover all that.

“Why am I here?” she asked him.

His eyes widened, and he leaned back in his chair to look her over. “You don’t know?”

Harri glanced down at the table he’d set for two. He’d made dinner, which accounted for the smell of spices in the house. Tonight, for the two of them, grilled salmon, asparagus, and potatoes that didn’t look or taste like potatoes but literally melted in her mouth. Sly cooked well and with intention. How he found time for it when he had the same crazy job she had, she couldn’t fathom. There was life in Sly’s house, and none in hers. The choices, she knew, had been intentional on both their parts.

She studied his face. “Forget I said that.”

“You okay? You seem a little . . . distracted. Bad day at work?”

She folded her napkin, noting just then that Sly had matched it to the pale-brown cloth over the table, and that the beige plates complemented both. It was this attention to detail, she knew, that also made him a good cop.

“Yes, but no. I’m seeing someone.”

It came out in a rush, but she knew right away from the look on Sly’s face that she’d said it wrong. His entire body tensed up. “Aiiight.”

She watched his expression go from open to guarded, and wondered what had happened, then realized what she’d actually said.

“No. Wait. I didn’t say that right. I’m seeing a therapist. A *doctor*.”

Sly’s shoulders eased, his smile returned. “Good thing I wasn’t eating when you threw that out there, I would have choked.”

She offered a sheepish grin. “Context would have helped.”

“So?” he asked, taking a sip from his wineglass. “How was it?”

She sat back in her chair. “Excruciating. Humbling. I didn’t come away with any miracle fix. Apparently, I’m expected to turn myself inside out and come up with the fix myself.” She gave him a long look. “Anyway, I took the first step.” Harri let her eyes look over the room, the table, the man. “I always seem to end up back here. I don’t think it’s the drums or the food, or even the sex.”

Sly’s eyes widened in surprise, catching himself before the spit take. He held his glass up. “You know I can choke on liquid, too, right?”

She went on as if she hadn’t heard him. “You’re here, RJ isn’t. In fairness, I pushed him away, and it was a hard push. More like a shove. I did the same to you, after what happened to G, but you stuck around. Why?”

She watched as he folded his hands in his lap, seemingly ready to have the conversation she’d been avoiding. There was music playing low in the other room from Sly’s old-school stereo system. Jazz. Something she didn’t recognize.

“Simple answer? I’m not your ex-husband. No offense, but he’s a damned fool. *Simpler* answer, I don’t get pushed away from a good thing, plus I play the long game. I figured time was on my side.” There was a glint in his eye. “And it’s not just about the . . . you know, for me either. Just making it clear.”

There was silence between them for a moment.

“Mind if I ask about the therapist?” he asked.

“She’s an ex-cop. No BS. She was injured on the job and had to rebuild everything . . . like me. I don’t think much gets past her.” Harri exhaled. “I’m tired, Sly. I’m carrying the world on my back. Can’t do it anymore.”

“I get it. You’re sick and tired of being sick and tired,” Sly said. “Now what happens?”

She pressed her lips tight, shook her head, still on wobbly ground. "I go back and talk some more. I deal with my crap." She looked around the comforting room. "More of this. Now, if I can just remember who I was before . . . everything," she joked, but only half humorously.

"I can help with that. What do you want to know?"

Harri stared at him not sure if she should be scared or not.

"Look, I was there. I clocked you the first day you walked into my district," Sly said. "You came in like you owned the whole city. Genuine badass. Bad *ass*. From what I can see, you didn't lose any of that. You just got knocked around a little bit. Didn't you ever wonder why I always seemed to be wherever you were?"

"I wasn't looking for anything," Harri said. "I was worse then, than I am now."

Sly shifted in his chair. "Hmm, well, you sure weren't picking up what I was throwing down, and I was throwing it hard. You're smart, but you're as clueless as a baby about some things."

Harri stared at him, then laughed, mystified to discover she'd had a benevolent stalker. "You do know that stalking is a Class 4 felony in Illinois, punishable by one to three years in prison and a fine of up to $25,000."

"Don't cop me," Sly said. "Cuz I'll cop you right back."

She felt lighter than she remembered feeling in a long time. She had a plan, a way out, a road to walk that didn't feel as though she would be traversing it barefoot and over broken glass. Thanks to a not-so-gentle push from Sergeant Sharon Griffin, her little Irish friend, and Dr. Roxanne Parker.

Harri raised her glass, then held it inches from her mouth before taking a sip. "I think I know why I'm here."

Sly stared back at her, smiling. "Shit. Took you long enough."

CHAPTER 16

The next morning, they made the 8:00 a.m. newscast. Three bodies; death investigation underway. No threat to the public. Same old vague details that ticked the boxes, but didn't open them. In this case, as in most others they had to deal with, Harri was glad for the broad sweep and the quick shift to the next sound bite.

They had five dead from suspected overdose from a drug it would take them weeks, maybe months, to identify. Toxicology took that long, depending on workload, understaffing, other priorities, and everything else that worked against them. Until they got a definitive, they'd have to make do knowing they were dealing with something in the opioid family. Not much to go on. Not nearly enough. But it was what it was. Harri watered the flourishing plant on her desk, then eyed a lone paper clip sitting on her desk blotter. Instead of scooping it up, gripping it for dear life, and slipping it into her pocket, Harri slid her top drawer open, purposefully swept the clip inside, and stood there for a moment, waiting to see if the world crashed in on her. It didn't.

Assembled at the office a little after eight, the team was joined by Streeter and Evans from the skate park and Detective George Pease, from Narcotics.

"These guys weren't kids," Streeter said. "What were they doing kicking around something like this? With the playoff game playing in the background?"

Vera looked confused. "What's the game have to do with it?"

Streeter looked at her as though she'd grown another head. "How do you watch a game half plastered?"

Vera's mouth hung open, disbelief on her face. "Are you *serious*?"

Griffin stood looming at the fringes of the hub of detectives. "Weeds, Li. Get out of them."

"We need to touch base with Grant," Harri said. "She won't like it, and she won't have much to tell us, but we have to follow through. Even a little something is better than nothing."

"Source," Matt said. "We concentrate on that."

Pease, a muscular, square-jawed human tackle dummy, said, "Think gangs. I can't say we've seen this Edge floating around in blue bags, but new stuff pops up on the regular. There's always *entrepreneurs*, independent operators changing shit up. A drug's a product like any other product. New and improved is always a good selling point."

Harri turned to Matt. "Any luck with Petey?"

He shook his head, pointed to Streeter and Evans. "I met with these guys. I was hoping to get a look at Mitchell's phone. They blew me off."

Evans scoffed. "Huh. You came in like a freight train . . . rubbed us the wrong way. Look, I get it. Family's family, but the heat we don't need. If we went full balls to the wall every time some kid stuck something up his nose or down his pipe, we'd never get anywhere on anything else."

Matt fumed, but held it in. Harri turned to Evans. "Where are you on things?"

Evans stood, defiant. "We followed steps. We filed the report. We determined no third party was on scene, and then we moved on."

He put his hands on his hips. "Like you and your partner did with McClintock, if I'm not reading it wrong."

He was right, Harri thought. He hadn't read it wrong. This was a case of one drop in the bucket turning into two drops and then into a flood no one saw coming. Now they were knee deep in blue bags and unanswered questions.

"Well, can we get a look at the phone?" Harri asked.

Evans gave Matt a nasty look. "Guess we all should be taking a look at it."

Vera stood. Harri could tell her mind was somewhere else, chewing on an idea. "This isn't a very wide spread, though, is it? Thirty-First Street at the park, McClintock's place a mile or so west of there. The poker game not far from that. So, wherever this stuff is coming from, it's not traveling far."

"*Yet*," Tony said, now on his second cup of coffee and fully into it. "We all know how it goes."

"And maybe we're not looking at one source," Harri said. "If it's gangs, there could be multiple sources, a dozen peddlers, all operating right in this area. Drugs, like guns, outnumber us by a trillion to one."

"Nothing's new there," Griffin said. "Doesn't change what we have to do. We have to stop this stuff and kill it."

"Hate to burst your bubble," Pease said, "but this *stuff*? It'll be called something else and look different this time next week. As soon as we get one sorted out, next day we got a handful more. Mutations, if you will. And until we know exactly *what* it is, we can't rule out simple pilot error. It might not be the drug at all. The stuff's poison, but it's not manufactured to snuff out its clientele after a single use. These dealers *do* want customers coming back for more. We'll work our contacts, see what we can get. We might get lucky."

Al groaned as he hooked his thick thumbs in behind his wide belt. "I love it when we gotta depend on lucky breaks to keep people from keelin' over."

"And just so you know," Matt said, back on Streeter. "It's not just *my* family I'm on this for. It could be any of your kids next. If it takes lighting a fire, I don't have a problem holding the matches."

Streeter lifted both hands in mock surrender. "All right, professor, don't get all hot under the collar."

Matt got red in the face and ripped his glasses off, ready to make something of it. "Hot under the . . . ? Look here—"

"Fighting each other sure isn't going to help," Harri offered calmly. "We find who's slinging this. We make them stop. That's it."

"Simple," Vera said, though the look on her face told Harri she suspected it was anything but.

Harri sighed, the magnitude of the work ahead of them getting to her already, and they hadn't even made it one hour into their shift. "We talk to Grant. We scour Mitchell's phone. We try the friends again. Then we go back to the McClintocks' and talk to the rest of her neighbors and anyone else she might have gotten this stuff from. We look for connections." She checked her watch. Nearly 9:00 a.m., a little shy of an hour into their shift. "Anything else we haven't thought about?"

There were a few grumbles, but no ideas.

"Anybody want to take the superintendent and the mayor?" Griffin asked. No one volunteered. "I didn't think so." She turned to go back to her office. "Heavy hangs the head that wears the fucking crown."

Matt brightened, sensing a kindred spirit.

"Don't *even*, Kelley," Griffin said, cutting him off. "Not in the mood." She slammed her door behind her.

"You know, we've heard a lot about her," Evans said. "Tough cookie. Not one to pour it down smooth, is she?"

Al chuckled. "*Pour* it down? Try *shove* it down."

Streeter nodded to Evans, and they grabbed their coats. "We'll take the phone. If we find something, or don't, we'll pass it on."

The team watched Streeter, Evans, and Pease take off, each waiting until their visitors were good and gone before talking again.

"Am I the only one thinkin' the phone was the easiest part?" Al groused. "We gotta run all over town like chickens with no heads, and they get to sit in the office and thumb through a phone . . . the *two* of them? No idea what Pease is gonna do. Plus, c'mon. If it was me, I wouldn't put my dealer's number in *my* phone, would you? That's one number I'd commit to memory just for *this* reason."

Tony couldn't hide his irritation. "Streeter and his buddy Evans don't look like they're too fired up about this. Served with a few guys like that. Always the last ones over the hill. Always the first to talk shit about it."

"We keep it moving," Harri said, gathering up her notes. "We hit Mitchell's friends first? Full-court press? Knock it out."

"Logical first step," Vera said.

"Me and Tony can take Ella's dorm," Al said, glancing over at Matt. "And Matt, seeing as we got zero chance of gettin' him to take a pass on this. I'm thinkin' roommates, right? Maybe somebody knows somethin', or saw somethin'. You three can take Mitchell's place. He's gotta have bros to tap. First team gets somethin' shouts out. Sound good?"

"Works for me," Vera said, slipping into her jacket. "Harri?"

Harri thought about her talk with Ella. The feeling she had that the girl was being evasive about her campus job. Four hundred dollars in cash was a lot of money for a college kid to carry around. And what kid dealt in cash these days anyway? Wasn't everything in their world digital? A tap of a card or phone here, a tap there? "Unless Matt would like to hang back and work on nailing down those blue bags and who might be putting them out there?"

"No way am I getting sidelined."

"It's not sidelining," Harri said, "it's giving us—"

Matt brushed past them. "We're doing this. I'll meet you two in the car."

Vera shook her head. "He used to be so nice. Not like Al or Tony here."

Tony cut his eyes at her. "Ain't *that* just nothing."

CHAPTER 17

Robert Mitchell's apartment was at Fifty-Fourth and University Avenue, less than a half mile from the campus on a block of quiet apartment buildings and single-family homes. In full spring and summer, the block would be leafy and busy. Now the trees were still budding, and mostly barren, and it was cold and damp. It was about 10:00 a.m. when they got there, but there was nowhere to park in front, so Vera parked two buildings down from Mitchell's and they all walked back. Parking was always at a premium in Hyde Park. Most of the streets had been designated for residential permit parking because of the traffic from the university, as well as tourists filing into Frank Lloyd Wright's Robie House, a five-minute drive away. The spots the permits didn't claim, the perpetually strapped city did, having saddled residents with a seventy-five-year parking meter contract that turned nickel-and-diming into an art form. Maybe their car would be there when they got back, maybe it wouldn't. Either the city would tow it, even with their city plates, or someone would steal it. Life was a gamble here in the city of broad shoulders.

They flanked out at the apartment door. Matt knocked.

"Smells like feet and guy pits," he said, his nose crinkled in displeasure.

"Eyes on the prize, Matt," Harri said as the door opened.

The pimply-faced twentysomething who stood inside blinked at the three of them, his mouth open. "We got more of them." He announced to whoever was inside, before stepping aside to let them enter. "Come on in. We may as well tell you what we told her."

Harri was confused. "Her?"

They were ushered into a very untidy front room occupied by two young men slumped on what looked like a secondhand slouch couch, and a slender Black woman standing over them in jeans and a beat-up leather jacket on top of a dark mock turtleneck. Harri's eyes traveled from head to toe, the toes covered by a pair of Nike running shoes that looked as though they'd been through the wars. But it was the hazel eyes, the slight grin, like something was funny, that made her think she was looking at one of their own.

"We get wires crossed somewhere?" Matt asked the woman, who'd yet to speak.

"I'm Detective Foster," Harri said. "Detectives Li, Kelley."

The woman's eyes took each one of them in turn. Keen, analytically, like a cop. She even stood like one, straight, facing the door, feet balanced, jacket open. She looked to be in her late thirties, athletically built, medium complexion, attractive, but not fussy about it.

"Where do you work out of?" Vera asked.

"My own office," the woman said, her voice strong, confident. "I'm a private investigator. And I was here first."

"And *why* are you here, exactly?" Harri asked.

"I would think for the same reason the three of *you* are, only I've been hired by the Mitchell family. They want what you're offering, only they want it faster and without the city tied up in it."

"So, they hired *you*?" Vera asked.

The PI caught the tone. "There any reason you think they *wouldn't*?"

The young men's heads swiveled from left to right as the exchange took place.

"Just one," Vera said. "We've got a lot of boots on the ground, and there's only one of you."

The woman said, "Well, none of your boots came this way until today, these guys told me, and Robby Mitchell died days ago. I was hired just this morning, and I made it here lickety-split. A lot of boots on the ground aren't always the godsend you think they are. Sometimes one pair of boots committed to the job is enough."

Matt didn't like it. Too many cooks in the kitchen on a case he wasn't about to see compromised. "We didn't catch a name?"

The woman pulled a face, then shook her head. "Nah. Too easy." She turned back toward the young men, then reached into her jacket pocket and pulled out her card and set it on the coffee table in front of them. She slid a look back at the three detectives staring at her and put another card down just for them.

"If you think of anything else," she told the young men, "give me a call. Day or night. I sleep lightly, when I sleep at all."

She brushed past the detectives. "Night. I expect I'll see you around. You know how paths cross."

Vera's mouth hung open. "Wait a minute. *Who* are you?"

"No time to coffee klatch, Detective Li. Boots, and all. We'll talk soon, I imagine."

The woman walked out and eased the door closed behind her. Harri could hear her jog down the stairs at a quick pace, whistling jauntily like she was off to work in a coal mine with six diminutive coworkers in tow.

"I don't think I've ever had that happen to me before," Matt said.

"Same here," Vera said. "Cocky, wasn't she."

Harri walked over to the table, picked up the card, and read it. "Cassandra Raines, Raines Investigations." She slid the card meant for them into her pocket. "Guess we know where to find her." She turned to Mitchell's roommates, down to business. "Now, let's start over. Tell us everything you just told her."

Harri was pleased with the information they'd gotten when they returned to the office with things to share. They spent the rest of the morning laying down foundation and ticking off boxes, slow work. Despite the number of boots they had at their disposal, as Vera was eager to tout, they knew that each pair only advanced one step at a time.

When they all assembled at the board later, Harri said to Al and Tony, "You first."

Al lifted out of his chair on a groan and a grumble, making that old man noise in response to stiff bones being slow to obey his brain's instruction. "Well, Matt will be pleased to know we didn't get any dirt on Ella. She's a good kid. No problem to nobody. Her and the skate park? Down to the last person, they wouldn't a guessed it."

Tony ingested his caffeine. "We got the same about Mitchell. He wasn't a troublemaker. More of a shoulder-to-the-wheel guy."

Al stretched out his back, emitting another groan. "One thing I found strange. I'm no Ricardo Montalbán, but—"

Al saw the curious looks he was getting but held up a hand to stop inquiries. "Nope. Movin' on. We looked around Ella's room. She's got two other girls in there with her. Nice kids, too, it looks like. Smart, like they could do your taxes, or somethin'. The strange thing was this. The other kids seriously looked like a bunch of ragpickers pulled off the street. Clothes hangin' off 'em. Holes in their jeans. If they weren't sittin' up in that building, I'd pick 'em up as vagrants."

Vera yawned. "Yeah, that's how college kids do it, Al. What's strange about that?"

He glanced over at Matt before he answered. "Like I said, I'm no Montalbán, but Ella had some spiffy stuff in her closet. High end, it looked like." He reached in his pocket and pulled out his phone. "Nothing sparkly or glitzy, but like quality made." He booted up his photo gallery and showed the photos around. "Tony was just as useless as me, so we asked the girls. They all figured Ella was rich and all this stuff came from Daddy. She wasn't stingy about sharin' it, so they had no complaints, overall."

Vera peered at the photos when the phone swiveled around to her. "Is that a Fendi handbag?"

Everyone drew in closer.

"Those sweaters look like cashmere," Harri added.

Al drew the phone back. "Like I said, no slouch in the clothes department."

"Our family's not rich," Matt said. "Maggie and Joe dug deep to send Ella to school. No way are they coming up with a Fendi handbag for a nineteen-year-old, you can count on that."

"Then where do you think she got it?" Harri asked.

Matt looked overwhelmed, out of ideas, scared. "She's working."

"Fendis go for a couple thousand and up," Vera said gently, watching Matt for his reaction, likely hoping he would take it well.

Tony, too, made every effort not to look Matt's way, finding an imaginary piece of something to pick at on his trouser leg. "I'm thinking there's a good explanation."

Matt jumped on it. "I'll ask her. I'll check with Maggie." He nodded. "Right. First chance I get."

Al took his seat. "Well, that's all we got. You guys' turn."

Harri handed the marker to Matt. "You want to take it?"

"Sure. Got it. Um. Well, we got the same on Mitchell. Good kid. But we got a lead on tracking where he got the stuff, maybe. We don't have the phone, so we don't know yet if this is a lie, but Mitchell's pals swear he didn't use or buy. We threw out the name Petey, and got nothing, but then one of the guys asked if we *meant P.D.* Ella said *Petey*, because she thought that's what she heard Mitchell say. But it's P.D. we're looking for. Every kid in that apartment has heard the name circling around campus. Apparently, P.D. is the worst-kept secret over there."

"That's it? P.D.? And nobody can finger him?" Al asked.

"*Her*," Matt said.

Al's face contorted into a displeased scowl. "Now *there's* a wrinkle I didn't see comin'."

Vera broke in. "They've heard of P.D., but they all claim they've never laid eyes on her."

Al twisted in his chair to look over at her. "And you believe 'em? Sounds like a crock."

"It could be," Vera said. "For it *not* to be a crock, I'd have to believe Mitchell and his friends are innocent guppies swimming in a very small fishbowl, and after our last case with the Colliers and their many secrets, I can't get myself there."

Tony said, "Colleges are like hospitals and police stations. Everybody knows *everybody's* everything. If they've *heard* of this P.D., *somebody's* seen her, and can point her ass out. We sweat the kids. Get them to crack, then sit them in front of a sketcher."

Harri shook her head. "Not there yet."

Matt held up the marker to regain the floor. "Anyway, I ran the initials earlier but came up empty. Not enough information." Matt jotted the initials on the board, then underlined them. He turned to face the room. "*P.D.* works the school fairly regularly. Her clientele must be robust enough to keep her coming back. Big campus. I'll bet she's got help. Right now, she's a ghost."

"If nobody knows her, how do they get in contact?" Tony asked.

"They say she just shows up. Word gets around and everybody interested makes sure they don't miss out. For her part, she's got to figure every weekend there's going to be a line of buyers." Matt frowned. "Party time, right?"

Al wasn't buying it. "And University Police don't have a handle on this? All this flies under their noses?"

"They're the same as us, I'd think," Matt said. "The flood's too great, not enough bodies to hold it back. It has to be like playing Whac-A-Mole. How long's a buy take? Three seconds? Slam, bam."

He walked over to his desk and picked up a folder. "Vera, Harri, and I were here about an hour before the rest of you slackers strolled in." He slid them a playful look. "I put in a call to University Police to see what we can get from them. Not sure pulling cameras will get us anything since we don't know where she hits or when. Like I said, it's a big school, spread out. There are a lot of nooks and crannies. So, for now, we have P.D. and that's all."

"We might want to give Gangs a ring too," Al said. "Maybe they know this P.D. She's slingin' for somebody. Independent operators don't last too long out there."

"Definitely," Matt said. "Anyway, P.D. is brick number one."

Tony scoffed. "One brick don't make a wall."

Harri rose from her chair. "But it's a start. We have a name. Ella connects P.D. to Mitchell. The roommates connect P.D. to the school. Now we have to find out where this P.D. comes from, who she's working for, and where she's getting this Edge."

"Yeah, I see all *those* connections," Al said, "but I don't see any that connect P.D. to McClintock or the poker guys."

Matt stepped away from the board. *"Yet."*

"Ella ever meet this P.D.?" Tony asked.

Matt reeled to face him. "Of course not. Why would she?"

Tony stood his ground. "Same fishbowl. Anybody ask her, or are we just assuming she never did?"

Matt's face colored, he was not pleased. "We're bashing victims now?"

"We're working the case, man. We follow where it goes. You expect something different because it's your niece?"

"That's not it, and you know it."

"*Thought* I knew it," Tony said. "Good you confirmed it."

After a moment's silence, Al said, "I think we can all see why there's good reason surgeons don't operate on their own family."

"I know what I'm doing," Matt shot back defensively. "I have it handled, and Ella's not in this . . . *okay?*"

Harri watched him, seeing the other side of the affable, easygoing Matt, the one she'd met at the hospital that Sunday. She knew there was a switch he could flip, and that he had obviously flipped it. Nothing good could come of that.

Out of the corner of her eye, Harri saw Griffin slip out of her office to stand and watch as they ran things down. Of course, she could feel the tension in the room, they all could. Harri hurriedly moved along, turning to her partner. "Vera, what've you got?"

Griffin leaned against a file cabinet, her arms crossed, all ears. Harri had been avoiding the boss since her session with Parker. Harri wasn't ready to talk about any of that with her, not that she was required to. Maybe it was that she just didn't want to admit to herself that Griffin had been right?

"I'm still on Faith Pope. I've been going through mug shots," Vera said.

Tony said, "Mug shots? Isn't that the preacher's wife? You think *she's* got a sheet? That's cold, Vera."

"How else would I know her face? It's not like we met in church."

Tony blinked. "You don't go to church?"

Vera's brows lifted. "Do *you* go to church?"

He began to play with his tie. "It's complicated. Get out my business, woman."

"Right," Vera said. "Well, I've found nothing yet, but I *know* I've come across her before. I'll keep at it. Meanwhile, I pulled what we had on the McClintocks' upstairs neighbors, the partying troublemakers? Their stuff's mostly domestic, like we learned from Reynolds. Nuisance calls for loud music, loitering, revving car engines at all hours accounts for the rest. Basically, they're the neighbors from hell.

"We've got a single mother, Lynette Thompson; her adult son, Reynard; an adult daughter, La'Kisha; and, according to the latest report, a couple of kids belonging to the two offspring, as well as an assortment of boyfriends and girlfriends who cycle in and out with alarming frequency. The apartment's rented to Mrs. Sybil Jackson, she's Lynette's mother. Nothing on her. There was a call for a wellness check from a relative about two months ago, but everything was fine. The landlord, Jerry Brown, is trying to get Lynette and her kids and *their* kids out of the place, according to one report, but they won't go, and Jackson, apparently, won't force them out. Age-old story."

"Nothing drug related," Harri stated, "or you would have said. Any complaints specifically from the McClintocks?"

"Or any dustups?" Tony asked.

Al rolled his eyes. "And somebody decided to settle it with skunk pills? Nuh-uh. That's a stretch stretched *way* out."

"Not when you consider the somebodies," Vera said. "Everybody up there's on paper, except for Jackson and the kids. Reynard's been in and out of jail—gang activity, aggravated theft. La'Kisha writes bad checks and steals, Lynette shoplifts. Both of them are on and off probation. They're just a trio of bad actors."

Al harrumphed. "I see why the landlord wants 'em out."

Vera scribbled her additions on the board. "It's the traffic going in and out there that might hold some promise. There's no telling who their friends are. Just because none of these people were charged with possession doesn't mean they aren't *in* possession. Anybody up there could have supplied McClintock, no problem. If she was desperate enough for relief that she turned to street drugs, she would have tapped almost anybody, and these misfits are just a floor up. So, we go, we check, see if our deaths tie in." Vera put the marker down and stepped away.

"Okay, one more thing." Harri tacked a business card to the board. "We ran into a private investigator at Mitchell's who says she's working for the parents."

Al frowned. "Thought *we* were workin' for the parents?" he groused under his breath.

Harri slid him a look. "And we'll keep doing it."

"And workin' to do what, *exactly*?" he persisted.

Harri turned to him. "What we're doing, only faster, she claims."

"And boy was she cocky, this PI," Vera said. "For a minute there, she had me thinking *I* was in the wrong place."

Matt reengaged. "Felt like we were."

"I asked around," Harri continued. "Raines is ex-CPD. Detective. She *was* us not long ago. Commendations up the arm. Decorated beyond that."

"Then why's she slumming?" Tony asked.

"She was shot in the line of duty," Harri said. "Forced to discharge her weapon to save her partner's life. After that, she quit, went private."

"Hero cop, one who took a bullet on the job?" Al nodded, impressed. "I don't hate it. I don't like the private part, though."

Harri turned to the group. "She has a reputation for being persistent."

"That's a polite way of sayin' pain in the ass," Al said.

Harri said, "Which means she's probably going to be a pain in *ours*."

Al raised his hand like he was in second grade. "In my experience, PIs are jumpy and real messy. Does her buzzing around mean we gotta play nice? If so, that ain't gonna sit well with me, even if she is ex-cop."

Harri glanced over at Griffin, who shook her head ever so slightly, just once to the left and back. That was a no on the playing nice. "We do our jobs. We don't get sidetracked, and we don't let her get under our skin. That work for everybody?"

"What's this PI look like?" Tony asked.

Vera looked over at him, eyes squinted, a visual clue to Tony that the ice he was gliding on was thin. "What difference does that make?"

"Just curious."

"She's very attractive," Matt said. "Cocky for sure, but cool about it."

Tony sat up. "No shit?"

"I didn't see a ring either," Matt offered, "but that's not always—"

Al bolted upright. "What the *hell* is this, *The Bachelor*? Can we get back to what we're *supposed* to be doin' instead of matchmakin' here for Tony Bigelow?"

Harri walked over to her desk, not wanting a single part of whatever was going on. "Okay. Grant first for me and Vera, then the McClintock neighbors." She pulled her bag out of her drawer and gathered her things as she watched Vera do the same.

"I'm deep diving on P.D.," Matt announced, slipping into his coat, giving Tony a nod. "No way I'm letting some PI take it."

Griffin pulled herself off the file cabinet, her eyes a steely pair of X-ray beams. "No. Kelley you're in the office running background, feeding information. You and P.D. do not cross paths."

Matt stood stunned. "What? You can't be serious. No way I'm riding a desk on this."

Griffin's eyes got harder. "That's exactly what you're doing. You work that computer and get us what we need when we need it."

Matt sputtered for a moment. Fumed. "There's no reason I can't do my job out there, and you know it." He jabbed a pointed finger in Griffin's direction. "You *know* that. This is *unbelievable*."

The room stilled; even the few cops across the room working on other cases stopped doing what they were doing. Nobody moved. The air didn't move. Harri could feel the heat radiating off Matt from where he stood three desks away. Her eyes clenched shut, she held her breath, hoping he had the good sense to shut his mouth. This was a standoff she knew from experience he couldn't win. It was career ending, if he took it too far. One more word. One more finger.

Griffin glared at him. "Considering the situation," she said slowly and with great care, "I'm going to let you keep that finger if it disappears in the next two seconds." She waited for Matt's pointed digit to lower. "Good. You're here until this is wrapped up, or you take some time and spend it with your family. Your choice. One-time offer. You don't want to know what comes next if you decline either option."

Matt angrily tossed off his coat and threw it at the back of his chair before fixing furious eyes on Griffin. *"This is bullshit."*

Griffin took a second before speaking. "Everybody's entitled to one *bullshit*. Kelley's had his. Anybody else want to spend theirs now?" She looked around the room. "Again, one-time offer. Going fast."

Al quietly slipped into his coat and plopped his worn driving cap onto his round head. Tony grabbed his coat, too, neither of them took Griffin up on her offer.

Griffin eyed the team. "No? No other *bullshit*s need to be aired at this time?"

No one said a word.

"Good. Then everybody but Matt *'Bullshit'* Kelley get back to work. You need anything from here, he's your guy."

Griffin turned and stormed back into her office. and the temperature in the room instantly rose above freezing.

Al put a hand on Matt's shoulder. "We got ya, pal. No worries."

Matt pulled his shoulder away, too angry to take any consoling. Instead, he plopped down into his chair and said nothing, his eyes glued to his computer, ignoring everything around him. Harri and Vera shared a look, then finished gathering their things, giving Matt plenty of space to regulate.

"He's not letting this go," Vera said as they rode down in the elevator.

"There's a line he won't cross," Harri said.

"Hmm."

Vera could say more with a *hmm* than most people could say in a full-blown conversation. Harri knew Vera was thinking about Krieg, and the line Harri had toed, but that was a discussion for another time, if ever. She got Vera, to a point, but when it came down to it, she didn't know Vera as well as Vera apparently knew her. Her fault. And something she could fix.

"Now you're curious," Vera said. "You want to get inside *my* head for a change."

Harri turned, stared at her partner, no blinking, no joke. "What am I thinking *now*?"

Vera grinned. "Something that would get you twenty to life, *partner*."

CHAPTER 18

The Cook County Medical Examiner's office was where they'd left it last time at Harrison and Leavitt. West Side. Rough side, where pockets of gentrified buildings and blocks did little to mask the blight that ringed them. Harri didn't care much for the building's architecture. The stone-colored building, all angles and tinted recessed windows, looked like a prison and was just about as appealing. Her expectations low, Harri walked inside with Vera, signed in, and waited for an escort back to autopsy. If given a choice of anywhere she'd want to be, Harri knew this place, this cold, hard, end place, was the one she'd never choose.

Across the lobby from them stood a Latinx family of five. Harri pegged them as mother, father, three offspring: two teenage boys—maybe sixteen, eighteen—and one preteen girl with ribbons in her long dark hair. The family huddled together for comfort, weeping softly, stunned looks on all their faces. They'd lost someone suddenly, perhaps violently, Harri surmised, and they had found themselves in this cold, hard place alone and adrift, strangers in a strange land. She'd stood in their shoes once. She recognized the look. She knew for a fact each of them would always remember standing in this lobby on this day and that the memory would grip them by the heart and never let go. Vera made no comment. Harri was glad.

"Detectives."

They turned to find Dr. Grant's diminutive, Borg-efficient assistant, Tybo Sawyer, standing behind them in green scrubs and a short white lab coat, her ID hanging from a county lanyard around her neck. Harri noted the same humorless expression on Tybo's ID photo as they were getting now. Her brown eyes always earnest and steady, the tight set to full lips not even hinting they were capable of being coaxed into a smile. It had become obvious to them that Tybo Sawyer's mainframe was not programmed in any way for levity.

"Which case are you here for?" Tybo asked.

"There are five suspected ODs," Harri said. "Which one has Dr. Grant gotten to?"

Tybo slid a compact tablet out of a wide pocket and started tapping on it, then looked up. "Robert Mitchell. Toxicology pending."

"Then we'd like to talk to her about *that* one," Vera said.

Tybo blinked at Harri, then Vera, the blinks slow and unaffected by the strictures of time. "The body has been released to the family."

"The report will do," Harri said.

Tybo's brows furrowed. "The report was sent. It's available in the system."

"We prefer the personal touch," Harri said, getting nothing back from Tybo. "If Dr. Grant has a moment."

"She's in the building, isn't she?" Vera asked. "You can time us if you want."

Tybo stowed the tablet back in the pocket, pulled a phone out of the other, and tapped on that. When she was done, she said, "Her schedule is full, but she'll see you in her office. Follow me."

Tybo marched off, her small feet housed in comfortable shoes squeaking across the tile. Up in the silent elevator, around the corner, they got deposited at Grant's office door.

"Ms. Sawyer, would you mind if I asked you a personal question?" Vera said.

Harri braced for what was coming, knowing who Vera was and having a feeling for who Tybo wasn't.

Tybo cocked her head to one side. "No, Detective."

With that she turned and marched down the hall to lord knows where.

Harri looked at Vera. "Told you."

"That is one scary little woman," Vera said.

They found Grant at her cluttered desk, her lab coat hanging over the back of her county-issued office chair. The county didn't splurge on luxury, unless it was for those who worked several pay grades up. For those who shoveled it out day in and day out, ate lunch at their desks, and got the blame when the shit hit the fan, a chair, a desk, a file drawer, a hook for your coat were all you got, and all of it was going to be more downtown alley than *Downton Abbey*. The only personal item in the dingy space was a framed 3 × 5 photo of Grant and her wife, which sat on her desk. In the photo, Grant was out of scrubs, smiling and bearing little resemblance to the Grant that faced them now.

"Where's Tybo?" Grant asked, taking a hurried sip from her mug. "I need her."

Vera jabbed a thumb toward the door. "She marched down the hall. There's a revolution to plan, apparently."

"Ah, Detective Vera Li. CPD's very own stand-up comedian."

Harri said, "We're here about the—"

"Tybo texted me already. Robert Mitchell. I sent the report. She said you preferred the 'personal touch.' What the hell's *that* about?" She put her mug down.

"Cuts down on the emails," Harri said.

Grant picked up the receiver on her office phone, a big green thing that looked like somebody had snatched it out of President Eisenhower's Situation Room. She listened to the dial tone, then dropped the receiver back in its cradle. "This works," she said. "But personal. All right. Here it is. Drug overdose. Fatal levels of opioids in his system. Cause of death, drug intoxication leading to severe cerebral edema. That's excess fluid building up in the tissues of his brain. No other contributing factors. Healthy young man otherwise." Grant stood, slipped into her coat. "Sad case. Yesterday I had the unpleasant duty of explaining it all to his devastated parents. And now I've got to do it again with another family, who've lost a seven-year-old to a gang bullet that came through their front window and struck him in the back of the head, killing him instantly. Anything else?"

"How long had he been dead when I found him?" Harri asked.

"I'd put time of death, allowing for the cold temps by the lake, at about one a.m. There was nothing you could have done to save him. Honestly, I'm surprised the girl with him survived. Maybe she didn't take as much, or maybe she took her share later than he did. I can't know. Maybe all we can do is chalk it up to the capriciousness of fate."

Vera homed in. "Opioid, you said. Was this particular one anything you'd seen before?"

"We're still testing it, but preliminarily, it presents like fentanyl likely laced with something else. I can't give you a definitive answer, and I can't say that I've seen this devastating an effect in such a short span of time. Five deaths." She watched them. "Of course, I'm worried about additional cases."

"Are we looking at the usual six- to eight-week time frame?" Harri asked.

"I requested a rush, given the circumstances. We may get lucky. This one might just hinge on legwork rather than lab work. Sorry about that."

"Marie McClintock," Harri said.

"She's on my schedule for tomorrow morning. Tybo hasn't yet scheduled the latest three. Anything else?"

"Yeah," Vera said. "When the tox comes back, will it be able to tell us not only what killed them but whether or not what killed them came from the same source?"

"If the chemical structure is the same, it might indicate a single source. One recipe, one kitchen, one unique fingerprint." Vera nodded.

"McClintock in the morning," Grant said. "The others as quickly as I can get to them. Good luck."

They stood in the hallway. Preparing to get back out there.

"Good luck, she says. Like we're rolling dice."

"It wasn't a diss, Vera." Harri zipped up her jacket. "And if you don't want it, I'll take it."

CHAPTER 19

Before the McClintock neighbors, while Matt was tied to a desk, Harri and Vera decided to pay a visit to Ella, Harri hoping they could talk to the girl without her parents hovering over her. News of their call would of course get back to Matt, but that was something they'd deal with later.

"You think she's lying," Vera said as they pulled up into the Byrne driveway on their neat little block on the northwest side. All the houses on the block looked much the same, spring wreaths on front doors, some houses with American flags flying. Clean windows, Harri noted, everything stable and uniform and safe.

"I think we didn't press her like we should have, or would have, if Matt hadn't been there." She sat watching the house. "Something doesn't add up. The timing for one. Mitchell died around one a.m. If we assume they took the drug together, Ella shouldn't be here. Amount would be a factor, like Grant said, body weight, all the physiological stuff. Can't rule out fate and good fortune either."

Vera sighed. "God, I hope she didn't lie to Matt. Lying to us, I can take. People lie to us all day long. But he's going to take it hard if he finds out the family's perfect little princess isn't so perfect."

Harri frowned. "There's no such thing as a perfect little anything."

They knocked on the door of the Byrne residence to find Ella alone when she opened the door. It surprised Harri, who had assumed Ella's parents wouldn't let her out of their sight for at least a little while longer until the shock of what happened died away. Trust, she had to imagine, would be another big thing they'd all have to work on. But there Ella stood in the doorway, her hair in a ponytail, her thin body swathed in comfortable fleece, looking worlds apart from the half-dead child Harri had encountered just over a week ago.

Ella appeared uncomfortable seeing them at her front door. "My parents aren't here," she blurted out. "They went to the store. The fridge is almost empty. I'm not supposed to leave the house while they're gone." Her mouth twisted disagreeably. "Like I'm a child grounded for life."

"We have a few more questions," Harri said, "if you're up for it."

"Questions? What kind of questions?"

Vera flashed her most disarming smile. "Easy ones. Promise."

Ella didn't step back to let them in right away. It took a few seconds. "Okay."

Harri went with small talk to ease in. "So, how are you doing?"

"I'm fine. I just feel like the biggest disappointment ever."

"No idea when you'll go back to classes?" Vera asked, scanning around the front room.

"It has to be soon. I can't get too far behind; I'd never catch up. Besides . . . I like being out on my own, you know?"

Ella looked around the entryway and the living room, well appointed, the curtains drawn. To Harri, it didn't look like the room got a lot of traffic. It was too orderly, not lived in, everything placed just so, tastefully, as though the Byrnes had plucked everything out of *House Beautiful*, and then cordoned off the room to keep anyone in the family from mucking it up. Ella bit down on her lower lip, seemingly in a quandary. "Can we talk on the patio? This room isn't very comfortable."

"Why is that?" Harri was curious.

Ella took in the room, her lips pressed into a tight line. "It's too . . . cold. But it makes a good first impression, Mother says. She cares a lot about that."

They followed Ella to the enclosed patio out back and sat with her in cushioned chairs the color of pea soup, overlooking a large sloped backyard with a mature oak in the middle. At the bottom of the yard sat a small garden plot still covered up for winter and what looked like a prefab toolshed with a gabled roof. Overhead, birds chirped, and there was a smell of woodsmoke in the air.

"Nice spot," Vera said, making conversation. "Have you lived here your whole life?"

Ella nodded, wringing her hands in her lap. Not a good start, Harri thought. She watched the young woman, but Ella did everything she could, it seemed, not to meet her eyes. Harri's hope that Ella had been truthful died right then.

"We can wait for your parents," Harri said, "if you'd rather do that."

"I wouldn't." The young woman lifted her chin off her chest, finally looked at them. "You know I lied. That's why you're here. I don't want my parents to know."

Harri sat back, let out a breath, her thoughts on Matt and what a hit this would be. Vera waded in first. "What'd you lie about?"

"I knew where Robby had gotten the pills," she said. "Everybody knows P.D., if they're into that sort of thing."

"And *you're* into it?" Harri heard how harshly the words came out of her mouth and took a second to regulate herself.

"Recreationally. I don't have an addiction problem, if that's what you mean. Edge, it's . . . it's no big thing. It just chills you out. Or that's what it's supposed to do. Last time was different. See, I've got a full course load. It's a tough school. Everything's coming at me a mile a minute every second of every day. You can't believe how competitive that place is. How much it's costing my parents. They remind me of it every semester."

"Is that why you took a job on campus?" Vera asked.

"I wanted my own money. I wanted to buy my own things. I wanted to be the one who decided." She lowered her head. "I want a lot of things."

"Why won't you tell us where you work?" Harri asked. "In fact, you're intentionally not telling us."

"Why's it important? It's just a job."

"A job that pays well enough for a Fendi handbag?" Vera asked.

Ella's eyes widened. "How'd you . . . you searched my room."

Harri stood firm. "Of course we did."

"You didn't have my permission."

"Your roommates granted access to the room. The bag wasn't hidden. Where do you work, Ella?"

"I work in Dr. Liebner's lab. Twenty hours a week. As an assistant."

Harri nodded. "Dr. Liebner's full name?"

"You don't believe me?"

"It's not about believing you or not believing you. I need the information, Ella, no games."

Ella paused, then said, "Dr. Alex Liebner."

"Thank you."

Ella hung her head. "I don't work in the lab anymore. I lost my spot. I'm only telling you because I know you'll check. I'm not working anywhere now, but I *did* work there. That wasn't a lie."

"Your parents know?" Harri asked.

Ella shook her head. Silence hung in the air for a few seconds.

"I'm tired of this whole thing," Ella muttered. "I just want it to be over."

"So, back to Saturday," Vera said. "Robby got the pills, or did you?"

Ella stared out over the yard of the place she no longer wanted to be. "Rob got them, but I knew he was going to, and I knew where he was getting them from."

"There's not a lot of quality control with street drugs," Harri said. "You could be taking anything and not know it. You think you're taking one thing only to find out it's laced with something else ten times more potent."

"That's how people die," added Vera.

"I know all that. It was dumb, and I know I was really lucky. Look at Rob. He had no idea. Neither of us did. I want you to know that. I didn't know what I was taking."

"P.D.," Harri said. "What can you tell us about her? A name would help, and where you think we might be able to find her. Does she hang out on campus?"

"I've never met her. I don't buy. I don't think anyone knows her real name, or anything. It's not really a relationship you want to get too deep into, you know? She moves around, I know that. You have to move around with her in order to get the stuff."

"How do kids manage that?" Vera asked.

"There's a text chain. I don't know who started it, or how P.D. taps into it, but when *she's* around, the *word* gets around. You show up."

"This time, Mitchell found her sometime Saturday?" Vera asked. "Sometime before the party. Did he say where?"

Ella pursed her lips, as if to keep words from tumbling out of her mouth inadvertently. Harri took in the bags under the girl's eyes, the gaunt look, her hollowed cheeks. If Ella was on the road to recovery, she sure didn't look it.

"Ella?" she pressed.

"In the park by the museum. Near the playground."

Vera's voice rose. "Across from the *grade* school?"

Ella squinched her eyes closed. "I know. It's bad. She stays off university grounds because of the University Police."

"When?" Vera asked, her jaw tight.

"Saturday. Early." Ella's face brightened, hoping no doubt for just a little squib of redemption. "No school on Saturdays, so there wouldn't have been any little kids around."

Vera wasn't having it. "*That's* your takeaway?"

Ella shrank into her sweatshirt. "We skipped the party, anyway. Went to the park instead."

"In the rain?" Harri asked.

"I don't mind the rain. Neither did Robby." After a pause she said. "We sat, we watched the cars fly by, we listened to the lake. We talked." Her eyes fixed in a miles-long stare before it broke.

"Did I say anything? When I came to, sort of?"

"You said, 'Uncle Matt.'"

"Those could have been my last words."

"They almost were," Vera said. "You could be where Mitchell is now. *Your* parents could be planning a funeral, crying their eyes out."

"Ella? We need the truth now," Harri said. "No more games."

Ella shook her head. "I'm entitled to my privacy. My parents, Uncle Matt . . . it's bad enough this happened. They don't need to know that I sometimes hang out with people who do drugs. It's no big deal. Not if I know what I'm doing. Not if I'm smart."

Harri inched a little closer. "You call what happened you being smart?"

Ella buried her head in her hands. "They're going to *kill* me."

"Ella, now's the time," Vera said. "Right now. We don't have any more time to waste. P.D.—anything you know about her. Anybody you know who possibly knows more. Right now."

Ella's lips clamped shut, like a child warding off a spoonful of medicine.

"Oh, we're not doing that," Harri said. "You want to be an adult, this is where you start acting like one. This has gone far beyond you now, people are dying."

The young woman turned her head away.

"Ella Byrne." The sharpness in Harri's tone brought a chill to the patio. Even the birds' chirping seemed to pause. "Stop this now."

Ella shot up from her chair. "I've told you all I know. It was all Robby, not me. I didn't do anything. I'm the one who almost died. I need to rest. I'm tired. I need you to leave." She tugged hard at her sweatshirt. "You should definitely leave before they get back. The best thing for all of us is to put this behind us."

Harri and Vera stood. Ella led them through the house to the front door but did so without chancing a look at either of them.

"One thing," Ella said as she held the door open for them. "Rob said P.D. is . . . hard. Tough. Not someone you want to play around with."

"Do you at least know how she comes and goes?" Vera asked, still salty from the sudden dismissal.

"No, I don't know. How could I, if I don't know her?"

As Harri and Vera walked back to the car, Harri's mind reeled with decisions to make.

"The classic pin-it-on-the-dead-guy approach," Vera said, sliding into the passenger seat. "She's in this some kind of way."

Moving in behind the wheel, Harri paused a second before putting the key in the ignition. "Money. Drugs. Lies. And a frightened kid."

"What are we going to tell Matt, if he asks?"

"The truth, or as much as we know of it," Harri said. "And we tell him, even if he *doesn't* ask. Anything less would be a lie." She started the car. "He processes it how he processes it. Bottom line, this isn't our mess to clean up, it's Ella's."

Vera cracked the passenger window for a bit of air. "Fine. But I'm standing behind you when you tell him his niece, the good kid, the star of the family, is lying her ass off. I'm not in the mood to get 'bullshitted' at."

"Meanwhile." Harri pulled out her phone and called Matt, who picked up on the first ring.

"Yeah," he spit out at the phone, obviously still pissed at getting benched.

Harri took the Band-Aid approach, one quick yank. "Matt, we need a camera pull. The park at Fifty-Sixth across from the Museum of Science and Industry. Saturday a week ago, the day before I found Ella. We're looking for an exchange in the playground. P.D. and Mitchell. Maybe start early, run through the entire day, if you can."

"P.D.?" he asked, an urgency to his voice. "What'd you do, double back to one of the roommates?"

Harri rolled her eyes at having to confront the stickiness of this entire thing so soon.

"No, we didn't, but we got a tip. Getting a look at the playground on Saturday would be helpful. Thanks."

Harri punched end, then sat peering out the windshield at the drizzle. "Remember when I said this isn't our mess?"

"Two minutes ago? Yeah."

"I was wrong."

CHAPTER 20

Faith Pope swore she'd never come back, yet here she stood in front of the house that had held so much misery for her. Everything bad in her life had happened inside that house. She shoved her hands into the pockets of her black leather jacket, which she'd retrieved from the back of her closet, a remnant of the life she'd lived before, and gripped the small Bible in her right hand, taking comfort in the feel of it, drawing strength from just knowing it was there.

This would be only the second time in twenty years she'd set foot inside the Gamon stronghold. She hadn't even come back for the funerals of her father and brothers. They had been dead to her long before any of them were buried beneath the willows. She'd left something behind, but she had no right to claim it now. It was a regret that would follow her to the grave, but one she could not hope to erase.

They knew she was coming, of course. You didn't walk up unannounced here and expect to get anywhere close to the front door alive. She had clocked the lookouts at the corner, and she knew there were others strategically placed around the perimeter and inside. The untrained guards stood sullen, young, expendable, at the curb, at the door, and in souped-up cars across the street. There was no sneaking up on the place. Even the bricks appeared to have eyes.

Faith didn't want to go in, but knew she had to. She'd made a mistake, a sinful error, and she needed to make it right. People were dying. Marie McClintock, leaving behind baby Emmanuel. The police were everywhere. Everything Faith held dear, her life, her God, her marriage, hung in the balance. There wasn't an amend she could make to turn back what had been done. She hoped only to do some good now. That's why she was here. To get it to stop, if she could, before everything burned down around her.

She slowly climbed the stone steps, her chin held high, her hand on the Bible. With every step, the new seemed to fall away and the old returned. Even her breathing shifted, the calm, the serenity she'd found, giving way to a cold, hard stillness that scared her. She'd left Vanessa Gamon behind, but she hadn't gone far. Her black heart had only been lying dormant. It took just the sight of the house, knowing what breathed inside it, for the darkness to resurface.

There was no need to give a name at the door. They knew her name and whose blood flowed through her. She sneered at the windows, the bricks as if *they* were the demons. This house, this life, this hell were the nightmare that haunted her sleep.

The young thug with his head in a do-rag and his pants around his upper thighs opened the door and then stepped aside to let her pass. No pleasantries. They hadn't been taught, and Faith wouldn't have accepted them anyway. It hurt her to be here, being here stung like a knife cut to the skin. Every breath seemed to sear her lungs and fill them with poison.

The loafing sentinels inside lounged around the front room, playing cards and video games, smoking and laughing and tracking her with predatory eyes as she walked through toward the office in back. Children. Corrupted children. Her footfalls made no sound on the carpet. To her the place smelled like death.

She'd changed her clothes, trading modesty for a statement, one of strength, the only thing respected inside these walls. Black from head to toe. Armor. Her one concession to the life she now led was the Bible in her pocket. Black was the color of the sinner. Black was the color of the heart God had not yet saved. Black was the color those in this house accepted without question.

They would check her for weapons when she got to the door at the end of the hall, but they'd find only a Bible. She was here for a very specific reason, and murder was not it. Besides, Faith knew that cutting off this head would not kill the snake. Many heads had fallen, and the snake had survived. There was always another head, always a new monster.

She lifted her arms so the thug could search her. She kept her face blank while he was doing it; it was better not to show emotion here. Here, like with weakness, emotion of any kind, any bow to love or feeling, empathy or care, was not allowed.

Having cleared Faith for entry, the banger opened the door and let her through, then closed the door behind her. The Black woman sitting at the big desk stared at her, wearing an amused look. It had been years since Faith had seen the face last. The woman was grayer, rounder, but the eyes were the same—empty, not alive. These were the eyes lightness had never touched. They were the eyes of a serpent in human skin.

The woman, dark, her natural hair cropped short, sat dressed as Faith was dressed. In her fifties, Faith knew, though she'd forgotten her exact age. She looked every second of it with worry lines along her forehead, deep creases around her mouth, wrinkles under her eyes. Stress. Anxiety. Hypervigilance. Those were the causes.

The devil raised her arms. "Never say never? You swore you'd never set eyes on this place again."

Faith glanced over at the young man sitting in a corner, an assault rifle resting on his lap. She knew that without hesitation he'd use it and that the devil would do nothing to discourage the impulse, blood or no blood.

"Give us a minute, Benzo," the woman told the man. "This won't take long."

Faith waited for the young man to get up and leave. "Hello, Cora."

Her sister laced her fingers across her stomach and stared at her. *"Vanessa."*

Faith hadn't heard her real name in so long, it took her a moment to recognize it as hers. She remembered Vanessa. The young girl trying to be hard, never allowed to be anything else. She had been caught in a cycle, low and far from heaven. In this place, cruelty was good, violence was good, fealty was required, love was not. Faith would never be Vanessa again.

All around this house people lived just above the poverty line, Faith thought as she scanned the familiar room chock-full of expensive things death had purchased. People just outside these doors were hungry, strung out, hopeless, uneducated, struggling, yet here Cora sat in a house built by a horrible trade, surrounded by bangers and killers, at a desk she had inherited from their father, who had started it all.

There was no need to pretend there was any real connection between them. Their family had never functioned on an emotional level. Everything with the Gamons was transactional, business, this for that, so she wouldn't waste time saying things she couldn't mean.

"People are dying, Cora," Faith said.

Cora angled her head. "Don't they always?"

"Whatever you're doing, you need to stop it. Shut it down."

Cora's left eyebrow lifted. "*I* do?" She leaned forward, those eyes from deep down below holding Faith's. "I don't understand why you are *here*, Vanessa. Your cut's not enough? Are you here to renegotiate? Because if that's the case, I really don't see how—"

"I'm here to wash my hands of it," Faith said. "To ask you to shut it down and walk away once and for all."

Cora laughed. "Walk away. Like *you* did?"

"These deaths can't be good for business, and this business has *never* been good for any of us."

Cora watched her sister closely. "Hasn't it been good for you? How much have I sent your way to hold on to that sad church that old man you married insists on wasting time on? You came with your hands out when the bank came calling. You were this close to losing the whole thing. You kept the money, Vanessa. You hold the bags, for a *fee*. You look the other way, and pretend you're not doing what you're doing, for money earned *here* in this house. Don't come in here now wanting to preach to *me*."

"You're right about all of it," Faith said. "I hold the bags."

"Hmm. A lot of folks hold a lot of bags. The trains I run, and you know this, run on a lot of tracks. More than you even remember. People are dying?" Cora snapped her fingers, then snapped them again, and again. "Every second somebody dies. Another one's gone." She snapped her fingers. "And another. That's life. But just so you don't go on thinking what you're thinking, not that it should matter to me, I had nothing to do with the screwup. If you really put your mind to it, you can guess who is." She grinned slyly. "Trying to impress me and run things on her own. She's a fool, reckless. Kind of like you back in the day before you took off without saying a damned thing to anybody. But she's been warned. She will learn, or she won't. Up to her."

"My fault. I doomed her to the life she's living. I sold her to the devil. *You.* That's my sin. I'm not the same as I was," Faith said. "But I can't undo anything. All I can do is help somebody else, *her* if she wants it."

Cora smirked. "Too late for that. You left her to the devil, remember? Why'd you *really* come here? Were you hoping she'd run into your arms and she'd forgive you?"

"There's no forgiving," Faith said. "I don't even hope for that. You don't think I knew this was not a place I should come for help? I knew. I know now. But the church does so much good. It helps so many people. I couldn't see it go under, not if there was a chance of saving it."

"So, you came to the devil. Nice."

Cora looked up and down, appraising her sister. "You haven't changed that much. I still see you in there. That old Bible thumper you married doesn't have a pot to piss in, never did. That old church is barely standing. The old grandmas show up every Sunday in their hats and pray and sing and carry on, but what ever changes?" Cora smiled, reading Faith's body language. "Oh, yes, I know all about Holy Land. Reverend Clevon Pope will be long dead before he gets anywhere close to getting what he needs to save that money pit. *That's* why you hold the bags while you pretend you *aren't* holding them. *That's* why we do all that unnecessary playacting with you and that Bible-study thing, so you, *Vanessa*, can make-believe you're not in it, when you are . . . *in* it. Offering up snacks and cookies while you hold the bags and take the money in the Bibles." Cora's eyes lasered in. "Too good for us, Vanessa. *Daddy* would say, too big for your britches. Don't you *dare* preach to me."

Faith knew Cora had come by her depravity honestly. Big Daddy Gamon had trained her, groomed her, and had tried to do the same for Vanessa, only it didn't take. Cora fell right into the family business, but Vanessa could never find the stomach for it. She found the taste for other things, instead, which led to years of addiction, pain, and hurt.

God, how low she'd been, when she'd wandered into Clevon's church and taken a seat in the very last pew, her spirit defeated, her soul ready to go. It was the end of her, and she'd felt it. Vanessa Gamon had run from the only life she'd ever known and had nowhere else to go.

It was Clevon who saw her, saved her. And she'd betrayed him. She had made a deal with the snake so he could save more lives like hers.

Maybe there was no way out now. In this life, you were either in or you were dead. But Faith wasn't here to save herself; she was here for others. Cora thought she held the cards. Maybe she did, but Faith held a few too. She wouldn't be here if she didn't.

"She sold to Marie McClintock, didn't she?" Faith asked.

Cora didn't answer.

"A vulnerable woman with a child and a husband," Faith said. "Gone when she shouldn't be gone. And four more. Cora, what are you doing? Stop this."

Cora sighed, appearing bored. "This is my business, not yours; I say, not you. And I've made the correction. It's never personal, Vanessa, you know that. It's dollars and corners and loyalty, something you know nothing about. Take the money, save your church, save all those lives. God will forgive you. That's what he does, isn't it? He might even one day wash *me* clean, what do you think?"

Cora was mocking her. She had expected nothing less.

Her voice barely above a whisper, Faith asked, "Where is she? You never send her. It's always a different three, but never *her*."

Cora grinned. "And it never will be. You don't deserve the reunion, do you? I'd rather see you stew in it. Suffer with your sin." Cora stood and walked from behind the desk and over to the window, her back to Faith. No danger. The glass was bulletproof. Big Daddy had insisted on it.

Faith wanted to strike, but knew she couldn't. Cora would not hesitate to kill her. "You're Big Daddy all over again."

Cora turned, her brows raised. "Thank you for the compliment. It *was* a compliment, wasn't it?"

"Do you even remember how old she is?"

"I know exactly how old she is," Faith said, seething. "Down to the minute."

"Oh. Okay. I wasn't sure. Do you also know that she was born with crack in her system? You might have suspected it, I bet. Do you know anything about crack babies, Vanessa? The problems they're faced with? The deficits? Might explain her impulsiveness in this situation, but it won't give her a pass."

Shame flooded over Faith, and her hands began to shake. The nightmare roared back. It was hard for her to catch her breath. Cora went on as if nothing was happening. "No thought for her. Instead, you ran off and saved yourself. You spit in our faces. Like you said, your sin."

"Gamons look out for themselves," Faith snapped back. "That's how we were raised. Like rivals, like animals. Animals that take and take and never give . . . I made a choice. I ran to the streets, and that was no place for a child. At least here"—Faith looked around the room, finding it distasteful—"she might have been warm and fed and protected, but you ruined her, didn't you? You didn't love her. You turned her into what *he* was, what *you* are, and you did it to hurt me."

Cora turned to face her sister. "Hmm. Maybe you're right. But you didn't come back for her, you came to help your grandpa preacher. You came for the money."

Cora walked back to her desk and sat. "I'll never send her. You won't *ever* see her. She belongs to this house, and your time's up. Our arrangement stands. You hold the bags; you take the money. You keep your mouth shut. And we all live happily ever after. I've put a stop to this new stuff that's killing my clientele, but the regular trade continues. Like Big Daddy said, 'We're in the business of tits and hits.'" She chuckled, then waved Faith away. "You can say as many of those prayers as you need to in order to get all that to go down smoothly, if it makes you feel better. You can see yourself out."

"It's not about family, is it, Cora?" Faith scanned the room, feeling as though the walls were closing in on her. She took in all the expensive things, the trophies of violence, the big desk, the ill-gotten wealth. "It's always been about this for you. You always wanted the chair and the money, even when he controlled it all, and you'd do anything to keep it now. I always wondered about that shooting. Big Daddy was always so careful, and no one asked any questions after . . . or at least *you* didn't. Now here you are surrounded by children willing to kill for you. Is there anything you *won't* do to keep all this?"

Cora stared at her, the eyes of the snake, as cold and bottomless as a watery grave. The mirthless smile was slow to form. "What do *you* think?"

Faith stood tall, refusing to bend. "I'm out, Cora."

"You might want to rethink that decision."

"Or what?" Faith asked, her head angled, the old eyes, Vanessa's eyes, as black as the clothes she was dressed in and just as deadly as the ones facing hers. "You'll have me killed too?"

"What good would that do me? I get *you* by getting someone else first." Cora eased out a breath. "First lesson I got from Big Daddy, you may have missed it. The dead can't strike."

Faith stood silently. In just that one moment, the goalposts had moved and the game had changed. She watched as Cora slid her bottom drawer open and retrieved a thick envelope and slid it across her desk to Faith. "Your next installment." Faith didn't move. She didn't want the money. "I'm curious," Cora said. "Does your husband know you're doing this? Have you come clean to him, at least?" Cora laughed. "No, I can tell by your face that you haven't. Also, I know you haven't because you're still sleeping alongside him and he hasn't cast you out. Lies, lies, lies, Vanessa. The Bible teach you how to lie so well?"

"I feel sorry for you, Cora."

Cora laughed, full throated, deep. "Don't. We'll go on as we have been, and we'll forget all about whatever *this* was." She pointed to the envelope. "All yours." Faith made no move to pick it up, the threat still fresh in her mind. After a moment, Cora shrugged. "I'm a Gamon. It's how we do it."

"I gave birth to her in this house," Faith said. "At least tell me what you named her."

Cora's face turned to a vengeful block of dark stone. "No."

Faith stared at the envelope sitting there as a temptation, but she was beyond that now. Cora had put them in a different place. Money for souls was no longer a thing she could do. Faith left the envelope where it sat, then turned her back and headed for the door.

Cora said, "Changes nothing, baby sister."

Shame. That's what Faith was covered in. It smothered her and filled her lungs. It weighed her down and pressed her organs together as though they were caught in a vise. Shame with something else attached, something she hadn't felt in a long time, rage. Pure, hot, unadulterated rage. It felt as if the good book literally burned a hole in her pocket. Faith stopped herself at the door, her hand on the ornate knob. The thugs were just on the other side, the ones with the feral eyes, the ones who killed on command, the ones who would not live to see an old man's rocking chair. Shame and rage killed as surely as bullets. It just took longer.

"Got more to say?" Cora asked, obviously enjoying herself.

Help me, Jesus. Faith squeezed her eyes shut, unable to pray her sins away, unable to put Vanessa away again. "You forget, Cora. I'm a Gamon too."

She flung the door open and stormed away. Down the hall, stopping short halfway to the door when she felt eyes at her back. She reeled, catching just a fleeting glimpse of someone darting into a doorway. She stood watching for a moment, before turning around and walking out of the house, into the sun, away from the snake.

CHAPTER 21

Vera set the drippy Italian beef down on the wax paper laid out over her lap to dab her fingers on the rough paper napkin before she checked the ding on her phone. "Grant," she said. "She's starting Marie McClintock."

Harri took a fast bite of her sandwich, minus the drip. She liked hers dry. Sacrilege here in the city, she knew, but she liked what she liked. "Good, but anticlimactic. We know why she's dead. We need to know who facilitated it."

Vera put her phone down and went back to the drippy mess she called lunch, giardiniera squirting out the sides of the soggy Italian bread as she bit into the thing again, leaning over the paper to save her pants and shirtfront. They had just twenty minutes to scarf lunch down and had stopped by Mr. Beef on Orleans to find a welcomed lull in the traffic at the door.

"You know, I really resent that show," Vera said. "Ever since it came on, the line to this place has been a real pain. Tourists tying up the line with all the *umms* and *ehs*. No idea what to order. There are rules, for fuck sake, learn them or go to McDonald's."

"Who stuck a bug up your ass?" Harri asked. "We got in all right."

Vera glowered at the door as a group of tourists snapped pictures of the Mr. Beef sign, took a series of group photos, and then wandered inside with silly grins on their faces.

"See? Look. There they go. I'll bet you one of them pulls out a credit card."

Harri smiled. "They'll only make that mistake once."

"It's just not right," Vera said, plucking a sliver of soggy beef off the soggy bread, and popping it into her mouth. "This isn't the Capital Grille."

Harri watched as Vera's sandwich all but disintegrated in her hands, beef au jus and oil coating her fingers.

"We haven't heard anything from Narcotics," Vera said. "Or from Streeter and Evans about Mitchell's phone. You figure Matt's following up?"

Harri wrapped the last bit of sandwich she couldn't finish in the paper and stuffed it into the greasy bag to throw away. "I know he is. I just hope he doesn't challenge Griffin in the meantime."

The car was filled with the smell of steamed beef, oil, giardiniera, and more beef, but their bellies were full, and they were ready to push on. The lingering smell would be the next shift's problem. Next stop, McClintock's neighbors.

The block was quiet, old cars parked along the street, even a beat-up old ice cream truck someone had left two doors down.

"Too early for that," Vera said, flipping up the collar of her peacoat against the spring chill. "By at least a couple months."

Harri glanced at the vehicle. It was an old Good Humor truck, its faded logo and menu selections painted over, with nothing replacing them. So not for commerce, she thought, only transportation.

"It wasn't here last time," she said. "Somebody's driving it."

"My childhood dream," Vera said, "to have my own ice cream truck."

Harri smiled. "What's stopping you?"

Vera glanced over at the old truck, sighed. "The cost of living. Some dreams aren't meant to come true."

—

"It's the police," Lynette Thompson called from her position behind the bedsheets that served as window curtains in the third-floor apartment. "They're back, and I bet you they're coming up here."

Her daughter, La'Kisha, bolted off the couch, nearly scattering the bowl of potato chips she was eating. "What they coming here for?"

Middle of the day, Sybil Jackson mused as she sat rocking in her chair as she did most days, and neither her daughter, nor *her* daughter, had a job to get to. Retired now, widowed, with a touch of arthritis in her back, Sybil had failed to raise her only child right. Now she was sad to say she lived in a den of vipers. After eighty years of good Christian living, a good woman for whom the Bible was her strength and salvation, she dwelled among no-accounts, and it pained her heartily to admit that she had birthed one of them, and that the one she'd birthed had begat others just as trifling as she was.

Sybil watched through clear eyes as one of La'Kisha's friends scurried around the place like a cheese-hoarding rat, grabbing up her jacket, shoes, and bags. Running, Sybil knew, from the police who, as Lynette surmised, were likely coming here. *Again.* In her day, they had a name for folk like this, but she was too good a woman to utter it out loud, all she could ever say was trifling.

In and out, Sybil thought. They came in and out at all hours, every day. Up all night, sleep most of the day. Trifling.

"I see 'em," La'Kisha said, peeking over her mother's shoulder to the street below. "It's the same ones from the other day."

They thought Sybil was too old to know what was going on right under her nose, so there Sybil sat in her own front room watching her stories on the biggest television she'd ever seen in her life, her Bible within reach, ready to ward off Satan and the ones who trailed along after them.

The bedsheets. Never in her life, Sybil noted, did she think she'd raise a woman who thought so little of herself and her children that she'd live like this instead of bettering herself, instead of working, instead of buying *curtains*. But when the devil calls, and a person picks up the phone, no amount of raising or training can help 'em, Sybil knew that for a fact.

If it weren't for the arthritis, Sybil wouldn't even be here. She'd be back home in Tennessee, Shelby County. She'd have moved back down there to be closer to her people when her husband, Herman, died fifteen years ago, if it hadn't been for Lynette and hers. Always a problem, Lynette. Always greedy and never wanting to do what needed doing. Always in the streets and not a church pew. Now here they all were unsaved, uneducated, unteachable, and a profound disappointment to Sybil. "Trifling," she muttered to herself, eyeing the two hiding behind the sheet. "Just plain trifling."

Sybil heard the downstairs door creak open, then bang shut, and the sound of footsteps on the stairs as the police made their way up to their door.

"Yes, ma'am, they coming here," Sybil said. "And you both know why." She glanced over at the sprinter in the baggy clothes as she raced for the back door. Sybil shook her head in utter disgust for the life she was forced to live and the unsaved she was forced to live with. "The devil's own."

The back door banged shut, just as there was a knock at the apartment door. Sybil eased her Bible over from the small table and set it in her lap, placing her hands on top. She could feel the holy Word as it moved through her fingers, and she closed her eyes to pray the evil away. The Lord could change a life, a heart, a direction just like that, and she prayed He'd do that for her kin. Her prayer was not new, but she was a patient woman, and she knew better than anyone that God moved in His time, not anyone else's.

"Don't let 'em in," La'Kisha whispered. "They can't come in if we don't let 'em. I saw that on YouTube."

Sybil sighed. Oh, the trials she had to endure. "Open the door, Lynette. Don't listen to La'Kisha. She flunked the fourth grade twice and ain't got a lick of good sense, and you know it. Besides, they likely saw both of you behind those sheets and can hear you whispering now through the door."

La'Kisha bristled up. "This ain't got nothing to do with you, Granny. We don't need no police in here causing trouble for us."

"More like it's you causing your own selves the trouble."

Sybil went back to her program, though the reception was bad, with wavy lines cutting in on occasion, almost always at the good parts.

There was another knock at the door. "Mrs. Thompson? Police. We have a few questions to ask you about the incident downstairs the other day."

Sybil smiled slightly at the *Mrs.*, knowing full well Lynette had never taken a husband her whole life, nor would one take *her*. That didn't stop her from having two good-for-nothing kids, though. La'Kisha, who was well on her way to following in her mama's footsteps, and Reynard, who did lord knows what to keep from working a real job.

Sybil knew the police knew there was someone home. Neither Lynette nor La'Kisha were dainty little flowers and had heavy feet. The McClintocks and the Reynolds woman downstairs complained all the time about the heavy walking at all hours. Sybil was sure the police had already heard the racing around up here. Lynette and La'Kisha stomping around along the floorboards like mules clopping up a mountain pass.

Lynette opened the door, looking just as guilty as a thief caught with their hand where it didn't belong. Sybil listened from the chair, as she always did. Too old for anyone to notice. The police had been here many times before since Herman died and Sybil let the devils in. They came about all the arguing and the drinking and whatnot. It was the whatnot that vexed Sybil most. It was one thing to ruin your own life, but quite another to spread that ruin around.

"We don't have nothing to say about what happened downstairs," Lynette said, her wide body blocking the detectives' view of the apartment.

Sybil shook her head, resigned. "Never was right in the head."

"I'm Detective Foster. This is Detective Li. It's just general information we're looking for, Mrs. Thompson. We won't take up much of your time."

Sybil watched as La'Kisha wrung the bottom of her shirt, her eyes wide, squirrelly, flicking nervous looks in the direction of the back door. Guilty as homemade sin. Sybil kept watching as La'Kisha then looked over at her mother, and a wave of sadness came over her as she thought about what could have been if Lynette had done right. She'd had dreams of Lynette becoming a teacher, like she had been, or even a nurse. It's why she'd worked so hard, two jobs, and two for Herman, to make sure Lynette had it better than they had it, only it didn't take. Lynette stepped aside and let the police in.

"We didn't even hardly know them," La'Kisha said in a voice Sybil barely recognized. It was softer, less harsh than La'Kisha's normal tone. La'Kisha was always hollering and fussing and cussing at folks. "Just to say hi in passing. It was them always complaining about us up here in our own apartment."

Sybil nodded, caressed the good book. Both Lynette and La'Kisha were afraid of the police. They were big talkers when they were drinking and carrying on, but the talk got real small when the folk with handcuffs came round. And it was presumptuous, Sybil felt, calling this their *own* apartment.

The apartment was *hers*, hers and Herman's. But when your daughter got kicked out of the place she was staying, and she had two babies with her, what could Sybil have done but let them in?

The detectives looked around the place. Sybil watched how they did it, real smoothly, like they weren't taking note of every little thing and filing it all away. There was one Black woman, and one Asian woman, both about half her age. Tall, slender, they looked like they could do something if they needed to, and she could tell they had guns under their jackets by the bumps at their sides and by how their jackets hung crooked. Big guns, if Sybil had to guess.

The women stood quietly, their backs to the wall. Smart women, Sybil could tell. A lot smarter than Lynette and La'Kisha, that was for sure. Sybil went back to her stories.

"Yes," Detective Li said. "We read the reports about the noise. But today we're here about Marie McClintock. Can you remember the last time you spoke with her or saw her?"

"It's sad what happened," Lynette said. "Her with the new baby."

Detective Foster turned to La'Kisha. "Are you La'Kisha?"

"Who told you my name?"

Sybil shook her head. Trifling.

Foster said, "Again, we read the reports."

"Oh, yeah, then I'm La'Kisha. La'Kisha Boyd. I live here with my mama and my grandmama."

The women looked over at Sybil, taking her in, offering a nod and a little smile. She could tell they weren't dismissing her. "And you're Mrs. Jackson? Nice to meet you, ma'am," Foster said.

Sybil nodded back. Of course they knew her name. All the times the police had been up here on Lynette's and La'Kisha's accounts. Still, she appreciated the good manners. She could tell these two women had been raised right by somebody.

"*So,* the last time you spoke to Mrs. McClintock?" Foster asked.

"Not in a while," Lynette said. "We weren't friends, we just lived in the same building."

"There was no conflict, bad feelings," Li asked, "over the complaint calls?"

Lynette and La'Kisha shook their heads.

"Do you remember where you both were between eight last Monday night and, say, six Tuesday morning?"

"Here. Sleeping, like regular people," Lynette insisted. "Like I said, we weren't social with them. We keep to our own business."

Detective Foster looked over at Sybil. "How about you, Mrs. Jackson? You were also here?"

"Where else would she be?" Lynette snapped. "She's old. Besides, she can't tell you nothing. She don't even get out that chair from one end of the day to the next."

La'Kisha scowled. "That's right. We the ones taking care of her."

Taking care of *her*. She was the one who'd opened up her home to the no-accounts. She had been doing just fine without them. Sybil could tell the detectives didn't like what La'Kisha had said. Their expressions changed; they didn't look so friendly anymore.

"I go to bed early," Sybil said. "I didn't hear anything untoward that night. Monday nights are usually quiet around here."

Foster asked, "So, no one heard anyone going in or out of the McClintock apartment Monday night. How about earlier in the day, or even a day or two before? Maybe you saw someone you may not have recognized, or who looked . . . off, like they didn't belong?"

A beat passed.

"Anyone at all?" Li asked. "Even Mr. McClintock . . . specifically Monday."

Lynette and La'Kisha shook their heads again, their mouths clamped shut.

"What about anyone who might have been visiting up *here*?" Foster asked. "Friends." She glanced over at Lynette. "Overnight guests."

Lynette bristled up. "What's who we got up here got to do with anything?"

La'Kisha held her arms out. "Besides, it's our property. We can do what we want."

"It's your *landlord's* property," Li said.

Lynette crossed her arms over her chest, then shot Vera a nasty look. "Don't matter *whose*. Now, you two have to leave. I got to get to work, and you all are holding me up."

Sybil scoffed quietly at the mention of work. Lynette didn't work. She didn't work outside in the streets, and she didn't do a lick of it in the apartment either. Sybil knew her daughter and granddaughter. Neither one of them was smart enough to lie well enough to fool the two women detectives, and watching them try was beginning to frustrate her to no end. She decided then and there that she could sit here and stay quiet and let the devils upset her spirit, or she could speak the truth, as the good book commanded, and rest in the arms of Jesus for all eternity when her time came. Either burn it all down or wallow in the darkness.

Sybil opened her Bible, laid her hands on the onionskin pages. "There's people up here most nights and days. La'Kisha's friends or else Reynard's. Lynette's men, when she can find herself one."

"Mama, don't be telling them that. It ain't got nothing to do with them, or you." Lynette slid a look at the detectives, nervous. "And *nothing* to do with Marie."

Sybil continued undeterred. "Coming and going. Nobody works. The drinking and what all starts the fighting." Her eyes held Foster's. "It's the what all they try and hide, thinking I don't know they're doing it."

"Mama! Stop talking to them."

"Drugs?" Vera asked, ignoring Lynette.

Sybil shook her head. "Not that I've seen, but I'd be surprised if there weren't any." She gripped her Bible, then angled her head toward La'Kisha. "Marie was up here talking to *that* one's friend. Not Monday, but a few days before she died. Thursday, I think. Marie was in a state; anyone could see that."

Li and Foster turned to Lynette and La'Kisha for explanation, but there was nothing coming, only wide eyes and cornered looks.

"She's got dementia," Lynette said. "You can't believe nothing she says."

Sybil shook her head. "Don't have dementia. Not yet anyway. Old don't mean crazy. La'Kisha's friend and Reynard are into something. There's a lot of whispering going on."

Lynette advanced. "Mama! I'll *make* you hush," she screeched.

"Stop," Foster called out. "You don't take one more step."

Lynette stopped in her tracks. "She's talkin' smack."

"Do you *want* to go to jail?" Li asked.

"For what?" La'Kisha squealed. "She didn't do nothing."

Sybil noticed the room felt different, tighter somehow, colder. Lynette had never put a hand on her before, neither had La'Kisha. They weren't smart, but neither was that dumb. Sybil was all that stood between them and the street, and they both knew it.

"Threatening physical violence is a crime," Foster said sternly. "And that's your *mother*."

Sybil grinned slowly. "Don't worry yourselves, officers. They're just scared."

La'Kisha spoke through gritted teeth. "I ain't scared of nothing, Granny."

Sybil looked her granddaughter straight in the face. "You're scared of life, La'Kisha. You're scared of trying. Just like your mama always was."

"Have a seat, ladies." Li took a step toward mother and daughter, the look on her face making it clear that *not* sitting wasn't an option.

Lynette and La'Kisha started cussing and carrying on but sat down on the couch as meek as lambs. Sybil paid them no mind.

"So, Mrs. Jackson," Foster asked. "Would you happen to know the name of La'Kisha's *friend*?"

Sybil nodded. "Like I said, I'm old, not crazy. She said her name's P.D., and she's about as next to nothing as nothing gets."

Foster and Li turned to La'Kisha, who averted her eyes to keep from looking back at them.

"P.D.?" Foster asked. "P.D. what?"

La'Kisha flicked her chin up. "I ain't got to say nothing to you."

"You have a coat, Ms. Boyd?" Vera asked pleasantly.

Lynette's eyebrows lifted. "What she need a coat for?"

Foster smiled. "Because we're going to ask her to join us at our place for a bit. Maybe she'll be more comfortable answering questions there."

La'Kisha shared a panicked look with her mother. Then La'Kisha's face fell. She turned to Foster. "What do y'all want to know?"

"Why is it no one ever wants to take a ride downtown?" Foster pulled her notepad out of her pocket. "Fine. Let's start at the beginning."

CHAPTER 22

"Finally, a last name. P.D. *Terry.* I can't believe we missed her by seconds," Vera said as they bounded down the stairs to the street. "La'Kisha still didn't explain how Marie McClintock knew what business she was in and that she could find her upstairs. And, let me just say, she folded way too quickly for me."

"You *wanted* us to have to wrestle with her?" Harri asked, shocked.

"No, of course not, but, I mean, I just hope she's nobody's repository of secrets. If she is, they're screwed."

They reached the second floor. Harri stopped and eyed Crystal Reynolds's door, then the McClintocks'. "Hold on. We've got new information. Maybe somebody can add to it. Pick one."

"I'll take McClintock, you take Reynolds," Vera said.

They each knocked at their respective doors and then stood waiting for an answer. Vera knocked again when the first knock went unanswered. She turned to Harri. "I guess he's still not back in."

"He might never be able to," Harri offered as the Reynolds door opened.

"Ah. Ms. Reynolds. Can we take just two minutes of your time?"

Crystal let them in. "I saw you two go upstairs. Now you see what I was talking about. It's Mrs. Jackson I feel for. She's a good Christian woman just trying to help family. But, whew, those two . . ."

"None of them mentioned Reynard," Vera said.

Reynolds shrugged. "Not much to mention, I expect. He's either in jail or squatting up there with the rest of them. When you don't see him for a while, he's locked up."

"And when did *you* see him last?" Harri asked.

"Not since around New Year's, I think. My guess? He caught a case."

"One question," Harri said, "and we'll let you go. You mentioned the noise and the arguing upstairs. Have you seen any evidence of drug activity?" Harri saw the wary expression on Reynolds's face. She took that as a yes. "So, Marie would know that if she went up there, she'd find someone who could either sell her something or put her in contact with someone who could."

"Why do you think the landlord was trying to get them out? We got kids here and we don't want them messed up in that. Marie, I know, felt the same way, so if she went up there, she must have really been going through it."

"Who's selling?" Vera asked.

Reynolds didn't answer.

"Do it for your kids," Foster said.

Reynolds drew her slouchy sweater around her. "They sit out on the back landing up there smoking weed and disturbing everybody. The alley's where they do it, like can't nobody see them standing there under the alley light passing stuff to cars that creep up at all hours. The only one I don't see out there is Mrs. Jackson. They got all kinds of folks hanging around up there."

"This building have security cameras?" Vera asked.

Reynolds laughed. "We lucky if we got lights out front and heat half the time. Why do you think they're so bold up there doing what they do right out in the open? They know as good as everybody in here, the police won't be coming around unless somebody gets shot or kills themselves." She glared pointedly at them. "You know it's true."

Standing out on the front stoop, breathing in fresh air, Vera eyed the spot where the ice cream truck had been. "Truck's gone."

"Yep."

"Want to check the drug alley?" Vera asked, buttoning her jacket.

"Yep."

Vera flicked her a look. "Still smarting from what Reynolds said?"

Harri walked off, still smarting from what Reynolds said. "I'll drive."

The alley was grungy, the asphalt pocked by ruts and divots with weeds popping up between the concrete, but it was not empty. Along with the rat-eaten garbage carts, thrown-away tires, rusty bed frames, bicycle wheels, and moldy clothes in half-opened plastic bags, there sat the ice cream truck parked behind the McClintocks' building. Leaning against it, smiling, her arms crossed in front of her, was Cass Raines, who'd beaten them to the punch . . . again.

Vera glared through the windshield. "Are you seeing what I'm seeing?"

Harri pulled up behind the truck. "I believe I am."

"How is she always one step ahead of us?" Vera shoved open the passenger door, bounded out.

"Vera—"

But Vera was already out of the car and gone. Harri got out, too, on a sigh of resignation. Harri knew Vera was competitive, so she knew that Raines getting here before them, again, would stick in her partner's craw. It didn't bother Harri who got here first. In her experience, first didn't mean squat, it was the results that counted. She knew Vera knew this, too, but everybody had a bug. Detective Vera Li's was that she hated to come in second . . . at *anything*.

Smiling slightly as she walked slowly to the truck, Harri watched the PI as the PI watched her. Formidable, Harri decided by the time she had reached her.

Raines pulled herself off the truck. "How's this for a meet-cute?"

"What're you doing here?" Vera eyed the truck, and not in a good way. She eyed it like it had just rumbled out of a reeking sludge pit covered in the devil's excrement. "Selling ice cream. In April. When it's forty degrees."

Harri took visual inventory of the truck. Out of habit, she glanced down at the license plate. The truck's tags had expired. *Ten months ago.* But she wasn't the ticket-writing police; she was the murder police. "Is anyone in there?"

Just then three heads popped out of the truck's side opening, a fat-faced Black man with a bald head and full beard, a Black woman in a leather aviator's hat with the flaps pulled down, and a gray-black calico cat with slightly crossed eyes and a head as round as a regulator clock. The cat wore a black bow tie, like he was on his way to the Oscars. The humans smiled and waved like they were greeting old friends, perfectly unbothered, it appeared, by the fact that they were driving around the city in an old ice cream truck in *April* with expired tags on their plates. The cat just stared.

"Izzy and Big Mic," Raines said. "That's Mic with a *c*, not a *k-e*." She jabbed a thumb toward the calico. "And Bigfoot."

Vera squinted at the cat. "And *they* are?"

Raines thought for a moment. "Boutique neighborhood watch, I guess you could say. Eyes and ears. We can't be everywhere, can we? Bigfoot, well, he's just a cat, right?"

"Yet you seem to *be* everywhere," Vera offered snidely.

Raines made a face. "I'm getting a whiff of irritation from you, Detective Li. Luckily, I can rise above it. In answer to your question, I'm here, in this filthy alley that Streets and Sans has somehow overlooked while it's busy up north scraping chewing gum off the pavement with a razor blade, doing my job. Same as you, only I work for myself and don't have to take any flak or punch a clock." Raines's grin widened. "Don't hate, just appreciate."

Harri flicked a chin toward the truck. "They're your backup?"

Raines turned serious. "I don't do backup anymore. Actually, Izzy and Mic are doing me a favor by letting me tag along. They keep close tabs on what goes down around town, at least on this side of Twelfth Street. They see who comes and goes and when. They know this alley, and they know the players who feed the traffic that rolls up and down here. Ice cream doesn't come out of the truck, information goes in." She jabbed a thumb in the truck's direction. "Through that wide window there. People are more comfortable talking to them than they are to you or me."

"Who're you here looking for?" Vera asked.

"P.D., of course." Raines anticipated their next question. "I work for the Mitchells, remember? Your side talks to them, they talk to me, I take next steps. All I'll say is that my client's son isn't shaping up to be the one driving the train."

Vera squinted. "What's that mean?"

Raines shook her head. "More to come. Bottom line, I'm following the same breadcrumbs you are. And since we're talking about it, you failed to mention that Ella Byrne was related to a member of your team. That would have been useful to know. I see why you didn't disclose it, but still. It would have saved me some shoe leather."

"You're not going to hound Ella Byrne." It came out as a firm statement, not a question.

Raines angled her head. "Hound? No. But if the road leads to her door, I'm going to knock."

"As much as we appreciate your commitment to this case," Harri began diplomatically.

Raines waved a dismissive hand. "Yeah, you don't give a Fig Newton about my commitment. You just want me out of your hair. I get it. *You're* not getting it, but I get your wanting it. It's simple. The Mitchells want P.D. found and brought to justice. That means I follow this all the way to the end. But they don't just want the who, they want the how, and then they want the how to stop. I give them what they pay for. Anything new on your end?"

"Not yet," Harri answered. "What've *you* got so far, besides the inside track from the Mitchells?"

Vera slid Harri a look as though her partner had just jumped lines and sided with the enemy.

"You first," Raines said.

Harri looked over at Izzy and Mic still hanging out of the truck. The girl didn't look much older than Ella Byrne. Izzy gave Harri a thumbs-up. "Explain this to me first. It doesn't feel smart."

"They're concerned citizens," Raines said, "like we all are. Mic is ex-military, now he DJs at a few clubs. He also hires out for parties. Say hi, Mic." The bald man stuck up a hand, gave them a nod. "Izzy is his daughter. Sharp as a tack. Eyes like an eagle. Also, ex-military."

Vera's mouth opened in surprise. "*Military?* She looks *twelve.*"

"Thank you!" Izzy called from the truck.

Raines smiled. "Chalk it up to good genes. Now back to P.D. Since you won't go first, I'll go, but only up to a point because I don't work for you two. And also, because I don't have time to stand out here in the cold next to an ice cream truck with my thumb up my you-know-what."

"And we *do*?" Vera said.

"I can imagine what you've got going," Raines said. "Six ODs, five fatal. Bosses tearing at your ankles. P.D. moves around. I know because I've been moving around looking for her. You're thinking she's nomadic, erratic. She's not. There's rhyme *and* reason to her madness. She's not hiding, she's just not standing in one spot waiting for you to catch her. Why? Because she's protected and therefore has no fear."

Harri focused in. "Gang protected?"

Raines shook her head. "Not in the traditional sense."

"She's *not* selling for the Double Dees?" Vera asked.

Raines shook her head. "She is *not* a Double Dee. She is the puppet master, not the puppet."

Vera lasered in. "Meaning?"

"Meaning P.D. supplies the stuff, but hires others to sling it. She has to run with *somebody*," Harri said.

Raines nodded. "You ever hear of a guy, now deceased, by the name of Big Daddy Gamon?"

"Gamon?" Vera's eyes widened. "I know that name."

"Most everybody out this way knows the name," Raines said. "Big Daddy got shot and killed in a turf war maybe fifteen years ago. He was into everything. Drugs, prostitution, guns, the whole nine. Then he started to get old, move slower. He took his eyes off the ball, and the youngbloods came for him. Age-old story. Lions always go after the wounded antelope. Big Daddy died, his business didn't."

"Do you know who P.D. is?" Harri asked.

Raines angled her head. "Don't you know by now?"

"I want to know if you know or whether you're fishing for information."

"P.D. Terry," Raines said. "That's from Mic and Izzy, who got it from somebody out here in these streets who also knows who the players are and where they play. Don't ask who. They won't tell you, and neither will I."

"Whose side are you on?" Vera asked.

Raines and Vera exchanged a contentious look. "I'm on the side that makes things right for folks out here. You know, the ones the city's too big to see."

"What do you think *we're* doing?"

Raines slid a look at Harri. "You know what I'm talking about." Turning back to Vera, she said, "I know what you're doing. I did it. What's right or wrong plays differently out here than it does down where the blue shirts hang out around the coffee machine. That's why nobody out here's ever going to be straight with you. I've seen your Narcotics guys out here putting out feelers. So obvious. They didn't get zip, I know. Mouths shut tight when badges come around."

Harri couldn't disagree with what Raines said. Things were complicated in the gray areas. You couldn't be a cop five minutes without bumping up against that fact. "What's Terry have to do with Big Daddy Gamon?" she asked.

"Gamon had kids. A son got killed with him, the other got killed a couple years after. His daughter Cora is running things now. You asked who was protecting her, *that's* who's protecting her. I'd like to know why, wouldn't you? I'm working on a lead. Meanwhile, this alley. Right in front of the truck, you'll see where they huddle up and sell their stuff. There are discarded cigarette butts and beer cans, and little blue bags that, I suspect, though I can't know for sure, since you haven't shared a thing with me, that your mystery drug came out of. Before you ask, Mic and Izzy didn't touch anything, and neither did I. We're not idiots." She pointed up at the light poles. "No camera there, but there's one on the back of the apartment building next door, and a POD around the corner. Everybody drives. Protected pushers get cocky and careless. Happy hunting." Raines moved around to the door of the truck, opened it. "Next time, *you* go first."

"Wait. Were you in the truck out front the whole time?" Vera asked.

Raines smiled, but didn't answer, then slid in and tapped the side of the truck for Mic to get it rolling. "Eyes and ears, Detective Li." The truck took off, leaving a cloud of black exhaust behind.

"Do you believe that?" Vera said. "She gets all that, while we get nothing?"

"It's not a competition," Harri said.

Vera glowered in the direction the truck had taken. "The hell it isn't."

Harri watched the truck go, then looked down at the drug debris strewn along the cracked and pitted asphalt, including at least a half dozen small blue bags. "She's good, all right."

Vera stomped back to the car. "I never said she was good."

Harri grinned, slid behind the wheel. "You didn't have to. She said it for you."

CHAPTER 23

"This is what I was afraid would happen," Cora said as she glared at Patrice across the desk. "You exposed me. Your little stunt could lose us everything. And all behind my back, like I wouldn't find out." She rose from her chair, walked around the chair Patrice was sitting in to loom over her from behind. "There are now police all over this, and according to my eyes on the street, a private investigator is going around asking questions about a P.D. Terry, who's selling bad pills to our buyers." Cora bent down close to Patrice's ear. It wouldn't take much for Cora to snap her neck.

Patrice flinched; her pulse spiked. Patrice could literally feel coldness behind her. They were both Gamons, family, but Patrice had always known it was family with a catch, a caveat. Power and money were all Cora *really* cared about. "They can't touch us," Patrice said. "We're bigger, stronger, smarter. We—"

Cora stood up. "Stop . . . talking. It takes only one crack in the wall, one snitch, one mole, one lapse, and all of this falls down around my head." She moved away from the chair, but didn't go far. "You're off product. I'll find something else for you to do to earn your keep. Something you can't mess up."

Patrice shot up from the chair, but the look in Cora's eyes compelled her to ease back down again. "You can't treat me like one of those fools outside. I've got a stake in this same as you. Goody's handling the new stuff, and I told you *I'd* handle him."

"Leave Goody to me. I've set up a meeting. I've already had one attempted defection. I need to head this off before there are more. We can't sell when we have no one to sell to."

Patrice rubbed her sweaty palms along her thighs. This was her second time in Cora's hot seat. She knew there would be no third time. "The police can't do anything. There isn't even a P.D. Terry for them to find. I know what I'm doing, even if you don't think so."

Cora walked back to her desk, sat down again, steepling her fingers under her chin as she studied the live wire across from her, the look on her face telling Patrice she thought she was anything but smart. "You're out of this. I'll clean this up. You wait until I find somewhere to put you."

Patrice stared at Cora, suddenly bold. "You can't treat me like some kid."

Cora let a moment pass, her fingers still steepled, her eyes still leveled at Patrice. "*I* will talk to Goody. *You* will hope the police come nowhere near here. You will learn your place. You will do what I tell you to do and *only* that. Nod. Let me know you've heard me this final time."

Patrice kept her mouth shut, but she was seething. Cora hadn't heard a word she'd said. She nodded, though, because she needed to get out of the room in one piece. Could Cora tell the nod was a lie?

"Good." Cora leaned forward. "Word of advice. I'd be careful if I were you. When you come for this seat, you'd better not miss." She leaned back again. "I didn't."

CHAPTER 24

Vera rushed into the office, bypassing pleasantries. She tossed her bag on the desk and, still in her jacket, logged on to her computer. She hadn't said hardly anything on the ride back, Harri noted, which meant she was worrying a problem and didn't want to lose the thread.

Harri looked around. No Matt, and Al and Tony looked a little sheepish. Harri sat down, took a sip from her water bottle, then one calming glance at her potted plant that sat thriving next to a stack of files.

"Where's Matt?" she asked.

"Said he had something he needed to do," Tony said. "Left about a half hour ago. Said he'd see us in the morning. First thing."

For a moment, no one said anything.

"He ain't dumb enough to flush his job down the crapper, if that's what you're thinkin'," Al said.

It was precisely what Harri was thinking, and she hoped Al was right.

He pointed to Vera. "What put a bee in her bonnet?"

"She'll tell us in a minute," Harri said. "Anything new on this end?"

Tony sighed. "We followed up with Pease. Narcotics' ears are to the ground, but they don't have any intel on a new thing on the street, so if this Edge *is* new, it's *really* new, like hot off the griddle new. Biggest pill throwers are the Double Dees, but no one's confirming anything or advertising anything. And P.D. as an identifier doesn't ring any bells."

"We have additional on that," Harri said. "Let's wait for Vera."

"Meanwhile, back at the ranch . . ." Al smirked and shot Vera an impatient look that she was too engrossed to catch. "Just FYI. There's apparently an uptick in the use of nitrous oxide. Can you believe it?" He shook his head. "The dumb crap people do to themselves out there. So, we got heroin, meth, and fent, and all the other variations, plus dummies out there sniffin' *laughin' gas*." He threw his hands up. "What the heck is everybody runnin' from? They can't get through a day without blitzin' themselves into a coma? You know, not to preach, or nothin', but for fuck's sake, face your shit, why don'tcha. Do you see me going out there getting blitzed on some mystery stuff? No. You know why?"

Tony grinned. "Because you're not far off from mandatory retirement and whatever you took would clash with your Lipitor?"

Al folded his arms across his chest and gave him a look that took no effort to decipher. "I got your Lipitor."

"Quiet," Vera commanded, the tapping furious now.

"Oh, for fuck's sake." Al stormed off in the direction of the fridge, no patience for suspense, no patience for anything.

Harri and Tony waited for him to return, each watching Vera like she had the answer to the mysteries of the universe at her fingertips.

"Any new sightings of that PI?" he asked.

Harri looked up at him. "What are you trying to do?"

He hit her with a look of innocence that was not even remotely genuine. "Can't a man be curious?"

"Maybe let it go?"

Al strolled back, eating a granola bar. "Sherlock still at it?"

Suddenly Vera bolted up from her chair, arms raised in victory, and they all jumped, startled.

"Got it," she crowed. "Eyes don't lie, and I *never* forget a face." They gathered around her computer to see the screen. "Vanessa Gamon a.k.a. *Faith Pope*."

"Gamon, as in Big Daddy Gamon?" Tony asked.

Vera looked like she might actually explode from excitement. "The one and the same. Two arrests. Drugs. Selling, and possession. Never any prison time. The name Gamon rang a bell when we got it from Raines, who got it from the ice cream truck . . ."

Al stopped chewing, looked around the circle, then went back to the screen, confused. "Just me, I guess."

Vera waved him off. "It's not a common name, so it popped right away. I assisted on one of the calls while I was still on patrol. Vanessa Gamon rode to jail in the back seat of *my* squad car. I *knew* I'd seen her before."

Tony squinted at her. "You're taking pride in *that*?"

Al leaned forward to look at the old mug shot. "Big Daddy Gamon, the pimp king. Go figure."

They all turned to face Al.

"*You've* heard of him?" Harri asked.

"You *haven't*? He ran all the girls on the South Side back in the day. If it stank or croaked, got stolen or went missin' and turned up floatin' in the lake, Big Daddy's hand was in it. I heard when he got popped and they buried him, they sat his body upright in an old Lincoln Continental instead of a casket. The guy was Chicago royalty . . . at least for the criminal set."

"Well, Faith Pope, the preacher's wife, is *his* daughter." Vera bathed in the glow of the revelation. "You can change your look, you can dress like a Sister Wife, you can change your voice and talk like Mary Poppins, but the eyes . . . you can't swap out the eyes."

"But how's she fit into all this?" Tony asked.

Harri said, "That gets back to who we ran into."

She gave them a quick rundown. Mic and Izzy, the ice cream truck. The PI. Harri then went to the board and ran a line from Mitchell and P.D. to P.D. and Marie McClintock, and then one from Big Daddy to Faith Pope, back to Marie. Harri turned toward the team, to the jubilant Vera. "I think we might be getting somewhere. Cora Gamon is the boss."

"What I remember is it was a whole family of Gamons," Al said. "Big Daddy, a couple of sons, I guess the two daughters there, Cora specific, musta stepped up when they got cut down. Might be a million of 'em by now."

"Are they connected to a gang, or are they strictly self-contained?" Harri asked.

Al considered the question. "We'd have to check that with Pease and his guys. Any info I got is decades old. I can't see them workin' for a gang. I can see them gettin' a gang to work for *them*, though."

"Meanwhile, you said you had more on P.D.?" Tony asked.

"P.D. *Terry*," Vera said. "But I just ran the name through. Nothing pops. Not even a driver's license or a state ID. It's obviously fake. Back to her being a ghost."

Harri picked up the thread. "A ghost who connects to two of our three scenes. We walked that alley, and behind the McClintock building we found a few blue bags, the same ones found at the skate park, next to McClintock's body, and on that poker table. A link, but not something we can lock anything down with. That alley, for one, is a drug hot spot. Those bags could have been dropped by anybody at any time. We can't tie those bags to P.D. or anybody in that apartment building, though Miss Sybil can place her inside her apartment."

Al finished his bar, balled the plastic it was in, and tossed it into Harri's trash bin. "The tie-in's gonna have to come through P.D., then. Same for hookin' Gamon or Pope to the rest of it. Just because Pope's connected to Big Daddy don't mean she's in on the business. In fact, it looks like she walked away from all of it and went straight."

Harri studied the board. "Maybe. At least I hope that's true."

"She's a link," Vera said. "Marie was a member of her husband's church. She even counseled her. Who's to say Marie didn't get the pills from Pope?"

Tony's brows lifted. "You really think the *preacher's wife* is slinging dope with P.D. Terry?"

"Hear me out," Vera said. "What if she *is* P.D. Terry? Stranger things have happened."

Al frowned. "Not *that* strange."

"Sometimes apples don't fall too far from the tree," Tony said.

"Well, *this* apple married a reverend and probably runs Sunday school classes," Al said. "I don't see her givin' marchin' orders to pushers on the side. And we ain't even started linkin' anythin' to those poker guys. I mean, they don't fit at all, you ask me. The kid I get. I even get McClintock. But three meat-packers in their forties meetin' up to play poker and talk shit? It's like that thing, which one of these ain't like the other?"

"I'm with Al," Tony said. "And we still have slow motion from Grant's office. That leaves us hanging."

Harri heard them, but was lost in thought, trying to work it out in her head. She turned to Vera. "And for sure the Gamon brothers are deceased? There aren't any others hanging around?"

Vera sat down again, tapped some more on her keyboard, after a couple of minutes, the excitement left her face. "Two sons. Antoine and Enoch. Definitely deceased. That leaves, as far as we know, Cora and Vanessa, a.k.a. Faith."

"And Vanessa," Tony said, eyeing the board, "could either be in or out."

Vera scrunched up her face. "I bet Raines knows."

"Yeah, about that," Al said. "Why is it she's poppin' up like crabgrass every time we roll up someplace? We need to get her to shut it down. PIs and cops do not mix, all right? We all know this."

Harri put the marker down and walked back to her desk. "She's licensed. She's not interfering. She's doing her job, and we have to do ours." She turned to the team. "Raines is not our focus here. Besides, the only person she's bothering is Vera."

"Hey," Vera protested.

Harri ignored her. "We get in touch with Pease *again* and see what he can tell us about Cora Gamon. Meanwhile, we see if there's a connection between Pope and P.D. and any of these people on this board." She glanced around the group. "Including Ella. P.D. is out there somewhere making money. We find out why she's so special that the Gamons are looking out for her. That's a lot. More than enough, in fact."

Harri checked her watch. It was after five. She glanced at the board again, but there didn't seem to be a thread they could pull with any great promise of a result, at least not tonight.

"We pick it up in the morning?" she suggested. "When we're fresh and full of ideas. We haven't had any new ODs, so that's good. Maybe whoever's putting this stuff out there is holding back until things cool off? I hope that's true. It would give us a chance to catch up."

"My experience?" Al said, "Nobody holds up on nothin'. It's about the money, not the body count."

Harri knew he was right. "Then that gives us more of a reason to get this done. See everybody tomorrow."

Harri watched as they all filed out, tired and dragging, leaving her and Vera the last ones. After slipping into her coat and grabbing her bag, Harri turned to Vera, who'd done the same. Vera had a kid and a family to get home to, a second shift after a routinely long and stressful one, with a three-year-old son, a husband, and a mother. Harri had a house with a roof over it and little else. Even two months ago, if asked, she would have said that it suited her fine. Today, the house, the box, felt constrictive, hollow, and she was in no hurry to get there. She slung her bag over her shoulder, flicked off her desk lamp.

She looked over at Vera. "Never forget a face. Good going, partner."

"It's nothing. We all have our talents. FYI? If I get home and there's an ice cream truck in front of my house with a PI in it, I'm going to need you to bail me out."

"Again, this *isn't* a competition."

Vera scoffed. "No, it isn't, but we're going to *win*."

CHAPTER 25

Harri waited outside the Byrne house in her car with rain streaking down her windshield. Kelley's car was in the driveway, parked behind the Byrnes' Audi sedan. She knew he'd be here. It's where she'd be if their situations were reversed. But he was going down the wrong road, which wouldn't put him in a good place. There was no telling how long he'd be in there, but she'd wait. She needed to talk to him, see where his head was at, pull him back, if she could. As she waited, she thought about her session with Dr. Parker, and how frightening it had been. She still couldn't decide what she was more afraid of, changing or not changing, feeling or not feeling. Harri wanted what she couldn't have, her son back. It was magical thinking. So, now what? She leaned her head back, exhaled. "What've you got in your bag of tricks for *that*, Dr. Roxanne Parker?"

She tuned in something soothing on the radio and watched the house, mesmerized by the warm light coming from the windows. The light gave the house a cozy glow. It made it look warm and inviting, yet Ella didn't want to be there. As with her, maybe it wasn't so much the space but the state of mind. If your head wasn't where it needed to be, if you weren't straight, no bed, no room, no house would ever be right. Where was Ella's head? What was she hiding?

It took more than an hour for the door to the Byrne house to open and for Matt to walk out. She checked her watch. It was now close to seven thirty. She watched as he kissed his sister on the cheek, then bounded down the stairs toward his car. Maggie Byrne looked as though she'd aged decades since Sunday last. Harri understood why.

She tapped her horn once, lowered the driver's-side window. Matt spotted her and came over.

"Anybody else, and I'd ask what you were doing here," he said.

Harri clicked the locks open. "Mind if we talk?"

He got in on the passenger side, flicking rain off his coat.

"Everything all right inside?" she asked.

Matt thought about it, rubbing his chin, the rasp of the five-o'clock stubble sounding like coarse sandpaper, twice as loud to the ear in the quiet car.

"I honestly don't know," he said. "I needed to check on her."

"I know."

"Griffin's got me chained to a desk *unnecessarily*, you know that, right? I can walk and chew gum at the same time."

Harri turned the radio off but said nothing.

Matt unzipped his jacket. "She's hiding something. Maggie and Joe aren't picking up on it, but I can *literally* see it in her eyes. Am I supposed to put my own niece in cuffs? I *knew* she was lying at the hospital." He turned to look at Harri. "You knew too. She said you and Vera came to ask more questions about Mitchell."

"*Not* about Mitchell."

Harri stared at the house, the lights blazing inside. From the outside one would never guess that there was turmoil on the other side of the custom curtains. When trouble came, when bad things happened, the misery it brought along with it didn't care how much you had in your bank account.

"We never get the truth, or at least the whole truth, the first time. We have to chip away at it, you know that." Harri told him what she and Vera had gotten on their visit. "She's holding back. What did you get in there?"

Matt shook his head. "She just kept pushing it all off on Mitchell. I'm not buying it."

"The money worries me," Harri said. "The designer stuff too. Your sister doesn't seem like the type who'd shower Ella in Fendi. Ella seems to feel a certain way about this house and not having any freedom. Good old-fashioned rebellion, or something else? For sure she wants out on her own in the worst way. Normal, sure. Or, again, something else. Any ideas?"

"You're reading it wrong," Matt said. "Ella's had everything a kid needs. There's no abuse or neglect, if you're looking that way."

Harri turned to face him. "I never said anything about abuse or neglect. But *something's* going on. Ella is not cooperating, and we need her to."

"Well, tonight, she admitted that she was *with* Mitchell when he met P.D. in the park. She can give us a description. She also said she heard that P.D. hangs out regularly enough in Kismet's coffee shop. Back table. I had to get kind of harsh to get that out of her. More cop than uncle. She may never speak to me again."

Harri watched the rain slide down her windshield. "Some of that, maybe all of it, will be a lie. Did Ella know P.D.'s last name when Vera and I spoke to her?"

"Yeah."

Harri sat with that for a moment. "The name's fake. *P.D.* won't be anywhere near that coffee shop now, if she ever was. She's been in contact with her friends. They say nobody's seen her since the day Mitchell died. So, we're no closer than before."

"We get Ella's description and hope at least *that's* real. And we scour cameras hoping we get a hit. *I'll* do that."

"Did she mention the name Gamon?"

"No, why?"

Harri told him about their encounter with Raines and her associates, and the background Vera had dug up on the Gamon family, past and present.

Matt ran his hands across his face in utter frustration. "Shit. Just when you think this thing can't get dirtier . . . no, the name never came up. I did check her phone. She had a number for P.D. I had her call it, but the number's dead. P.D. likely ditched it days ago. You can just imagine how Maggie and Joe are taking all this. They're talking therapy, rehab, tough love . . . this person is out there right now selling to somebody else. It's like waiting for a bomb to go off."

He looked over at her, empathy on his face. "Nobody knows that better than you. Don't mind me. I'm just babbling . . . I want to punch something, but I've got nothing to punch. That doesn't mean I've lost my grip like Griffin seems to think I have. I don't need to be grounded like I swiped the car keys and broke curfew."

"It never hurts to be reminded where the line is," she said. "When you can't see straight. When you want to *punch* something." She flicked him a look. "This is just between you and me. And Vera, the Carnac of the Midwest . . . and Griffin and her creepy bobblehead. She was right to bench you. You don't want the trouble you seem to be so eager to borrow. Ella's in a good place, with a strong family around her. She may have to suffer some consequences. You might not be able to shield her from that, no matter how much you might want to."

"You came here to talk me out of throwing my badge away."

She smiled. "I just came to talk."

Matt let out a loud groan and laid his head back against the headrest. "I'll talk to the boss in the morning."

Harri smiled. "*After* she's had her coffee. And though you might not like it, we really *could* use you on the desk. There are cameras to tap from the park and that coffee shop, if we can get them. We might catch a break."

"Right." He rezipped his jacket, a signal that he was done talking. "I'll serve my penance. No way to it but through it, I guess."

"That's what they tell us," Harri said. "They leave out the part about how hard 'through it' can be."

"Mind if I ask a personal question?" he said; his eyes looked as though he'd been up for weeks.

Harri shook her head, a little wary about what might be coming. She'd already drained herself with Parker. The last thing she wanted was to have to dig up any more emotional sludge.

"That line you almost crossed," he said, "how much did it scare the hell out of you?"

She let a beat go. "It wakes me up in a cold sweat. There's not much that separates us from anybody else, is there? Nothing brings that home quicker than when someone comes after somebody we love." She turned to face him. "And the line's always there. We have to toe up to it every time we go out."

"Well, this line's a tough one." He placed his hand on the door. "One more, then I'm going home to try and get some sleep. Vera said you order your Italian beef *dry*. That can't be right, can it?" The slight grin that followed told her he was joking. A joke to make the hard stuff go down easier, no doubt.

Harri, relieved by the diversion, chuckled. "I don't like the dripping and the soggy bread. Now get out. Go home."

He opened the door, gave her a wink. "See you in the morning. Get some sleep. You look like you're about to fall over too."

"Appreciate that," she offered sourly.

He got out, but leaned back in. “If I have to ride the desk on this, I’m going to ride it like Willie Shoemaker.”

Harri started the car. “Counting on it.” She watched him jog across the street, get into his car, and drive off in the opposite direction.

She shook her head, smiled, then pulled away. “Smart-ass.”

CHAPTER 26

A black Town Car pulled up in front of Holy Land Church and stopped under the streetlights, their dull glow insufficient to illuminate the street in the misty rain. The sandstone-colored church, cracked, sagging, and past its prime, stood eerily in the murk, giving it a ghostly, haunted feel. The driver idled at the curb while from the back seat Cora Gamon watched the night people hunker in doorways across the street. She was perfectly safe, she knew. Those in the neighborhood recognized her car on sight. No one was dumb enough to mess with it.

Cora lowered the window and peered out at the church. It was dark, with rusted security gates over the front door, as though there was something inside worth taking.

"There was a time when church doors stayed unlocked day and night," Cora said. "In case anyone needed to go inside to pray or hide, or just be." She glanced around to scowl at the dingy street, the people scurrying between the raindrops like frightened rats in search of a hole. "No sanctuary anymore."

Patrice sneered. "I can't see you going to church."

"Not for me."

"And this place doesn't look like much."

Cora's mouth twisted in a frown, as though she were sniffing something odorous and foul. She wanted her niece to see the church, see what living outside the Gamon fold could look like for her. It was mighty cold out in the cold. The visual reminder was a courtesy, a one-time offer. What came next, if Patrice didn't straighten up, wouldn't be pleasant.

"I've seen it before, anyway," Patrice said. "You think I don't know what's going on? I've been paying attention. I get it. She didn't want no baby holding her back, so she bounced. Cut ties. Whatever."

"Hmm." Cora wrapped her coat tighter around her shoulders. "Then this field trip was unnecessary. Not a child. Fine. Paying attention. Very well." She looked over at the girl at the window. "But still with a lot to learn."

Patrice reeled. "Then *teach* me. I can do more than pass bags around. Who do you think's running the street part, anyway? *Me*. Who's getting our packs out and around without anyone catching on? *Me.* And *I'm* the one you just sat down? I don't need to see some stupid, broken-down church, Cora, I need to be let *in*. I need to get some respect around here."

"You're under the impression that this is a collaboration. It is not. You need to learn your place."

Patrice scoffed. "Well, *this* sure isn't it. I can't believe she chose this over . . ."

"The important thing to remember is where the line is. To know who's inside it, and who isn't. *She* isn't."

Patrice turned back to glance out the window, smiling. "Why'd she come? I saw her, but she didn't see me. She wants to make some kind of deal, doesn't she? She came back to us to beg for something, didn't she?"

"She's already made the deal. I just have to remind her of that. I will. In a bit. I want her to worry over it first."

"You do that a lot," Patrice said. "Make people worry. I made Goody worry too. He won't be any kind of problem."

"Self-preservation is a powerful impulse," Cora said.

"I know."

Patrice rolled down her window, breathed in. "It smells like a storm's coming."

Cora took her own deep breath, mimicking her niece's. "Funny, all I smell is . . . money to be made." She tapped the back of the driver's seat to get the car moving.

Patrice settled into her seat and turned her head away from Holy Land. "It's a shitty church. Someone should burn it to the ground."

CHAPTER 27

Harri sat in her front room in one of two chairs she owned in the sparsely furnished house that now, instead of insulating her and giving her a place to shelter, felt like a tomb. It suddenly surprised her how little she had let in over the last six years. Where had she gone?

The inventory didn't take long. There was a small couch, a coffee table, one lamp, one shade, one woven area rug. Everything else, everything from before, was either in storage or she'd tossed it away.

The house was a box. Utility. When she made a sound, when she coughed or sneezed or muttered a word to herself, no one heard it. She held no great affection for the place. Only now did Harri feel as though she were stumbling out of a fog into another country. It was a revelation, of sorts, realizing that she had done this to herself. She didn't have to ask why. She knew. The world had yanked her heart out of her chest.

Harri could sense the big tree breathing outside her front window and hear the wispy fluttering of its spring leaves as it awoke from deep sleep. The tree was alive, her son wasn't. Reg. He'd died right at the foot of that tree. Alone. A bullet in his chest. The thought that he'd called for her as he died haunted her every other thought. It made her heart race and scared her awake in the middle of the night. *We serve and protect.* It was written on the side of every CPD squad car in the city she worked for, and yet she hadn't done either for Reg. What good had her gun and badge done either of them that fateful day? Useless thinking, she'd come to accept. Accept that she couldn't have what she wanted—Reg and G alive, Eddie Noble in prison until he died. Accept that Krieg had outwitted them and likely wouldn't pay for it. Why, she wondered, did acceptance feel like defeat?

Guilt eats away at living things. Grief stills the wings of even the strongest bird. Harri hated the tree but didn't know if she was strong enough to leave it. She hated her dungeon cell, too, but . . . the *tree*. Near the door, just inside the entryway, sat a large vase nearly filled with colorful glass marbles. She'd placed the first marble in the vase the day of Reg's funeral and one every day since to mark the days of loss. Six years, 2,191 marbles. Six years of countless paper clips and thumbtacks, pieces of string, buttons, thin dimes, pen caps, snatched up and buried in a pocket to grip or caress as interminable minutes and hours passed. She'd made it through. Harri was still breathing, like the tree. Maybe the tomb no longer served her. *Maybe?*

She stared at her case board, much like the one at the office. She'd hung it on a barren wall and now studied it to see where they needed to go next. The lines and question marks, the photos, the timelines, all copies of the board at work, taunted her here just as they did there. She could see clearly some of the connections, and they made sense. P.D. to Mitchell and Ella, McClintock to P.D. through her neighbors, but how did the three meat-packers fit? And how many more deaths would there be? Was the drug they'd all taken tainted? If so, purposefully? Was there more of it floating around out there ready to take someone else's life? No new cases. That was good, she thought. Maybe this was as bad as things would get. Five deaths were five deaths too many.

She stepped closer to the board, staring at the photos of the three meat-packers. Normal middle-aged guys. Union workers. Not rave kids. They didn't fit. Neither did Marie McClintock, but Harri could follow the trajectory to see how she might have gotten caught up in everything. Faith Pope, or Vanessa Gamon, connected to Marie through Holy Land Church, but not at all to Ella and her friend. Was the Gamon family the connector? P.D., protected by them, Faith, one of them, at least by blood? What were they missing?

Too tired to ask another question, too fatigued to get her brain to clear and think logically, Harri called it for the night. She needed sleep, if she could get it. She had to turn it all off for at least a few hours.

She turned her back on the board, kept her eyes off the front window. Even though the curtains were drawn, she sensed the tree looming, breathing, waiting to hurt her. There had been whole days when she stared at nothing but the tree. Harri knew it so well she could draw every crack, every line in its bark, account for every leaf, so why was she having such a hard time looking at it now? Why did it feel as though it was watching *her*?

We serve and *protect*. The city. *Other* people's sons. A half life instead of one that was full. A cell, a tomb. An uneasy alliance with acceptance. Wanting and needing something nothing on earth could give her. Harri rubbed tired hands across her face, almost nothing left in the tank tonight.

"Clock out." It was an order to herself. "You can take a few hours." She glanced around the room, her brain not cycling down an inch. The pieces swirling in her mind. "Faith Pope. Big Daddy Gamon. Not someone she'd come right out and own. But P.D. and Gamon connect. Raines's ice cream–truck friends had learned the woman was being protected by them. Pope and the Gamons also connected. Family ties." She turned back to the board and looked over all the blank space under the three men's names. "How do *they* fit? We figure *that* out and we might just solve this whole thing." She went back to her notes. "An opioid cut with . . . something?" She thought fentanyl. Fentanyl powder in the pills. The easiest, cheapest additive, as far as she knew. Narcotics wasn't her area, but she had been out on the streets long enough to know a little about what poison flowed through them. Fentanyl would fit with what she'd seen at the skate park. Mitchell's and Ella's blue lips, blue in Ella's nail beds as Harri had rubbed the girl's hands, trying to get warmth back in them.

"Ella," she muttered. "She's lying. Chemistry major. Job in a lab." She scribbled the words *Breaking Bad*, before crossing them out with an angry pen and slamming the pad closed. "Now I'm just making shit up." Harri checked her watch. Almost 9:00 p.m. She should rest. She should be living. There should be food in her refrigerator and life in her home. There were a lot of things Harri should do, a lot of things she should have, but the one thing she wanted now was answers. Solving this—getting the drug off the streets, forward motion—was as good as a thumbtack or a marble, or a piece of string.

Sleep or keep going? She stood in the middle of the room and tried to decide. It was only nine. She'd done sixteen-hour shifts on nothing but stubbornness and caffeine. If she checked one more thing, putting in just an hour more, she could still get a decent night's sleep. Maybe. She recalled the nightmare, the dark figure in her room. The feeling that she was being visited. Then there were all the emotions she'd dug up with Parker, things she hadn't allowed herself to look at, things she'd actively avoided sharing with anyone. There was a lot of headwork for her to do, and at this moment, it all felt insurmountable. Could she sleep, even if she should? What dark thing awaited her in her dreams? Work was easier. Work she knew how to do.

Chickening out, she grabbed her jacket and keys and headed back to the office. Halfway to the car, she remembered Vera and the flak she'd given her when Harri followed a lead without including her. The look Vera had given her had been cold enough to frost glass. It was not a look Harri cared to see again. From the car, she sent Vera a quick text.

Going back for an hour. Want to check something. No need for you to come back out. Keep you posted.

Feeling virtuous, all bases covered, Harri tossed her phone onto the passenger seat and started the car, but it beeped with an incoming text before she even got her foot on the gas pedal. Vera.

Seriously? Don't you ever sleep? What's up?

Harri's thumbs hovered over the screen for a bit while she thought of what to write.

Poker guys. Background. Looking for a tie to P.D. Has to be one.

Harri waited as the undulating text bubbles moved from right to left. She didn't think her decision to put in a little more time had warranted a conversation, yet the bubbles kept moving.

I could have been there and back by now, Harri fired off. If I find something, you'll be the first to know.

More bubbles. Five minutes already at the curb. Finally, Vera's response popped in.

OK, but you sound a little snippy.

Sound? "OK? All that for *OK*?" Peeved, Harri tossed the phone down again and pulled away. "Now that I've checked in with my work wife, I guess I'm cleared to go."

Harri passed the tree, but kept her eyes averted. The breathing was enough.

CHAPTER 28

The driver slowly pulled Cora's car into the dark alley. She sat upright and imperious in the back seat, not in a benevolent mood. She had arranged to meet with Goodlow Dixon, here, away from prying eyes and attuned ears. This was business. *Her* business. Cora didn't appreciate having her hand forced. No one could be allowed to go behind her back, and she needed to reestablish her hold over the organization, to send a message, to Goody, as she had done with Patrice. This was what had gotten her here at midnight.

"What a hellhole," she muttered. "A bomb could go off here, and nobody would even notice."

She knew the neighborhood, the alley. Her people plied their trade on these streets. But more importantly the neighborhood and the alley knew her, and gave her the respect, and the fear, she deserved. Here in the dust and grime and dark, where no one likely felt safe, Cora Gamon couldn't have felt safer if she were at home in her own bed. Only the ones who ruled the street, owned the street, got to walk the street without fear.

She peered out the tinted window as the car pulled to a stop halfway in. There were no cameras or lookouts here. Nobody cared one way or the other about what went down in this part of town. There were apartment buildings all around her, and likely curious eyes peeking out windows, but no one would bat an eye at the black car. Everyone knew who it belonged to. Around here, noses stuck where they didn't belong got shot off.

Classical music played on the radio, the soft melodic tones as soothing to Cora's dark soul as a child's lullaby or mother's prayer. The music, art, and expensive things she'd surrounded herself with were in glaring contrast to where she'd started, to how she had to be as a Gamon. Cora had been raised hard to be hard, and she'd made sure Patrice had gotten the same message. Now the child had the nerve to rise up, to challenge her. *Her.* She'd done well hiding her fury. Cora considered it a personal triumph, growth, that her niece had walked away unscathed.

Still, Cora did not trust her. She trusted no one entirely, no one but herself. It was safer that way. Hadn't everyone let her down? Hadn't Big Daddy always said, you either lived hard or died soft? She glanced at Crow in the driver's seat, taking in the stoic back of his head. She knew the money she paid him fastened him to her side, that's why she paid him very well. But she could never leave herself open completely. It's why the gun was in her bag. It's why her eyes stayed open, alert. She didn't trust so much as rely on the power of the transactional agreement. Money for protection and loyalty. Fear of pain or death to ensure compliance.

It wasn't the drug she objected to. How could she? Drugs and flesh and metal were how she made her living. It was the deal behind her back she could not allow. Goody knew better, or so she had thought. Did he really think she wouldn't find out he and Patrice were working together? That their secret experiment *might* just impact the family's stake? They couldn't afford to give an inch to their competitors. An inch meant millions lost.

Cora checked the time on the dashboard, suddenly impatient. She would wait for Goody just five minutes more. If he didn't show, it was as good as him signing his own death warrant.

Just then, a car turned into the alley from the north end. It was a familiar maroon Chrysler 300. Goody.

"He cut it close, didn't he, Crow?" she asked her favorite killer.

Crow didn't bother to answer; Cora knew he wouldn't.

She watched the car approach, suddenly feeling a slow crawl of dread snaking up her spine.

"What's your feeling, Crow?"

His hard gaze held hers in the rearview mirror, his eyes unreadable, as they always were. The man gave her one slow nod. Even after all the years, Cora wouldn't get anything more from Crow.

"Flick the lights," she instructed, and then waited for the approaching car to do the same, as it did right on cue.

She and Goody were going to have a little talk. They were going to talk about loyalty and who exactly he thought he worked for. Goody would have to decide here and now whether he worked for her or if he was tired of living. There would be no third option.

"It's about control," Cora said. "I know you know this, Crow. It's about respect, which I have earned, and she has not. The radio."

Crow leaned over and turned the radio off, plunging the car into silence. Through the windshield Cora watched the Chrysler slowly ease in front of them, stop a few yards from their front bumper, and then idle. She expected Goody to step out to beg for his life, but the driver's door didn't open.

"I know he doesn't expect *me* to come to him. Flick the lights again, Crow."

He flicked the lights, but the doors to Goody's car stayed closed, the engine humming, time wasting. Cora grumbled, "He's going to be a problem."

Crow tapped the horn twice. The Chrysler didn't budge, but the engine cut off. Cora's uneasy feeling, that dread, grew. "This is nonsense." She picked up her phone and sent Goody a text.

Get out of the car. You have one minute.

Cora fixed angry eyes on the car, but no one got out. The hairs began to stand up at the back of her neck, telling her she was in danger. Cora waited for a return text, but when it came, it froze her to her seat. The message read: I got my kids to think about. It was you or them.

Cora's blood froze, her breathing hitched. She'd been lured, tricked. Slowly, she reached for her gun. She didn't have to wonder who got her here, she knew. As she stared at the back of Crow's head, she knew something else too. Someone else had been feeding her killer. Someone had paid him more than she had.

"Crow? Get me out of here." Her words were slow, cautious, a test, that she knew instinctively, as Big Daddy had known, she would fail.

Crow turned the engine off, his eyes straight ahead, his mouth set. Cora turned to look behind her as a black SUV with its headlights out slowly turned into the alley. The Chrysler in front, the SUV behind, she was boxed in. She tried again. "Crow, what are you doing? Ram the car. Get me *out* of here."

Crow started the car again but didn't put it in gear. Cora wet her lips, her mind spinning. No one got out of the Chrysler, no one got out of the SUV. Cora gripped her gun tight. Getting out wasn't an option.

She lifted her gun to the back of Crow's head. "*Ram the car*," she ordered. *"Now."*

Somewhere close a dog began to bark. The alley was so quiet she could even hear the wail of a police siren blocks away. She hated the police, but at that moment, she would have taken every last one the city had to offer. A jail cell was a lot better than a grave.

"Go," Cora yelled. "Ram it."

Crow didn't move. Cora pulled the trigger, but all that came back was clicks. The gun was empty. She lowered the useless thing to her lap. "How?" Crow met her eyes in the rearview.

"Wasn't hard," he offered without emotion. "Look."

The driver's door to the SUV opened, and one of her own men got out. Clifford Drake, Little C. "That traitorous bastard," she hissed. "I'll double your money. Take him out. Take him out *now*."

Crow didn't move.

The driver's door on the Chrysler opened, but it wasn't Goody stepping out. It was another member of her crew, Holt Buck. Big men, hard men, killers she'd thought worked for her until tonight.

Cora stared at Crow in the rearview. "What'd she offer you?"

Crow slid down the back windows. "Enough."

"She'll cross you too," she said, "Worse, when she finds out what you did, how she got here."

Crow's eyes held hers in the mirror. "I never expected to die old in my bed, Cora, did you?"

"I'll take that answer with me, if you don't mind."

In a flash, Little C and Holt had the car covered, one stood at her left window, the other at her right, their guns pointed at her face. When she looked at Crow again, his eyes were locked on hers in the mirror. "Business," he said.

She glanced down at her Glock 25. It had been a gift from Big Daddy for her sixteenth birthday. As she held it tight, her hands on the grip, Cora should have prayed, but she'd never been taught how. Anyway, Gamons didn't pray. They were the ones other people prayed never to see.

"You can tell her when you see her," Cora said, "she'll never wash my blood off her hands. And she'll never fill the chair." She sat back and counted the breaths she took, knowing she didn't have many more.

"Well, which one of you is going to do it?" she asked grimly, an undertone of ferocity in her voice, even now. "Or don't *any* of you have the guts. Crow? Why not *you*?" He didn't answer. "Ah. I don't get even that much respect from her? She'll let two low-level hitters take me out instead of the top man?" She stared at the hitters hovering outside her window.

Holt grinned at her, his crooked teeth capped in gold her money had paid for. "Nothing personal, boss lady."

Crow tossed a small blue bag with two tablets in it onto the back seat. "Pick it up."

Cora stared at the bag and almost laughed. "The infamous Edge. And now she wants *me* to be her next lab rat?"

"Just take it, Cora," Little C said. "Don't make this hard."

Cora paused, then picked up the bag and tossed it out the window. Her eyes locked with Crow's. Her right hand, her betrayer. The one she would have trusted if she had been able to trust. "*You* do it." She flicked a look at her useless gun.

Crow's eyes stayed steady on hers. "No more orders, Cora. We already decided who."

A beat passed. Someone shouted her name.

"Cora!"

She turned toward Holt, but it was just a fake. Little C was the one chosen. She heard a click, and that was all. For only a second, she could feel herself chasing the world as it fell away. The last thing her conscious being heard was a bored sigh from the big man at her window, and the last half beat of her own heart.

CHAPTER 29

Cass Raines pulled to the curb across the street and a half block down from the alley. Close enough. She shut off the car, turned to Whip in the passenger seat.

"How solid is this tip?" she asked him.

"First off, I don't leave my house on bullshit. You been looking for this girl for days now. You put feelers out, I put feelers out on top of your feelers, and now we're here. Are we getting out of the car and walking to that alley or are we just going to sit here playing twenty questions?"

Cass stared at him. "I don't think I like the attitude, dude."

Whip didn't look concerned. "It's cold. It's damp. It's late. I got to be at the diner at four a.m. And I am not in this life anymore, okay?"

"You insisted on coming," she shot back.

"Because *you* don't know when to let up."

"You didn't say that when I saved your ass from a banger bullet not too long ago. You were real happy to see me then, weren't you?"

"True dat, my friend. That was a true come-to-Jesus moment, for sure. But in this case? I really don't think either one of us want to go down this road. Nothing to do with the Gamons is going to turn out in the positive. *Ever.*"

"I need to know if it's P.D. Terry in that car," she said. "Your tip, whoever it is, just said a Gamon hit. Could be anybody connected to the family. If it's her, my job's done. The rest is up to the police, okay?"

Whip, a big guy, dark, mean looking to those who didn't know he was a big, soft teddy bear who'd hurt you if he had to, opened the passenger door to get out.

"Nuh-uh. Just me," Cass said.

Whip faced her, his mouth open. "Are you out of your mind? You think I'm going to sit here in this car while you walk your lanky behind into that alley where somebody just blew a Gamon away?"

"Allegedly," Cass said. "I haven't made visual confirmation. There might be nothing in that alley, which means you and I came out of warm beds for nothing. And I had a hot man in *mine*. I'll walk down, take a look, walk back."

Whip looked at her like she was crazy. They'd known each other since they were children, more like siblings than friends. He knew better than most how stubborn Cass could be. He frowned. Nothing else he could do. "You got something?"

She pushed the driver's door open. "My sparkling personality enough?"

"Cass, goddamn it. You know what I mean."

She smiled. "Yeah, I got something, but I won't need it. I'm just going to take a look. Be back in five minutes. If I'm *not* back in five minutes and it looks like something jumped off, do *not* let them put me in a frilly dress at the funeral home. I want to be buried in my leather biker jacket, so I look cool when I get to the pearly gates."

"That supposed to be funny? Because it ain't, all right? If you're not back in five minutes, I'm coming in there after you. Got me looking like a side piece in a bitch seat." He checked his watch. "Clock's ticking. I mean it."

"All right. Jeez." She slammed the door and headed up the street, her eyes scanning the block, finding it empty, then focusing on the mouth of the alley. When she got there, she saw a black car with its left back passenger door open. Just where Whip's tipster said it would be. She turned back toward the car and gave Whip a thumbs-up. In return, he held up his wristwatch and pointed at its face, letting her know the clock was still ticking. She waved him off and then walked toward the car, checking the alley for threats.

There was no movement that she could see, no one hiding in shadows. The alley was so eerily quiet that she imagined even the city rats that called this alley their turf had scurried someplace else.

The car was not running; all its lights were off. Just a black Town Car with a surprise inside, left vulnerable to whoever. She feared that she'd find the young woman she'd been looking for inside the car. Whip's information hadn't been specific. All his contact knew was that something went down here, and that it had to do with the Gamons. Maybe there was no one inside. Maybe if there was someone inside, it wasn't Terry. There were a lot of maybes possible, she thought, as she slowly approached.

A dog barked from somewhere, a low, hoarse woofing that had to be keeping people awake. She glanced up at the windows in the apartments overlooking the alley, but lights were out in all but one or two. Burrowing into her puffer jacket, her hands in her pockets, Cass walked up to the car's back bumper, noting the plate. Standard, it wasn't personalized. Only an idiot drug dealer and flesh peddler would tool around the city with a vanity plate on the back of their car.

Giving the car a wide berth, she moved around to the rear door, bracing herself for what she might find. She was used to seeing the remnants of violent death, but that didn't mean she liked it or was never shocked by it. There was a body in the back seat, slumped over on its right side. A woman in black. Cass moved just a little closer, peered in the driver's-side back window. Black. An older woman. Not P.D. Terry. Not even close.

"Cora Gamon."

Cass recognized her face from the countless newspaper articles written about her and the news footage she'd managed to find of

Gamon waltzing into court on a butt-load of charges even prosecutors knew they had a snowball's chance in Hell of pulling off. Cora Gamon was like Teflon dressed in designer attire. Nothing stuck to her, *ever*, and now it looked like nothing ever would.

Cass noted the Glock in Gamon's bloody lap. She appeared to have been shot in the back of the head, which ruled out suicide. There was brain matter and viscera in the lap, too, the round appearing to have gone in the back, out the front, bringing some of Gamon's brain along with it.

The front seat was empty, the back windows, right and left, lowered.

"Security breach," Cass muttered. "Intentional. A hit."

Cass moved to the front to peer inside the driver's window. The driver's seat had been slid back to accommodate a taller person. Made sense. It didn't make sense that Gamon had been driving herself and then jumped in the back seat to be killed. Someone else drove her here to die.

Stepping back, she checked the ground. There were tire tracks in the mud in front of Gamon's car, the mud a remnant of the recent rain they'd been having. "She'd been blocked in."

A deal gone bad? Something tied to the ODs? A rival making a play, taking advantage of the chaos? With Cora Gamon dead, was the entire drug trade on the South Side up for grabs? And what about Terry? She was still in the wind. Now without protection? Or was this *her* doing?

"Messy, messy." Cass stepped away from the car, careful where she placed her feet. There was nothing else she could learn without touching, and she couldn't do that. This was police work now.

She backed up, taking one last look at the alley and the car, then turned to walk the way she'd come. Fast. If she stayed much longer, the police would eventually show up, and she'd likely have to spend what was left of the night in a holding cell at the district for trespassing on a crime scene, and who needed that?

She turned the corner and jogged to the car, just as Whip started to get out of it. Her five minutes were up. He got back in when he spotted her running toward him. She hit the driver's door, slid behind the wheel, and started the car, ready to put distance between herself and the alley.

"Yup. Your tip was good," she told Whip. "It's Cora Gamon."

Whip shook his head. "Noo. Oh, that is *not* gonna be good for nobody."

"Nope." She grabbed her phone, dialed 911.

"What are you doing?"

"Calling it in."

Whip growled in frustration. "Of course you are."

She looked at him. "You wouldn't?"

"My experience with the police is a little different from yours, remember? Five-O ain't never my first impulse."

Cass relayed address and issue to the dispatcher but declined to leave her name. It wasn't pertinent to the situation, as far as she could see. She hadn't killed Cora Gamon, nor did she know who did. When she ended the call, she handed her phone to Whip. "We're out of here."

"Oh, you don't want to wait for the officers to show up so you can walk 'em through it?"

Cass pulled a face. "Now you're just being an ass."

Suddenly she heard the faint sound of approaching sirens. Nothing got squads moving like the discovery of a body in an alley. "Here they come." She reversed, U-turned, and drove away while the getting was good.

"Why're *we* running?" Whip asked.

"Because *we* don't want to spend the night in jail for walking all over a crime scene."

"You didn't touch anything, did you?"

She flicked him a look. "I beg your pardon?"

Whip sat back in the seat. "Just checking. You can get carried away."

"That's a lie."

Whip chortled. "Two words. Fire. Warehouse."

She rolled her eyes, turned toward the Drive to head south. "You're real mouthy for a wingman."

Whip yawned. "You want good, or you want quiet?"

She smiled. "Both would be nice, just once."

He chuckled. "Well, you ain't getting both. Take me home. I got a bed with my name on it."

Cass sped up. "Demanding too."

Then she had a thought, and slowed, pulling the car over to the side of the street.

"What the hell?" Whip said. "You don't know how to evade the police?"

She let a moment pass in which she thought about *not* calling the number. After all, she didn't work for them, she worked for the Mitchells, and for herself. They'd get the call, eventually, they didn't need her filling them in. "Who died and made me the Helper Fairy, anyway," she said as she eyed the business card slipped into the visor.

Whip frowned. "What?"

But with her foot on the brake, the car in gear, she couldn't just leave it. She shook her head. "You're just too good, Cassandra. A saint, in fact. Saint Cass, patron saint of the woe begotten and of overworked cops."

Whip stared at her like she needed an exorcism. She ignored him, put the car in park, grabbed the card, took her phone back, and dialed. "Look at me, working for CPD, like I have a paycheck coming at the end of the week," she groused.

Whip grabbed his head in his hands. "What're you doin'?"

"Sprinkling a little goodwill."

She couldn't ignore the interdependence that came with swimming in the same dirty pool with the badges. Even though one hand rarely washed the other, it didn't hurt to play nice with the folks who controlled the bat computer and who sometimes could be persuaded to part with a lead here or there, if she asked nicely. She considered this good business, a gesture of cooperation that she hoped would not come back to bite her.

"Foster," the woman on the other end answered, sounding as though Cass had woken her up.

"Yeah, this is Raines. Cora Gamon is dead." She relayed the address. "You're welcome, and just so you know, I'm running a tab." She ended the call without waiting to see what Foster had to say.

"Glad somebody's getting some sleep," she muttered, feeling just a tad virtuous.

"That was the dumbest thing I've ever seen you do," Whip said, shaking his head, a look of pity in his eyes. "You still got cop tendencies. You can't help yourself, can you?"

She pulled away from the curb. "I'll be fine." She checked the rearview to make sure there were no blue lights behind her. "It'll be good."

She punched on her radio, cranked up the oldies station. Gladys Knight and the Pips were taking that midnight train to Georgia. Cass thought of the cantankerous Detective Li and smiled. Li was likely getting a call from her partner right now. Oh, to be a fly on that wall, she thought.

Cass grinned. "She's gonna *love* this."

CHAPTER 30

Patrice eased down into Cora's chair and ran her hands along the top of the big desk. It was all hers now.

Though late, the next day, in fact, 2:00 a.m., she hadn't been able to sleep. Too wired. Too excited. Too many things to do. She'd increased security around the house, doubled the lookouts. If their rivals came for her, they'd have to work for it. Then she'd called in Crow and the others. She wanted to know how it all went down.

There was a knock at her office door, then the door opened, and Crow, Little C, and Holt walked in and stood in front of her.

"It's done," Little C said.

Patrice looked at Crow. He'd been Cora's enforcer. Could he be hers? Time would tell.

"Who did it?" she asked.

Holt said, "It was C."

Patrice's eyes held Crow's. "Why not you?"

Crow said nothing. Patrice couldn't read anything on his face. It was like looking at a cardboard cutout of a man instead of the man himself.

"Did she say anything? Did she know it was coming?"

"It went like we planned it," Holt said. "She didn't say a whole lot."

Patrice grew anxious. She wanted details. "What *did* she say?"

Little C said, "She had a message for you. She said her blood was on your hands, and you would never be able to wash it off."

"That's it?"

The men nodded, but Patrice had a feeling they were holding something back. She decided to let it go for now. Instead, she sat back and thought about Cora's last words. "I think I can live with that."

"You sure about that?" Crow said.

Crow speaking startled her; he startled Little C and Holt, too, from the surprised looks on their faces. She'd never heard him utter a single word to her before, and now, here, he'd uttered four.

"Yeah, I'm sure. Now you three had better be sure. Either you're in or out. Either you work for me, or you don't work anywhere. Don't let my age fool you. You're not dealing with Cora anymore. We go hard and fast from this point on. Anybody not up for that say so now." She looked at each man, waiting for anyone fool enough to object. "Good. Then it's business as usual."

She opened the desk's bottom drawer, keyed in the combination she'd commandeered months ago. Drawing out three short stacks of hundreds. Five thousand each. Payment enough for ridding her of a problem before the problem got rid of her. It was all about timing, Patrice knew, and Cora had been too slow off the mark.

Little C and Holt took their stacks and left, Crow remained behind, his stack still on the desk. Their eyes locked. An understanding reached. Patrice picked up the stack and put it back where it'd been and closed the drawer.

"We're good, then," she said nervously.

Crow didn't answer. He looked right through her.

"You're with *me* now," she said, her hands on the armrests of *her* chair. "We keep the bags moving. We go bigger. The police will be here to ask questions about Cora. Handle them and get me Goody on the phone."

Crow didn't move a muscle. "I don't make phone calls. I don't handle police." His eyes swept over the big desk. "You're in the chair. If you can keep it. All that's you."

There was something in the way he said it that made Patrice begin to shake. She was the boss now, but was she? Had Cora truly been? How would she handle the chair, the business? Could she trust Crow? One day would she be in the back of a Town Car with a gun to her head?

She mustered up just enough courage to put on a convincing show. "Careful, Crow. You work for me now. Cora's dead. She was in a dangerous business and had a lot of enemies. Who can say which one finally got her? Close the door on your way out."

Crow turned and left, leaving the door open.

And Patrice began to worry.

CHAPTER 31

Matt beat the shift clock out of restlessness and a growing feeling of foreboding. Unable to sleep, tired of tossing and turning, disturbing his wife, he finally got up and dressed and headed into the office to do something, *anything*, that would move the needle on the ODs, praying Ella wasn't in any deeper than he feared she may be. His niece was lying to him, to everybody, he didn't even have to be a cop to know that. He needed to know why and what about.

He glanced around at the overnighters scattered around the desks, waiting for tragedy to strike and a call to come in. What a business to be in, he mused, waiting for violent death. He sighed, sat at his desk, too keyed up to do otherwise. His kids were at home in their beds, thank God. Too young yet to get into the kind of trouble Ella was in. *Yet.* Something *else* to worry about.

He hadn't found anything on the street-camera footage he'd reviewed earlier, but he had hours of it yet to go over, concentrating on the park where Ella said Mitchell had made the buy, and the streets around it on the Saturday before the skate park. If he could find P.D., see where she came from and where she went, maybe they could track her down and bring her in. Then he'd know how deeply Ella was involved. When he knew, *then* he could fix it.

"At least get a plate," he muttered as he turned on his computer. "See who the car is registered to. *Something.*"

He rolled up his sleeves, pushed all the papers and files on his desk away, and settled in. He'd find it. He'd find *her*. He'd get it done.

Hours later, his eyelids heavy, a dull headache from stress, Matt stared at the grainy black-and-white video images as they played out before him on the screen. Cars coming and going, people walking in and out of the frame, nothing, nothing, having to do with Ella or Mitchell or Terry.

He'd gone through the entire Saturday but had found no one walking into or out of that park that even resembled Mitchell. Another lie.

"Damn it, Ella," he hissed.

He clenched his fists, bit down on his lower lip, keyed up on caffeine and a lack of sleep. How far was he willing to go to protect his family? It was a question he honestly didn't know the answer to. Matt cued up more footage, widening the scope, this time focusing on the Friday before Harri found Ella and Mitchell. He couldn't give up. He had to know. He had to help Ella, if he could. If he couldn't, he'd still have to be there to get the family through it all. It took until four in the morning until he found it. He'd almost missed it as his eyelids drooped and his headache raged, despite the Tylenol tabs from his drawer. Not in the park, as she'd said, but outside the Japanese Garden a couple of blocks south. Friday, not Saturday. The Garden, not the park. Lies on top of lies. Matt stood, his eyes glued to the monitor. A grainy figure, a Black woman in loose clothing, her head hidden under a dark hoodie, walking toward the swings. And *Ella*, not Mitchell, waiting there. A quick exchange: money for a bag, and the woman was gone again.

Matt noted the time. 1400 hours. He sat down again, advanced the video, looking to see where the woman in the hoodie went. She walked away from the buy, then turned west, away from the lake and the MSI, out of range of the camera. He'd have to request footage from another POD.

For now, though, he zoomed in, hoping to get a look at the pusher, only the closer he zoomed, the muddier the image became. This was the best he was going to get.

"But Ella knows *exactly* what she looks like. Maybe even where to find her."

His phone buzzed. It was a text from Harri sent to the entire team. Cora Gamon was dead. Ella was his first thought. He picked up the phone and dialed his niece's number, letting it ring before voicemail clicked in. He started to leave a message but stopped himself. This was a conversation he needed to have in person. He grabbed his coat, then hesitated. He should leave the information for the team. That was his job. But what if there was some explanation for Ella being there? He had to give her one last chance to come clean, to explain it all. Besides, Gamon's death would be the biggest fire. He glanced over at Griffin's door, then around the room, making a choice, a decision, the only one he felt he could make, knowing it would cost him.

CHAPTER 32

Harri and Vera had spent the early hours standing in the alley Cora Gamon died in, freezing to death in a light rain, while techs and cops and rats did their thing around the pusher queen's luxury car. By the time they made it into the office at eight, both had already put in half a shift extra, they'd briefed Griffin, and the stakes couldn't be higher.

"Cora Gamon," Harri started as she stood at the board. She'd underlined Gamon's name. "Taken out. We'd be stupid to think her murder was unrelated to what we're working on, but before we talk about that." She turned and scribbled the name Tasha Jackson on the board. "*She* closes a circle."

Vera, Al, and Tony sat around the board while Griffin sat off to the side, watching. Harri knew the boss wasn't happy. She hadn't been when she called her in the middle of the night to inform her of the Gamon hit, and her mood darkened even more when she relayed that the tip had come in from Raines just ahead of the first squad arriving on scene. Now here they all were with the clock ticking, with moves being made. They were almost there, Harri could feel it.

Vera glanced over at Matt's chair. "We're missing somebody. Anybody hear from Matt?" Harri flicked a look toward the door, half expecting to see him rush in, only he didn't. After the talk they'd had, she wasn't sure if she should worry. He was in a weird place, and now with the news of Gamon's murder, she didn't know what he'd do to shield Ella.

"Try calling him?" Harri asked.

Vera picked up her phone and dialed Matt's cell, then waited, and waited, then hung up. "No pickup. You think there's a problem?"

Harri turned toward Griffin but got only a get-on-with-it look.

"Let's move on," Harri said.

"First, I heard from Streeter on my way in," Al said. "Follow up to me buggin' him about Mitchell's phone. P.D. wasn't in the kid's contacts *or* his logs."

This had to be the information Raines had been holding back. The more to come. Her proof that Robby Mitchell hadn't been the one "driving the train." P.D.'s number was in Ella's phone, according to Matt. She eyed his empty chair. "Damn it."

"He could have had a second phone," Vera said, "or a throwaway. Kids are devious."

"Yeah, well, all that's true," Al said, "but then where's the other phone? It wasn't on him. His folks didn't find it in his room at home, and it wasn't in his apartment. And none of his pals copped to seeing Mitchell jugglin' two phones. If he had one, *I'm* thinkin' he *wasn't* thinkin' about hidin' it when he set off to that skate park with Matt's niece. He wasn't expectin' to die out there. So, if *he* didn't call Terry . . ."

Harri faced the team. "Ella could have."

She told them about Ella lying to them, and Matt going through the girl's phone. Matt's personal stuff, the worries about his family, she kept to herself.

"This shit is startin' to get sticky." Al pulled his phone out of his pocket. "I'm callin' him again. We gotta lock this down." He looked over at Griffin. "No worries, boss. We got this. It's all good."

They all waited while Al's call went unanswered. Harri and Vera exchanged a look. Griffin got up from her chair and disappeared into her office.

"And there's that," Harri muttered.

"Do you think Raines is on Ella's trail?" Vera asked.

"I would be," Harri answered. "We should be too."

Vera had a serious look on her face. *"Raines."*

Harri said, "She's doing *her* job, *this* is ours. I know you're competitive . . ."

Vera bristled. "So are *you*."

"But something about Raines in *particular* is rubbing you the wrong way, what is it?"

"She's cocky," Vera said.

"*You're* cocky," Harri shot back.

"She's beat us to the punch *twice*."

"And you hate coming in second," Harri said.

Vera threw her hands up. "Who likes coming in second?"

"We're wasting time." Harri pointed to the new name on the board. Matt and Raines and whoever would have to wait. "Let's do this so we can get back out there." She picked up the marker. "Tasha Jackson." She'd already underlined the name last night and drawn a bold line from it to the name of one of the three meat-packers. "Anthony Beadnell. Father. Daughter." She turned to the team. "I found a missing person report filed by Beadnell. Tasha has been missing for over a month. *This* time. She's a chronic runaway. I found at least six runaway reports. Classic story. Divorce. Teenage rebellion. Kid shuttling from parent to parent. Kid takes off, comes back when she's hungry or needs something, gets it, takes off again."

Tony frowned. "Beadnell couldn't get a handle on that?"

Vera turned to him. "What'd you expect him to do, tie her to a chair?"

Tony took another sip of life from his mug. "It's a start."

Harri banged the marker against the board to keep everyone from getting sidetracked. "*Six* reports. Tasha's been running since she turned sixteen. She's now twenty, wherever she is."

"Not to be heartless, or nothin', like Tony here," Al said, "but what's Beadnell's runaway kid got to do with what we're on?"

Harri walked back to her desk, picked up a copy of Jackson's arrest history. "Tasha has been picked up for shoplifting, trespass, destruction to public property, pickpocketing . . ."

Al scoffed. "She ain't exactly Dillinger."

Harri tacked the sheet up to the board under Jackson's name. "She's also a drug lookout."

Al noted the location of that arrest. "That'd be the Dees' territory."

"It would. It is," Harri said. "But they didn't come to retrieve her. The Gamons did." She scribbled a name on the board below Jackson's. "I looked it up. Her lawyers? Jack Wellner and Associates."

"Sounds pricey," Al said. "How'd the runaway kid of a meat-packer come up with all that scratch?"

"I don't think she did," Harri said. "I went back and pulled up other Gamon gang arrests. They all got bailed out, and pretty quickly, by Wellner and his *associates*."

"So, Jackson's with the Gamons?" Tony said. "As their . . . whatever."

Vera stood. "And if Jackson's with the Gamons, and P.D.'s with the Gamons, and P.D. is connected to our first two ODs, and Jackson to one of our last, we've got dot-to-dot connection. And *that* brings us to the late Cora Gamon. Coincidence? I don't think so."

Harri stepped away from the board. "Pease filled us in on Gamon. She ran a pretty big operation, until last night. Someone executed her and then placed a little blue bag with pills in it into her right hand. That ties that to us. It's the pills. It's the ODs. It's all of it rolled up together."

"Sending a message," Tony said. "Any ideas?"

"Not yet," Harri said. "But information is flowing in from *somewhere*. Raines called it in. Then she called *me*."

"Walked all over the crime scene, too, I'd bet," Vera added, folding her arms across her chest. "Like she's Sherlock Holmes, and we're the ones holding his pipe and hat."

"We'll talk to her about it," Harri said. "I made some calls. She's not on the job anymore, but she's still got a lot of friends who are. We know where to find her."

"Anyway, back to this." She circled Faith Pope's name. "Cora Gamon dead. Faith, a.k.a. Vanessa Gamon, alive. It'd be naive to think there has been no contact between the two. And Faith's probably the only one we can leverage for information without sending in SWAT to the Gamon nest. The leads on the Gamon scene will follow through. They'll be in touch." Harri put the marker down. "We have this end. So, we double back. We talk to Faith. We see what Raines has that we don't. We get tougher with Ella. We keep working it." She recalled her notes. "Tony and Al, maybe follow up with the campus lab Ella says she worked at? For Dr. Liebner."

"You really think Matt's niece is tangled up in all this?" Tony asked.

"Her lying sure makes it seem that way," Vera said.

"Maybe it's because she doesn't want to get grounded by her parents, or disappoint Matt," Harri said, giving the girl the benefit of the doubt even now. "We approach her again. And we probably all agree Matt can't be in on that. He's too close."

Al said, "He's gotta step back, that's for sure."

Tony thought about it. "It's no big leap from buying to selling, if a kid gets in too deep. Maybe that's what she's hiding?"

The loose threads flew around in Harri's head, the possibilities, the angles. Despite the dots, they needed more.

"Right," she said absently.

Tony looked over the board. "Meat-packer gets the pills from his runaway kid who's slinging for the Gamons. The circle closes."

"No new ODs. That's somethin'," Al said.

Harri slid her phone out of her pocket, dialed Matt's cell again. No answer. "He always picks up. Why isn't he now?" She looked over at his desk and his computer and made a beeline for it.

"What're you doing?" Vera asked.

"Checking to see what he was working on last," Harri said as her fingers flew over the keyboard. "Might tell us something."

They gathered around her, their eyes on the monitor.

"He had the street cameras up," Harri said.

"And look what time he was viewing it," Vera said, pointing toward the last log-in details. "He was here most of the night. Up until . . ." Her eyes slid down the screen. "Four a.m.? *What?*"

"He was here when you texted us about Cora Gamon," Vera said.

Harri sat down in Matt's chair, her eyes focused on the screen as she reran the last bit of footage he had reviewed. "This isn't the park Ella told us about. It's near the Japanese Garden." She slowed down the grainy images and watched them frame by frame. Minutes went by, but no one moved. Finally, there it was.

"And *that's* not Mitchell," Harri said, leaning back. "It's Ella." She leaned forward again and zoomed in to see what looked like a woman walking into the frame in baggy clothes and a hoodie pulled over her head. "And that's P.D. Terry, or whoever she really is. No good shot of her face, but she knows that. And she just walks off into a blind spot. She knows what she's doing."

"The reason we can't find P.D. Terry," Vera said, "is because there *is* no P.D. Terry. No car to connect her to, no face to run through facial rec. No record tied to that bogus name. What do you want to bet she's one of them?"

"Family," Harri said. "Faith Pope might be able to tell us who she is, then."

"She's a Gamon," Al said. "She ain't gonna tell you squat."

Harri considered for a moment. "She appears to have turned her life around. She's heavily into her husband's church. Isn't 'Thou shalt not lie' one of the top rules for living a Christian life?"

Tony scowled. "You never heard of Christian hypocrisy? Look around. Plus, she's a *Gamon*. Are we going to have to get into a nature/nurture discussion here?"

"We go see," Harri insisted. "We ask."

Al stared at the images freeze-framed on Matt's monitor. "Yeah, meanwhile, that right there's why Matt ain't here."

"He's running interference," Tony said. "Getting ahold of Ella before we can get ahold of her. The ice he's skating on can't get any thinner."

Harri closed down the computer. Got up out of Matt's chair. She didn't want to think about the Matt part of things, but she had to. "Okay. We put eyes on Matt *and* Ella. We bring her in and treat her like we'd treat anybody else. Also, we follow up with Faith Pope. Her sister's just been murdered. Maybe she'll be willing to talk to us now."

She turned to Vera. "We'll take Raines and Pope, if that's okay with you? We find out if Raines has any more information from her contacts that she hasn't passed along, and I hope the answer to that is no."

CHAPTER 33

Cass burst through the door of Deek's diner, wide-eyed and primed for confrontation to find Foster and Li sitting in *her* booth. She couldn't believe it when she'd gotten the call from Muna, her favorite waitress, who'd given her the heads-up as only she could.

"You better get your long, tall behind down here," she had whispered into the phone. "You got two tough-looking cops down here askin' for you, and they sat their butts right down in your booth before I could even say nothing."

Cass had sat up in bed, her head crowded with images of Cora Gamon's wasted life swimming around in it. "What do they look like?"

"Women. Dead-eyed serious. One Black. One Asian. Tallish. Lanky like you," Muna said. "Foster and Li, they said. Looks like they could both run down a banger across three states without even workin' up a good sweat. How come you can't ever piss off slow cops? Why you gotta always get on the bad side of the ones who look like they actually take their jobs serious?"

"Like *I* choose," Cass said. "Tell them to get out of my spot."

There'd been a pause.

"I love you to death, you know that," Muna said, "but I ain't about to tussle with no handcuffs trying to save a seat for you and your pancakes. Get down here. *Now.*"

She'd dressed lightning fast and jumped in the car for the three-block trip from her apartment building to Deek's front door, then tumbled in to glare at the badged-up interlopers, who appeared mighty pleased with themselves, especially Li, whose satisfied grin she caught all the way across the room. Finally, she'd gotten someplace ahead of her, and Li looked like she was enjoying it.

The place was quiet, as expected for a Tuesday morning, only a few tables occupied, and all the booths open, except for the one Cass claimed for herself years ago. The smell of bacon, biscuits, and hot coffee threatened to divert her attention, but she managed to hold on to the affront.

Muna waved her over to the counter. "If you gonna need bail money, I'mma need a heads-up. I'd have to clock out and then get to the bank way across town. I don't do that money-transfer mess, you know that."

Cass's eyes were on her booth, the cops' audacity an offense to her very soul. She was territorial; she'd be the first to admit it. She was also a creature of habit; she'd freely cop to that too. So, having two uninvited guests in her spot was not sitting well. "How'd they know that's where I sit?"

Muna, dark, rotund, solid, not the least bit shy, or fearful of confrontation, hence the Louisville Slugger under the counter, said, "Somebody dropped a dime on you, *that's* how. Could be anybody, really. Everybody who knows you knows you either in your office, here, or runnin' around jumpin' into lakes or off roofs, or some foolishness." She leaned closer. "What they got on you?"

Cass waved Muna off. "Nothing." She thought of the alley with maybe one or two of her footsteps left in the mud around Cora Gamon's Town Car. "Much."

Muna glowered at the booth. "Hmm. That don't look like not much. You got A Team back there, my friend. They don't send A Team for not much." She turned to look Cass over, long and hard. "You always get yourself into trouble. How come you just can't do normal things? You know most folks don't have police doggin' their every step."

Cass scowled, held up a hand. "Not today, Muna. Bigger fish to fry." Cass flicked a look toward the door that led to the kitchen. "Deek in there?"

Deek was the grouchy owner/cook of this greasy Michelin Star–ignored establishment. He never had a kind word, and mostly communicated in grunts, growls, and spatula slams to his busy grill.

Muna nodded. "And you know how he feels about the po-po in his place, so you better make whatever that is back there go away like poof."

Cass turned to walk back to the booth, but Muna grabbed her by the arm. "No shoot-outs in here either. You know Deek just had the place painted."

Cass pulled her arm free. "Shoot-outs? *Really?* Who do you think I am?"

Muna wisely refrained from giving a response. Cass approached the booth as though she were walking her last mile. Harri and Vera, who were sitting facing the front door, saw her coming, their butts warming the Naugahyde-covered seats. Cass could have not shown up, sure. Let the cops cool their heels for a while, but that would only have postponed whatever *this* was.

Cass loomed over them. "Foster. Li. What a surprise."

"Raines," Harri said.

Cass really did not like being encroached upon, hilarious when she considered she spent most of her time encroaching on other people's space.

"Look who got here first," Vera said, smiling like a cat in the catbird seat.

"Don't start with me," Cass shot back. "What's all this?"

"We'd like to talk," Harri said. "We figured you'd be more comfortable here. We don't have a lot of time. Neither do you, I imagine. Let's start with Cora Gamon."

Cass slid into the booth opposite them. "First, how'd you know where *here* was?"

Vera smiled. "We have friends too."

"Who do *you* know that knows *me*?"

There was only silence.

"Oh, that's what we're doing?"

Vera said, "You seem a little miffed."

Cass pressed her lips tightly together to keep the naughty words inside. "Yes, let's make this quick. I'm hungry."

"Don't let us stop you," Harri said. "We can talk while you eat."

Cass pulled a face. "Um. No. I don't like to eat with strangers, especially strangers as strange as Li over there."

Vera's grin widened—she was obviously enjoying herself.

Harri slid the laminated menu away from her, as though it might bite and leave rabies behind. "I appreciate your call last night. Did you also place the 911 call? The caller, a woman, wouldn't identify herself."

"Sounds like you," Vera said.

Muna was back from the kitchen, but appeared to be avoiding the booth like it was a rattler with her name on it.

"I'm still on how you two are *here*," Cass said.

"We asked around," Vera said. "We learned this was your place. Nice booth too. Out of foot traffic. Close to the back door. It gives you a good view of everybody coming in and going out. You think like one of us."

"Yeah, we've gone over that already. I need to know who to scratch off my Christmas card list."

Harri smiled. "How did you find out about Cora Gamon? Was it a tip from the ice cream–truck people?"

Cass's brows raised. "That's what you're calling them? It's Mic and Izzy. Easy. One syllable on the first name, two on the second. Hold on. I need tea." She held up a hand for Muna, who came quickly over.

"What can I get you all? Coffee? Juice?" She shot Cass a look, then lowered her voice to a whisper. "A lawyer?"

"Tea, please," Cass said. "Hold my regular order till this is done."

"Pancakes," Vera said. "Sausage on the side."

Cass shot her a petulant look. "Seriously, what are we doing? Who? *Who?*" She leaned forward. "And since we're on it. What's with you, Li? Did I run over your dog or something?"

Muna fake coughed, the word *bail* croaked out. It was reminder enough. She then turned on her heels and disappeared into the kitchen. Cass sat back in the seat that wasn't on the side of the booth she preferred to sit on. No, Li was in *that* one. "I went first last time. Your turn."

"Cora Gamon is dead," Harri said.

Cass blinked.

"A bullet to her head," she added.

Cass blinked again.

"Pills in a blue bag placed in her hand."

Cass perked up. Finally, information she didn't already have. "The same bags we've been chasing?"

Vera said, "Appears so."

"That connects Gamon's murder to your ODs," Cass said. "Questions are, why hit Gamon now, and whether the hit came from inside the castle or outside of it."

"There's been very little chatter, according to Gangs," Harri said. "No one's talking. No one's bragging. We don't know yet who steps into Cora Gamon's shoes. Nothing's transparent."

"That'll say a lot," Cass said. "Maybe the Gamon bubble bursts and a rival takes over."

Muna was back with a silver teapot, tea bags, and a ceramic cup with Deek's name stenciled on the side, which she sat on the table before hurrying away again.

"So, *who* tipped you?" Harri asked.

Cass selected a tea bag. Earl Grey. Decaffeinated. "I'm not going to tell you who. I'll only say they heard something and said something. They aren't into anything the Gamons are into."

"So, you got the tip and showed up to the crime scene and took a good long look," Vera said.

"To confirm, and the only thing I touched was the ground beneath my shoes. This isn't my first case." She poured hot water into her mug, then dunked the tea bag a couple of times before letting it steep. "And, again, *Li*, I don't work for you, so you can ease up on the chewing out. I'm not interested in the Gamons. They're *your* problem, sorry to say."

"You're after *Terry*," Li said.

Cass looked at her, then Harri. "We all know there is no Terry, right? But there's somebody calling herself that, somebody who's hawking the Gamons' wonky product. I'm wondering where the name even came from. Who started it? Why even? It feels amateurish, like something out of a bad movie." She sipped her tea. "Tell me about Ella Byrne."

Harri said, "Why?"

"Because there were *two* kids at that skate park. One walked away. And because I covered that campus and learned some interesting stuff. Enough people know the alias, but they also know Byrne. Some folks say she is quiet, studious, some say she can be haughty, and a bit of a snob. There's nothing that says she can't be both, of course, but it makes me wonder who we're dealing with, really."

Vera's eyes narrowed. "What're you saying?"

"Most operations like the Gamons' are comprised of a series of concentric circles. At the center you had Cora and a small band of trusted folks. At the outer circle you have your pushers, your lookouts, your bag guys. The closer you get to the center, the more important you are. The further away, the more expendable you become. I'm not telling you two anything you don't know." Her eyes held Harri's. "The students I talked to know Ella and Mitchell. One or both of them had to get the drug from someone in the Gamon universe. Who, that's the question mark. My money's on the fake P.D." She searched their faces. "You've found something."

"We'll admit Byrne hasn't been entirely truthful," Harri offered diplomatically. "We'll circle back."

"There's something else you're not saying," Raines said.

Harri's eyes held steady. "The same with you."

"Not showing your cards," Raines said, eyeing Harri, an understanding passing between them. "Inconvenient, but I get it."

Harri smiled. "I don't think there's a lot that gets by you."

Raines let a moment go. "You all have been handling Byrne with kid gloves. Hands off. Softball approach. It has to have occurred to you that maybe, just maybe, Ella Byrne is P.D.'s connection." She watched them both carefully. "Of course it has. That's why you've been slowboating it with her. Meanwhile, she's leading the two of you and the rest of your team around by the nose, giving you all the little-lost-lamb routine."

"I hope that's not the case," Harri said.

Cass stared at her with a look of pity. "I'm sure you do. You'd be wrong, though. We're dealing with kids here. Kids who are afraid of Mommy and Daddy catching wind of what they're really doing when they should be studying, again not telling either of you anything you don't already know. Self-preservation is a great motivator. The link between the Gamons and Byrne is what I'm looking for now. *Somebody* gets paid. Cora Gamon being dead is telling. Maybe she crossed somebody or maybe her clock just ran out, and the pills are to get you all spinning your wheels. There are a lot of buckets still to fill."

"We haven't been shielding Ella, if that's what you think," Vera offered defensively.

Cass pinched off half an inch of space between her thumb and index finger. "Um. Lil bit. I get why. She's a kid. She's one of your own's family. That makes her *your* family. I know how it works, and I'm not knocking you for it. But it's gotten in the way." She took a sip of tea. "Now that we know. Ella Byrne has secrets. And, depending on how deep into this she is, whether she's a faraway circle or one closer to the center, we have to worry about what the Gamons are thinking, if there are any Gamons left."

Harri had listened intently, half her mind on Matt and where he was, and on where Ella was now. Raines was right. The Gamons weren't about to let one kid lead cops to their door.

"It seems clear where *I* go from here," Cass said. "How about you two?"

Harri and Vera exchanged a look. Cass read it. "You handle your side of it; I handle mine. We stay out of each other's hair. Deal?"

"Fair enough," Harri said.

Cass put her mug down. "And no one has dibs on Ella Byrne."

For a moment, no one spoke. It appeared they'd come to an impasse.

"Concentric circles," Vera said, staring at Cass. "Are you always so sure of yourself?"

"Not always. Today? About this? Yes. You two done warming my seats?"

Harri's eyes flicked up to the door as a couple walked in and claimed a table. Vera's had done the same. Cass, feeling exposed, vulnerable, glowered at her visitors. "You're killing me here, you know that, right?"

Harri knew that asking Cass to back away from Ella was a lost cause, and so she didn't bother. Instead, she watched the PI take another sip of tea while she squinted, amused, at Vera, who glared back.

"Sabers at dawn, then, Li?" Cass eyeballed Vera. "You know what this is? It's your competitive nature. I get it."

"And *yours*," Vera said.

Cass shrugged. "What are we going to do, right? We are as God made us."

"What's your next move?" Vera asked, fairly certain she'd get no answer.

Cass looked down at her mug. "I'm going to drink my tea and eat my pancakes, then get back to work. What're *you* two going to do?"

Vera smiled. Cass smiled back. Cage fight averted. The cops stood up, zipped their jackets.

"Aww, see? I tell you everything, and you tell me nothing. How is that fair?"

"Everything?" Vera balked. "You've given us practically zip."

Cass pointed toward the ceiling. "Ah, the operative word here being *practically*."

"We'll talk to you later, Raines," Harri said as the two walked away, relinquishing the PI's booth.

Cass quickly changed sides so that she faced the door, settling in on the right side of the table at last. "Not if I see you coming first," she muttered as she signaled for Muna, getting her attention. "Pancakes, please."

Harri and Vera stood out on the sidewalk, a chilly breeze skittering over their faces, their backs to the diner windows.

"Damn it, she's starting to grow on me," Vera said.

Harri headed to the car, reaching in her pocket for the keys and her phone. "That's because you're the same person in different bodies."

"Oh, now you're just being mean," Vera said, following.

"The truth hurts."

Vera sighed. "Boy, does it ever."

Harri dialed Matt's number and again got no pickup. "Damn it."

Vera eased into the passenger seat. "Not good."

"No," Harri said, worried. "It isn't."

CHAPTER 34

Faith sat in a middle pew in Holy Land Church. Alone. Cora was dead. Killed like Big Daddy and their brothers. Lives of violence ended the same way. She stared at the altar with weary, sinful eyes, not feeling at home, not feeling worthy of being here. Sin. Old sin. New sin. "Or all have sinned," she whispered in the hallowed place, "and fall short of the glory of God."

What did she feel for Cora? There was only nothing where her feelings should be. Faith couldn't even muster pity for herself at not being able to feel sadness or empathy or grief. She'd run, but she hadn't run far enough. She'd changed, but the change had not reached her soul. What was she doing here? What was she playing at?

"Faith?"

Clevon. She squinted her eyes closed. How had he known she was here? Wasn't she even allowed a moment's solitude?

She opened her eyes, turned to face him as he stood at the church door. She got up from the pew and stepped into the aisle to wait for him, dutiful, ever dutiful. Or as dutiful as a Gamon could be. Gamons were bad seeds from evil roots that no amount of singing, praising, praying, or masking could make right.

"Clevon."

He walked toward her. "Everything all right? You sitting here in the dark like this. Is your spirit troubled?"

Is her spirit troubled? The man had no idea who he'd married. Not a clue. He knew nothing of her past, nothing about the evil root.

"Just taking a moment to be thankful," she said, forcing a smile. She decided then, in that moment, to test a truth, to see if it unburdened her. "I've had bad news from back home." She knew he had no idea where home was, she'd made sure of that. "A death."

His face flooded with sympathy, and he clasped her hands in his. "I am so sorry to hear that." He gathered her in his arms, and she nestled her face in his chest, breathing in his cologne, a mix of cedar, cloves, and leather. "Who?"

Faith pulled herself out of the embrace. "My sister."

She watched his face for a reaction, and found only an empathy she didn't feel worthy of. She'd never shared anything about her family, her past. They had both accepted each other where they'd met each other, agreeing to let what came before die away to make room for what was new.

He took her hand and led her back into the pew, and they sat side by side. Clevon Pope then bowed his head, closed his eyes, and prayed silently while Faith, suddenly unable to, watched and wished she were good enough to try. Cynically, she wondered what good prayers would do for Cora, whom she doubted would see heaven's gates.

"Thank you."

He opened his eyes. "I don't know about your people."

Faith sighed. One truth was enough, wasn't it? "Sometimes the people we leave aren't good ones."

He exhaled, then smiled. "Well, I'm a good listener, for whatever you're wanting to say. You know as well as I do that none of God's creatures is without fault, though we are called to strive for moral perfection."

His calming words echoed in the quiet church. The one he cherished, the one Faith had done the unimaginable for. She did not rush to respond. There were so many places she could start, but somehow, she couldn't bring herself to bare her soul, even here where confessions were encouraged.

And then she opened her mouth to speak, only to have the sound of the church door still her words and turn their heads to face it. Faith stood, Clevon too. In the doorway stood a tall, dark man in sunglasses and dressed all in midnight blue. The sight of him erased years and religion and replaced them with hate and vengefulness, all in one moment, in less time than it took to blink or swallow or draw in a breath. She knew Crow. Crow knew her. The Gamons weren't the only ones she'd run from. Standing beside her was a young woman who had her eyes. Faith stopped breathing. It was as if the world had jolted to a sudden stop, gravity suspended, sending her hurtling through the air as she fought to stay on her feet. Every sin, every mistake, every failing, faced her now in the form of a person, and she was unprepared for it. The impulse to run as she had before was overwhelming, but like before, she had nowhere to go. What did the girl know? How much had Cora told her? Twenty years, she thought, and it'd come to this. Faith felt for the Bible in her pocket, squeezed it for strength and courage and for the right thing to say to this child who was both hers and not hers.

"Can we help you?" Clevon asked, open, unknowing.

Faith moved to stand between him and the two at the door. They were there for her, not him. The woman held a backpack, much like the ones she'd accepted in the past. Faith knew what was inside. She knew there would be a Bible with an envelope tucked in it. A sacrilege. The bag. The one she'd told Cora she would no longer hold.

The woman, dark, petite, young, cold eyes, held the bag up, a smirk on her face. "I think you forgot something." She tossed the pack, and it landed halfway between them.

Faith stared at Crow. He'd been with the Gamons for years. He'd been Big Daddy's right arm and had been Cora's, though Faith knew he could never be trusted, now it appeared he would kill for . . . it hit Faith again like an angry punch. She had no idea what Cora had even named the baby. She'd had no right to ask, no need to know. She couldn't even admit to being curious about it. When she'd escaped, she'd left everything behind and severed every family tie.

But now with every second, every breath, Faith could feel herself melting away and Vanessa Gamon returning. She gritted her teeth and tried to hold on to who she was, but she couldn't grab enough of her as she disappeared. This was no reunion, no tender moment. Hallmark had no place here. This was business, Gamon business. Life and death. It was about power and dominance and retribution.

Inner turmoil. What did the Bible say about it? She couldn't think, couldn't remember now. Clevon would know, but Clevon had no place in all this. This was her horror to live.

"*I* say we're still in business." The young woman took a step forward. "*I'm* in charge." She smiled. "Last one standing, or at least the last one who counts."

"Not even in her grave yet, and you're doing this?"

She went on as though Faith hadn't spoken, too high on herself, it appeared, to hear a word she said. "I've got new stuff. Fresh blood. The chair. I'm going to own this town."

Faith stared at her, then at the bag sitting on Clevon's floor, in his church. Death. Darkness. *Here.* It was all her fault. She wanted to scream, fight, hide, all of it, all at once. She could feel the shift, the change, but couldn't stop it, just as she couldn't when she walked back into that house. Her eyes shifted to the man in blue. Loathing him.

It wasn't Faith that moved from the spot. It wasn't her who walked up to the bag, picked it up, and flung it back at the woman's feet. "She obviously meant very little to you."

An arrogant smile disappeared. "Turns out about as much as I meant to her . . . or *you.*"

Faith searched the young woman's eyes for something that resembled humanity, and could literally have wept when she found no trace of it. She had absolutely no right to lament the loss, but she did anyway. "Did you do it, or did *he*?" She avoided looking at Crow.

Patrice grinned. "It got done. All that matters. I run it now."

Faith watched her, then let a moment go. "Not *here.*"

The shock on the young woman's face slowly turned to feigned amusement. "*Here* and everywhere."

Faith could tell the girl's amusement wasn't real. It masked uncertainty, nervousness, fear. She wasn't ready for the seat. She wasn't nearly as hard as she believed herself to be or would need to be to live long term.

"What do they call you?" The woman didn't answer. "Your *name*, child."

Patrice drew herself up in defiance. "Name's Patrice *Gamon.*" The emphasis on the last name told Faith how much the girl valued it.

"Patrice." She let the name circle her brain for a moment, then let it go, having no claims on it either. "Well, Patrice *Gamon*, either you pick it up and take it, or I burn it. It's up to you."

Crow stood, unmoving, seemingly unbothered by what was playing out in front of him. Faith knew he was eyes and ears and bullets and nothing else.

Patrice ignored what she'd said. "You know Crow."

Faith's eyes slid again to the killer, then back, but she said nothing. Yes, she knew Crow. What she also knew was that Patrice didn't know Crow as well as she needed to.

Patrice flicked a chin toward Clevon. "Maybe *he* wants it." She glanced around the church. "Seeing as it paid for *this.*"

Faith was gone. Vanessa took another step forward and spoke slowly and clearly. "Take your garbage. Get out of this church. It would be a mistake for either of you to come back."

Patrice's face went glacial. Crow's expression never changed. She stared at the bag sitting in front of her. Faith knew Patrice couldn't afford to leave it. There were thousands of dollars' worth of death inside. She'd have to take it, but taking it would make her look weak, so Patrice had a decision to make—save face or break herself. Either way, it was not Faith's problem.

Patrice reached around and pulled a gun out of her waistband, then held it down by her side, making herself look weaker. "That's all you got to say to me? After all this time?"

Faith didn't flinch. She knew then the advantage was hers. Weak, frightened people brandished guns when they had nothing else to rely upon but the threat of violence. This was what Cora had created in her absence.

Behind her, Clevon gasped at the sight of the weapon. Faith could hear him praying under his breath. It was yet another sin to atone for. The gun didn't scare her. She was gifted her first one at the age of eight. Big Daddy had it custom-made with her initials in diamonds on the grip. That was what Gamons did.

"I've said all I need to," Faith said.

"Crow," Patrice barked. "Bring it to me."

Faith felt a pang of pity for the girl. Patrice didn't know who Crow was. She didn't know that he didn't fetch or carry; he didn't bow or blindly serve. Faith watched Crow not move a muscle. She then turned to stare at the girl who didn't realize she was playing a dangerous game while standing next to its most lethal player.

"If you have any hope of surviving," Faith said, "you should know who your people are and what they will and will not do for you." She looked down at the gun, at the unsure hand that held it. "And unless you intend to use that, you might want to put it away and stop defiling the Lord's house."

Patrice glared at her but held on to the gun. After hesitating for a moment, she meekly walked over to the bag and picked it up. "You owe me. I won't forget."

Faith's eyes held steady. What she owed Patrice, she could never repay, but it did neither of them any good destroying themselves over it. This was what she'd learned, if nothing else. "Go home, child."

Behind her, Clevon breathed heavily. It was the gun, the man in the suit, though Faith knew he had no idea what he was truly seeing. There would be questions she wouldn't know how to answer, and things that needed to be said that she wouldn't want to say. But right now, the threat was in front of her.

Patrice's hands tightened on the grip of the gun. She bit down onto her lower lip. Faith could see the indecision, the calculation. "Nobody calls me *child*."

Faith was looking at her sister's killers, she was sure of it. In the Gamon family, it was always a short journey from cradle to grave. For Gamons, blood meant everything, until it meant nothing.

"Look at me," Faith said, sadness, shame, punctuating every syllable she uttered. "What do you see?"

Patrice scoffed, looked disinterested, bored even. "I see a broke-down old woman actin' like she all *that*. Livin' up here with a broke-down old man in a broke-down old church."

Faith knew this bravado was as fake as the amusement had been but let a second go as a chilling stillness settled in deep. She remembered the disconnected feeling and knew where it led. Yet she took another step closer, unable to stop herself. "Look closer. Then believe what you see."

For a moment there was only silence, then suddenly Patrice shoved her gun in her waistband. "I'll be back."

"*Don't* come back," Faith said. "There's nothing for you here."

"Who's going to stop me?"

Faith stood firm. "Ask *him* who." She meant Crow.

Patrice turned to look, then headed for the door, Crow not yet. Faith and Crow locked eyes for a moment. They had history, some of which was about to walk out the door ahead of him.

"One word of advice," Faith said, turning Patrice back around. "Open your eyes. You don't have what you think you do. That was Cora's mistake."

"I got everything I need, no thanks to you."

Patrice snarled at her, then stormed out with her chin high. Crow took one last look at Faith and then followed without a word. She watched them go and kept her eyes on the door until it banged shut behind them and the church was quiet again.

Avoiding Clevon's eyes, she took a deep breath, then sat back down in the pew. She lowered her head, focusing on her sinful hands as they lay cold in her lap. They were Gamon hands. The hands of one who lied and ran in order to live. Hands with secrets. Hands that had to come clean now.

One truth could be two, she thought, her head hung low. Two could be many. Now. Or never.

"Clevon, I need to tell you who I am."

CHAPTER 35

Vera shook her head, slipped her cell phone back into her pocket. "Well, that's that. Grant can't help us. She's gotten through Mitchell, McClintock, and one of the poker guys. Same cause of death. Pretty simple. Bad drug. Specifics unknown for weeks yet. Oh, and look, a text from Al. He and Tony went all through the chemistry department at U of C. There's a Dr. Alex Liebner, there's a lab, the lab's got assistants. Ella is not, nor has she ever been, one of them. She's lied about *everything*. I'm so sick of this. What are we even *doing*?"

Harri drove. "We're doing what we always do."

Vera glanced over at her. "Right. And we're not making a dent. Next week, next case, more bodies."

Harri said nothing. Didn't have to, as far as she saw it. Every cop everywhere cycled through the same pessimistic thinking a hundred times a day, even the usually jovial Vera Li.

Harri slid Vera a side look. "You good?"

Vera stared out the window, looking glum. "I think it's the weather. It's been shit raining and miserable all week. And I *hate* this case. Dead kids. Dead mothers. Dead meat-packers. A baby without a mama. Most days I can deal with it. I go home, kiss my kid, put it behind me. Today?" She sighed. "I want to do something else today. Feed the animals at the zoo, work the candy counter at the movies, sell shoes at Nordstrom."

Harri didn't know what to say. She agreed with Vera but knew that neither of them was suited for much else but what they were doing. "Might be nice for a breather, but we're so deep into this now, we couldn't *not* do it if we tried. One minute you'd be selling shoes, the next you'd be chasing down a shoplifter. Lord knows what you'd do at the zoo."

Vera smiled, drew her hand to her chest. "I'm touched. You get me. You *really* get me."

"Everybody *gets* you. Nice dream, though."

Harri parked in front of the Byrne house, staring at the brown Ford sedan in the driveway. Matt's car. Her heart sank.

"Oh, c'mon. *Nooo*," Vera said. "What's he *doing* here?"

Harri scanned the neat block of single-family homes, reluctant to make a move. It was a nice house, which she'd observed before. A steady-looking home that matched all the others on the block. But something was definitely going on behind the Byrnes' doors that wasn't normal and wasn't right, and now it had become obvious.

"Try again," Vera said.

Harri held the phone, but didn't dial again. "No use. We go in, we do this, and let the chips fall."

"One more minute," Vera said. She stared out the window, inhaling, exhaling slowly. "Wow. You can literally eat off the sidewalks. And where are the potholes?"

Harri pulled a face. "There are none. Streets and Sans works harder up here."

Vera glowered at the even pavement. "That's just wrong. There's a pothole on my street right now deep enough to swallow a Mini Cooper."

"Call your alderman," Harri said.

Vera glared at the even street. "I've already called him everything I can think of."

They both sat in the car, staring at the house, as reticent as a death row inmate headed toward a lethal injection.

"If all *this* doesn't work," Harri mused, "what does?"

"I wish I knew," Vera said. "We could be wrong?"

Harri watched the street. "It doesn't feel like we're wrong. College kid pretty much financing her own life. Supposedly working at a lab job, only she isn't. Parents don't look too closely. They're just proud of the kid's industriousness. Then—"

Vera sighed. "Then there's a street buy, and now we're someplace neither one of us wants to be."

Harri glanced down at her phone. No text or missed calls from Matt. "We wrap this up. We close the loop. Then maybe we go sell shoes."

They got out, rang the bell, but no one answered.

Vera tilted her head up to a gloomy sky, her eyes clenched closed. "Can this end already, *please*?"

They turned when a car pulled into the driveway behind their car. It was Maggie Byrne, Ella's mother, who got out of a silver Audi sedan carrying a workout bag and a Starbucks cup. She didn't appear shocked to see them, but she did look worried about seeing Matt's car in her driveway.

"What's going on? What's happened? Where's Matt?" She looked at Harri and Vera. "Why are you two here?"

Vera held out a hand for a shake. "I don't believe we've met. I'm Detective Vera Li."

Byrne shook it, her eyes wide. "What's the problem?" She looked at Harri for the answers. "Has something new come in? Has there been an arrest?"

"We'd like to talk to Ella," Harri said. "No one answered when we rang."

"Why do you need to talk to Ella?" Harri could feel the woman's mom shield rise as she spoke. "I mean, she's given you all she has. Now all we want to do is put this behind us. Get her the help she needs and get her back on track, back in school."

"We want that too," Harri said, "but we have a few more questions."

Byrne stared at them for a time, but it didn't look like she believed them. Finally, she said, "She's inside. I left her asleep a couple of hours ago." She flicked a look at her brother's car. "Not sure why Matt would be here, unless something's happened." She brushed past them to put her key in the door. "She's spending a lot of time in her room lately. Avoiding us."

Vera noticed Byrne's gym bag and the yoga mat rolled up under her arm. "Just back from the gym?"

"It was either that or go crazy sitting around the house. The chaos is killing us. We've got an appointment for a therapist for Ella first thing Monday morning. We are determined to turn this around."

They stood behind Byrne, then heard the woman gasp. "The door's not locked." Byrne shoved the door in, then reeled around to face them. "The alarm's off. I know I turned it on when I left, and I know I locked the door." She moved to rush inside, but Harri pulled her back by the arm.

"Stay here," she said, unzipping her jacket. "We'll check."

"But what if—"

Vera moved in front of Byrne. "We've got it. Hang tight."

They moved in, closing the front door behind them, then stood listening to the house for any creaks or bumps or footsteps. The place was quiet, nothing seemed out of place.

"Ella," Harri called out. "It's Harriet."

Nothing came back. If there was someone else in the house who shouldn't be there, they didn't want to announce themselves as cops and elevate things. Harri and Vera exchanged a look, and wordlessly decided to split up, one upstairs, one downstairs.

Vera headed toward the back of the house. "Ella? You home? Matt?"

Harri mounted the stairs, slowly, gun at her side, placing her feet lightly on the risers to cut down on the creaks. "Ella? You here? Just stopped by to check on you."

As she passed the framed Byrne family photos mounted up and down the wall, her eyes landed on a smear of red maybe a couple of inches long. She looked closer. There was what looked like a partial fingerprint in the smear. Blood. The gun went up. Harri's cautious unease quickly shifted to all pistons firing. Not wanting to call out to Vera, she waited on the stairs, listening for human noises—footsteps, whispers, whimpers, but all she heard was the house breathing.

"Pssst."

Harri turned to find Vera on the bottom stair. Vera shook her head. The downstairs was clear. Harri cocked her head toward the smear and waited for Vera to make her way up to take a look.

"Shit," Vera whispered.

They counted to three, then took the rest of the stairs. At the top, Vera branched off, Harri went left, quietly, eyes focused. Two bathrooms. All clear. Master bedroom. Clear. A kid's bedroom, two twin beds inside. All clear. At the end of the hall on Vera's side, there was a small craft room, empty, save for the odds and ends of Maggie Byrne's hobbies—bolts of colorful yarn, knitting needles on the table, assorted paints and brushes, an easel leaned against a far wall. A small spare bedroom was empty too.

Harri and Vera met up where they'd parted at the top of the stairs, with just one room left to check. Ella's. They knew it was hers because there was a wooden sign hung from it with the girl's name painted in colorful letters. Harri turned the knob, checked that Vera was ready, and then they pushed inside into a sea of sunflower yellow and dainty pink.

A twin bed, empty, its frilly comforter disrupted and balled up. Posters of teen heartthrobs on the wall, fuzzy slippers and fuzzy pillows and frilly things. All a flipped-up mess. Every book had been pulled off the bookshelves and tossed, every drawer in the dressers had been pulled out and their contents scattered all over the floor, the closet had been gutted, clothes off hangers and strewn about. Someone had slashed the mattress and the pillows and thrown every shoe into the center of the room. But there was no Ella.

Harri checked deep into the closet, there was no one hiding inside. Vera stood at a closed door on the opposite side of the room, braced, and then pushed the door open.

"Harri."

Harri reeled, rushed over. They were in a small bathroom, toilet and sink only, and on the tile floor lay Detective Matt Kelley, his head a bloody mess, streaks of it congealed on the left side of his head.

Vera knelt down. "Matt?"

"Is he breathing?" Harri asked, already pulling her phone out of her pocket to dial for an ambulance. She watched as Vera checked for a pulse, as Harri's heart beat nearly out of her chest.

Vera felt a pulse, a strong one. "Yeah, he's alive. Looks like somebody whacked him over the head good, though." She searched for a towel and pulled one off a narrow towel rack, turning to soak it in cold water from the sink, then ring it out. "Do you see what they hit him with?"

Harri's eyes skimmed over the room but saw nothing that could have accounted for the wound. The only blood she could see was on Matt, which got her wondering about the smear on the stairs. She pedaled back a few steps just out of the bathroom to see if she'd missed anything, then made the call for backup and got an ambulance moving their way.

She watched as Vera placed the towel against Matt's head and tried to rouse him. "Matt?" Vera calmly offered as she gently shook him. That's when his eyes began to flutter, and he moved.

"There you go," Vera said. "Up and at 'em."

Grimacing, Matt slowly sat up, his eyes unfocused. When he struggled to stand, Vera stopped him. "Nope. Cop a squat. We've got help coming."

Harri watched as Matt came around. She noticed that his gun was still in his holster. Whoever hit him hadn't taken it, nor had they used it on him. Two good things.

Vera stood. "I think he'll be all right." She bent over in front of Matt's face and held up two fingers. "How many fingers am I holding up?"

He squinted, his face pale as buttermilk. "Two. I'm good," he croaked out. "Somebody conked me, that's all."

But Vera wasn't ready to declare him good yet. "Who's the president?"

Matt sneered up at her. "Are you *trying* to kill me?"

Vera stood, looked over at Harri. "He's good."

"We'll let the doctors decide that. Ambulance is coming."

Matt staggered to his feet. "I don't need a doctor."

Harri avoided looking at him. Now that the shock and immediacy of the situation had passed, now that she knew Matt was okay, a wave of anger came over her that she didn't want anyone to see. Her hands were clenched into fists, *again.* Matt had taken an unnecessary risk. He'd defied orders, and it could have gotten him killed. She and Vera could have just as easily found him dead on that bathroom floor. Thoughts. She had a ton of them, none suitable for conversation.

She turned to face the room, the mess, then proceeded to walk slowly through it again, her eyes sweeping across the floor. Where was Ella? Harri heard the ambulance pull up in front, its siren wailing. When she heard them enter the house and trundle up the stairs, she turned to face the two paramedics who rushed in with their gear in tow. She pointed at Matt.

"Seriously, I don't need the hospital," he said. "I'm fine. It's Ella I'm worried about."

There were a lot of things in the paramedics' bags, but it didn't appear that Matt needed most of it. After a brief assessment, the wound on his head was bandaged up with gauze and tape.

"You really should get an X-ray," one of the medics advised. "Make sure nothing's fractured."

Matt pulled a face. "I'm okay."

The second paramedic shook her head. "Seriously, this might look minor, but it'll be better to make sure nothing's going on internally. For safety's sake."

Harri watched the exchange. Matt was being obstinate, and she had a feeling there was something he wasn't saying.

"Give us a minute, please?" she asked the paramedics.

She waited until the pair stepped into the hallway and moved away from the door before she spoke again. She kept her voice low and steady.

"What happened?" Harri asked.

There was a moment's pause, which told her everything she suspected. "Not sure."

"Where's Ella?"

Matt didn't answer. Harri took a moment longer. It was for her, but also for Matt. "I don't think this is how you want this to go, is it?"

Their eyes locked. She could see he was lying. She could also see that he knew she knew it.

"Your lying to us is not going to help her. Your running interference for her is also not going to help her. The *truth* helps her."

"We saw the video from the Garden," Vera said. "That's why you came over here. You waited for Maggie to leave so you could talk to Ella alone, hoping she'd finally tell you the truth."

"When *you* found it," Harri said, "you should have told *us*. This could have been avoided. One more chance," Harri said. "Then we can't help you."

He palmed the towel, looked up at them. "Yeah, I saw the exchange. It wasn't Mitchell. I came to get the truth out of her. She denied everything. I asked her who she was selling for, and she lost it. She trashed the room, screaming, crying. I told her I had to bring her in, that she was going to have to answer for what she did. I was about to call Maggie to have her meet us at the district with a lawyer. The next thing I know, I'm out. You know the rest." His eyes pleaded with them. "She doesn't know what she's doing. She's all turned around."

"Where's your phone?" Vera asked.

Matt checked around his feet. "I must have dropped it."

Vera searched the floor. There weren't a lot of places for a phone to disappear to in a small bathroom. She didn't find it. "Not here."

Matt shut his eyes. "Then I've got no idea."

"You're wrong," Harri said. "She knows what she's doing. Where would she go?"

"I don't know," he said. "Her car was out front when I got here."

"It's gone now," Vera said.

"She's either running away," Harri said, "or running to somebody. The Gamons would be my guess."

"No way." Matt tried to stand, but halfway up thought better of it, and sat back down. "We don't know she's in with them. There's no way she'd run to drug dealers. She can't be in that deep. Look, I know I shouldn't have stepped out on this, but I . . . I had to try and help her." He looked at Harri, then Vera. Maybe it was understanding he was looking for.

"You get that right? You see why."

"Go to the hospital," Harri said.

"Look, Harri—"

She held up a hand to stop him from talking but couldn't follow up with words that wouldn't lead to bad feelings. All she could think about was what might have happened. How easily this could have ended up another way.

"Go get checked out," Vera said. "We'll take it from here."

"I screwed up," he admitted to Harri.

He had. And she had no idea what she could do to get him out of the jam. She called for the paramedics, and they came back in and led

Matt out. Then she returned to searching the floor. It's what she could do now instead of punching a wall.

Vera helped in the search. "He might not think he needs a doctor now, but he's going to need one when Griffin finds out about this."

Harri poked through the things on the floor with her foot. She walked over and peered into the girl's closet. There was nothing much to catch the eye, no designer things, no expensive handbags. Not in this house. "We need to find Ella. She could be in trouble."

Harri walked over to the window. The curtains had been slashed. Assuming that was Ella's doing, too, it was obvious the girl was out of control and maybe even a danger to herself.

Back at the floor with her foot, Harri's toe hit something solid in the pile. A cell phone in a yellow case. It had to be Ella's. She bent down and picked it up at almost the same time that Vera bent down across the room and picked up another cell phone.

"Matt's," Vera announced.

Harri swiped a thumb across the screen of the phone she held. It was password protected. "And this has got to be Ella's. Techs are going to have to break it, unless her parents have the code. Can't see her leaving without a phone. She must have access to another one."

"And she left the one we could easily track," Vera said.

Harri nodded. "And maybe took one we can't."

Vera brushed the back of her hand across her brow. "She is not making this easy for us."

"We put out alerts," Harri said. "We get units looking for her. We go back to her dorm. We put a flash on her car. And we hit the Gamons." She turned to Vera. "Did I miss anything?"

"You think we're going to just walk up to the Gamons and get anything out of them?"

"Of course not, that would be stupid. We touch base with Narcotics and see if they have any ideas. With Cora Gamon dead, there's a power shift. They should know something. Meanwhile, we do the next best thing."

"Faith Pope," Vera said.

Harri nodded. "A.k.a. Vanessa Gamon. Her sister's dead. Estranged, or not, she's got to have some insight."

"And Matt?" Vera asked.

"We can't worry about him right now."

Vera smiled. "But we will anyway."

CHAPTER 36

Harri squinted out the windshield at the small fenced-in park two blocks from Holy Land Church. She could see Faith Pope sitting alone on a bench, staring out into space, her hands in the pockets of her long black coat.

Harri sighed. "Another park."

Vera looked up from her phone, then back at it. "Yep. The city's got tons of them. This is from Al. Matt's fine. Not even a concussion. Hard head, I guess. His wife's taking him home. He and Tony are going over to meet with Gangs and Narcotics since it's looking like all roads lead to the Gamons' front door."

"Griffin?" Harri asked.

"Eerily quiet."

They both knew what that meant, neither of them needed to comment on it.

Harri turned off the car. "Right. Let's do this. Ella's out there trying to get herself killed."

Faith Pope didn't hear them walk up, her mind was somewhere else or on something else. Harri could tell by the thousand-yard stare. She wasn't dressed this time like she was a member of some strict religious sect. The black coat was over a simple gray sweater and black pants. Black ankle boots had replaced the dowdy flats from before. There also seemed to be a different feel to the woman, Harri noted. Steel, strength where before she'd gotten the impression that the opposite was true.

"Mrs. Pope," Harri said.

The woman looked up, took them in, seemingly unfazed.

"We were more than happy to meet you at your home, or the church. Where you'd have been more comfortable," Harri said as she glanced around the empty park, and then up at a gray spring sky.

Pope smiled slightly, but there wasn't an ounce of joy in it. "I've visited enough sin on my house. I won't bring any more." She folded her hands in her lap, inhaled, then let the breath slowly out. "I've been estranged from my family for years, decades. I had nothing to do with them until a year ago when we were close to losing the church. No bank would lend to us." She slid them a wry look. "Churches don't make money. I went to Cora. We made a deal. My soul for enough to keep Clevon's doors open."

"What sort of deal?" Vera asked.

"Gamons sell things," Faith said. "Drugs, people. In exchange for keeping the church afloat and out of arrears, I agreed to hold drug bags. There are Gamon drug bags hidden all over this city. I suspect the young woman you're looking for now, the one you mentioned on the phone, holds them, along with many more young people just like her."

"Who's she reporting to, now that Cora's dead?"

Pope scanned the half-barren trees, the empty playground a few yards away, the traffic whizzing down the street before she answered. "My daughter, Patrice Gamon." She watched them. "Don't look so hopeful, Detectives, she's a stranger to me, no one I know. I left her behind when she was two days old. I hadn't seen her since . . . until this morning when she showed up with a bag that I refused to accept."

"How'd she know about your deal if there was no contact?"

"Cora would have been happy to tell her. She would have been happy to tell her all kinds of things, whether or not they were true.

Patrice was Cora's protégé. Her leverage over me. She was grooming her to take over the family business, eventually." Pope's eyes hardened. "Patrice didn't want to wait."

"Patrice killed her?"

Pope pressed her lips tightly. This was obviously a question she was not going to answer. "If the girl you're looking for holds the bags and is now missing, you already know what could happen. If you're hoping that I have some pull with Patrice because we share blood, that's not the case. I can't waltz into the Gamon house any more than you can."

"How would someone like Ella Byrne even get hooked up in the Gamon business?" Vera asked.

Pope considered the question. "Money or habit. Or both? You've seen it all before."

"Patrice is P.D. Terry," Harri said.

"She's probably used a lot of names. Gamons are chameleons when we have to be. The girl would be a fool to go there. *You* would be a fool to go there. Your badges mean nothing to them. They might let you walk in, but there's no guarantee they'd let you walk out again. I don't know anything else that will help you." Pope stood, the meeting apparently over. "If the girl is smart, she'll be far from here right now. If she isn't . . ."

"We could go in," Vera said.

Faith frowned. "Not without someone dying."

Harri searched for a solution. "Then what would compel Patrice to come *out*?"

Pope looked at them. "Money."

"She wouldn't come out for *you*?"

"If it was to kill me, yes. Otherwise, no. That's how it is."

Harri didn't understand the nonfeeling. Even estranged, even complicated, the bond between mother and child was a powerful one that was not easily broken. But somehow Faith Pope had chosen to ignore all that. Maybe for her own sake, maybe for Patrice's. Harri wondered what price she had to pay.

"Money only?" she asked.

"Money mainly. She took the chair. She wants the respect and the fear that comes with it, but she's not smart enough or old enough or patient enough for the responsibility. She knows it. That's what makes her far more dangerous than Cora was. She has to prove otherwise. But she's not the one to worry about."

"Who is?" Vera asked.

"His name is Crow," Faith said. "Cora's right arm." Faith looked over the park, as if it grounded her and calmed her soul. "And Patrice's father. It was not a love match, it was rape. I don't think Patrice knows. That would be a secret Cora would hold on to to use when she needed it. Secrets were Cora's power, her ace in the hole. Our father was like that."

"I'm sorry," Harri said, meaning it.

Faith met her eyes. "What is there to say? I'm not the first. Unfortunately, I won't be the last."

"Edge," Harri said. "What can you tell us about that?"

Faith shook her head. "I held the bags. I didn't ask what was in them. I don't think it was Cora responsible. She was greedy, power hungry, brutal, if she had to be. I have a feeling Patrice is responsible for Edge. That may be why she had Cora killed. She wanted to move things in a new direction. I looked into her eyes. I made it a point to. She's what Cora made her. I don't think she'd lose any sleep over people dying."

"If we need you," Harri said, "would you be willing to help us?"

Pope thought about it. "I never want to go back. The sad part is I took it all with me. I couldn't understand why the church, Clevon, even God, couldn't lighten my spirit or make me feel clean. I finally figured it out. It's because of the secrets. Hiding who I was, what I was, what happened to me. All of it was still in there, blocking the good from getting in. I've given up every last secret now. Clevon knows everything, and he still accepts me. That's the blessing. I'm not Vanessa Gamon anymore. The good can finally get in." She stared at Harri. "There is no limit to how far I would go to keep that."

Harri knew all about things you buried, about how heavy those things could become. Seeing Pope trying to dig herself out from under in real time echoed the human struggle, and hers.

Harri pulled out her notepad. "Where's a good number we can reach you?" After she jotted it down, she reached into her pocket and got a business card, which she handed to Pope. "If you can think of anything else that might help, I'd appreciate a call. We'll be in touch."

Pope read the card, then slipped it into her pocket. "It's a choice, you know. To live in the light or suffer in darkness. I don't think Patrice will last long enough to find that out. Gamons usually don't."

"Luckily, you did," Vera said.

Pope frowned. "Gamons have never been lucky either."

CHAPTER 37

The team stood facing the bobblehead in Griffin's office, waiting for the boss to explain why she'd called them all in. Harri had an idea, and she was sure the others did too. They were all trained detectives, each smart enough to make the leap.

Harri fought the impulse to check her watch for how long they'd been standing here. It felt like forever, seeing as there were things they needed to get done. Ella was still unaccounted for. She hadn't gone back to campus; she hadn't gone home. There was no telling what state of mind she was in, and everybody hoped she was nowhere near the Gamons.

Finally, Griffin sat forward. "Matt."

It's what Harri expected. Matt hadn't come in after being released from the hospital. He'd made no contact with any of them, but it now appeared Griffin had reached out. A call from your boss after defying a direct order, an act of defiance that could have cost you your life, couldn't have been a pleasant conversation.

"He's taking a few days," Griffin said.

Al harrumphed. "Takin' 'em or you gave 'em to him?"

"How's that matter to you?" Griffin asked.

"Alls I'm sayin' is, you gotta give the guy some leeway on tryin' to help the kid. I mean, would you bring your own kid in without tryin' to help 'em first?"

"Yes," Griffin answered without missing a beat. "In cuffs. *My* cuffs. Why, you ask? Because I did not raise my kids to be lawbreakers, and I will not have lawbreakers living in my house. I will not feed or clothe lawbreakers, and I will not aid or abet them just because I brought them into the world and have their baby teeth in a tiny little box in a pretty little decorated chest with their name on it."

Tony smirked. "You're kidding, right?"

Griffin's eyes landed on his. "Does it look like I'm kidding?"

Tony stood confused, and a little scared. "You'd get the kid a lawyer, though, wouldn't you?"

Griffin blinked twice. "Sure."

Al grimaced. "How many kids you got there, Griffin?"

"Three. Each one of them model citizens. Anybody else got any more questions not relevant to this discussion?"

Vera raised her hand. "Excuse me. Can I ask about the bobblehead?"

Griffin's eyes swung back. "Are your affairs in order?"

Vera's lips pressed tightly together for a moment. "Never mind."

Griffin sat back. "As I said, Kelley will be taking a few days. He is *not* working this case. You are not to operate as if he *is* working this case. If you see Detective Matt Kelley working this case in any capacity, you are to tell him to knock it the hell off and then report it to me. If you are thinking that you will not do that, in an effort to show solidarity toward your coworker or friend, think again. If any of you are thinking about also going rogue believing that the ends justify the means, think again. If you think I don't know you're thinking this, I repeat, *think again*. Kelley is out until he's not out. Out means out. We have Narcotics and Gangs coming in to coordinate. We've got what, we've got who, now all we have to do is wrap this up. Go do that. Any questions?"

"Yeah, I got one," Al said. Fearless, it appeared, seeing as he was just a handful of years off retirement. "I hear what you're sayin'. Rules are rules. But I think we need to cut some slack here."

Griffin stood, squared her shoulders. "Kelley got his slack. He walked out of that house instead of having to be carried out in a body bag."

There was silence in the room.

"I've said what I needed to," Griffin said, retaking her seat. "Get out. Bring in whoever you need to. Don't take all year. There's more where this came from."

They all turned to leave, but Griffin wasn't done. "Foster. Li. Hang back."

Harri could almost hear Vera groan, though she knew her partner was smart enough not to emit a single sound in front of Griffin or the leprechaun. The two stood in front of the desk waiting for the next round.

"What's going on with Ella Byrne?" Griffin asked.

Harri filled her in, as much as they knew. Everything short of her current whereabouts. As she talked, Griffin lasered in, not missing a beat, as far as Harri could tell. When Harri finished, she turned to Vera to see if she wanted to add anything. Wisely, she did not.

"So, she could be long gone," Griffin said, "or in deep with the Gamons."

"That sums it up," Vera said.

"I didn't just fall off a turnip truck," Griffin said. "I get the delicacy here. We're either saving her or catching her."

"Yes," Harri said.

Griffin looked at them both. The silence in the room felt interminable. Harri was in no position to judge Matt. She knew Griffin knew all that.

Finally, Griffin said, "All right. If it's the latter, add assault on a police officer. Let's see if consequences can turn this kid around. That's all."

Harri and Vera walked out of the office. Griffin couldn't have been clearer. She left them not an inch of wiggle room where Matt was concerned. But that didn't change a thing, and Harri knew that Griffin knew it too. Vera turned to her partner, confusion on her face. "Seriously, what's up with the *bobblehead*?"

CHAPTER 38

Detective George Pease, a big guy with thinning red hair and a mustache and short beard to match, ran his hands across his face. It had been a long day.

"Knowing a thing," he said, "and proving a thing are two different things. We can't justify a warrant. Cora Gamon's body isn't even cold. No one in that house scares easy. They've been in the game too long."

"We got this thing nailed, though," Al said, leaning back, his shirtsleeves rolled up, his blazer hanging on the back of his chair. "We just need somebody to come out and fess up. That could be Ella, if we can find her."

"We have Faith Pope," Harri said, as she stood at the board, marker in hand, looking over the lines and circles, threads leading here and there. "The power play with the Gamons is likely what led to Cora Gamon's murder. She's willing to keep the lines of communication open. And we might be able to use her in some way to get close to Patrice."

"The way you explained it," Tony said, "the only way she's going to be any use to us is as bait. Is that what we're thinking?"

"No."

Vera and Harri said it together, definitively.

"We're not throwing her to the sharks to close our case," Harri said. "That'd be the same as killing her ourselves."

"We've got nothing on this Patrice Gamon," Pease said. "We've kept tabs on the Gamons for years. Big Daddy we had. The brothers. We knew there were two daughters, Cora and Vanessa. All of them bad to the bone. How the hell did they keep Vanessa's kid off our radar? And why bother? It's not like they're worried about their reputation or protecting her from the business. Hell, from what you've said, Cora was grooming her to join right in on all of it."

Harri slid him a look but held back the detail of Faith's assault. "We won't know that until we get Patrice or somebody else in our interview room."

Al chuckled sourly. "We got a fat chance of that happenin' the way we're goin'. No signs of Ella's car drivin' around. Neither Matt or the parents know where she is, as far as they're sayin', and God help him if he's keepin' mum on that. He'd be lucky to keep his CPD baseball cap let alone his badge if that's the case."

Pease walked up to the board, the sound of his hand scratching against his beard loud in the room. "We don't do all of this over in Narcotics. But you can put up there that nothing at that crime scene leads anywhere. The only thing connecting Cora Gamon's death to this is that blue bag in her hand. The car was clean, nobody left a print or DNA anywhere, except for the victim. The round pulled out of her doesn't match any weapon in our database. We got zero leads. Cora Gamon is just . . . gone, and unless somebody stands up and says 'Hey, I killed her,' we'll be spinning our wheels on that from now until the end of time."

Vera stood at her desk, her eyes on the board. "We need Ella. We need her safe, of course, but we also need her to get to Patrice. If the Gamons are putting Edge out there, no one inside their bubble is going to say anything." She looked around at the others in the room, her hands on her hips. "So, how're we going to do this?"

Harri put the marker down. "Ella gets us Patrice. Patrice gets us Cora's killer and the source of the ODs. If we get something that sticks, we get the head of the Gamon organization and bring it all down."

Pease didn't look convinced. "You say that like it's going to be easy or like it's going to make some big difference. One head topples, there's always a new one to take its place."

"Pope mentioned an enforcer named Crow," Harri said.

"Oh, we know Crow," Pease said. "His name always comes up when you're talking about the Gamons, but we can never catch him at whatever he's doing. Personally, I think he's the reason Cora lasted as long as she did. Mention his name on the streets and people literally piss their pants right in front of you. Good guy to have on your side. Wrong guy to know if he's on somebody else's."

"Maybe he helped Patrice clear the way?" Vera asked.

"Maybe. If she offered him a better deal. Word is Crow does what he wants. You take it or leave it."

Tony flicked his chin at the board. "And her being his kid, like Pope said, wouldn't he be even more motivated to protect her?"

"Hmm," Vera mused. "I don't think standard rules apply in this family."

Harri turned away from the board. There was nothing else she could glean from it, and she was tired of staring at it trying to make the scribbles make sense. "Then we have to find out which ones do." She turned to the team. "Can anyone think of anything else we can do tonight to get us somewhere? What stone haven't we turned over?"

"Nope," Al said. "Only other thing is to drive the streets all night looking for Ella Byrne, and we already got uniforms with their eyeballs peeled."

"I have a feeling Matt will be doing that too," Vera said, "despite what the bobblehead said."

•

“Guess that’s it,” Pease said. “We push on. Call us if you need us. The Gamons are slippery as hell, or at least Cora was. This Patrice is a new development, but I wouldn’t expect anything different. Gamons don’t spill. And, not to pop anybody’s balloon, but we don’t have a single witness who will say they saw or heard *anything* in that alley. We couldn’t even get anyone within three blocks to admit they heard the squad cars roll up. One call to 911. Unknown source.”

“Not so unknown,” Harri said. “The call was placed by a PI named Cassandra Raines.”

“She’s slippery too,” Vera offered.

“She followed up that call with a call to me,” Harri said. “She’s not working against us.”

“Then we’re back to where we were,” Pease said. “In need of a break.”

Harri sighed. “We need to keep going. What would surveillance on the Gamon place look like?” She turned to Pease, who shook his head.

“Suicide,” he said. “Either we go in hot and heavy, or there’s no point in putting targets on our backs.”

Al stood. “Look, we’re at a standstill right now. I say we take a couple hours, get some sleep, then hit it again in the morning. What good are we if we’re half keelin’ over and stressed out?”

Harri didn’t want to give it up. Ella was out there. Edge was out there. They needed to be out there.

Vera said, “Al’s right. Harri? It’s been a day.”

Harri looked around the room at the tired cops who were pushing themselves just as much as she was. “We try again tomorrow.”

CHAPTER 39

Harri lay on her bed in the dark, crying into her pillow, missing all she'd lost. When the tears stopped, when she was close to drifting off, she rolled over, startled to see two figures standing against the wall.

She gasped, reached under her mattress for her service weapon, prepared to defend herself, only there was something about the figures that felt warm, familiar. She peered into the dark, her chest exploding.

"Who's there?"

"It's okay, Mom," Reg said. "It's us."

Us? Her son stepped forward, his face, his beautiful face, came into full view. Coming with him was her partner and friend, Glynnis Thompson, G.

Harri gasped, dropped the gun, wanting it out of her hands, and her eyes flooding with tears. "Oh my God. Oh my God."

Reg smiled, his big brown eyes twinkling. "Hi, Mama."

His voice was clear and soothing and broke her heart anew. She thought she'd never hear that voice again, never see her baby's face. Harri kept her eyes open. She didn't want to miss a single second.

"You look like crap on a stick," G said, then laughed, the trill of it familiar, light, like she remembered it. "Get to a spa, girl."

Harri scrambled out of bed, reached toward the two of them, but the more she reached, the farther away they got. She felt like she was advancing toward them, but she never seemed to close the distance. It was frustrating, it made her angry. She wanted to hold her son. She wanted to wrap her arms around her baby and never let go again. Why couldn't she? Why couldn't she move?

"Why can't I reach you?" she yelled out, her heart desperate and aching for the feel of her son. Gone six years. So many days. The last time she'd seen him he was lying in a casket that she had prayed was big enough for the both of them. "Reg! Come to me."

He shook his head. "Can't, Mom. But it's okay. You don't have to be so sad anymore, okay? Look, I'm good." He glanced around the empty room, the one she hadn't bothered to fix up or make homey. The room she just slept in, but didn't live in. "Ick. I don't like this house." His eyes held hers, worry in them. "You shouldn't be here, Mama. This place is . . ."

"It's a dump," G said. "What're you doing here? You couldn't even buy a chair, for crap's sake?"

"I'm . . ." Harri started, but could find no easy explanation. "I needed to be alone."

Glynnis looked skeptical. "You're hiding. This place sucks."

"I'm not . . . hiding, I'm . . ."

"Yeah, you are, Mom. I don't want you to do that. That's what I came to tell you. I'm okay. Now you have to be okay, too, all right?"

Harri shook her head at the impossibility of the ask. "I'll never be okay, Reg. Never."

"But you can be better," he said. "You can have more than this, right?"

G nodded. "He's saying, you don't have to lie down in a grave before it's your time to lie down in a grave."

Harri reached again, tried to get closer again. She just wanted to touch him, hold his face in her hands, hold him. This was torture. Her efforts to move futile. She could sense time slipping away. She knew Reg and G wouldn't stay long.

"I messed up," she said. "I wasn't there. I should have been. I . . . I could have done something."

"You didn't do anything wrong, Mom," Reg said calmly. "Things just happen. It doesn't matter anymore because I'm okay. I'm not sad. I'm not alone."

"I got him, H," Glynnis said. "He's with me." She gave Harri a playful wink. "He's my kid now. And thanks for what you did for me and my family, my kids. I knew you'd figure it all out. I knew you'd move Heaven and earth. Get it? Heaven and earth." G chuckled. "I'm here all eternity, partner." Then G turned serious. Harri knew the look. "Live, Harri. You only get one shot at it. Don't squander it living here, under a rock, alone. We'll see you when you get here. Not too soon, though. Promise?"

Harri could feel them move farther from her and panicked. "Wait. Not yet." She reached for them again.

"See you, Mom," Reg said, waving goodbye. He was happy, just like he always had been. His spirit felt light and serene. She could see the calmness in him.

Harri shook her head, the lump in her throat too massive, too heavy to ignore. "Don't, Reg. Stay."

Reg and G began to lose shape, to fade from the room. She was losing them again. "Please. No, wait. Don't go. Reg, G, wait. Stay just a little longer." They were merely shadows now, growing smaller. "Please, come back."

They were gone.

Harri startled awake and sat up in her bed, her T-shirt drenched in sweat, her mind grabbing for fading images she wanted more than anything to see again. Gasping for air, her heart ached, she looked around the darkened bedroom, realizing in a crushing instant that it had all been a dream. Reg and G hadn't really been there. It was all her brain playing tricks, her soul screaming out for comfort.

Harri tore herself from the bed, her body trembling with anger, with hurt, feeling as though she had lost Reg and G all over again. Fresh pain, fresh loss. She wanted to yell; she wanted to pummel something until she was too weak to move. Turning around in a slow circle, scanning the emptiness of where she was, she remembered the message. That the house was crap. That she was hiding here. That she needed to live her life. That her son was fine, happy, and cared for. That G had her back.

On her wrist Harri felt the watch, the one she rarely took off. It had been Reg's. She'd plucked it out of the bag of his personal effects when they'd been released to her, and she had placed the watch on her wrist, finding the steady sweep of its second hand comforting, reassuring. Reg's heart had stopped, but his watch still kept the time. Tick, tick, tick.

Standing in her bedroom, shaken, Harri listening to . . . nothing. This house didn't breathe. There was no settling, no bumps, no creaks. How could it when it was a dead place? That's what Reg and G had come to tell her. That she was living in a dead place, and that if she stayed much longer, she would be as dead as the house.

A strange peace came over her. Her baby was okay. He wasn't hurting. He wasn't cold and dead in a deep hole. She didn't have to beat herself up anymore because she couldn't protect him. G was there. G would protect her son, and Harri would protect G's kids. It was a strange peace, an instant release. A shift. More magical thinking?

She'd wanted more time. She would have given anything for just one more hug. Now it felt like maybe she'd gotten just what she'd needed.

"You're okay, Reg," she muttered to the dark. "Thank you, G."

She sat back down on the bed, lowered her head in her hands. "They're okay." She squeezed her eyes shut, releasing fear. *"They're okay."* And she believed it.

Almost as quickly as a finger snap, the house felt oppressive, tight, like a vise around her ribs. She scanned the room, taking in all the nothing she'd been settling for, seeing it as if for the first time, and Harri knew she needed to get out. Bolting out of bed, she pulled herself up straight, anxious suddenly, the feeling of being entrapped strong and frightening. It was as if she could actually hear a clock ticking down, as if she'd just woken up from a six-year sleep. What had she done? What was she doing? *Get out. Go.*

CHAPTER 40

Goodlow Dixon saw the black car drive up in front of his place, and his blood ran cold. How had he gotten himself into this? Then he remembered. Money. He'd needed the money. He had a chemistry degree, no job, and a wife with a baby on the way, and entry level at the day job wasn't cutting it. That's when his friend Ulysses from the neighborhood recommended him to the Gamons. That was two years ago. This was now. Cora Gamon was dead, and Patrice Gamon was in charge. The minute he'd heard that Cora had been shot, he knew who'd done it. How low did you have to be, he thought, to ice a member of your own family? He'd known it before, but he really knew it now. Patrice was a psychopath.

Goody stepped away from the window and tried to compose himself before his visitors reached the front door.

"Cool. Keep it cool," he whispered under his breath. "Just give them what they paid for. Don't ask questions." He wrung his hands out, bounced on the balls of his feet, like a boxer getting ready for the bell. "Keep it business. Keep it tight. Keep it moving. Stay alive."

The bell rang. Goody waited a moment and then walked over and opened the door to find Patrice Gamon and Crow standing there. The sight of Crow almost gave him a heart attack. Crow was like a stroke, a silent killer. The final Gamon was too young for the job. She was at least two decades younger than he was, and yet there she stood in a black boss suit at midnight on a Wednesday, flanked by a big quiet man who'd likely kill his own mother and then sit down and eat the meal she'd cooked for him. They made a pair, Goody thought, a deadly pair.

He knew why they were here, and he had what they wanted, but he also wanted out and he had no idea how to have that conversation and leave it breathing. It was true with things like this, people like this, that you could get in with little effort, but it was almost impossible to get out.

His son, Omarr, was two now. His crisis was over. And he wanted out. He wanted away from the dope and him feeling dirty about cooking it up. But Patrice and Crow were not people you crossed, not people you threw over.

"Where is it?" Patrice asked as she stood in the room, a distasteful grimace on her face, as though she were smelling something offensive. "It's late."

His operation was in the basement, a veritable home-based lab that churned out temptation to those who could not withstand it. Kids. The broken and disheartened looking for a moment's peace. Goody was killing them. He'd been killing, only their deaths hadn't made the six o'clock news.

Goody had the bag that held the small second batch he'd been ordered to produce. He grabbed it from the table, handed it to Crow, and waited while he opened it, peered inside, and nodded to Patrice that it was all there. From her bag, Patrice pulled a thick envelope with Goody's blood money in it.

Those at the top didn't normally make the exchange themselves, Goody knew, but this Gamon was different. She was harder, coarser, than Cora. She was an impulsive thug.

"This better be good stuff," Patrice said, "or I'll be on your ass, you know I will."

"I told you; you rushed me. I wasn't sure of the mix. But you just kept pushing. That's on you, not me. Take the stuff. It's the best I can do."

Patrice stared at him, her beady little eyes as unreadable as a shark's. "Why are you looking so nervous? All jumpy?"

"It's late," Goody said, having had enough. "I've done enough."

Patrice handed the bag to Crow. "We're going to try this again. Maybe Cora put up with BS. I don't."

Goody gripped the envelope, knowing for sure he couldn't do this anymore. "We need to talk, actually. I got a job. More money. Legit. Omarr." He didn't mention the job or where it was, and that he'd already bought tickets to California. There wasn't even a job waiting, that was a lie, but he wanted out of this, away from *her*. He ran his tongue over dry lips, fighting off the urge to pee. "Maybe I can help you find a replacement? Somebody who needs the money." He got zero reaction from the two in front of him. "If you need me to do that. Job starts in a month. I have to pack, get my stuff together—"

Patrice held a hand up to stop Goody from talking. "You work for us. You work *here*. There's enough in that envelope to keep you happy." She took a step forward. "You unhappy, Goody?"

He swallowed hard. "It's just that it's a steady job with a lot of opportunity. Benefits." He added that part knowing that the only benefit that mattered to him was walking away without a bullet to the back of his head. "I can pass along all my notes and everything to the new person. You won't lose anything."

Patrice took him in, her shark eyes probing. "No. It's not a good time to make any changes. The new and improved Edge is barely off the ground. My business comes first."

Goody found strength from somewhere. He really wanted to wash himself clean of this, and this was his only chance. "The thing is—"

Patrice stopped him with a look. "Crow."

It was all she said. Just the one word. Goody looked at Crow, but there was no reaction from him. The pack was still in his hands. The threat was implicit. Goody knew what could come next.

He swallowed hard. “I hear you. Your business first.”

Patrice grinned, a victory. “I knew you’d get it. Get back to work, Goody. I’ll need double next time.”

Goody’s eyes widened. “*Double?* But—”

Patrice’s grin disappeared. “You got a problem with that, Goody? Get your people back on this. Full time. Overtime.”

He hesitated before nodding. “No problem. Full time.”

That was it. In and out. Goody watched them go from the front window and stayed glued there until the black car pulled away from the curb and disappeared down the street.

“Full time,” he muttered. “That’s it. I’m *done*.”

CHAPTER 41

The Gamon greystone in Bronzeville stood quiet in the early morning. Nothing stirred on the street. Not even the Gamon sentries were out yet. Harri noticed that in every house and apartment building on the block, the curtains were closed, blinds down, and doors were locked and fortified with either bars or storm doors. She had a facetious thought, though it wasn't quite true, that there were more locks within a hundred-yard radius than blades of grass. She worried about the children, the vulnerable, those who couldn't fend for themselves, having to live life fearful of wayward bullets, blue bags, and menace every hour of every day. What CPD could do, what she could do, wasn't much when the threat was on every corner, and lost people, angry people, sick people, didn't care who they killed or when.

She turned to Pease, who'd gotten them all here to take a look. "When'd you set this up?"

"Overnight. This block's never really off our radar," he said. "It's mecca, actually, for all that's wrong with this neighborhood. After our meet last night, I remembered we set up here a couple years ago. Good spot. Right across the street with a clear view of the Gamons' front door. It's a lot safer here than in a car out in the open. We haven't seen Byrne yet, but I figured your team would want to share the watch. It's quiet now, most of their business takes place at night, but it'll start hopping soon. They've got money to make."

"And they have no idea you're watching from over here?" Vera asked, glancing around the room at the handful of drug cops milling around in tactical vests.

"We're keeping it small. Just us here, a couple cars cruising close. The rest on standby ready to roll, if we need them. They've got watchers everywhere, not just out in front, so we keep it mobile, loose, but ready to initiate. We have to outsmart the fish to catch the fish. If they knew we were here, they'd have shot us up or burned us out. My thinking? After Cora, things are up in the air. They're not on their game. That works for us."

Harri turned to look around the front room of the small bungalow. Besides three Narcotics guys with Pease, she, Vera, Tony, and Al were there peeking behind curtains at a drug house across the street, gambling on a break that might not come. Her eyes landed on the owner of the house, an elderly man named Mr. Hosea Moore, who seemed to be having the time of his life. Pease had introduced them. Moore was ninety-three years old, but didn't look it, and was already dressed for the day at 6:00 a.m. in old man pants held up by actual suspenders, a red flannel shirt with eyeglasses tucked in the breast pocket, with a comfortable pair of "house shoes" on his swollen feet. Strong grandpa vibe, Harri noted with a smile. Moore had opened his home to them, taking a risk that he maybe should not have, Harri thought. Though safe now surrounded by police, what would happen to the old man when they left? She hoped Pease and his team knew what they were exposing the old man to.

Al sat on the couch, watching the watchers. "Ever consider pullin' up stakes, Mr. Moore? Somewhere quieter? Not sure I'd want to see all that outside my front window day in, day out."

"*Me* move? I was here first. Me and Olive moved into this place in 1971. This house used to belong to Olive's grandmother, Mrs. Ida Jean Simpson. When Miss Ida died, the house came to us, and we were happy to have it. Married couple like we were, we couldn't afford to move into a place like this, not at that time. Us with kids, and all. We raised four children here. Two sons, two daughters. All grown now with kids of their own. Me and Olive were doing all right, till she died, oh, going on thirty years now. Cancer." He pointed his cane toward the window. "I was here even before Big Daddy moved over there. They used to have all kinds of chippies running in and out of that place."

"Chippies?" Vera said.

Al filled her in. "Hookers."

"Whatever you call them," Moore said. "Used to make Olive so mad. There's none of that over there now. Oh, Cora and them was still in the business, but the girls weren't working out of the house anymore."

Tony stood next to Moore's chair, his hands in his pockets. "That must have been something to see. Nobody called the police? Have them raided?"

Moore chuckled. "Oh, we saw plenty of police over there. Politicians too. Whole lot of men drivin' in from the suburbs on a Friday, Saturday night. Raids, though?" He shook his head. "Not a one. It's like you folk don't want to see what's right in front of your faces. My neighbor down the street got his windows shot out not too long ago. He called 911, police came lights blazin'. Next day, the Gamons burned him out. He didn't get killed, thank Jesus, but he lost his home. Had to move in with his daughter who lives in Ohio."

"Knowing that, you're still helping us, why?" Vera asked.

Moore looked at her. "Because it's the right thing to do. I'm an old man, young lady. At this point in my life, I don't fear nothin', not even the grave."

Harri smiled. The old man reminded her of her own grandfathers, who'd died decades ago. Honest men, principled men, men who did the right thing when it was called for. "You must know a lot about that house," she said.

Moore's chin lifted with pride. "Sure do. Everybody up and down this block could tell you the stories. All kinds of things go on over there.

"That house used to belong to a bootlegger who they say worked for Al Capone. It's got all kinds of hiding spots, secret doors leading every which way, even a tunnel that runs underground, they say. I know a couple of houses on that side where the tunnel ends up. Those neighbors passed some years ago, so I don't know if the new folks know that in their basements, they got a piece of history just sitting there. For sure, the Gamons know it. And I'd bet you, they been keeping them tunnels open and ready to use when they need 'em. Might be the reason they so hard for y'all to catch. They like little rats scurrying around in the dirt, going this way and that. Matter of fact, this whole block back in the twenties and early thirties had nothing *but* killers and dirty politicians, bathtub gin and South Side mobsters, all working for Capone or in his pocket. You get in there; you're going to need a map."

"Do you have a tunnel in *your* basement?" Vera asked.

Moore shook his head. "The tunnel don't run on this side of the street for some reason, at least not as far as I know. And I got nobody to ask really, seeing as all the old folk have gone to glory and we got young people who don't know nothing from nothing. Could be the tunnel runs all the way to city hall. I wouldn't put it past them."

Moore pointed his cane at the window again. "Three houses down. The Carters? The tunnel goes that far, I know. I remember when old Enoch Carter bolted that door shut on his end. He had a heart attack, they say, soon after. Then that way, going toward the lake, three doors down, the Howards? They got a door too. Taylor Howard died, oh about fifteen years ago. Had a stroke in his bathtub is what they said, and he drowned."

Al's eyes narrowed. "You're kiddin'."

Moore shook his head. "Wish I was, but I ain't. Seemed mighty convenient to me, too, but I got no way of proving otherwise. Folks there now probably don't know what they got under them. For sure, one of them Gamon secret doors lead right down there, if the police ever do get a notion to bust their way in."

"That's some interesting stuff," Tony said. "Tunnels, bootleggers."

"But you haven't seen a young woman in her twenties go in or out recently?" Harri asked, getting back to their present situation. "White. Thin. Young."

"Nope. Don't get a lot of young white folk. Could have missed her, though. I don't sit at this window all day long. I play cards down at the senior center on Tuesdays and Thursdays. Then I got my doctor's appointments and such. My granddaughter drives me to them." He pointed at a flat-screen television set in the corner. "I got that for Christmas, but I hardly play it. Everything's too loud and too dumb."

"But you still keep watch on the Gamon place?" Vera asked.

He brightened. "I figure somebody ought to be paying attention."

Al's brows lifted. "You ain't scared they're goin' to catch you lookin' and shoot your place up?"

Moore laughed. "Nobody pays attention to old folk, young man. We're doggone invisible. Besides, I got a little sumthin' sumthin' for 'em, if they come looking for it. I didn't just fall out the pumpkin patch. You familiar with a little thing called the Korean War?"

Al sat up, enthralled now, practically salivating with interest. "Are you kiddin'?"

"I was there," Moore said. "Heard of the Tuskegee Airmen?"

Now Moore had everyone's attention, except that of Pease, who monitored the street through a pair of high-powered binoculars and had likely heard the old man's stories before.

"They were there too. Air support. I wasn't one of them, but me and everybody else was happy to see their bombers flying over us. So, I ain't scared of no droopy-pants thugs, is what I'm saying."

"Let's hope it doesn't come to that," Harri said, turning back to the window and the street beyond it. As the minutes passed, the street slowly filled up with watchful-eyed Gamon bangers who took their positions in front of the house, staring daggers at every car that drove down the street. They were armed. There was no reason why they wouldn't be, Harri thought as she watched the thug ballet play out in front of her eyes. It began to rain again, at first lightly, a thin, misty sprinkling that soon gave way to a veritable deluge. Still, the bangers held their spots, duty bound to protect the Gamon house and the dealers inside. After a couple of hours of tedium watching the guards move around in the rain, a tan Chevy Impala rolled to a stop in front of the Gamon house and two surly-looking Black men got out. One then reached into the back seat, grabbed up a white girl, and pulled her from the vehicle. Harri gasped. It was Ella.

"No, no, no," she muttered, turning to look over at Pease as he put down his binoculars and picked up a camera to take photos of the girl getting out of the car. Harri turned to the others. "It's Ella."

"Damn it," Al said. "That ain't good."

Harri turned back to the window, her eyes glued to Ella's face, seeing the fear in it, as well as a large, fresh bruise on her right cheek. "They're holding her," she said. "She's not here willingly."

"What you think they want with her?" Moore asked from his chair.

Vera and Harri exchanged a look of dread. "She's got something they want," Vera said.

Pease kept snapping, his lens capturing every step the thugs and Ella made up the walk, up the front steps to the house, and until the door opened and the thugs dragged the girl inside.

Pease put the camera down. "She's in trouble. The clock just started ticking." He slid his phone out of his pocket. "Let's plan it out. We got to move quickly. Or the girl's good as dead."

Harri called Griffin, and she and the team hovered around her cell phone on speaker as she relayed developments. Their viewing party had quickly escalated to a police action, and they needed authorization to proceed in conjunction with Narcotics, or else they were off book and on the hook, just like Matt. Pease already had his team getting in place. Time was of the essence.

"You're sure it's her?" Griffin asked, ever cautious.

"Positive ID," Harri shot back. "We go or don't go." There was a moment's silence on the other end of the line as she sweated, knowing everyone else was sweating too. Unable to take the silence a second longer, Harri said, more forcefully, "We have to *move*."

"Go," Griffin snapped. "If any of you come back dead, I swear to *God*, I'll kill you."

Griffin hung up. Everyone in the room looked at each other. Unpacking what Griffin had just threatened them with wasn't an option. It was go time.

They sketched out their plan on the back of a Walgreens prescription fact sheet Moore had sitting on his dining room table. Pease and his team, Harri and hers, hovering over the paper while Pease drew *X*'s and *O*'s and arrows that represented cops and access points.

"This is jumping off way too quick," Tony said. "We're not going to take time to troubleshoot the variables here? No telling what they've got stockpiled in there."

"Exigent circumstances," Pease said curtly, his eyes on Tony. "Imminent danger." He turned to the others. "We ram the front and back. Simultaneously. Shock and awe. That's us. That leaves the tunnel." He looked at Harri. "That's you guys. If Moore's got it right, you should be able to split up and block it from both ends."

"I got it right," Moore called from the chair. "Nothing wrong with my mind, or my memory, thank you very much."

"Grab as many POs as you need. We'll grab some too," Pease continued, taking no time to entertain the old man. "Suit up. We move in five. Heads in the game."

Harri had parked their unmarked car in Moore's unused garage, and she and Vera hustled to it now to grab their vests, flashlights, and cuffs out of the trunk. They'd decided. Al and Tony would go east; they would take west. If it came to a tunnel escape, they'd have Ella's captors hemmed in. Harri slid the Kevlar vest over her head, her mind on the problem. Tunnel. Confined space. Numerous opportunities to get it wrong. Pease and his team would have it easier. Front and back. Ram. Shock and awe. But if the rats scurried and ran for the tunnels, that meant them. She secured the Velcro straps tightly, flattening her chest, the armor adding six pounds to what her body usually carried around. She watched as Vera, Al, and Tony did the same. No one said anything, but Harri was sure they were all thinking about Ella and how they were going to get her out of the Gamon house safely.

"Kidnapping. Battery." Tony ticked the charges off. "Unlawful restraint."

"Yeah," Al shot back. "Drug house. Shoot-out. Bodies everywhere."

Vera adjusted her vest with harsh tugs on the straps. "You would think they'd design one of these things to be comfortable for women, wouldn't you? Granted, I don't have much upstairs, but still, it's like wearing waffle iron plates on your chest."

"Wrong time," Harri said, knowing Vera joked to deal with tension.

"Oh, don't I know it," Vera shot back. "We can't find Ella anywhere, but *somehow* the Gamons put hands on her? How does that happen?"

"If they'd wanted to kill her," Harri reasoned, "she'd be dead already. They need her for something. That gives us time."

"The place is locked up tighter than tight," Tony said. "This is going to take some shit. I think we need a lot more than a sketch on the back of a piece of paper."

"In a perfect world," Harri said, "you'd be right, but we're never going to get that."

Al shook his head. "None of this feels right."

They were silent for a time, all of them no doubt feeling the same, but dismissing it.

Al suited up, noticing everyone else was too.

Harri said, "You all heard the boss. Nobody comes back dead."

CHAPTER 42

Patrice walked around the chair Ella Byrnes sat trembling in, watching the young woman as Crow stood by.

There was no one in the office but the three of them. This was a private conversation. About loyalty and money. Patrice fought to command the space, deepening her voice, keeping her face hard, mimicking Cora so that her youth and inexperience didn't show. She was sure she fooled the girl, but she knew she wasn't fooling Crow. It galled her that she didn't appear to impress him. She would have to assert herself more, then talk to Crow about showing her some respect.

"Where's my product," Patrice asked again. "I gave you the bag. You were supposed to sell what was inside to your egghead friends." She leaned over, her face in Ella's. "Instead, you and your *boyfriend* decided to have a little party by the lake. All the bags. All the spots. *You're* the one that didn't bring my money back. You OD'd instead." She straightened. "Greedy rich girl. Brought all this attention down on *my* head. Where's my money? Where's my *bag*? Where's my pills?"

Ella's face was flushed, her hair wet with sweat. She squeezed her eyes shut while she trembled in fear. "I told you; I don't have it. I'm *sorry*. After . . . after what happened, I got rid of them. I killed my *friend*. I couldn't take the risk of killing anyone else. Can't you see that?"

"What do you mean, 'got rid of them'?"

Ella didn't want to say. She hesitated. "I flushed the pills. I had to. I couldn't have them near me. What if my parents found out?"

Patrice stopped, looked over at Crow. "This white girl flushed my product . . . so her *parents* wouldn't find out. You hear that, Crow?"

Ella whimpered. "Did you want me to take the bag to the *police*? I *protected* you. I lied to everyone about everything so they wouldn't find out."

"*You* protected *me*?" Patrice walked over to the big desk and sat behind it, her hands folded in her lap, as she'd seen Cora do countless times. "You protected *yourself*. There was $20,000 worth of pills in that bag. What do you have that's worth that much to me?"

"I just want to go home," Ella pleaded. "I'm sorry. I just want to go *home*."

Patrice smiled. "You *are* home. It's either dollars or you work it off in trade. I'll leave it up to you what you want to do."

The room fell silent, even Ella's crying stopped. Patrice was learning quickly, though her methods were far harsher than Cora's had been.

"Well?" she asked, knowing she'd won, loving the power in that, determined to enjoy every second of it. "What did you decide? You're either going to sell a lot or make a lot . . . for me."

Ella fixed terrified eyes on the young woman behind the desk. "I won't do either thing. Let me go or . . ."

Patrice leaned forward, curious, amused. "Or what?"

Ella didn't answer.

"Right," Patrice said. "What I thought. I decided already anyway. You're going to do both." Ella began to weep. Patrice laughed. "It's going to take a lot more than that, white girl."

Suddenly Patrice heard the sound of feet running, loud voices beyond her door. Something was happening. She looked over at Crow for confirmation. A nod of the head told her he'd heard it too. There was a frantic rap at the door. "Five-O! Five-O!" one of the guards outside yelled. "They comin' in." The alert was followed by the booming sound of a battering ram against the front door and back doors.

Patrice shot up from the desk as Crow rushed to the door and opened it to get the news. The thug outside told it in a hurry, no time to waste. "Cops all over the place. Y'all better get out of here."

Patrice grabbed her gun out of the top drawer, raced around the desk, and yanked Ella to her feet, gripping her arm so tightly her knuckles blanched. "What's the play, Crow?"

Crow took point, leading them out of the office toward the back of the house. "Tunnel's this way," he barked.

"*What* tunnel?" Patrice snapped. Cora had never said anything about a tunnel. That bitch, she thought, her brain exploding in red-hot heat, that backstabbing *bitch*.

Crow ignored her question. "Keep moving. Quick."

As they ran, Ella tried pulling away from Patrice, but her hold was too tight, her fingers literally biting into her skin like talons. "Let me go, *please*."

"Not a chance. I *own* you."

The three of them hit a hidden panel Patrice had never noticed before just as the front and back doors burst open and shouting started, rough voices barking commands to disarm and get down on the ground. "*Down, down, down*," the cops shouted. The panel was a door that led into an old wooden stairwell. On the other side, hidden from the raid, Patrice put her gun to Ella's head.

"One word," she warned. "One sound and I drop you right here."

Crow flicked on a switch, and a string of overhead bulbs came to life, illuminating a short, rickety flight of dusty steps and what looked like a passageway beyond them. It was cold, damp, dank in the confined space, and the uncirculated air carried a strong scent of earth, sewer, and rancid water.

"Follow me," Crow said, taking the stairs. "Quick."

"Who put this here?" Patrice asked as she followed behind him, dragging Ella with her. "And when was anybody going to tell *me* about it?" Her blood boiled. She'd lived in this house her entire life, and no one had told her there was a way out of it that didn't involve walking out into the open. "That evil *bitch*." In that moment, as she descended each dusty step, she wished she could have Cora killed a second time.

"You knew," she said through clenched teeth. "And you didn't say a *thing*."

"Between you and Cora," Crow said. "Keep up."

Was she supposed to just trust him? Where was she following him to? Maybe this was some kind of trap. She gripped her gun tighter, handled the girl just a little bit rougher, her anger getting the better of her, as they descended the stairs. Patrice drew Ella closer for another warning. "You slow us down; you die down here in the dirt." Above them, the sound of creaking floorboards and the commotion caused by many feet running around the house grew fainter the farther down they went. Then suddenly there was the unmistakable *pop* of gunfire, the sound of chaos, raised voices, barks, commands, the confusion of footsteps. Mayhem.

"Faster," Patrice ordered, gripping her prize, following Crow down in the dim light. "They're shooting up the place. Somebody snitched!" She glared at Ella. "*You* did." She stopped on the steps, whirled the girl around to face her. "You working with them. You're wearing a wire."

Ella buried her head in her hands. "I'm not. I don't have anything. I swear. Please, just let me go. *If you let me go, I'll get you your money. I promise.*"

Patrice wasn't listening. She slipped her gun in her waistband and started to search Ella, head to toe, roughly, every pocket, every inch of her, even her shoes. She had never thought to search her before, and kicked herself now, knowing Cora would have. "Lucky for you." She shoved the girl onward. "Walk."

Ella tried pulling away again. Patrice wouldn't let her. "They can't help you now. Keep going. You'd better walk." Crow came to the door to the tunnel and reached for the key to the lock that hung from a peg just over his right shoulder. He'd walked this passage, unlocked this door, traversed the tunnel many times over the years, familiarizing himself with the terrain, just for a time such as this. Big Daddy had worked overtime securing the passage, making sure it would work as an escape for him if things went horribly wrong. They only had to get there and come out the other end, where they'd be as good as gone.

Once through the door, the temperature dropped like a stone, cold became freezing as the tunnel, dark and tight, close and unforgiving, loomed in front of them, seemingly endless. Sewer stink was overwhelming. Their feet slushed around in a quarter inch of sewer runoff. In the dim light, Patrice saw rats as big as cats skittering along the tunnel walls. Down this far, the little light they'd set up here didn't do much. Though Crow knew the tunnel, he squinted into its depths, adjusting to the darkness, momentarily unsure. After a few steps, he stopped short.

"What are you doing?" Patrice asked. "Go."

"Right or left," Crow said. "Decide."

"What difference does it make?"

Crow turned, glared at her. *"Decide."*

Patrice suffered a moment of indecision. Was he setting her up? Deliberately trying to slow them down? Was he challenging her here, *now*? She drew her gun, held it down at her side, her other hand gripped around Ella's arm. The threat was unmistakable. "Don't play games with me, Crow. I can drop you just as easy as I can drop her."

Crow didn't flinch. "You put too much stock in that gun. Use your head. *Choose*."

Their eyes locked. What felt like a year passed. "Left," Patrice said, "and if it doesn't lead out, you'll rot down here with *her*."

CHAPTER 43

Harri and Vera stood at the tunnel exit in the Carters' basement, staring at a metal door that looked as though it hadn't been opened since Prohibition. The current owners knew about the legend of the bootleggers' tunnel but hadn't spent a lot of time thinking about it, relegating it mostly to Chicago myth. They knew about the door in their basement, too, but had paid it no mind, either, going so far as to stack plastic bins of clothes and boxes of old VHS tapes and shoes and disused appliances in front of it to maximize the space. They had no idea if it even opened. If it didn't, Harri worried they were dead in the water. She hoped Al and Tony and whoever they'd commandeered were having an easier time on their end.

With them was a patrol officer they'd grabbed on their way down, Officer Essex Maxwell, a stocky redhead with chestnut-colored eyes, who was the only one on scene who appeared willing to descend into a tunnel behind two homicide cops, no questions asked. Maxwell hadn't even blinked at the request. She just tucked right in.

Harri looked over at her. "Mind if we go first names from here on out? Seeing as how we might have to go through some stuff."

"You can call me Ess, no problem," she said.

Vera put out a hand. "I'm Vera. She's Harri. I hate tunnels. Basements too." She grinned. "Long story. I'll save it for the bar."

Ess looked like she could handle herself as their backup. They assumed they were going to encounter Patrice Gamon and Crow in the tunnel, seeing as they'd gotten a report over the radio that Pease and his team hadn't found either of them, or Ella in the house when they'd breached the doors. Patrice and Crow might even have backup with them. That put the odds in their favor. Harri hoped the element of surprise evened things up.

"We have to move this stuff," Vera said. "Fast."

Harri exhaled. "All right. We shove everything away from the door and get at it."

They started lifting and shoving bins and boxes and things aside, Harri all the while praying the lock turned and the door opened when they were done.

"They didn't teach us anything about tunnels in the academy," Ess said as she shoved a plastic bin full of teacups and plates away from the door.

Harri looked over at her while shoving a banker's box to the side. "Hard to anticipate everything. Training-wise, we're clearing a room. Close quarters, just the three of us, we limit our exposure. Left and right sweeps. How we'll do it will depend on how much space we have. Slow and precise. Got it?"

Ess nodded. "Roger that."

"Also, cross fire," she said. "We've got people coming from the opposite end. We don't fire in this tunnel, unless we have to, and preferably aiming the other way. Tight shots, if we have to take them. Nobody dies."

Ess nodded again. "Understood."

Vera kicked a box of tapes to the side, then reached for a box to lift and put down somewhere else, before picking up another, and another, as Harri did, her back straining, sweat pouring down her face, adrenaline pumping. This was the work before the work. They had the door cleared in short order. Harri reached for the knob, squeezed her eyes shut, and twisted, her eyes popping open in complete surprise to find the door wasn't locked and that years of disuse, as far as the homeowners knew, hadn't sealed it shut.

"No way," Ess offered, just as surprised as Harri was.

"Think about it," Harri said, "what use would the tunnels be to the Gamons if they couldn't get out of them when they needed to?"

Vera wiped her brow with the back of her hand. "I don't know how secure I'd feel with a doorway to killers in my basement. You'd think the Carters would have sealed this up. Unless they were persuaded not to?"

"We'll see about that when this is done," Harri said. "Right now, radios off. I don't think we'll get a lot of reception down here, but the less noise we make, the better." When they'd all silenced their radios, Harri pulled the door open wide, and rancid tunnel flew out and up their noses. An old string of single bulbs lit the way forward, but the dim light did little to banish the shadows and the murkiness. They drew their weapons; she turned to Ess. "Single file. We think before we act. Deliberate movement."

"Got it," Ess said.

"Low and slow," Vera added.

Ess nodded. Harri and Vera shared a look.

"Okay, let's go." Harri stepped off into the dark, Vera and Essex behind her.

CHAPTER 44

Crow turned and headed left, as instructed. He thought about what would happen when they reached the end. He hadn't noticed when Patrice retrieved her gun from the drawer. That was on him. He didn't like knowing there was a gun at his back. Surreptitiously, he eased his weapon out of his shoulder holster and slipped it into his waistband.

"Faster," Patrice ordered. "It stinks down here."

Crow read the markings on the rock walls. Arrows and numbers scrawled in bold white chalk, the numbers correlating to the addresses of the houses they were passing under. The end, the house they needed, came after a slight turn in the passage, indicated by a circle with an *X* inside it. He estimated they were maybe five hundred feet of twists and turns from that. He was prepared for the trek, but wasn't sure Patrice or her pet were. The girl was already crying and shaking and slowing them down.

"Where to when we get to the end?" Patrice asked.

"Car," Crow said.

"*What* car?"

Crow ignored the question. "Then we ditch *that*."

He meant the girl. The anchor around their necks. Crow knew the police hadn't broken in for him. It was the girl they wanted. If it came down to him or her, Crow knew he wouldn't hesitate to take her down, Patrice, either. Crow took care of Crow. Every day, all day, always.

"She ain't going nowhere until she makes good," Patrice said. "Know *that.*"

Crow stopped, turned, and sneered at Patrice. "Does it look like she has your money? *Think*, girl."

Patrice shoved Ella to the ground, pointed the gun at her head, then slowly turned it in Crow's direction. "Enough of your '*girl.*' If it comes to it, I got no problem being the only one who gets out of here."

Crow looked past the gun, staring instead into Patrice's jumpy eyes. He knew it didn't take much to threaten, that talk was cheap, bravado even cheaper than that. He could see Patrice was over her head. And now she had gone too far. He didn't say a word. He'd said too many already from where he stood. The look he gave her, the death riding in on every blink, said all he needed to. He didn't have a problem with being the only one who got out of the tunnel breathing either. In that, he and the girl were alike.

Patrice put her gun away, grabbed Ella. "Let's go. I want out of this hole."

Crow picked up the pace, knowing Patrice Gamon had just sealed her fate.

CHAPTER 45

They didn't speak. Sound traveled, even a whisper, so they communicated by hand signals and gestures. They moved slowly, eyes focused, scanning the tunnel, listening to the steady drip of water seeping in and the scratchy scampering of raggedy rats who called the tunnel home. Vera was unusually sedate. Harri figured it was the closed space, the stagnant air, the potential for death farther up.

Harri checked back on Ess, who appeared dialed in and ready, but tense, afraid, as they all were. Harri gestured, her palm down, for Ess to take a second to breathe, waiting for the PO to draw in a calming breath before moving forward again. Vera gave Ess a thumbs-up for encouragement. The last thing they needed was for something to jump off in this tunnel that led to one of them getting killed. Calm, steady, easy. That's what she wanted.

Harri wondered about what was going on at the other end of the tunnel, whether Al and Tony had made it down and were there for the squeeze they'd planned. She didn't see any offshoots along the passage yet, it seemed to be just a straight track running east past the Gamon house and west to where they'd entered it. Easy, Harri muttered under her breath, knowing this was anything but. At that moment, she stopped short. She thought she'd heard something ahead of them and waited to hear it again. It didn't take long, and this time Vera and Ess nodded that they'd heard it too. It was the sound of footsteps sloshing in water, the same water the three of them were working their way through. On top of that there was the sound of strained breathing. Someone was coming toward them fast.

They had no cover. The door out was behind them. They needed to hold the line, here in the dark. "Ess?" Harri whispered, just to check.

"I'm good," she whispered back.

The sound of the sloshing footsteps grew louder. More than one person was coming their way. Harri hoped one of them was Ella Byrne. She'd saved her once; she didn't want to lose her now. She pressed herself to the tunnel wall and stayed low and ready, as did Ess and Vera. This would be the time for prayers and entreaties, for appeals for divine providence and safekeeping. Harri sent the thoughts up past the tunnel ceiling as sweat rolled down her back.

Harri saw them first, a tall dark man leading two women, one a petite Black woman with mean eyes, the other Ella, horribly pale and nearly catatonic, shuffling along like a chain gang inmate, locked in the Black woman's grip. The woman and man were armed, guns in hand and at their sides. She assumed the man was Crow, the woman the phantom they'd been chasing, P.D. Terry, a.k.a. Patrice Gamon. Harri looked at Vera and Ess. She could tell that both recognized their sticky situation had just gotten a lot stickier. No one decided, there was no time for them to draw straws, Harri pushed off the wall, raised her weapon as the trio got closer. "As far as you go," she said, her words ricocheting off the slimy, stinking walls. "Police. Drop your weapons. Move away from the girl."

"There's nowhere to go," Vera added, backing her partner's play. "Guns down. Back up."

Crow, in the half second it took for him to register their presence, and Patrice stood stunned, a look of shocked malevolence on both their faces. Ella just appeared in shock, listless, a rag doll dragged along for the ride.

The tunnel was too narrow, too low, too compact for bullets, the chance of injury or death was too great. They needed an easy takedown with no one harmed. Would they get it?

Patrice pedaled back, pulling Ella with her, using her as a human shield. "Nuh-uh. Back up. Back *up*. Or I take her out."

Harri's eyes shifted from Patrice to Crow and back. Two guns. Two killers. One Ella.

"We can't do that," Harri said. "You're Patrice, right? Patrice Gamon?"

Patrice shook her head, adamant that she would not yield. "I'm not playing with you. I mean it. This white girl don't mean nothing to me. I'll kill her *and* you. I'll blow this whole thing up."

"No one wants to get hurt here, Patrice," Harri said. "We don't want to hurt you." She watched Crow, his hands, his gun, ready for the slightest twitch, the subtlest move. Two guns. Two killers. A lot to think about in the narrow tunnel.

"Back. *Up*," Patrice screeched. "Crow, you better do something. You better kill these cops."

Harri's eyes shifted to Crow. "You really want her to die down here? Like this? She doesn't have to. You don't either. This can end with everyone walking out of here." She could feel Vera and Ess tense beside her. They needed to de-escalate. "Guns down," Harri ordered. "On the ground. Back away." Her eyes held Crow's. "Do the right thing. For her."

Confused, Patrice ambled forward. "What're you talking about for *me*? Crow does what I tell him to. *I* got the chair."

"She can still have a life," Vera added. "So can you."

Crow sneered, began to move back. "Only life that counts is mine." He flicked Patrice a look, smiled. "Three guns to two guns. You can count, can't you?" He took a step back.

Patrice's mouth dropped open. "You son of a *bitch*. You *coward*. You piece of *shit*." She pulled Ella back closer to her chest. "I'll take you out *and* them too."

Crow glared at Patrice. "I got no problem doing the same."

"We don't have time for a family feud," Harri said, her voice sterner now. They had to get out of this tunnel. She felt Vera and Ess move slightly to the right. Better position. Better coverage. No one moved for a time. "*Tell* her, Crow. Maybe she thinks she's got nothing to lose."

Crow smiled, scoffed, took another step backward, farther into the dark. "Do what you have to do. Blood ain't money in my pocket."

She'd hoped there was some family feeling in the man, but there didn't appear to be anything there. Apparently Patrice was just the result of a heinous, violent act, and he'd attached no connection to her at all. Bad for Patrice, but bad for them too.

"Don't take another step," Harri ordered. She didn't want a desperate Crow meeting Al and Tony down the tunnel. But she gave up on the appeal for decency. Crow was too far gone, Patrice too. "All right. Guns down. Let go of Ella. Now."

"Do it," Vera added, matching her partner's hardness. They'd ticked up to a new level, a place where there could be no compromise. *"Now."*

"You won't get past us," Harri said, "and we have backup coming from the other end. This is where it ends. Don't make it any worse than it already is."

Patrice glared at Crow, her hand tightening on the grip of her gun. "You got us down here. I knew this was a trap. Now what, Crow? Now *what*?"

Crow flicked Patrice a look of disgust as he turned slowly toward her. "Shut up, fool."

"Who you calling a *fool*?"

Harri's heart seized. She could almost feel the tunnel contract. "Stop! Both of you. Right now! Guns down. Do it now!" She looked over at Ella, standing uselessly in the line of fire.

Seconds. That's all it took. Harri saw the flicker in Crow's mean eyes, and the same in Patrice's. Her breath held, Harri silently counted the breaths she wasn't taking. This wasn't going to end the way they'd wanted. They wouldn't all walk out. It took a split second, less, for Crow to raise his gun, to decide. He was gone before he got a chance to fire. Harri's round hit him squarely in the chest, and she watched with regret, but not sorrow, as he fell backward, arms splayed out, into the gunky water. She shifted to Patrice, who stood stunned, and indecisive, her gun aimed at her. Harri's pulse raced. She was locked in, but there was no shot with Ella plastered to Patrice's chest.

"Drop it. Drop it *now*!" Harri yelled.

"You shoot me, you shoot her too," Patrice screamed. "And I know you don't want to do that. You think this is all me?" She tugged Ella by the hair. "She's in it just as much as I am. She moved the pills same as me. What're you all going to do to her, huh? Nothing. Little Miss Priss gets to walk away. I get the time, though, right?"

"We'll work all that out up top," Vera said. "Right now, let go of her. Let her walk this way,"

Harri stared down the sight of her gun, hands melded to her grip. *We serve and protect.* The motto might as well have been emblazoned on her brain. Her priorities were clear. Everyone left had to walk out, if they could. Crow had made his choice; there would be a time and place to deal with hers, but this was not it. Ella began to pull away from Patrice, to struggle against the hold, petrified by the gunfire and the dead man at her feet. Harri focused on Patrice's hand, the gun, and Ella. Hand and gun. They were Harri's entire world at that moment.

Vera shouted, "Ella, stop moving!"

"I want to go *home*," Ella cried, fat tears streaking her dusty face, her green eyes swimming in desperate water. "I'm sorry. I made a mistake, and did something horrible, but I just want to go *home*. *Please*, let me go home?"

"Drop it," Harri ordered. "I won't ask again."

Patrice stared at Crow, confusion written all over her face. Finally, she did the math. It was now three guns to one. Harri knew it would come down to how badly Patrice wanted to live and how much she was willing to lose.

"I didn't kill her," Patrice screamed. "It was Crow."

"Gun. *Down*," Harri barked. *"Last time."* All the while she prayed like she hadn't in a long time. She prayed that she would not have to kill this child. Prayed that she wouldn't have to fire again. She prayed as hard as she'd prayed for her son not to be dead. Harri prayed as her heart raced, prayed as she gripped the gun tighter, prayed that Patrice would give up and decide to live. Time seemed to slow, every second felt precious. Harri stood ready. Slowly, Patrice bent over and placed her gun on the ground, though she held fast to Ella. Harri took a breath, relief filling her. She would not have to kill a child. She would not have to live with that weight pressed to her heart like a millstone. It would only be Crow who haunted her.

"Kick it this way," Vera commanded. "Then let Ella go and get down on the ground. Do it fast."

With a last burst of frustrated anger, Patrice shoved Ella toward them with such ferocity that it sent the girl stumbling to the ground, where she balled up into the fetal position and began to wail like a hobbled animal. As quickly as a lightning strike, Vera and Harri rushed forward, acting as buffer between Ella and Patrice while Ess bolted forward, grabbed Ella under the arms, and dragged her deadweight beyond Patrice Gamon's reach.

"Get off me," Patrice cried, as Harri and Vera held her down and got the handcuffs on her. "I didn't do anything. I never killed anybody. Let me *go*."

She bucked and kicked and screeched, but they contained her. Harri looked over at Ess, the weeping Ella in her arms. "Get her out of here. Go." She and Vera watched as Ess bolted back toward the door, Ella in tow. Safe. Again.

"Vera! Harri!" It was Al and Tony's voices coming toward them from the opposite end of the passage. "Say something! Call out!"

"You could have just given up," Harri said. "No one had to die."

They lifted her up, prepared to walk her out.

"We're good," Vera yelled back. "It's over."

"Almost there," Al called back. "Stay put."

Patrice grinned. "*You* killed him, I didn't. But he got what he deserved. He was a coward. He was supposed to *protect* me. Instead, he was just gonna *run*. I could tell. He was gonna run and leave me down here."

Vera and Harri shared a look.

"That coward was your *father*," Vera said. "Some family, huh, partner?"

Harri glanced at Crow. "That's not what I'd call it."

Patrice struggled to get out of their grip, but she wasn't going anywhere. She turned her head to look at Crow's body. "You *lie*. You're both dirty *liars*. Say it? Say you're *liars*. I hate you. I didn't do anything. Let me go."

"You have the right to remain silent," Harri began before taking a pause.

Vera looked at Harri, concerned. "You okay?"

"Yep," Harri lied.

"He gave you no choice. It could have just as easily been my shot," Vera said.

Harri nodded. "I know."

A moment passed. Patrice had gone quiet, thankfully. Harri wanted fresh air. She wanted out of the tunnel and away from Crow and Patrice Gamon.

Vera clenched her eyes closed. "Remember when I said I wanted to sell shoes, or something?"

Harri nodded. "I didn't think you were serious."

"I wasn't. Now I am. This tunnel business is for the birds."

CHAPTER 46

Four cops, one Gamon, climbed the narrow stairs out of the tunnel and back into the Gamon house. All of them looking as though they'd worked an entire shift as coal miners, their faces streaked with sweat and dust, their shoes destroyed by silt and grime. The fresh air felt good on Harri's face as she walked out of the house onto the street clogged with cop cars and ambulances, fire trucks and curious neighbors, who finally, it appeared, felt bold enough to stand in front of the Gamon house without fear of being shot dead in the street.

Harri knew it was only a temporary reprieve. Patrice was going, Crow was gone, but the game they had been in wouldn't stop. Harri spotted Faith Pope in the crowd, standing dour and silent, watching as the last of her blood met her fate. Patrice saw her, too, and went crazy, trying to run, pulling away from Tony, kicking, screaming, cursing her from a distance. There had been failures everywhere and lives were destroyed. Harri would have to come to terms with the one she'd taken.

"Get her away from me! I'll *kill* her," Patrice screamed at the top of her lungs. "I don't want to see her. She doesn't get to be here. It's *my* chair. It's *mine*."

Faith appeared unmoved. Her face revealed nothing. She stood there until Patrice was put into a squad car, and then she simply turned and walked away. Back to her church, Harri presumed.

Big Daddy gone. Her brothers gone. Cora gone, now Patrice. She was the last Gamon standing, and as Harri stood on the street covered in tunnel, glad to be alive, truly glad, she wondered what would become of Faith. How would her life play out? What lesson could Faith Pope offer *her* as she stepped out on her own road of recovery?

Ella was safe. She was with her family headed to the hospital to get checked out. She was alive, fortunate, but she had a lot of hard things coming. As Harri turned to head back to their car, to face the next difficult things coming for her, she spotted the ice cream truck with Izzy, Mic, Raines, and the big-headed cat leaning out the side window. She hated to admit it, and she knew Vera surely did, but their help had been crucial, and they owed them their thanks.

"Got the girl, I see," Izzy said when she and Vera reached them. "Saw her come out with that big Black cop who looks like he could eat a Buick. Boy, y'all went through it, huh?"

Raines lifted her chin. "Tunnel versus cops, cops win. What next? Fistfight in a coal mine?"

Mic stared at them. "I don't think they pay y'all enough for this."

"I know, right?" Vera said, deadly serious.

"I counted twenty-two Gamon flunkies taking a ride," Raines said. "Plus the head Gamon. How's *that* for bumping up that clearance rate?"

"I fully expected to run into you down there," Vera said, "seeing as you like to get everywhere ahead of us."

"And risk getting shot in the face by some punk? Pass, besides, my job was over the second Ella Byrne got walked out. I'm with Mic. They don't pay either of you enough."

"Thanks for your help," Harri said.

Raines smiled. "No problem. Just remember *that* the next time I need a cop favor. You two owe me *big*."

Vera was suspicious. "How big?"

"Don't worry. Somewhere between helping me move and bailing me out of jail." She turned to Mic. "Ready to pack it up, Mic?"

"Eh, one more question," Vera said. "Why's the cat named Bigfoot?"

Izzy grinned. "He's got extra toes on his front paws. They're massive. Want to see?"

Vera held up a hand. "No, I'm good."

Mic nodded and slid behind the wheel. "Well, case closed," he announced as he backed the truck up, turned, and drove away. Izzy and Raines waved goodbye. Harri and Vera waved back as though bidding a fond adieu to old friends.

"I think I'm going to miss that pesky PI," Vera said.

Harri walked away. "You're going to miss arguing with her."

"That's what I said."

Harri laughed, then stopped laughing. There was still Patrice to square away and Ella to deal with. And Matt. And Crow.

"Tough decision," Vera said, concern on her face. "But you know we share this. It's not all on you."

It was kind, but it wasn't true. She'd taken the shot, not Vera.

"Let's go give Griffin proof of life," Harri said.

Vera groaned. "Right after I get tunnel off me."

CHAPTER 47

Days passed before they could get Ella into an interview room, detained, waiting to be questioned, flanked by her parents and a lawyer. And Matt wasn't allowed anywhere near her. Ella had made a terrible mistake and now there were consequences.

Patrice Gamon had been charged with a long list of offenses, running the gamut from the manufacture and delivery of a controlled substance to resisting arrest, kidnapping, solicitation of murder, and assault on a police officer. She was currently in the Cook County Jail at Twenty-Seventh and California, hoping a lawyer could get her out.

Things felt strained in the office. Harri wasn't quite sure what to say to Matt, and apparently neither did anyone else, so they just watched, and did their jobs, hoping somehow the spell would break and things would go back to the way they were.

On a sigh, Harri got up from her chair, grabbed her mug, and headed for the coffee machine. "Matt, got a minute?"

She could feel the team hold their collective breaths, but no one said anything. Matt followed her to the kitchen alcove. Not in a rush, she filled her mug, found a wooden stirrer, plucked a tiny plastic carton of half-and-half out of the caddy, poured it in the mug, stirred, took a sip, winced. Coffee wasn't her thing. She could take it or leave it, mostly leave it, but the lure of coffee had been the bait, and now she was committed. Matt looked like he hadn't slept in months. Harri waited for the acidy mud to hit her stomach before she started anything.

"How's it going, Matt?" She took another sip, pulled a face, then decided that was it. No more. She put the mug down, turned her back on it. His hands flew up. "She's going to have to face some charges. She'll tell what she knows, and she'll have to testify against Patrice. She might get a deal. First offense. But anyway you cut it, she's in serious trouble."

"Maybe she won't have to testify. There are people streaming in to stick it to Patrice. We have Goodlow Dixon, who made the stuff. He alone might be enough to lock this whole thing down and put her away. And there's Faith Pope. Ella's only a small piece." She stared at his pinched face, the worry lines between his eyes. It looked like this whole thing had taken years off his life.

"We had no idea she had all this going on," he said, his voice sad, disappointed. "That she could even consider something like this." He exhaled heavily. "But she's young. She can do better. We'll all get through it."

"Yeah, you will."

He managed a smile. "Griffin's still pissed. The team? Everybody's walking around me like I'm radioactive."

"They're giving you space."

"I screwed up."

"We *all* screw up," she said. "All we can do is keep things moving." She thought of Krieg sunning himself in the Solomon Islands, beyond her reach. She thought of having to let go of the ones she'd lost, and the life she'd taken.

"Vera and I are going in there, and we're going to close this case. You good with that?"

"Yeah," he said. "Have to be."

She nodded. "Okay then. Welcome back, by the way."

"I cut it close, didn't I?"

She smiled. "Next time, don't."

Ella told them everything, and each revelation put another nail in Patrice Gamon's coffin. Her parents looked bereft as Ella laid it all out, even the lawyer looked as though someone had kicked his dog down a flight of stairs. Ella was slinging Edge for the Gamons in exchange for a Fendi lifestyle. After she had unburdened herself, Harri just had to know. "Why did you even get involved in this? It's one thing to take the drug yourself, even share it with your friends, but you took the bags, you *sold* it. You were a *pusher*, Ella."

Ella lowered her head, picked at her cuticles as her hands lay in her lap. "It didn't feel so bad. The money was good. I wasn't really thinking about anything else, I guess. But when I wanted to stop, after Robby . . . she wouldn't let me. She said she *owned* me. I thought if I ran, if I went somewhere else for a while, things would blow over, but Uncle Matt showed up. He wanted to *arrest* me. I flipped. I had to get out of there."

"Where'd you go?" Vera asked, her arms crossed in front of her.

"I booked a spot in the Grant Park garage. I slept in my car. Nobody noticed. I knew I couldn't go home after what I'd done. Somehow I convinced myself if I could *talk* to her, tell her I didn't have her drugs, I could work something out?"

Maggie Byrne squeezed her eyes shut. "Oh, Ella."

"I called her, and we were supposed to meet at a neutral place. A coffee shop. Only she didn't come herself, she sent two of her people. They forced me into the car and drove me to the house."

"How'd you get that bruise on your cheek?"

"I tried to get out of the car. The one in the back seat with me. Holt. Hit me."

Ella's father's face went pale. It looked like he wanted to vomit, but he said nothing.

"Patrice wanted $20,000," Ella said. "She wasn't going to let me go. That's when the police showed up. If they hadn't, I . . . I'd be dead, I think."

It was all they needed. Harri turned to the two-way mirror, knowing Matt was there watching. The end of this, she knew, only ended *this*. There would always be more people like the Gamons, more bags, more victims, more tragedies, and she had accepted the duty, as Vera and the others had.

Harri rubbed Reg's watch for assurance. This time, there was no pain attached to it, only calm, only peace. She had things to do, and she now felt like it was okay to do them without feeling that she was stealing something that didn't belong to her.

She looked down at Ella, knowing she'd have to get some things back, too, starting now.

CHAPTER 48

Harri stared at Parker's cane as it leaned against her chair, considering what she'd said about it being imperfect but strong. Parker sat back in her chair, her legs crossed, her hands folded in her lap.

"That was some dream," she finally said. "Doesn't take much to interpret that one. How'd you feel about it?"

Harri pulled one thumbtack out of her pocket. Just one. There were no other found coping objects accompanying it. Progress? "I *felt* . . . anxious, and then less anxious. Sad, then less sad. Okay, not great." She'd told her about the marbles in the vase, how she had dropped one marble in each day since her son died. "No marbles since I had it." She stared down at the tack. "Those things don't seem to work anymore anyway."

"Why do you think that is?"

"I was hoping you'd tell me."

Parker shook her head. "This is your story, not mine. All I am is ears, remember? . . . Ready to talk about what happened at work? Not a small thing having to take a life. Most cops don't. You've joined an exclusive club. You'll ride a desk for a while. You good with that?"

She wasn't ready. "Maybe we stick a pin in that?"

"All right. Let's try family. Your mother, brother, his family. How do they fit in?"

"I worry them," Harri said. "I don't mean to." She clasped her hands in her lap, then slid Parker a look. "They need me to be better . . . maybe we could stick a pin in that too?"

"Okay. Lot of pins here."

Harri glanced over at all Parker's fancy degrees hung on the wall, thinking Parker might have wasted her money and her time if ears were all she had to offer. Parker caught her looking.

"It was money well spent," she said, smiling. She took a moment. "I'm glad you came back. A lot of cops don't."

She recalled her talk with Sly. "I'm sick and tired of being sick and tired."

Parker's brows lifted. "Good. Hat tip to Ms. Hamer, of course. Do you cook, Harri?"

Harri thought for a moment, not sure how they'd gone from Fannie Lou Hamer and the hat tip to cooking. "No."

"Did you ever?"

"Sure."

"Why'd you stop?"

Harri paused. "I had no one to cook for."

"*You* have to eat. Weren't you somebody to cook for?"

Harri's eyes flashed. Parker was slick as goose grease. "I see what you're doing."

Parker grinned. "Good. Then let's get to it. I'm listening."

ACKNOWLEDGMENTS

My deepest gratitude to my agent, Evan Marshall, who has guided me with sure hands through eight books, two publishers, and a lot of writer jitters. He is steady and kind and has been a great champion for my work. Thank you, Evan, for everything and more. Thank you also to the wonderful editing team at Thomas & Mercer, all champs—Gracie, Miranda, Alicia Lea. My work is in *excellent* hands. To my editor at T&M, Liz Pearsons, who's always there with the plan, keeps the train on the tracks, and who, by the way, is a very good egg. I can't tell you how much I appreciate all you do. To Clarence Haynes, that eagle-eyed editor god, who takes my messy, confusing, malformed, windy *horror* of a manuscript, and whittles it down to uncover the art beneath, words cannot adequately express how much I am thankful you were assigned to me.

It takes a village to make a writer. None of us gets a book out of our brains and out the door by ourselves. Thanks to my family, who endures pensive moods and a lot of faraway gazing when the words don't come. I eventually make my way back to the real world, once the fantasy world has been nailed down, but I freely acknowledge the rough patches. Thanks for your patience and understanding.

To my book family, my community, my fellow word warriors in Crime Writers of Color, Mystery Writers of America, Sisters in Crime,

Rogue Women Writers, and beyond, thank you. There is strength in advocacy; there is personal fulfillment in the support of others. I think we've all found this out. Writers write, sure we do, but we also know that the gifts we were given were meant to be passed along. Thank you to all those who passed it along to me so that I could pass it along to someone else. Thank you to all those who have offered advice, encouragement, friendship, inclusion, and direction. Much gratitude, and right back atcha.

Thanks to the readers who have found Detective Harriet Foster and have grown to love her as much as I have. Harriet's not easy, but she's worth the effort, I think. Aren't we all?

Finally, a special shout-out to Ron Oberman, whom I met at a book signing not too long ago. Mr. Oberman, a retired educator, had been chewing on a character for decades and wanted to get him out there. He graciously offered the character to me because he thought I just might be the one who could do it. I gave it a shot. Ron, Frank Streeter is for you. However, I would love to see what *you* might do with him. It's never too late to put pen to paper. Best wishes.

Until next time!

ABOUT THE AUTHOR

Photo © 2022 Bruno Passigatti / Bauwerks Photography

Tracy Clark is the author of the Cass Raines Chicago Mystery and Detective Harriet Foster series, award-winning books that feature tough, smart, Black female characters working the mean streets of the Windy City. Her debut novel, *Broken Places*, was CrimeReads' Best New PI Book of 2018 and made *Library Journal*'s Best Crime Fiction list that same year.

A finalist for Anthony, Lefty, Macavity, Edgar, and Shamus Awards, Tracy has won two G. P. Putnam's Sons Sue Grafton Memorial Awards and one Sara Paretsky Award. She is a proud member of Crime Writers of Color, Mystery Writers of America, and Sisters in Crime and sits on boards at Bouchercon and the Midwest Mystery Conference.

When not writing, Tracy watches old black-and-white movies, reads, or putters around. She roots equally for the Cubs, White Sox, Bears, Blackhawks, Sky, and Fire. As a proud Chicagoan, it's deep-dish and hot dogs, no ketchup—vegan schmegan. And she can toss a (fictional) dead body anywhere and make it work. *Dare her.*